SUDDENLY IT'S A WORLD WITHOUT ADULTS, AND NORMAL HAS CRASHED AND BURNED...

'We can't just go around arresting people without some kind of system,' Albert said.

'Yeah, Sammy,' Howard said with a smirk. 'You can't just go all laser-hands whenever you decide you don't like someone.'

Dekka shifted in her seat, hunching her strong shoulders forwards. 'No, so instead we let little girls be kicked out of their own homes and terrorised.'

'Look, once and for all, we can't have a system where Sam is judge, jury and executioner,' Astrid said.

MORE GRIPPING TITLES FROM MICHAEL GRANT

GONE

HUNGER

LIES

PLAGUE

FEAR

LIGHT

BZRK

BZRK RELOADED

BZRK APOCALYPSE

MESSENGER OF FEAR

EVE & ADAM

with Katherine Applegate

MICHAEL GRANT

First published in Great Britain 2010
by Egmont UK Limited
This edition published in 2015
by Electric Monkey, an imprint of Egmont UK Limited
The Yellow Building, 1 Nicholas Road, London W11 4AN
First published in the USA 2010
by HarperTeen

Published by arrangement with HarperTeen
a division of HarperCollins Publishers, Inc.
1350 Avenue of the Americas, New York,
New York 10019, USA

ISBN 978 1 4052 7706 8

www.electricmonkeybooks.co.uk

A CIP catalogue record for this title is available from the British Library

Typeset by Avon DataSet Ltd, Bidford on Avon, Warwickshire, Great Britain
Printed and bound in Great Britain by Clays Ltd, St Ives plc

46556/18

For Katherine, Jake, and Julia

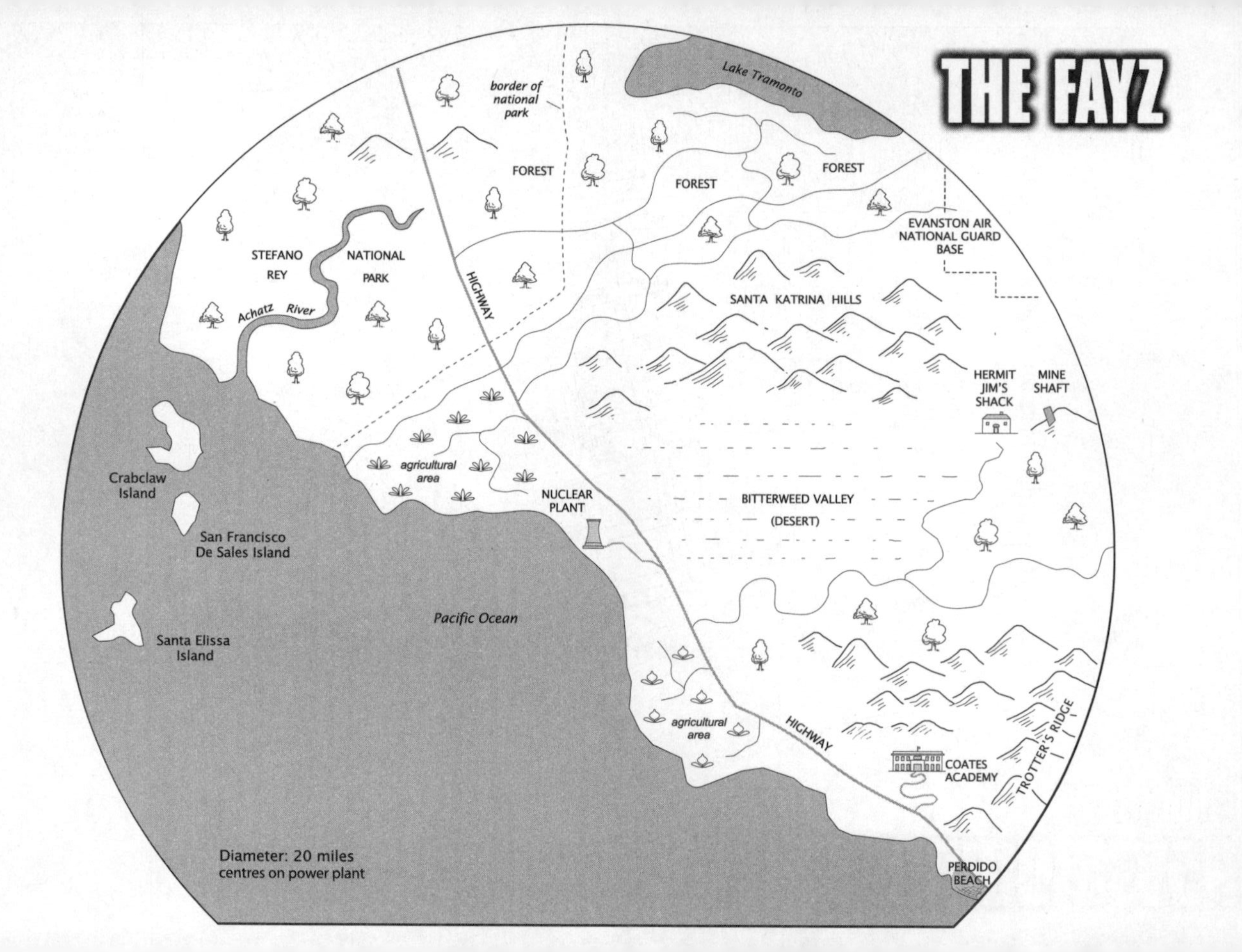

THE FAYZ
Lake Tramonto
border of national park
FOREST
FOREST
FOREST
EVANSTON AIR NATIONAL GUARD BASE
STEFANO REY
NATIONAL PARK
Achatz River
HIGHWAY
SANTA KATRINA HILLS
HERMIT JIM'S SHACK
MINE SHAFT
agricultural area
NUCLEAR PLANT
BITTERWEED VALLEY
(DESERT)
Crabclaw Island
San Francisco De Sales Island
Santa Elissa Island
Pacific Ocean
agricultural area
HIGHWAY
COATES ACADEMY
TROTTER'S RIDGE
PERDIDO BEACH
Diameter: 20 miles
centres on power plant

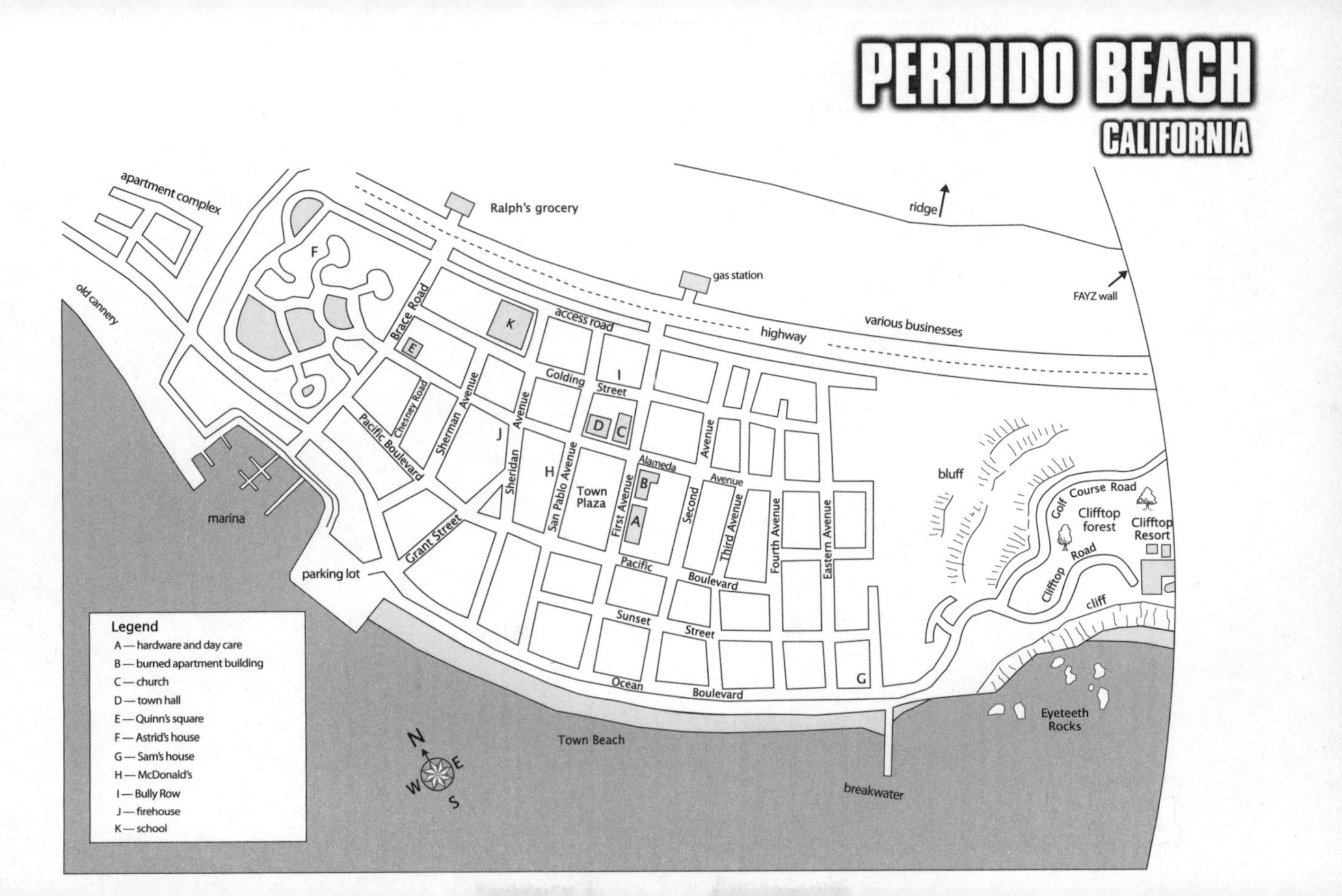
PERDIDO BEACH
CALIFORNIA
apartment complex
Ralph's grocery
ridge
gas station
FAYZ wall
old cannery
access road
highway
various businesses
Brace Road
Golding
Street
Chesney Road
Sherman Avenue
Avenue
Pacific Boulevard
Sheridan
San Pablo Avenue
Town Plaza
Alameda
Avenue
First Avenue
Second
Third Avenue
Fourth Avenue
Eastern Avenue
Grant Street
Pacific
Boulevard
Sunset
Street
Ocean
Boulevard
marina
parking lot
Town Beach
breakwater
bluff
Golf
Course Road
Clifftop
forest
Clifftop
Resort
Clifftop
Road
cliff
Eyeteeth
Rocks
N
E
W
S
Legend
A — hardware and day care
B — burned apartment building
C — church
D — town hall
E — Quinn's square
F — Astrid's house
G — Sam's house
H — McDonald's
I — Bully Row
J — firehouse
K — school

ONE

66 HOURS 52 MINUTES

OBSCENE GRAFFITI.

Smashed windows.

Human Crew tags, their logo, along with warnings to freaks to get out.

In the distance, up the street, too far away for Sam to want to chase after, a couple of kids, maybe ten years old, maybe not even that. Barely visible in the false moonlight. Just outlines. The kids passing a bottle back and forth, taking swigs, staggering.

Grass growing everywhere. Weeds forcing their way up through cracks in the street. Trash: chip bags, six-pack rings, supermarket plastic bags, random sheets of paper, articles of clothing, single shoes, hamburger wrappers, broken toys, broken bottles, and crumpled cans – anything that wasn't actually edible – formed random, colourful collections. They were poignant reminders of better days.

Darkness so deep, you'd have had to walk off into the wilderness in the old days to experience anything like it.

Not a street light or a porch light. Electricity out. Maybe forever.

No one wasting batteries, not any more. Those, too, were in very short supply.

And not many trying to burn candles or light trash fires. Not after the fire that burned down three homes and burned one kid so bad, it took Lana, the Healer, half a day to save him.

No water pressure. Nothing coming out of fire hydrants. Nothing to do about fire but watch it burn and get out of its way.

Perdido Beach, California.

At least it used to be California.

Now it was Perdido Beach, the FAYZ. Wherever, whatever, and whyever that was.

Sam had the power to make light. He could fire it in killing beams from his hands. Or he could form balls of persistent light that would hang in the air like a lantern. Like lightning in a bottle.

But not too many people wanted Sam's lights, what kids called Sammy Suns. Zil Sperry, leader of the Human Crew, had forbidden any of his people to take the lights. Most of the normals complied. And some freaks didn't want a bright advertisement of who and what they were.

The fear had spread. A disease. It leaped from person to person.

People sat in the dark, afraid. Always afraid.

Sam was in the east end, the dangerous part of town, the part Zil had declared off-limits to freaks. He had to show the flag, so to speak, demonstrate that he was still in charge. Show that he wouldn't be intimidated by Zil's campaign of fear.

Kids needed that. They needed to see that someone would still protect them. That someone was *him*.

He had resisted that role, but it had come to him, anyway. And he was determined to play it out. Whenever he let up, whenever he lost focus, tried to have a different life, something awful happened.

So he walked the streets at two in the morning, ready. Just in case.

Sam walked near the shore. There was no surf, of course. Not any more. No weather. No vast swells crossing the Pacific to crash in magnificent showers of spray against Perdido's beaches.

The surf was just a soft whisper now. *Shhh. Shhh. Shhh.* Better than nothing. But not much better.

He was heading towards Clifftop, the hotel, Lana's current home. Zil had left her alone. Freak or not, no one messed with the Healer.

Clifftop was right up against the FAYZ wall, the end of Sam's area of responsibility, the last part of his walk-through.

Someone was walking down towards him. He tensed, fearing

the worst. There was no question that Zil would like to see him dead. And out there – somewhere – Caine, his half brother. Caine had been helpful in destroying the gaiaphage and the psychopath Drake Merwin. But Sam didn't kid himself into believing that Caine had changed. If Caine was still alive, they would meet again.

And God knew what other horrors were out in that fading night – human or not. Out in the dark mountains, the black caves, the desert, the forest to the north. The too-calm ocean.

The FAYZ never let up.

But this just looked like a girl.

'It's just me, Sinder,' a voice said, and Sam relaxed.

'T'sup, Sinder? Kind of late, huh?'

She was a sweet Goth girl who managed mostly to stay out of the various wars and factions raging within the FAYZ.

'I'm glad I ran into you,' Sinder said. She had a steel pipe in one hand, the grip cushioned with duct tape. No one walked around without a weapon, especially at night.

'You OK? You eating?'

That had become the standard greeting. Not, 'How are you?' But, 'Are you eating?'

'Yeah, we're getting by,' Sinder said. Her ghostly pale skin made her seem very young and vulnerable. Of course the pipe, the black fingernails, and the kitchen knife stuck in her belt made her seem not entirely gentle.

'Listen, Sam. I'm not someone who, like, you know, wants to tell on people, or whatever,' Sinder said. Uncomfortable.

'I know that,' he said. He waited.

'It's Orsay,' Sinder said, and glanced over her shoulder, guilty. 'You know, I talk to her sometimes. She's kind of cool, mostly. Kind of interesting.'

'Yep.'

'Mostly.'

'Yeah.'

'But, you know, weird maybe, too.' Sinder made a wry grin. 'Like I'm one to talk.'

Sam waited. He heard the sound of a glass bottle shattering and high-pitched giggling from the distance behind him. The kids throwing their emptied bottle of booze. A boy named K. B. had been found dead with a bottle of vodka in his hand.

'Anyway, Orsay, she's at the wall.'

'The wall?'

'On the beach, down by the wall. She's like, she thinks . . . Look, talk to her, OK? Just don't tell her I told you. OK?'

'Is she down there now? It's, like, two a.m.'

'That's when they do it. They don't want Zil or . . . or you, I guess, giving them a hard time. You know where the wall runs down from Clifftop to the beach? Those rocks out there? That's where she is. Not alone. Other kids are there, too.'

Sam felt an unwelcome tingle running up his spine. He'd

developed a pretty good instinct for trouble over the last few months. This felt like trouble.

'OK, I'll check it out.'

'Yah. Cool.'

''Night, Sinder. Take care.'

He left her and continued walking, wondering what new craziness or danger lay ahead. He climbed the road up past Clifftop. Glanced up at Lana's balcony.

Patrick, Lana's Labrador, must have heard him because he gave a short, sharp warning bark.

'Just me, Patrick,' Sam said.

There were very few dogs or cats still alive in the FAYZ. The only reason Patrick had not ended up as dog stew was because he belonged to the Healer.

From the top of the cliff Sam looked down and thought he could make out several people on the rocks, right down in the surf that wasn't quite surf. They were big rocks, dangerous back in the days when Sam would take his board out there with Quinn and wait for a big one.

Sam didn't need light to scale down the cliff. He could have done it blind. In the old days he'd done it hauling all his gear.

As he reached the sand, he heard soft voices. One speaking. One crying.

The FAYZ wall, the impenetrable, impermeable, eye-baffling barrier that defined the boundaries of the FAYZ, glowed almost imperceptibly. Not even a glow, really, a suggestion of translucence. Grey and blank.

A small bonfire burned on the beach, casting a faint orange light over a small circle of sand and rock and water.

No one noticed Sam as he approached. So he had time to identify most of the half-dozen kids out there. Francis, Cigar, D-Con, a few others, and Orsay herself.

'I have seen something . . .' Orsay began.

'Tell me about my mom,' someone cried out.

Orsay held up her hand, a calming gesture. 'Please. I will do my best to reach your loved ones.'

'She's not a cell phone,' the dark girl beside Orsay snapped. 'It is very painful for the Prophetess to make contact with the barrier. Give her some peace. And listen to her words.'

Sam squinted, not quite able to recognise the dark-haired girl in the flickering firelight. Some friend of Orsay's? Sam thought he knew every kid in the FAYZ.

'Begin again, Prophetess,' the dark-haired girl said.

'Thank you, Nerezza,' Orsay said.

Sam shook his head in amazement. Not only had he not known that Orsay was doing this, he hadn't known she'd acquired her own personal manager. Not someone he recognised, the girl called Nerezza.

'I have seen something . . .' Orsay began again, and faltered as though expecting to be interrupted. 'A vision.'

That caused a murmur. Or maybe it was just the sighing sound of the water on the sand.

'In my vision I saw all of the children of the FAYZ, older kids, younger, too. I saw them standing atop the cliff.'

Every head swivelled to look up at the cliff. Sam ducked, then felt foolish: the darkness concealed him.

'The kids of the FAYZ, *prisoners* of the FAYZ, gazed out into a setting sun. Such a beautiful sunset. Redder and more vivid than anything you've ever seen.' She seemed to be mesmerised by that vision. 'Such a red sunset.'

All attention was again focused on Orsay. Not a sound from the small crowd.

'A red sunset. The children all gazed into that red sun. But behind them, a devil. A demon.' Orsay winced as if she couldn't look at this creature. 'Then, the children realised that in that red sun were all their loved ones, arms outstretched. Mothers and fathers. And all united, all filled with longing and love. Waiting so anxiously to welcome their children home.'

'Thank you, Prophetess,' Nerezza said.

'They wait . . .' Orsay said. She raised one hand, waved it towards the barrier, fluttered. 'Just beyond the wall. Just past the sunset.'

She sat down hard, a puppet whose strings had been cut. For a while she sat there, crumpled, hands open, palms up on her lap, head bowed.

But then, with a shaky smile she roused herself.

'I'm ready,' Orsay said.

She laid her palm against the FAYZ wall. Sam flinched. He knew from personal experience how painful that could be. It was like grabbing a bare electrical wire. It didn't do any damage, but it sure felt like it did.

Orsay's narrow face was scrunched up in pain. But when she spoke her voice was clear, untroubled. Like she was reading a poem.

'She dreams of you, Bradley,' Orsay said.

Bradley was Cigar's real name.

'She dreams of you . . . you're at Knott's Berry Farm. You're afraid to go on the ride . . . She remembers how you tried to be brave . . . Your mother misses you . . .'

Cigar sniffled. He carried a weapon of his own devising, a toy plastic lightsaber with double-edged razor blades stuck into the end. His hair was tied back in a ponytail and held with a rubber band.

'She . . . she knows you are here . . . She knows . . . she wants you to come to her . . .'

'I can't,' Cigar moaned, and Orsay's helper, whoever she was, put a comforting arm around his shoulders.

'. . . when the time comes . . .' Orsay said.

'When?' Cigar sobbed.

'She dreams that you will be with her soon . . . She dreams . . .

just three days, she knows it, she is sure of it . . .' Orsay's voice had taken on an almost ecstatic tone. Giddy. 'She's seen others do it.'

'What?' Francis demanded.

'. . . the others who have reappeared,' Orsay said, dreamy now herself, as if she was falling asleep. 'She saw them on TV. The twins, the two girls Anna and Emma . . . she saw them . . . They give interviews and tell . . .'

Orsay yanked her hand back from the FAYZ wall as if she had just noticed the pain.

Sam had still not been seen. He hesitated. He should find out what this was about. But he felt strange, like he was intruding on someone else's sacred moment. Like he would be barging into a church service.

He sank back towards the cliff's deepest shadows, careful not to be heard over the soft *shush . . . shush . . . shush* of the water.

'That's all for tonight,' Orsay said, and hung her head.

'But I want to know about my dad,' D-Con urged. 'You said you could do me tonight. It's my turn!'

'She's tired,' Orsay's helper said firmly. 'Don't you know how hard this is for her?'

'My dad is probably out there trying to talk to me,' D-Con wailed, pointing at a specific place on the FAYZ barrier, as if he could picture his father right there, trying to peer through frosted glass. 'He's probably right outside the wall. He's probably . . .' He choked up, unable to continue, and now Nerezza gathered him to her as she had Cigar, comforting him.

'They're all waiting,' Orsay said. 'All of them out there. Just beyond the wall. So many . . . so many . . .'

'The Prophetess will try again tomorrow,' the helper said. She raised D-Con to his feet. 'Go now, all of you. Go. Go!'

The group rose reluctantly, and Sam realised that they would soon be heading straight for him. The bonfire collapsed, sending up a shower of sparks.

He stepped back into a crevice. There wasn't a square inch of this beach and this cliff that he didn't know. He waited and watched as Francis, Cigar, D-Con, and the others climbed up the trail and away into the night.

An obviously exhausted Orsay climbed down from the rock. As they passed, arm in arm, the helper bearing Orsay's weight, Orsay stopped. She looked straight at Sam, though he knew he could not be visible.

'I dreamed her, Sam,' Orsay said. 'I dreamed her.'

Sam's mouth was dry. He swallowed hard. He didn't want to ask. But he couldn't stop himself.

'My mom?'

'She dreams of you . . . and she says . . . she says . . .' Orsay sagged, almost fell to her knees, and her helper caught her.

'She says . . . let them go, Sam. Let them go when their time comes.'

'What?'

'Sam, there comes a time when the world no longer needs heroes. And then the true hero knows to walk away.'

66 HOURS 47 MINUTES

Hushaby, don't you cry,
go to sleep little baby.
When you wake, you shall have
All the pretty little ponies . . .

IT WAS PROBABLY always a beautiful lullaby, Derek thought. Probably even when normal people sang it, it was beautiful. Maybe even brought tears to people's eyes.

But Derek's sister, Jill, was not a normal person.

Beautiful songs could sometimes take a person out of themselves and carry them away to a place of magic. But when Jill sang, it was not about the song, really. She could sing the phone book. She could sing a shopping list. Whatever she sang, whatever the words or the tune, it was so beautiful, so achingly lovely, that no one could listen and be untouched.

He wanted to go to sleep.

He wanted to have all the pretty little ponies.

While she sang, that was all he wanted. All he had ever wanted.

Derek had made sure the windows were shut. Because when Jill sang, every person within hearing came to listen. They couldn't help it.

At first neither of them had understood what was happening. Jill was just nine years old, not a trained singer or anything. But one day, about a week ago, she'd started singing. Something stupid, Derek recalled. The theme song to *The Fairly OddParents.*

Derek had stopped dead in his tracks. He'd been unable to move. Unable to stop listening. Grinning at the rapid-fire list of Timmy's wishes, wanting each of those things himself. Wanting his own fairy godparents. And when at last Jill had fallen silent, it was like he was waking up from the most perfect dream to find himself in a grey and awful reality.

It took only a day or so before Derek figured out that this was no ordinary talent. He'd had to face the fact that his little sister was a freak.

It was a terrifying discovery. Derek was a normal. The freaks – people like Dekka, Brianna, Orc, and especially Sam Temple – scared him. Their powers meant they could do whatever they wanted. No one could stop them.

Mostly the freaks acted OK. Mostly they used their powers to do things that needed doing. But Derek had seen Sam Temple in the middle of a fight. Sam against that other mega-freak, Caine Soren. They had destroyed a big part of the town plaza trying to kill each other. Derek had curled up in a ball and hidden as best he could while that battle raged.

Everyone knew the freaks thought they were special. Everyone knew they got the best food. You never saw a freak reduced to eating rat meat. You never saw a freak eating bugs. A few weeks earlier, when the hunger was at its worst, Derek and Jill had done that. They'd caught and eaten some grasshoppers.

Freaks? They never had to sink that low. Everyone knew that. At least that's what Zil said.

And why would Zil lie?

And now Derek's own little sister was one of *them.* A mutant. A freak.

But when she sang . . . when she sang, Derek was no longer in the dark and desperate FAYZ. When Jill sang, the sun was bright and the grass was green and a cool breeze blew. When Jill sang, their mother and father were there, along with everyone else who had disappeared.

When Jill sang, the nightmare reality of life in the FAYZ faded away to be replaced by the song, the song, the song.

Derek was in that place now, soaring on magical wings towards Heaven.

When I die, hallelujah by and by . . .

A song about death, Derek knew. But so beautiful when Jill sang it. It pierced his heart.

Oh how glad and happy when we meet . . .

Oh how happy, even though they sat in the dark in a house full of sad memories.

The beam of light was startling.

Jill stopped singing. It was devastating, that silence.

The beam of light shone through the gauzy curtains. It played around the room. Found Derek's face. Then swivelled until it had lit up Jill's freckled face and turned her blue eyes glassy.

The front door of the house flew open with a crash. The strike plate shattered.

The intruders spoke no words as they rushed in. Five boys carrying baseball bats and tyre irons. They wore an assortment of Halloween masks and stocking masks.

But Derek knew who they were.

'No! No!' he cried.

All five boys wore bulky shooter's earmuffs. They couldn't hear him. But more importantly, they couldn't hear Jill.

One of the boys stayed in the doorway. He was in charge. A runty kid named Hank. The stocking pulled down over his face smashed his features into Play-Doh, but it could only be Hank.

One of the boys, fat but fast-moving and wearing an Easter Bunny mask, stepped to Derek and hit him in the stomach with his aluminium baseball bat.

Derek dropped to his knees.

Another boy grabbed Jill. He put his hand over her mouth. Someone produced a roll of duct tape.

Jill screamed. Derek tried to stand, but the blow to his stomach had winded him. He tried to stand up, but the fat boy pushed him back down.

'Don't be stupid, Derek. We're not after you.'

The duct tape went around and around Jill's mouth. They worked by flashlight. Derek could see Jill's eyes, wild with terror. Pleading silently with her big brother to save her.

When her mouth was sealed, the thugs pulled off their shooter's earmuffs.

Hank stepped forwards. 'Derek, Derek, Derek,' Hank said, shaking his head slowly, regretfully. 'You know better than this.'

'Leave her alone,' Derek managed to gasp, clutching his stomach, fighting the urge to vomit.

'She's a freak,' Hank said.

'She's my little sister. This is our home.'

'She's a freak,' Hank said. 'And this house is east of First Avenue. This is a no-freak zone.'

'Man, come on,' Derek pleaded. 'She's not hurting anyone.'

'It's not about that,' a boy named Turk said. He had a weak leg, a limp that made it impossible not to recognise him. 'Freaks with freaks, normals with normals. That's the way it has to be.'

'All she does is –'

Hank's slap stung. 'Shut up. Traitor. A normal who stands up for a freak gets treated like a freak. Is that what you want?'

'Besides,' the fat boy said with a giggle, 'we're taking it easy on her. We were going to fix her so she could never sing again. Or talk. If you know what I mean.'

He pulled a knife from a sheath in the small of his back. 'Do you, Derek? Do you understand?'

Derek's resistance died.

'The Leader showed mercy,' Turk said. 'But the Leader isn't weak. So this freak either goes west, over the border right now. Or . . .' He let the threat hang there.

Jill's tears flowed freely. She could barely breathe because her nose was running. Derek could see that by the way she sucked tape into her mouth, trying for air. She would suffocate if they didn't let her go soon.

'Let me at least get her doll,' Derek said.

'It's Panda.'

Caine rose through layers of dream and nightmare, like pushing his way through thick curtains that draped his arms and legs and made his every move tiring.

He blinked. Still dark. Night.

The voice had no obvious source, but he recognised it, anyway. Even if there had been light he might not have seen the boy with the power to fade away and almost disappear. 'Bug. Why are you bothering me?'

'Panda. I think he's dead.'

'Have you checked his breathing? Listened to his heart?' Then another thought occurred to him. 'Why are you waking me up to tell me someone's dead?'

Bug didn't answer. Caine waited, but Bug still couldn't say it out loud.

'Do what you gotta do,' Caine said.

'We can't get at him. He didn't just die. He got in the car, right? The green one?'

Caine shook his head, trying to wake up all the way, trying to make the trip back to full consciousness. But the layers of dream and nightmare, and memory, too, dragged at him, confused his brain.

'There's no gas in that car,' Caine said.

'He pushed it. Till it got rolling,' Bug said. 'Then he jumped in. It rolled on down the road. Until he got to the bend.'

'There's a railing there,' Caine said.

'He went through it. Crash. Bumpety-bump all the way down. It's a long way down. Me and Penny just climbed down, so I know it's a long way down.'

Caine wanted this to stop. He didn't want to have to hear the next part. Panda had been OK. Not a horrible kid. Not like some of Caine's few remaining followers.

Maybe that explained why he would drive a car off a cliff.

'Anyway, he's totally dead,' Bug said. 'Me and Penny got him out. But we can't get him up the cliff.'

Caine got to his feet. Legs shaky, stomach like a black hole, mind filled with darkness. 'Show me,' he said.

They walked out into the night. Feet crunched on gravel now interrupted by tall weeds. Poor old Coates Academy, Caine thought. It had always been so meticulously maintained back in the old days. The headmaster would definitely not have approved of the big blast hole in the front of the building, or the garbage strewn here and there in the overgrown grass.

It wasn't a long walk. Caine did not speak. He used Bug sometimes; Bug was useful. But the little creep was not exactly a friend.

In the pearly starlight it was easy to see where the railing had been ripped apart. It was like a steel ribbon, cut then left half curled, dangling over the side.

Caine peered through the darkness. He could see the car. It was upside down. One door was open.

It took a few minutes for him to locate the body.

Caine sighed and raised his hands. It was near the limits of his range, so Panda didn't come flying up off the ground. He sort of scuffed and scooted along at first. Like an invisible predator was hauling him away to its lair.

But then Caine got a better 'grip' and Panda rose off the ground. He was on his back, staring up at the unreal stars, eyes still open.

Caine levitated the boy up from the crash, up and up until he brought him to as gentle a stop as he could. Panda lay now on the road.

Without a word, Caine started walking back to Coates.

'Aren't you going to carry him back?' Bug whined.

'Get a wheelbarrow,' Caine said. 'Carry your own meat.'

63 HOURS 31 MINUTES

THE WHIP CAME down.

It was made of flesh, but in his nightmare it was a snake, a writhing python that sliced the flesh from his arms and back and chest.

The pain was too terrible to endure. But he had endured it.

He had begged for death. Sam Temple had begged to die. He had begged the psychopath to kill him, to end it, to give him the only relief possible.

But he had not died. He had endured.

Pain. Too small a word. Pain and awful humiliation.

And the whip kept coming down, again and again, and Drake Merwin laughed.

Sam woke up in a bed of tangled, sweat-soaked sheets.

The nightmare did not leave him. Even with Drake dead and buried under a mountain of rock, he had Sam under the control of his whip hand.

'Are you OK?'

Astrid. Almost invisible in the darkness. Only the faintest starlight filtered through the window and framed her as she stood there in the doorway.

He knew what she looked like. Beautiful. Compassionate, intelligent blue eyes. Blonde hair all wispy and wild since she'd just gotten up from her own bed.

He could picture her all too easily. A picture more detailed than real life. He often pictured her as he lay alone in his bed. Far too often, and for too long. Too many nights.

'I'm fine,' Sam lied.

'You were having a nightmare.' It wasn't a question.

She came in. He could hear the rustle of her nightgown. He felt her warmth as she sat at the edge of his bed. 'The same one?' she asked.

'Yeah. It's getting kind of boring now,' he joked. 'I know how it ends.'

'It ends with you alive and well,' Astrid said.

Sam said nothing. That had been the outcome: he had survived. Yes, he was alive. But well?

'Go back to sleep, Astrid,' he said.

She reached for him, fumbled just a little, unable to find his face. But then her fingers touched his cheek. He turned away. He didn't want her finding the wetness there. But she wouldn't let him push her hand away.

'Don't,' he whispered. 'You just make it harder.'

'Is that a joke?'

He laughed. The tension broke. 'Well, not an intentional one.'

'It's not that I don't want to, Sam.' She bent over and kissed his mouth.

He pushed her away. 'You're trying to distract me. Make me think about something else.'

'Is it working?'

'Yes, I'd say it's working very well, Astrid.'

'Time for me to go.' She stood up and he heard her moving away.

He rolled out of bed. His feet hit the cold floor. 'I need to do a walk-through.'

She stopped in the doorway. 'Sam, I heard you come in two hours ago. You've had almost no sleep. And it will be dawn in a couple of hours. The town will survive that long without you. Edilio's kids are on duty.'

Sam pulled on a pair of jeans and zipped them up. He considered telling her about Orsay, about this latest craziness. But there would be time for that later. No rush.

'There are things out there that Edilio's guys can't handle,' Sam said.

'Zil?' Astrid said. The warmth was rapidly draining out of her voice. 'Sam, I despise Zil as much as you do. But you can't take him on yet. We need a system. Zil is a criminal, basically, and we need a system.'

'He's a punk creep, and until you come up with your great system, someone needs to keep an eye on him,' Sam snapped. Before Astrid could react angrily to his tone, he said, 'Sorry. I didn't mean to take it out on you.'

Astrid came back into the room. He hoped it was because she was just too attracted to him to leave, but that wasn't it. He could barely see her but could hear and feel that she was very close.

'Sam. Listen. It's not all on your shoulders any more.'

'You know, I seem to remember a time when you were all in favour of me taking on the responsibility,' Sam said. He pulled a T-shirt over his head. It was stiff with salt and smelled like low tide. That's what happened when you washed clothes in salt water.

'That's right,' Astrid said. 'You're a hero. You are without a doubt the biggest hero we have. But, Sam, we're going to need more in the long run. We need laws and we need people to enforce laws. We don't need . . .' She stopped herself just in time.

Sam made a wry face. 'A boss? Well, it's just kind of hard to adjust that quickly. One day I'm just me, minding my business. Then the FAYZ comes and suddenly everyone is telling me to step up. And now you all want me to back off.'

Orsay's words came back to him, up from the fuzzy, sleepy

recesses of his memory. *The true hero knows when to walk away.* It could have just as easily been Astrid saying that.

'I want you to go back to bed is all,' Astrid said.

'I know how you can get me to go back to bed,' he teased.

Astrid pushed him playfully, palm on his chest. 'Nice try.'

'Truth is, I can't go back to sleep now, anyway,' Sam said. 'I might as well take another walk.'

'Well, try not to kill anyone,' Astrid said.

It was meant as a joke, but it bothered Sam. That's what she thought of him? No, no, it was just a joke.

'Love you,' he said as he headed for the steps.

'Me too,' she said.

Dekka never remembered dreams. She was sure she had them because sometimes she woke up with a shadow on her mind. But she never really recalled details. The dreams or nightmares must have come – they said everyone dreamed, even dogs – but all Dekka retained was a sense of foreboding.

Her dreams – and her nightmares – were all in the real world.

Dekka's parents had sent her away. They'd sent her to Coates Academy, a boarding school for troublesome kids. In Dekka's case the 'trouble' was not the few incidents of misbehaviour she'd been involved in. Nor was it the occasional fight – Dekka had a habit of defending girls who had no other defender, and sometimes that resulted in a confrontation. Nine times out of ten, the fights went nowhere. Dekka was big and strong and fearless, so bullies usually found an excuse to walk away once they realised Dekka wouldn't. But on half a dozen occasions blows had been traded.

Dekka won some and lost some.

But the fights weren't the problem for her parents. Dekka's parents had taught her to stand up for herself.

The problem had been a kiss. A teacher had seen her kissing a girl and had called her parents. It wasn't even at school. It was in a parking lot outside a Claim Jumper Restaurant.

Dekka remembered every detail of that kiss. It was her first. It had scared her like nothing before ever had. And later, when she'd caught her breath, it had excited her like nothing before ever had.

It had upset her parents. To put it mildly. Especially when Dekka used the 'L' word openly for the first time. Her father was not going to have a lesbian daughter. He'd put it quite a bit more crudely than that. He had slapped her face, hard, twice. Her mother had stood there dithering and ineffectual, saying nothing.

So it was off to Coates to be with fellow students who ranged from decent kids whose parents just wanted to be rid of them, all the way to the brilliant, manipulative bully, Caine, and his creep of a henchman, Drake.

Her parents imagined she would be under constant discipline. After all, Coates had a reputation for fixing damaged kids. And a part of Dekka wanted to be 'fixed' because that would make life so much easier. But she had never chosen to be what she was, any more than she had chosen to be black. There was no 'fixing' her.

But at Coates, Dekka had met Brianna. And all thought of changing herself, of becoming 'normal,' evaporated.

She had fallen in love with Brianna at first sight. Even back then, long before Brianna became 'the Breeze', she had a swagger and a style that Dekka found irresistible. A feeling she had never shared with Brianna. Probably never would.

Where Dekka was gloomy and internal, Brianna was loud, brash, and reckless. Dekka had looked for some evidence that Brianna might be gay, too. But when she was honest, Dekka had to admit that this didn't seem to be the case.

But love wasn't rational. Love didn't have to make sense. Neither did hope. So Dekka held on to her love and to her hope.

Did she dream about Brianna? She didn't know. Probably didn't want to know.

She rolled out of bed and stood up. It was pitch-black. She found her way to the window and pushed back the blinds. Dawn was still an hour off, at least. She had no clock. What was the point?

She looked towards the beach. She could just make out the

sand and the faint phosphorescence of the water's edge.

Dekka found the book she was reading, *The Unknown Shore.* It was one of a series of seafaring books she'd found in the house. It was an unusual choice, but she found it strangely reassuring to inhabit a very different world for a while each day.

She carried it downstairs to the one light in the house. That light was a small ball that floated in mid-air in her 'family room'. A Sammy Sun, kids called them. Sam had made it for her, using the weird power he had. It burned night and day. It was not hot to the touch, had no wire or other source of energy. It simply burned like a weightless lightbulb. Magic. But magic was old news in the FAYZ. Dekka had her own.

Dekka rummaged in her cupboard and found a cold, boiled artichoke. There were a lot of artichokes to be had in the FAYZ. Not exactly bacon and eggs and hash browns, but better than the alternative, which was starving. The food supply in the FAYZ – the mordantly named Fallout Alley Youth Zone – was tenuous, generally unpleasant, and, occasionally, literally sickening, but Dekka had endured protracted hunger in earlier months, so a breakfast artichoke was fine with her.

In any case, she'd lost some weight. She supposed that was a good thing.

She felt more than heard a rush of air. The door slammed, a sound that arrived at the same time as Brianna. Brianna came to a vibrating stop in the middle of the room.

'Jack's hacking up a lung! I need cough medicine!'

'Hi, Brianna,' Dekka said. 'It's kind of the middle of the night.'

'Whatever. Nice pj's, by the way. You pick those up at Gap for Truck Drivers?'

'They're comfortable,' Dekka said mildly.

'Yeah. For you and your twelve closest friends. You've got curves – unlike me – you should show proud, that's all I'm saying.'

'Jack's sick?' Dekka reminded her, hiding a smile.

'Oh, yeah. Coughing. All achy and grumpy.'

Dekka suppressed her jealousy that Brianna was caring for a sick boy. And Computer Jack, at that. Computer Jack was a tech genius who, as far as Dekka could tell, had absolutely zero moral centre. Wave a keyboard under his nose and he'd do whatever you wanted.

'Sounds like the flu,' Dekka opined.

'Well, duh,' Brianna said. 'I didn't say he had anthrax or black plague or whatever. But you don't get it: Jack coughs, he doubles up, right? Maybe stomps his foot or smacks the bed, right?'

'Ah.' Jack, much to his own dismay, had developed a mutant power. He was as strong as ten grown men.

'He broke my bed!'

'He's in your bed?'

'He didn't want to smash any of his stupid computers at his stupid place. So he came over to my place. And now he's smashing my place. So here's my plan: You come over, right? And you levitate him, right? If he's in the air, he can't do any damage.'

Dekka peered at Brianna. 'You're loony, you know that? If there's one thing we have plenty of, it's houses. Stick him somewhere unoccupied.'

'Huh,' Brianna said, sounding a bit deflated. 'Yeah.'

'Unless you just want me to come over and keep you company,' Dekka said, hating the hopeful tone in her own voice.

'Nah, that's cool. Go back to bed.'

'You want to check upstairs for cough medicine?'

Brianna held up a half-empty bottle of some red liquid. 'I already did. You were talking. Saying something. Thanks.'

'OK,' Dekka said, unable to entirely conceal her disappointment that Brianna had refused her offer of help. Not that Brianna would notice. 'Flu usually goes away on its own after a week or so. Unless it's a twenty-four-hour flu. Either way, Jack won't die of it.'

'Yeah, OK. Later,' Brianna said. And she was gone. The door slammed.

'Of course, sometimes flu can be fatal,' Dekka said to emptiness. 'A girl can hope.'

FOUR

62 HOURS 33 MINUTES

THEY BROUGHT HIM a leg. A calf, to be specific. Caine was still the leader of the dwindling tribe of Coates kids, after all. Down to fifteen of them now, with Panda gone.

Bug had found a wheelbarrow and rolled Panda to the school. He and some of the others had built a fire of fallen branches and a few desks.

The smell had kept everyone awake through the rest of the night.

And now, in the hour before dawn, their own faces smeared with grease, they'd brought him a leg. The left one, Caine guessed. A token of respect. And an unspoken desire that he join them in their crime.

As soon as Bug left, Caine began trembling.

Hunger was a very powerful force. But so were humiliation and rage.

Down in Perdido Beach the kids had food. Not much, maybe, but Caine knew that the threat of starvation had receded for them. They weren't eating well in Perdido Beach. But they were eating much better than the kids at Coates.

Everyone who could have defected from Coates already had. Those who were left were kids with too many problems, too much blood on their hands . . .

It was down to Caine and Diana, really. And a dozen creeps and losers. Only one was any real help in the event of trouble – Penny. Penny, the monster bringer.

There were days when Caine almost missed Drake Merwin. He'd been an unstable mental case, but at least he'd been useful in a fight. He didn't make people think they were seeing monsters, like Penny. Drake *was* the monster.

Drake wouldn't have stared at this . . . this thing on the table. This all-too-recognisable object, charred and blackened. Drake wouldn't have hesitated.

An hour later, Caine found Diana. She was sitting in a chair in her room, watching the sunlight's first rays touch the treetops. He sat on her bed. The springs creaked. She was in shadow, almost invisible in the faint light, nothing but the glitter of her eyes and the outline of a hollow cheek.

In the dark, Caine could still pretend that she was her old self. Beautiful Diana. But he knew that her luscious dark hair was brittle and tinged with rust. Her skin was sallow and rough. Her arms sticks. Her legs unstable pins. She didn't look fourteen any more. She looked forty.

'We have to give it a try,' Caine said without preamble.

'You know he's lying, Caine,' Diana whispered. 'He's never been to the island.'

'He read about it in some magazine.'

Diana managed an echo of her old snarky laugh. 'Bug read a magazine? Yeah. Bug's a big reader.'

Caine said nothing. He sat still, trying not to think, trying not to remember. Trying not to wish there had been more to eat.

'We have to go to Sam,' Diana said. 'Give ourselves up. They won't kill us. So they'll have to feed us.'

'They will kill us if we give ourselves up. Not Sam, maybe, but the others. We're the ones responsible for turning out the lights. Sam won't be able to stop them. If not freaks like Dekka or Orc or Brianna, then Zil's punks.'

The one thing they still had at Coates was a pretty good idea of what was going on in town. Bug had the ability to walk unseen. He was in and out of Perdido Beach every few days, sneaking food for himself, mostly. But also overhearing what kids were saying. And supposedly reading torn magazines he didn't bother to sneak back to Coates.

Diana let it go. Sat quietly. Caine listened to her breathing.

Had she done it? Had she committed the sin herself? Or was she smelling it on him now and despising him for it?

Did he want to know? Would he be able to forget later that her lips had eaten that meat?

'Why do we go on, Caine?' Diana asked. 'Why not just lie down and die. Or you . . . you could . . .'

The way she looked at him made him sick. 'No, Diana. No. I'm not going to do that.'

'You'd be doing me a favour,' Diana whispered.

'You can't. We're not beat yet.'

'Yeah. I wouldn't want to miss this party,' Diana said.

'You can't leave me.'

'We're all leaving, Caine. All of us. Into town to be taken out one by one. Or stay here and starve. Or step outside as soon as we get our chance.'

'I saved your life,' he added, and hated himself for begging. 'I . . .'

'You have a plan,' Diana said dryly. Mocking. One of the things he loved about her, that mean streak of mockery.

'Yeah,' he said. 'Yeah. I have a plan.'

'Based on some stupid story from Bug.'

'It's all I've got, Diana. That, and you.'

Sam walked the silent streets.

He felt unsettled by his encounter with Orsay. And unsettled, too, by his encounter with Astrid in his bedroom.

Why hadn't he told her about Orsay? Because Orsay was saying the same thing Astrid was saying?

Let it go, Sam. Stop trying to be all things to all people.

Stop playing the hero, Sam. We're past all that.

He had to tell Astrid. If only to have her walk him through it, make sense of this thing with Orsay. Astrid would analyse it clearly.

But it wasn't that simple, was it? Astrid wasn't just his girlfriend. She was the head of the town council. He had to officially report on what he had learned. He was still getting used to that. Astrid wanted laws and systems and logical order. For months Sam had been in charge. He hadn't wanted to be, but then he was, and he'd accepted it.

And now he was no longer in charge. It was liberating. He told himself that: it was liberating.

But frustrating, too. While Astrid and the rest of the council were busy playing Founding Mothers and Founding Fathers, Zil was running around unopposed.

The thing with Orsay at the beach had shaken him. Was it possible? Was it even slightly possible that Orsay was in contact with the outside world?

Her power – the ability to inhabit others' dreams – was not in doubt. Sam had once seen her walking through his own dreams. And he had used her to spy on the great enemy, the gaiaphage, back before that monstrous entity had been destroyed.

But this? This claim that she could see the dreams of those outside the FAYZ?

Sam paused in the middle of the plaza and looked around him. He didn't need the pearly light to know that weeds now choked the formerly neat little green spaces. Glass was everywhere. Windows not broken in battle had been shattered by vandals. Garbage filled the fountain. On this site the coyotes had attacked. On this site Zil had tried to hang Hunter because Hunter was a freak.

The church was half destroyed. The apartment building had burned down. The storefronts and town hall steps were covered with graffiti, some just random, some romantic, most of it messages of hate or rage.

Every window was dark. Every doorway was in shadow. The McDonald's, once a sort of club run by Albert, was closed up. There was no electricity to play music any more.

Could it be true? Had Orsay dreamed his mother's dreams? Had she spoken to Sam? Had she seen something about him that he had failed to see in himself?

Why did that thought cause him such pain?

It was dangerous, Sam realised. If other kids heard Orsay talking that way, what would happen? If it was bothering *him* this much . . .

He was going to have to have a talk with Orsay. Tell her to knock it off. Her and that helper of hers. But if he told Astrid, it would all get too big. Right now he could just put a little pressure on Orsay, get her to stop.

He could just imagine what Astrid would do. Make it all about free speech or whatever. Or maybe not, maybe she'd see the threat, too, but Astrid was better with theories than she was with just walking up to people and telling them to stop.

In one corner of the plaza were the graves. The makeshift markers – wooden crosses, one inept attempt at a Star of David, a few just boards shoved upright into the dirt. Someone had knocked most of the headstones over and no one had yet had time to put them back.

Sam hated going there. Every kid buried in that ground – and there were many – was a personal failure. Someone he had not kept alive.

His feet stepped on to soft earth. He frowned. Why would there be dirt clods?

Sam raised his left hand over his head. A ball of light formed in his palm. It was a greenish light that darkened shadows. But he could see that the ground was disturbed. Dirt everywhere, not piled up, more like clods and shovels full had been thrown.

In the centre, a hole. Sam brightened the light and held his hand over the hole. He peered down inside, ready to strike if something attacked. His heart was hammering in his chest.

Movement!

Sam leaped back and fired a beam of light down into the hole. The light made no sound, but the dirt hissed and popped as it melted into glass.

'No!' he cried.

He tripped, fell on his rear in the dirt, and already he knew he'd made a mistake. He'd seen something move, and when he fired the searing light he'd seen what it was.

He crawled back to the edge of the hole. He looked over the edge, illuminating the scene with one cautious hand.

The little girl looked up at him, terrified. Her hair was dirty. Her clothes were muddy. But she was alive. Not burned. Alive.

There was tape over her mouth. She was struggling to breathe. She had a doll clutched tight. Her blue eyes pleaded.

Sam lay flat, reached down, and took her outstretched hand.

He wasn't strong enough to lift her cleanly up. He had to drag and haul, reposition, haul some more. And by the time she made it up out of the hole she was covered in dirt from head to toe. Sam was almost as dirty, and panting from the effort.

He pulled the tape from her face. It wasn't easily done. Someone had wound it around and around. The little girl cried when he pulled the tape from her hair.

'Who are you?' Sam asked.

He noticed something strange. He raised the level of light. Someone had written in magic marker on the girl's forehead.

The word was 'Freak'.

Sam's palm went dark. Slowly, careful not to scare her, he put his arm around the girl's heaving shoulders.

'It will be OK,' he lied.

'They . . . they said . . . why . . .' She couldn't finish. She collapsed against him, weeping on to his shirt.

'You're Jill. Sorry, I didn't recognise you at first.'

'Jill,' she said, and nodded and cried some more. 'They don't want me to sing.'

Job one, Sam told himself: take care of Zil. Enough. Whether Astrid and the council liked it or not, it was time to take care of Zil.

Or not.

Sam stared at the hole from which he'd pulled Jill, really seeing it for the first time. A hole in the ground where none should be. Something about it . . . something terribly wrong.

Sam gasped, sucked air sharply. A chill ran up his spine.

The horror here was not that a little girl had fallen into a hole. The horror was the hole itself.

FIVE

62 HOURS 6 MINUTES

SAM TOOK JILL to Mary Terrafino at the day care. Then he found Edilio, woke him up, and walked him to the town plaza. To the hole in the ground.

Edilio stared at it.

'So the girl fell in, walking around in the night,' Edilio said. He rubbed sleep out of his eyes and shook his head vigorously.

'Yeah,' Sam said. 'She didn't make the hole. She just fell in.'

'So what made the hole?' Edilio asked.

'You tell me.'

Edilio peered more closely at the hole. From the first need, Edilio had taken on the grim duty of digging the graves. He knew each one, knew who was where.

'*Madre de Dios*,' Edilio whispered. He made the sign of the cross on his chest. His eyes were wide as he turned to Sam. 'You know what this looks like, right?'

'What do you think it looks like?'

'It's too deep for being so narrow. No way someone did this

with a shovel. Man, this hole wasn't dug *down*. It was dug *up*.'

Sam nodded. 'Yeah.'

'You're pretty calm,' Edilio said shakily.

'Not really,' Sam said. 'It's been a strange night. What . . . who . . . was buried here?'

'Brittney,' Edilio said.

'So we buried her when she was still alive?'

'You're not thinking straight, man. It's been more than a month. Nothing stays alive that's in the dirt for that long.'

The two of them stood side by side, staring down into the hole. The too-narrow, too-deep hole.

'She had that thing on her,' Edilio said. 'We couldn't get it off her. We figured she's dead, so what's it matter, right?'

'That thing,' Sam said dully. 'We never figured out what it was.'

'Sam, we both know what it was.'

Sam hung his head. 'We have to keep this quiet, Edilio. If we put this out there, the whole town will go nuts. People have enough to deal with.'

Edilio looked distinctly uncomfortable. 'Sam, this isn't the old days. We have a town council now. They're supposed to know whatever's going on.'

'If they know, everyone will know,' Sam said.

Edilio said nothing. He knew it was true.

'You know that girl Orsay?' Sam asked.

'Of course I know her,' Edilio said. 'We almost got killed together.'

'Do me a favour and kind of keep an eye on her.'

'What's up with Orsay?'

Sam shrugged. 'She thinks she's some kind of prophet, I guess.'

'A prophet? You mean like those old dudes in the Bible?'

'She's acting like she can contact people on the other side. Parents and all.'

'Is it true?' Edilio asked.

'I don't know, man. I doubt it. I mean, no way, right?'

'Probably should ask Astrid. She knows this kind of stuff.'

'Yeah, well, I'd rather wait on that.'

'Hey, hold up, Sam. Are you asking me to not tell her about that, either? You got me hiding two big things from the council?'

'It's for their own good,' Sam said. 'And for everyone's good.' He took Edilio's arm and drew him close. In a low voice he said, 'Edilio, what kind of experience do Astrid and Albert really have? And John? Not to mention Howard, who we both know is just a jerk. You and me, we've been through every fight there's been since the FAYZ came. I love Astrid, but she's so into her ideas about how we have to get everything organised that she's not letting me do what I need to do.'

'Yeah, well, we kind of do need some rules and stuff.'

'Of course we do,' Sam agreed. 'We do. But in the meantime, Zil is kicking freaks out of their homes, and someone or something just dug its way up out of the ground. I need to be able to deal with stuff without everyone looking over my shoulder all the time.'

'Man, it isn't cool to lay this on me,' Edilio said. Sam did not respond. It would be lousy to pressure Edilio any further. Edilio was right: it was wrong to ask this of him.

'I know that,' Sam said. 'It's just . . . look, it's temporary. Until the council gets its act together and comes out with all its rules, someone still has to keep things from falling apart. Right?'

Finally Edilio sighed. 'Right. OK, I'll get us a couple shovels. Fill this in quick before people start coming out.'

Jill was too old for the day care. Sam had known that. But he had dumped her in Mary's lap anyway.

Great. Just what Mary needed: one more kid to look after.

But it was hard to say no. Especially to Sam.

Mary cast a weary glance around the day care. What a mess. She'd have to round up Francis and Eliza and some of the others and take another shot at bringing some order to this disaster. Yet again.

She glanced with bitterness at the milky plastic sheet that covered the blown-out wall between the day care and the hardware store. How many times had Mary asked for some help dealing with it? The hardware store had been looted many times and the axes and sledgehammers and blowtorches were mostly gone, but there were still nails and screws and tacks strewn everywhere. Kids had to be watched constantly because they absolutely would crawl under the plastic and end up poking one another with screwdrivers and then crying and fighting and demanding Band-Aids, which had run out long ago and . . .

Mary took a deep breath. The council had a lot to do. A lot of problems to deal with. Maybe this wasn't their top priority.

Mary forced a smile for the girl, who watched her solemnly and clutched her doll.

'I'm sorry, sweetie: what's your name again?'

'Jill.'

'Well, it's nice to meet you, Jill. You can stay here for a while until we work something else out.'

'I want to go home,' Jill said.

Mary wanted to say, *Yeah, we all do, honey. We all want to go home.* But she had learned that bitterness and irony and sarcasm didn't really help when dealing with the littles.

'What happened? Why were you out on the streets?' Mary asked.

Jill shrugged. 'They said I had to go.'

'Who?'

Jill shrugged again, and Mary gritted her teeth. So sick of

being understanding. So deeply, deeply sick of being responsible for every stray child in Perdido Beach.

'OK, then, do you know why you left your house?'

'They said they would . . . hurt me, I guess.'

Mary wasn't sure she wanted to pry any deeper. Perdido Beach was a community in a permanent state of fear and worry and loss. Kids didn't always behave too well. Older brothers and sisters sometimes lost it when dealing with their siblings.

Mary had seen things . . . things she would never have believed possible.

'Well, you can stay with us for a while,' Mary said. She gave the girl a hug. 'Francis will tell you the rules, OK? He's that big kid over in the corner.'

Jill turned away reluctantly and took a couple of hesitant steps towards Francis. Then she turned back. 'Don't worry: I won't sing.'

Mary almost didn't respond. But something about the way Jill had said it . . .

'Of course you can sing,' Mary said.

'I better not,' Jill said.

'What's your favourite song?' Mary asked.

Jill looked bashful. 'I don't know.'

Mary persisted. 'I'd like to hear you sing, Jill.'

Jill sang. A Christmas carol.

What child is this who laid to rest
on Mary's lap is sleeping?
Whom angels greet with anthems sweet
While shepherds watch are keeping . . .

And the world stopped.

Later – how much later, Mary could not know – Jill sat down on an unoccupied cot, cradled her doll close, and fell to sleep.

The room had fallen silent as she sang. Every child standing stock-still, as if they'd been frozen. But everywhere eyes were alight and mouths formed dreamy half smiles.

When Jill stopped singing, Mary looked at Francis.

'Did you . . .'

Francis nodded. There were tears in his eyes. 'Mary, you need to catch some sleep, hon. Eliza and I will handle breakfast.'

'I'm just going to sit down, rest my feet for a while,' Mary said. But sleep took her anyway.

Francis woke her what seemed like mere minutes later. 'I have to go,' he said.

'Is it time?' Mary shook her head to clear it. Her eyes didn't seem to want to focus.

'Soon. And I have some goodbyes to say first,' he said. He put his hand on her shoulder and said, 'You're a great person, Mary. And another great person has come to see you.'

Mary stood up, not really following what Francis was

saying, just knowing that someone was there to see her.

Orsay. She was so slight and fragile looking Mary instinctively liked her. She seemed like one of the kids, almost, one of the littles.

Francis touched Orsay's hand and almost seemed to bow his head as if in prayer for a moment. 'Prophetess,' he said.

'Mother Mary, the Prophetess,' Francis said, performing a very formal introduction. Mary felt like she was meeting the president or something.

'Orsay, please,' Orsay said in a soft voice. 'And this is my friend, Nerezza.'

Nerezza was very different from Orsay. She had green eyes and olive skin and hair that was black and lustrous, gathered in a sort of loose wave on one side. Mary did not recall having seen her before. But Mary was trapped in the day care most of the day; she didn't socialise much.

Francis grinned a little nervously, it seemed to Mary.

'Happy *rebirthday*,' Nerezza said.

'Yes. Thank you,' Francis said. He squared his shoulders, nodded to Nerezza, and to Orsay said, 'I have some more people to see, and not much time. Prophetess, thank you for showing me the way.' And with that, he turned away quickly and left.

Orsay seemed almost sickened. As though she wanted to spit something out. She nodded tersely to Francis's back and gritted her teeth.

Nerezza's face was unreadable. Deliberately, Mary thought, as though she was concealing an emotion she felt strongly.

'Hi . . . Orsay.' Mary wasn't quite sure what to call her now. She'd heard kids talking about Orsay being some kind of prophet and she had dismissed it. People said all kinds of crazy things. But clearly she'd had some profound effect on Francis.

Orsay didn't seem to know what to say next. She looked at Nerezza, who quickly filled the void. 'The Prophetess wishes to help you, Mary.'

'Help me?' Mary laughed. 'I actually have enough volunteers for once.'

'Not that.' Nerezza waved that off, impatient. 'The Prophetess would like to adopt a recently arrived child.'

'Excuse me?'

'Her name is Jill,' Orsay said. 'I had a dream about . . .' And then she trailed off, as though she wasn't quite sure what the dream was. She frowned.

'Jill?' Mary repeated. 'The little girl who was terrorised by Zil? She's only been here a few hours. How did you even know she was here?'

Nerezza said, 'She was forced out of her home because she was a freak. Now her brother is too scared and weak to care for her. But she's too old for the day care, Mary. You know that.'

'Yes,' Mary said. 'She's definitely too old.'

'The Prophetess would care for her. It's something she wants to do.'

Mary looked at Orsay for confirmation. And after a few seconds, Orsay realised it was her turn to speak and said, 'Yes, I would like to do that.'

Mary didn't feel quite right about it. She didn't know what was going on with Orsay, but Nerezza was clearly a strange girl, brooding and even, it seemed to Mary, a little tough.

But the day care didn't take older kids. It couldn't. And this was hardly the first time Mary had temporarily sheltered an older kid who then found another place to get her meals.

Francis seemed to have been vouching for Orsay and Nerezza. He must be the one who had told Orsay about Jill while Mary was sleeping.

Mary frowned, wondering why Francis had been in such a hurry to leave. *Rebirthday?* What was that supposed to mean?

'OK,' Mary said. 'If Jill agrees, she can live with you.'

Orsay smiled. And Nerezza's eyes glittered with satisfaction.

Justin had wet his bed sometime in the night. Like a baby. He was five years old, not a baby.

But there was no denying he had done it.

He told Mother Mary and she told him it was no big deal, it happened. But it didn't used to happen to Justin. Not when he had a real mommy. It had been a long time since he had peed the bed.

He cried when he told Mother Mary. He didn't like telling her because Mother Mary seemed like she might be getting sick or something. She wasn't as nice as she used to be. He usually told Francis if he had to. Some nights he didn't pee because he didn't drink any water for practically all day. But last night he'd forgotten about not drinking water. So he had, but just a little.

He was five now, older than just about all the kids at the day care. But he was still wetting his bed.

Two big girls had come and taken the singing girl away. Justin had no one to take him away.

But he knew where his house was, his real house with his old bed. He never used to wet that bed. But now he had a stupid bed on the floor, just a mattress, and other kids stepped all over it, so that was probably why he was wetting his bed again.

His old house wasn't very far away. He'd gone there before. Just to look at it and see if it was real. Because sometimes he didn't believe it was.

He had gone to check and see if Mommy was there. He hadn't seen her. And when he opened the door and went inside he had gotten too scared and he had come running back to Mother Mary.

But he was older now. He'd only been four and a half then, and now he was five. Now he probably wouldn't be scared.

And he probably wouldn't pee in his bed if he was at his real home.

SIX

57 HOURS 17 MINUTES

DAYLIGHT, BRIGHT AND clear.

Sam and Astrid walked through the Mall. It didn't take long. There was the fish stand, already almost bare, with just two small octopi, a dozen or so clams, and a small fish so ugly, no one had yet been brave enough to buy it.

The fish stand was a long folding table dragged from the school cafeteria. Plastic bins were lined up, the grey plastic kind that were used to bus dishes. A droopy cardboard sign held in place by duct tape hung from the front of the table. It read, 'Quinn's Seapreme Seafood.' And below that, in smaller print, 'An AlberCo Enterprise.'

'What do you think that fish is?' Sam asked Astrid.

She peered closely at the alleged fish. 'I think that's an example of *Pesce inedibilis*,' she said.

'Yeah?' Sam made a face. 'Do you think it's OK to eat?'

Astrid sighed theatrically. '*Pesce inedibilis?* Inedible? Joke, duh. Try to keep up, Sam, I made that really easy for you.'

Sam smiled. 'You know, a real genius would have known I wouldn't get it. Ergo, you are not a real genius. Hah. That's right: I threw down an "ergo".'

She gave him a pitying look. 'That's very impressive, Sam. Especially from a boy who has twenty-two different uses for the word "dude".'

Sam stopped, took her arm, and spun her towards him. He pulled her close. 'Dude,' he whispered in her ear.

'OK, twenty-three,' Astrid amended. She pushed him away. 'I have shopping to do. Do you want to eat, or do you want to . . . *dude*?'

'Dude. Always.'

She looked at him critically. 'Are you going to tell me why you were covered with mud this morning?'

'I tripped and fell. When I saw the girl, Jill, in the dark, I tripped over my own feet.' Not exactly a lie. Part of the truth. And he would tell her all of the truth just as soon as he'd had a chance to sort it out. It had been a weird, disturbing night: he needed time to think and work out a plan. It was always better to go to the council with a plan worked out; that way, they could just say OK and let him get on with it.

The Mall had been set up on the playground of the school. That way the younger kids could come and play on the equipment while older kids shopped. Or gossiped. Or checked each other out. Sam found himself looking a bit more carefully at the faces. He didn't really expect to see Brittney walking around here. That was crazy. There had to be some other explanation. But just the same, he kept his eyes peeled.

What he would do if he did actually see a dead girl walking around was something he'd have to think about. As strange as life in the FAYZ could be, that was still one problem he hadn't had to face.

In no particular order the Mall consisted of Quinn's Seapreme Seafood; the produce stand named Gifts of the Worm; a bookstall identified as the Cracked Spine; the fly-covered stall of Meats of Mystery; Totally Solar – where two enterprising kids had scrounged a half dozen solar panels and would use them to charge batteries; the Sux Xchange where toys and clothing and miscellaneous junk were bartered and sold.

A wood-fired barbecue grill had been set up a little apart. You could take your fish or meat or vegetables there and have them cooked for a small charge. Once grilled over the coals, pretty much everything – venison, raccoon, pigeon, rat, coyote – tasted the same: smoky and burned. But none of the stoves or microwaves worked any more, and there was no more cooking oil, certainly no more butter, so even the kids who chose to cook their own food ended up duplicating the same experience. The only alternative was boiling, and the two girls who ran the place kept a big pot simmering. But everyone agreed that grilled rat was far superior to boiled.

The 'restaurant' changed names every few days. It had already been Smokey Sue's, Perdido I Can't Believe It's Not Pizza Kitchen, Eat and Urp, In 'n' Get Out, Smokey Tom's, and Le Grand Barbecue. Today the sign read, 'WTF?' and in smaller letters, 'What the Food?'

Kids lounged at two of the three rickety dining tables, chairs tilted back, feet up. Some were eating, some just hanging out. They looked like a junior version of some kind of end-of-the-world movie, Sam thought, not for the first time. Armed, dressed in bizarre outfits, topped with strange hats, men's clothing, women's clothing, tablecloth capes, barefoot or wearing ill-fitting shoes.

Drinkable water now had to be trucked from the half-empty reservoir up in the hills outside of town. Gasoline was strictly rationed so that the water trucks could be kept running as long as possible. The council had a plan for when the last of the gas was gone: relocate everyone to the reservoir. If there was still any water there.

They calculated they had six months till they ran out of water. Like most council decisions it seemed like bull to Sam. The council spent at least half their time concocting scenarios they would then argue over without ever reaching a decision. They'd been supposedly drafting a set of laws for pretty much the whole time they'd been in existence. Sam had done his best to be patient, but while they were dawdling and debating he still had to keep the peace. They had their rules, he had his. His were the ones most kids lived by.

The Mall lined the western wall of the school gym so as to take advantage of the shade. As the day wore on and the sun rose, the food stalls would run out of stuff and close down. Some days there was very, very little food. But no one had starved to death – quite.

The water was brought down in five gallon plastic jugs and given away free – a gallon per person per day. There were 306 names on the water list.

There was rumour of a couple of kids living out of town in a farmhouse. But Sam had never seen evidence of it. And made-up people were not his problem.

The remaining sixteen known people in the FAYZ were up the hill at Coates Academy, all that was left of Caine's isolated band. What they ate and drank was not Sam's concern.

Away from the school's wall, over in the lesser shade of a 'temporary' building, a different group was at work. A girl read tarot cards for one 'Berto. The 'Berto was short for 'Albert'. Albert had created a currency based on gold bullets and McDonald's game pieces. He'd wanted to call the currency something else, but no one remembered what. So, 'Bertos they were, a play on 'Albert', coined by Howard, of course, who had also come up with 'the FAYZ' to describe their weird little world.

Sam had thought Albert was nuts with his obsession with

creating money. But the evidence was in: Albert's system was producing just enough food for kids to survive. And a lot more kids were working. Far fewer were just hanging out. It was no longer impossible to get kids to go into the fields and do the backbreaking work of picking crops. They worked for 'Bertos and spent 'Bertos, and for now at least starvation was just a bad memory.

The tarot reader was ignored. No one had money to waste on that. A boy played a guitar of sorts while his little sister played a professional drum set they'd liberated from someone's home. They were not good, but they were making music, and in a Perdido Beach without electricity, without recorded music, without iPods or stereos, where computer hard drives grew dusty and DVD players were untouched, even pitiful entertainment was welcome.

As Sam watched, a girl placed a quarter of a melon on the musician's tip plate. They immediately stopped playing, broke the melon into pieces, and wolfed it down.

Sam knew there was a second market, out of sight but easy enough to find for those who were interested. That market sold alcohol and pot and various other contraband. Sam had tried to put a stop to the alcohol and drugs, but he had not accomplished much. He had more pressing priorities.

'New graffiti,' Astrid said, looking up at the wall behind the meat stand.

The black and red logo formed a crude 'H' and 'C.' Human Crew. Zil Sperry's hate group.

'Yeah, it's all over town,' Sam said. He knew he shouldn't keep talking, but he did, anyway. 'If I weren't on a leash I'd go over to Zil's so-called compound and put an end to this once and for all.'

'What do you mean? Kill him?' Astrid said, playing dumb.

'No, Astrid. Haul his butt to town hall and stick him in a locked room until he decides to grow up.'

'In other words, put him in prison. Because you decide to. And for as long as you decide to keep him there,' Astrid said. 'For a guy who never wanted to be in charge, you're awfully willing to be a dictator.'

Sam sighed. 'OK, fine. Whatever. I don't want to fight.'

'So, how is the little girl from last night?' Astrid asked, changing the subject.

'Mary was taking care of her.' He hesitated. Looked over his shoulder to make sure no one was within range to overhear. 'Mary asked her to sing. She says it's like the world stops when she sings. Like no one talks, no one moves, the whole preschool just practically froze. Mary says it's like an angel is singing. Just to you.'

'An angel?' Astrid said sceptically.

'Hey, I thought you believed in angels.'

'I do. I just don't think this little girl is one.' She sighed.

'More like a siren.'

Sam stared blankly at her.

'No,' Astrid said. 'Not like a police car siren. Like Odysseus. Ulysses. The sirens. The ones who when they sang no man could resist them?'

'I knew that.'

'Uh-huh.'

'I did. They did a parody on *The Simpsons.*'

Astrid sighed. 'Why am I with you?'

'Because I'm incredibly attractive?'

'You are mildly attractive, actually,' Astrid teased.

'So, I'm a kind of really hot dictator?'

'I don't recall saying "really hot".'

Sam smiled. 'You didn't have to. It's in your eyes.'

They kissed. Not a big passionate kiss, but nice like it was always nice. Someone hooted derisively. Someone else yelled, 'Get a room.'

Sam and Astrid ignored all that. They were both aware that they were the 'first couple' of the FAYZ, and their relationship was a sign of stability to kids. Like seeing Mom and Dad kissing: kind of gross, but kind of reassuring.

'So what are we going to do with the Siren now?' Astrid asked. 'She's too old to stay with Mary.'

'Orsay took her in,' Sam said. He waited to see whether the mention of Orsay would get a reaction from Astrid.

No. Astrid didn't know what Orsay was up to.

'Excuse me. Sam?'

He turned around to find Francis. Not the best time to be interrupted, not when he was trying to discuss his attractiveness with Astrid.

'What's up, Francis?'

Francis shrugged. He looked confused and awkward. He stuck out his hand. Sam hesitated; then, feeling slightly ridiculous, he shook Francis's hand.

'I felt like I had to say thanks,' Francis said.

'Oh. Oh, um . . . cool.'

'And don't take it like it's your fault, OK?' Francis said. 'And don't be mad at me. I tried . . .'

'What are you talking about?'

'It's my birthday,' Francis explained. 'The big One-Five.'

Sam felt a bead of sweat roll down his back. 'You're ready, right? I mean, you've read the write-up on what you have to do?'

'I've read it,' Francis said. But his voice betrayed him.

Sam grabbed his arm. 'No, Francis. No.'

'It's going to be OK,' Francis said.

'No,' Astrid said firmly. 'You don't want to do this.'

Francis shrugged. Then he grinned shyly. 'My mom, she needs me. She and my dad just broke up. And, anyway, I miss her.'

'What do you mean they just broke up?'

'They've been thinking about it a long time. But last week my dad just took off. And she's alone, right, so –'

'Francis, what are you talking about?' Astrid demanded irritably. 'We've been in the FAYZ for seven months. You don't know what's going on with your parents.'

'The Prophetess told me.'

'The *what*?' Astrid snapped. 'Francis, have you been drinking?'

Sam felt frozen, unable to react. He knew instantly what this was about.

'The Prophetess told me,' Francis said. 'She saw . . . she knows and she told me . . .' He was getting more and more agitated. 'Look, I don't want you to be mad at me.'

'Then stop acting like an idiot,' Sam said, finding his voice at last.

'My mom needs me,' Francis said. 'More than you do. I have to go to her.'

'What makes you think the poof takes you to your mother?'

'It's a door,' Francis said. His eyes clouded over as he spoke. He wasn't looking at Sam any more. He was inside his own head, his voice sing-song, as if reciting something he'd heard. 'A door, a pathway, an escape to bliss. Not a birthday: a *rebirthday*.'

'Francis, I don't know who is telling you this, but it's

not true,' Astrid said. 'No one knows what happens if you step out.'

'*She* knows,' Francis said. 'She explained it to me.'

'Francis, I'm telling you not to do this,' Sam said urgently. 'Look, I know about Orsay. I know, all right? And maybe she thinks this is true, but you can't risk it.'

He felt Astrid's penetrating gaze. He refused to acknowledge the unspoken question.

'Dude, you are the man,' Francis said with a soft smile. 'But even you can't control this.'

Francis turned and walked quickly away. He stopped after a dozen feet. Mary Terrafino was running towards him. She waved her stick-thin arms and yelled, 'Francis! No!'

Francis raised his hand and checked his watch. His smile was serene.

Mary reached him, grabbed him by the shirt, and yelled, 'Don't you leave those children. Don't you dare leave those children! They've lost too much. They love you.'

Francis slipped off his watch and held it out to her. 'It's all I have to give you.'

'Francis, no.'

But she was holding air. Yelling at air.

The watch lay in the grass.

Francis was gone.

SEVEN

56 HOURS 30 MINUTES

'**WHAT** ELSE HAVEN'T you been telling us, Sam?'

Astrid had immediately called a meeting of the town council. She hadn't even yelled at him privately. She'd just nailed him with a poisonous look and said, 'I'm calling a meeting.'

Now they sat in the former mayor's conference room. It was gloomy, the only light coming through a window that was itself in shade. The table was heavy wood, the chairs deep and luxurious. The walls were decorated – if that was the right word – with large, framed photos of past mayors of Perdido Beach.

Sam always felt like a fool in this room. He sat in a too-big chair at one end of the table. Astrid was at the other. Her hands were on the table, slender fingers flat on the surface.

Dekka sat scowling, irritated, though Sam wasn't sure at whom she was directing her dark mood. A piece of something blue was stuck in one of her tight cornrows – not that anyone was foolish enough to point it out or laugh.

Dekka was a freak, the only one besides Sam in this room.

She had the power to temporarily cancel gravity in small areas. Sam counted her as an ally. Dekka was not about talking without end and getting nothing done.

Albert was the best-dressed person in the room, wearing an amazingly clean and seemingly un-salty polo shirt and relatively unwrinkled slacks. He looked like a very young businessman who had stopped by on his way to a round of golf.

Albert was a normal, though he seemed nevertheless to have an almost supernatural ability to organise, to make things happen, to do business. Looking at the group through hooded eyes, Sam knew Albert was probably the most powerful person in the room. Albert, more than any other person, had kept Perdido Beach from starving.

Edilio slumped, holding his head with both hands and not making eye contact with anyone. He had a submachine gun propped against his chair, a sight that had become all too normal.

Edilio was officially town marshal. Probably the mildest, most modest and least-assuming person in the council, he was in charge of enforcing whatever rules the council created. If they ever got around to actually creating any.

Howard was the wild card in the group. Sam still wasn't sure how he had managed to talk his way on to the council. No one doubted that Howard was smart. But no one thought he had an honest or ethical bone in his body. Howard was chief toady to

Orc, the glowering, drunken boy-turned-monster who had fought on the right side a couple of times when it had really counted.

The youngest member was a sweet-faced boy named John Terrafino. He was a normal, too – Mary's little brother. He seldom had much to say and mostly listened. Everyone assumed he voted however Mary told him to. Mary would have been there, but she was simultaneously indispensable and fragile.

Seven council members. Astrid as chairperson. Five normals, two freaks.

'A few different things happened last night,' Sam said as calmly as he could. He didn't want a fight. He especially didn't want a fight with Astrid. He loved Astrid. He was desperate for Astrid. She was the sum total of all the good he had in his life, he reminded himself.

And now she was furious.

'We know about Jill,' Astrid said.

'Zil's punks. Who wouldn't still be doing stuff like that if we'd shut them down,' Dekka muttered.

'We've voted on that,' Astrid said.

'Yeah, I know. Four to three in favour of letting the sick little creep and his sick little friends terrorise the whole town,' Dekka snapped.

'Four to three in favour of having some kind of system of laws and not just fighting fire with fire,' Astrid said.

'We can't just go around arresting people without some kind of system,' Albert said.

'Yeah, Sammy,' Howard said with a smirk. 'You can't just go all laser-hands whenever you decide you don't like someone.'

Dekka shifted in her seat, hunching her strong shoulders forwards. 'No, so instead we let little girls be kicked out of their own homes and terrorised.'

'Look, once and for all, we can't have a system where Sam is judge, jury, and executioner,' Astrid said. She softened it a bit by adding, 'Although if there's one person I would trust, it's him. Sam's a hero. But we need everyone in the FAYZ to know what's OK and what's not. We need rules, not just one person deciding who is out of line and who isn't.'

'He was a really good worker,' John whispered. 'Francis. He was a really good worker. The prees are totally going to miss him. They loved him.'

'I only found out about this last night. Actually, early this morning,' Sam said. He gave a brief description of what he'd seen and heard at Orsay's gathering.

'Could it be true?' Albert asked. He seemed worried. Sam understood his ambivalence. Albert had gone from being just another kid in the old days, a person no one even really noticed, to being the person who in many ways ran Perdido Beach.

'I don't think there's any way for us to know,' Astrid said.

Everyone fell silent at that. The idea that it might be possible to contact parents, friends, family outside of the FAYZ was mind-boggling. The idea that those outside could know what was happening inside the FAYZ . . .

Even now, with some time to digest it, Sam felt powerful and not necessarily pleasant emotions. He had long been plagued by the fear that when the FAYZ wall somehow, some day, came down, he would be held responsible. For lives he had taken. For lives he had not saved. The idea that the whole world might be watching, dissecting his actions, questioning every panicky move, every desperate moment, was disturbing, to say the least.

So many things he didn't want to have to ever talk about. So many things that could be made to look awful.

Young master Temple, can you explain how you sat by while kids wasted most of the food supply and ended up starving?

Are you telling us, Mr. Temple, that children were cooking and eating their own pets?

Mr. Temple, can you explain the graves in the plaza?

Sam clenched his fists and steadied his breathing.

'What Francis did was commit suicide,' Dekka said.

'I think that's a little harsh,' Howard said. He leaned back in his chair, put his feet on the table, and interlaced his fingers over his skinny belly. He knew this would irritate Astrid. In fact, Sam guessed, he did it for just that reason. 'He wanted to go running home to Mommy, what can I say? Of course, it's hard for me to believe that anyone would choose to step out of the FAYZ. I mean, where else do you get to eat rats, use your backyard for a toilet, and live in fear of nineteen different kinds of scary?'

No one laughed.

'We can't let kids do this,' Astrid said. She sounded quite sure.

'How do we stop them?' Edilio asked. He raised his head, and Sam saw the distress on his face. 'How do you think we stop them? When your fifteenth birthday rolls around, the easy thing is to take the poof. You gotta fight to resist it. We know that. So how are we going to tell kids this isn't real, this Orsay thing?'

'We just tell them,' Astrid said.

'But we don't *know* if it's real or not,' Edilio argued.

Astrid shrugged. She stared at nothing and kept her features very still. 'We tell them it's all fake. Kids hate this place, but they don't want to die.'

'How do we tell them if we don't know?' Edilio seemed genuinely puzzled.

Howard laughed. 'Deely-O, Deely-O, you are such a doof sometimes.' He put his feet down and leaned towards Edilio as if sharing a secret with him. 'She means: We *lie.* Astrid means that we lie to everyone and tell them we do know for sure.'

Edilio stared at Astrid like he was expecting her to deny it.

'It's for people's own good,' Astrid said in a low voice, still looking at nothing.

'You know what's funny?' Howard said, grinning. 'I was pretty sure we were coming to this meeting so Astrid could rank on Sam for not telling us the whole truth. And now, it turns out we're really here so Astrid can talk us all into becoming liars.'

'Becoming?' Dekka snarled with a cynical look at Howard. 'Wouldn't exactly be a transformation for you, Howard.'

Astrid said, 'Look, if we let Orsay go on with this craziness, we could not only have kids stepping out on their fifteenth. We could have kids not wanting to wait that long. Kids deciding to end it right away and thinking they'd wake up on the other side with their parents.'

Everyone at the table leaned back at once, taking that in.

'I can't lie,' John said simply. He shook his head, and his red curls shook, too.

'You're a member of the council,' Astrid snapped. 'You have to abide by our decisions. That's the deal. That's the only way it works.' Then, in a calmer voice, she said, 'John, isn't Mary coming up on her fifteenth before long?'

Sam saw the jab hit home. Mary was perhaps the single most necessary person in Perdido Beach. From the start she had stepped up and run the day care. She'd become a mother to the littles.

But Mary had her own problems. She was anorexic and bulimic. She ate antidepressants by the handful, but the supply was rapidly running out.

Dahra Baidoo, who controlled the medicines in Perdido Beach, came to Sam secretly and told him that Mary was in every couple of days, asking for whatever Dahra might have. 'She's taking Prozac and Zoloft and Lexapro, and these aren't just nothing little meds, Sam. People have to go on and off these things carefully, according to the book. You don't just grab whatever and mix them all up.'

Sam hadn't told anyone but Astrid about it. And he'd warned Dahra to keep it to herself. Then he'd made a mental note to talk to Mary, and had forgotten to ever follow up.

Now, from John's stricken expression, Sam could guess that he was far from certain that Mary wouldn't give in to the poof and step out.

They took a vote. Astrid, Alberto, and Howard shot their hands up immediately.

'No, man,' Edilio said, shaking his head. 'I'd have to lie to my own people, my soldiers. Kids who trust me.'

'No,' John voted. 'I . . . I'm just a kid and all, but I would have to lie to Mary.'

Dekka looked at Sam. 'What do you say, Sam?'

Astrid interrupted. 'Look, we could do this temporarily. Just until we find out if Orsay is making this all up. If she came out later and admitted it was all fake, well, we'd have our answer.'

'Maybe we should torture her,' Howard said, only half kidding.

'We can't just sit by if we think kids are going to be dying,' Astrid pleaded. 'Suicide is a mortal sin. These kids won't be getting out of the FAYZ, they'll be going to hell.'

'Wow,' Howard said. 'Hell? And we know this, how exactly? You don't know any more than any of us do about what happens after a poof.'

'So that's what this is about?' Dekka asked. 'Your religion?'

'Everyone's religion is against suicide,' Astrid snapped.

'I'm against it, too,' Dekka said defensively. 'I just don't want to be getting dragged into the middle of some kind of religious thing.'

'Whatever Orsay represents, it's not a religion,' Astrid said icily.

Sam heard Orsay's voice in his head. *Let them go, Sam. Let them go and get out of the way.*

His mother's words, if Orsay was telling the truth.

'Let's give it a week,' Sam said.

Dekka took a deep breath and blew it out all at once. 'OK. I'll go with Sam on this. We lie. For a week.'

The meeting broke up. Sam was the first out of the room, suddenly desperate for fresh air. Edilio caught up to him as he was running down the steps of town hall.

'Hey. Hey! We never told them about what you and me saw last night.'

Sam stopped, looked towards the plaza, towards the hole they had refilled.

'Yeah? What did we see last night, Edilio? Me, I just saw a hole in the ground.'

Sam didn't give Edilio the chance to argue. He didn't want to hear what Edilio would say. He walked quickly away.

EIGHT

55 HOURS 17 MINUTES

CAINE HATED DEALING with Bug. The kid creeped him out. For one thing, Bug had become less and less visible. It used to be that Bug would do his disappearing act only when necessary. Then he started doing it whenever he wanted to spy on someone, which was pretty frequently.

Now he would become visible only when Caine ordered him to.

Caine was betting everything on Bug's story. A story of a magical island. It was insane, of course. But when reality was hopeless, fantasy became more and more necessary.

'How much farther to this farmhouse of yours, Bug?' Caine asked.

'Not far. Stop worrying.'

'You stop worrying,' Caine muttered. Bug was walking invisible through open fields. Nothing but depressions in the dirt where he stepped. Caine was all-too-visible. Broad daylight. Across a dusty, ploughed field under a bright, hot sun. Bug said no one was in these fields. Bug said these fields had nothing growing and that none of Sam's people knew about the farmhouse, which was practically unnoticeable, off a dirt road and looked abandoned.

Caine's first question had been, 'Then how do you know about them?'

'I know lots of stuff,' Bug answered. 'Besides, a long time ago you said to keep an eye on Zil.'

'So how does Zil know about this farmhouse?'

The voice above the impressions of invisible feet said, 'I think one of Zil's guys used to know these kids. Back in the day.'

Caine's next question: 'Do they have food there?'

'Yeah. Some. But they also have shotguns. And the girl, the sister Emily? She's some kind of freak, I think. I don't know what she does, I ain't seen her do anything freaky, but her brother is scared of her. So is Zil, kind of, only he doesn't show it.'

'Great,' Caine muttered. He noted that Zil was a kid who wouldn't let himself show fear. Maybe useful.

Caine shaded his eyes with his hand and scanned around, looking for telltale dust plumes from a truck or car. Bug said the Perdido Beach people were low on gas, too, but still drove when they needed to.

He was confident that he could take on and defeat any one freak from Sam's group. With the sole exception of Sam himself.

But if it was Brianna and Dekka together? Or even that little preppy nitwit Taylor and a few of Edilio's soldiers?

But right now the real problem was simply that Caine was weak. Walking this distance – miles – was hard. Very hard when his stomach was stabbing him again, and his navel was scraping his spine. His legs were wobbly. His eyes sometimes became unfocused.

One good meal . . . well, not really a good meal . . . was not enough. But it was keeping him alive. Digesting Panda. Panda energy flowing from his stomach through his blood.

The farmhouse was hidden by a stand of trees, but otherwise right out in the open. A long way from the road, yes, but Caine couldn't believe Sam's people had never found it and searched it for food.

Very strange.

'No closer,' a young male voice called from the front porch of the house.

Bug and Caine froze.

'Who are you? What do you want?'

Caine couldn't see anyone through the dirty screen.

Bug answered, 'We're just –'

'Not you,' the voice interrupted. 'We know all about you, little invisible boy. We're talking about him.'

'My name is Caine. I want to meet the kids who hang out here.'

'Oh? You do, huh?' the unseen boy said. 'Why should I let you do that?'

'I'm not looking for trouble,' Caine said. 'But I guess it's only fair to tell you that I can knock your little house down in about ten seconds.'

Click click.

Something cold touched the back of Caine's neck.

'Can you? That must be something to see.' A girl's voice. Not two steps behind him.

Caine had no doubt that the cold object laid against the nape of his neck was a gun barrel. How had the girl gotten so close? How had she snuck up on them?

'Like I said, I'm not looking for trouble,' Caine said.

'That's good,' the girl said. 'You wouldn't like the kind of trouble I can bring.'

'We just want to . . .' Caine couldn't actually think of precisely what it was he just wanted to do.

'Well, come on inside,' the girl said.

There was no movement. No walking, no climbing the steps. The farmhouse seemed to warp for a second, and then it was suddenly around them. Caine was standing in a gloomy living room. There were plastic slipcovers on the sagging couch and on a corduroy La-Z-Boy.

Emily was maybe twelve. Dressed in jean shorts and a pink Las Vegas sweatshirt. As Caine had expected, she was holding a huge, double-barrelled shotgun.

The boy came in from outside. He seemed completely unsurprised to see that Caine and Bug were standing in his living room. As though this kind of thing happened all the time.

Caine wondered if he was hallucinating.

'Have a seat,' Emily said, indicating the couch. Caine sat gratefully. He was exhausted.

'That's a pretty good trick,' Caine said.

'It's useful,' Emily said. 'Makes it hard for people to find us if we don't want to be found.'

'You have any electricity?' the brother asked Caine.

'What?' Caine peered at him. 'In my pocket? How would I have electricity?'

The boy pointed mournfully at the TV. A Wii and an Xbox were attached. All indicator lights off, of course. Game cartridges were stacked high.

'That's a lot of games.'

'The other ones bring them to us,' Emily said. 'Brother likes the games.'

'But we can't play them,' the boy said.

Caine looked at him closely. He did not strike Caine as any sort of genius. Emily, on the other hand, seemed shrewd and focused. She was the one in charge.

'What's your name?' Caine asked the boy.

'Brother. His name is Brother,' Emily supplied.

'Brother,' Caine said. 'OK. Well, Brother, those games aren't much fun if you don't have electricity. Are they?'

'Those others told me they'd get some of that.'

'Yeah? Well, only one person can bring electricity back,' Caine said.

'You?'

'Nope. A kid named Computer Jack.'

'We met him,' Brother interjected. 'He fixed my Wii, long time back. Games still worked back then.'

'Jack works for me,' Caine said. He sat back and let that sink in. It was a lie, of course. But he doubted Emily would know that. She wouldn't know that Jack was in Perdido Beach. And that according to Bug he was sitting in a squalid room reading comic books and refusing to do anything.

'You can get the lights on?' Emily asked with a glance at her anxious brother.

'I can,' Caine lied smoothly. 'It would take about a week.'

Emily laughed. 'Kid, you look like you can't even feed yourself. Look at you. You look like a scarecrow. Dirty, hair falling out. And lying like a rug. What *can* you do?'

'This,' Caine said. He raised one hand and the shotgun flew out of Emily's hand. It hit the wall so hard, the barrel stuck in the plaster like a crossbow bolt. The wood stock quivered.

Brother leaped up, but it was like he hit a brick wall. Caine threw him casually through the window. Glass shattered.

There was a loud crash as the boy landed on the screened porch.

Emily was up in a heartbeat and suddenly the house disappeared around Caine. He found himself with Bug, standing in the yard.

'That's definitely a neat trick,' Caine yelled. 'Here's an even better one.'

With hands outstretched he yanked Brother straight through the porch screen. The mesh wrapped around the boy's body like a shroud. And he began to rise into the air, struggling feebly, calling out to his sister to save him.

Emily was instantly a foot from Caine, face-to-face.

'Try something,' Caine snarled. 'It'll be a long drop for your idiot brother.'

Emily looked up, and Caine saw the fight go out of her. Brother was still rising, higher and higher. The fall would maybe kill him. It would at the very least cripple him.

'See, I haven't been spending my days and nights here on the farm,' Caine said. 'I've been in a few fights. Experience. It's kind of useful.'

'What is it you want?' Emily asked.

'When the others get here, you let them walk on in. I have to have a little conversation with them. Your shotgun has had it. And your little tricks won't save you or him.'

'I guess you really want to talk to those boys.'

'Yeah. I guess I do.'

*

Lana heard the knock at the door and sighed. She'd been reading a book. Meg Cabot. A book from a million lifetimes ago. A girl who became a real-life princess.

Lana read a lot now. There were still plenty of books in the FAYZ. Almost no music, no TV or movies. Plenty of books. She read everything from fun chick lit to heavy, boring books.

The point was to keep reading. In Lana's world there was awake time. And there was nightmare time. And the only thing keeping her sane was reading. Not that she was at all sure she was sane.

Not sure of that at all.

Patrick heard the knock, too, and barked loudly.

Lana assumed it was someone needing healing. That was the only reason anyone came to see her. But from long habit and deeply ingrained fear, she lifted the heavy handgun from the desk and carried it to the door with her.

She knew how to use the weapon. She was very accustomed to the feel of the grip in her hand.

'Who is it?'

'Sam.'

She leaned in to look through the peephole. Maybe Sam's face, maybe not: there were no windows in the hallway outside, and so, no light. She threw the dead bolt and opened the door.

'Don't shoot me,' Sam said. 'You'd only have to heal me.'

'Come on in,' Lana said. 'Pull up a chair. Grab a soda from the fridge and I'll get the chips.'

'Well, you still have a sense of humour,' Sam said.

He chose the easy chair in the corner. Lana took the chair she had turned around to face the balcony. She had one of the better rooms in the hotel. In the old days it must have cost hundreds of dollars a day with this great view looking out over the ocean.

'So, what's the emergency?' Lana asked. 'You wouldn't be here if there wasn't some kind of problem.'

Sam shrugged. 'Maybe I'm just here to say hi.'

It had been a while since she had seen him. She remembered the awful damage that had been done to him by Drake. She remembered all too well placing her hands on his flayed skin.

She had healed his body. Not his mind. He was no more completely healed than she was. She could see it in his eyes. It should have created some sympathy between them, but Lana hated seeing that shadow over him. If Sam couldn't get past it, how could she?

'No one ever comes just to say hi,' Lana said. She pulled a pack of cigarettes from her bathrobe pocket and lit one expertly. She inhaled deeply.

She noticed his disapproving look. 'Like any of us are going to live long enough to get cancer,' she said.

Sam said nothing, but the disapproval was gone.

Lana looked at him through a cloud of smoke. 'You look tired, Sam. Are you getting enough to eat?'

'Well, you really can't get enough boiled mystery fish and grilled raccoon,' Sam said.

Lana laughed. Then she sobered. 'I had some venison last week. Hunter brought it to me. He wondered if I could cure him.'

'Did you?'

'I tried. I don't think I helped much. Brain damage. I guess it's more complicated than a broken arm or a bullet hole.'

'Are you doing OK?' Sam asked.

Lana fidgeted and began stroking Patrick's neck. 'Honestly? And you don't talk to Astrid about it so she comes rushing over here trying to help?'

'Between you and me.'

'OK. Then, no, I guess I'm not doing OK. Nightmares. Memories. It's hard to tell which is which, really.'

'Maybe you should try going out more,' Sam said.

'But none of that is happening to you, right? Nightmares and all?'

He didn't answer, just dropped his head and looked down at the floor.

'Yeah,' she said.

Lana stood up abruptly and went to the balcony door. She stood there, arms crossed over her chest, cigarette burning forgotten in her hand. 'I can't seem to stand being around people. I get madder and madder. It's not like they're doing anything to me, but the more they talk or look at me or just stand there, the angrier I get.'

'Been there,' he said. 'Still am there, I guess.'

'See, you're different, Sam.'

'I don't make you angry?'

She laughed, a short, bitter sound. 'Yeah, actually you do. I'm standing here right now and a part of me wants to grab anything I can put my hands on and smash it against your head.'

Sam got up and went to her. He stood just behind her. 'You can punch me, if it helps.'

'Quinn used to come see me,' Lana said, as though she hadn't heard him. 'Then he dropped a glass and I . . . I almost killed him. Did he tell you? I grabbed the gun and I had it pointed right at his face, Sam. And I really, really wanted to pull the trigger.'

'You didn't, though.'

'I shot Edilio,' Lana said, still looking down towards the water.

'That wasn't you,' he said.

Lana said nothing, and Sam let the silence stretch. Finally, she said, 'I thought maybe Quinn and I . . . But I guess that was enough for him to decide to move on.'

'Quinn is working a lot,' Sam said, sounding lame. 'He's out there at, like, four in the morning, every day.'

She slid open the balcony door and flicked the cigarette butt over the rail. 'Why did you come, Sam?'

'I have to ask you something, Lana. Something's going on with Orsay.'

'Yeah.' She pointed towards the beach below. 'I've seen her down there. It's been a couple times. Her and some kids. I can't hear what they're saying. But they look at her like she's their salvation.'

'She's saying she can see through the FAYZ wall. She says she can sense the dreams of people outside.'

Lana shrugged.

'We need to try and figure out if there's any truth to it.'

'How would I know?' Lana asked.

'One of the possibilities . . . I mean, I wondered . . . I mean, if it's not a lie, and maybe Orsay really believes it . . .'

'Go ahead, Sam,' Lana whispered. 'You want to say something.'

'I need to know, Lana: is the Darkness, the gaiaphage, is it really gone? Do you still hear its voice in your head?'

She felt cold. She crossed her arms over her chest. Squeezed herself tightly. She could feel her own body, it was real, it was her. She felt her own heart beating. She was here, alive, herself. Not there in the mineshaft. Not a part of the gaiaphage.

'Don't ask me about that,' Lana said.

'Lana, I wouldn't if it wasn't –'

'Don't,' she warned. 'Don't.'

'I . . .'

She felt her lips twist into a snarl. A wild rage swelled within her. She spun to face him. Stuck her face right in his. 'Don't!'

Sam stood his ground.

'Don't ever, *ever* ask me about it again!'

'Lana –'

'Get out!' she screamed. 'Get out!'

He backed quickly away. Out into the hallway, closing the door behind him.

Lana fell to the carpeted floor. She dug her fingers into her hair and pulled, needing the pain, needing to know that she was real, and here, and now.

Was he gone, the gaiaphage?

He would never be gone. Not from her.

Lana lay on her side, sobbing. Patrick came over and licked her face.

NINE

54 HOURS 42 MINUTES

ZIL SPERRY WAS feeling very good. He'd spent the day waiting for the blow to fall. Waiting for Sam and Edilio to show up at his compound. If they had, he could have made a fight out of it, but he wasn't crazy enough to think he would have won. Edilio's soldiers had machine guns. Zil's Human Crew had baseball bats.

He had more serious weapons, too, but those were not in the compound. Not with that freak Taylor able to pop in anywhere, any time and see whatever she wanted.

And then, there were the other freaks: that glowering lesbian thug Dekka, the brat Brianna. And Sam himself.

Always Sam.

The compound was four houses at the end of Fourth Avenue, past Golding. The street dead-ended there in a sort of cul-de-sac. Four not-very-big, not-very-fancy houses. They'd set up a roadblock of cars to form a wall across Fourth Avenue. The cars had to be pushed into place – the batteries were all dead, all except the few vehicles Sam's people kept in running condition.

At the centre of the roadblock was a narrow gap, an opening. A square and blocky once-white Scion was in position to one side of the opening. It was light enough that four kids could push it across the opening to block the gate.

Dekka could of course simply lift the thing into the air. That and the rest of Zil's defences.

But they had not come after him. And Zil knew why. The town council was too gutless. Sam? He would have come after him. Dekka? She would love to come after him. Brianna had zipped through the compound a few times already, using her freak speed to blow past sentries almost unseen.

Zil had strung wire after that. Let Brianna come through again, she'd get the surprise of her life.

Sam was the key. Kill Sam, and Zil might be able to handle the rest.

At noon, when everyone would be scrounging lunch, Zil led Hank, Turk, Antoine, and Lance out of the compound, across the highway, and north to the foothills of the ridge.

The farmhouse. That freak Emily and her moron brother. At first Turk had mentioned it as a place he knew from back, before. He'd attended a birthday party there for the boy named Brother. Brother and Emily were homeschooled, and Turk knew them from church.

Turk had been surprised to find Brother and Emily still

there. And they'd all been surprised to find that Emily was a seriously powerful freak.

But they had agreed to let Human Crew hide things there.

So Zil had put up with them, made them promises, given them games they couldn't really play in order to have the farm as a safe house. But when the time came . . . well, a freak was still a freak, even if she was useful.

Reaching the farmhouse meant getting past the heavily guarded gas station first. Fortunately there was a deep ditch, an open storm drain running parallel to the highway and behind the gas station. There were no more storms, so it was dry and choked with weeds. But there was a path there, and as long as they kept quiet, Edilio's soldiers at the gas station wouldn't hear them.

Once past town they walked down the highway for a while. All the pickers would be in the fields having lunch. No one would be hauling produce to town.

The highway was eerily empty. Weeds grew tall on the shoulders of the road. Cars that had crashed there during the first few seconds of the FAYZ still sat empty, dusty, useless. Relics of a dead era. Their doors were ajar, trunk lids raised, windows often shattered. Every glove compartment and trunk had been searched by Sam's people or by scavengers for food, weapons, drugs . . .

One of those cars had been the source of Zil's small arsenal.

They'd found the guns, along with two bricks of compressed marijuana and a couple of fat Baggies stuffed with meth. Antoine had probably snorted half the powder already, stupid tweeker.

He was a problem, Zil realised. Drunks and drug addicts were always a problem. On the other hand, he could be counted on to do what he was told. And if some day Antoine just lost it totally, Zil would find someone else to take his place.

'Keep your eyes sharp,' Hank said. 'We don't want to be seen.'

Hank was the enforcer. Weird, with him being a runty little kid. But he had a vicious streak, Hank did. There was nothing he wouldn't do for Zil. Nothing.

Lance, as usual, walked a little apart. Even now it amazed Zil that Lance was part of his core team. Lance was everything the others were not: smart, handsome, athletic, likeable.

And Turk? Well, Turk gimped along on his bad leg and talked. 'In the end we're going to have to be totally freak-free,' he was saying. 'The big ones, the dangerous freaks, we're going to have to take them out.

'Terminate them. With extreme prejudice. That's what they used to say when they meant "assassinate". Terminate with extreme prejudice.'

Sometimes Zil wished he'd just shut up. He reminded Zil in some ways of Zil's older brother, Zane. Always talking, never shutting up.

Of course what Zane talked about was different. Mostly what Zane talked about was Zane. He had an opinion on everything. He knew everything, or thought he did.

His whole life Zil had barely gotten a word in edgewise around Zane. And when he did manage to contribute to the endless family discussions, Zil mostly earned condescending, even pitying, looks.

His parents hadn't meant it to be that way, probably. But what could they do, really? Zane was the star. So smart, so cool, so good looking. As good looking as Lance.

Zil had realised very early on that he would never, ever, ever be the star. Zane owned that role. He was charming, handsome, and ever-so-smart.

And he was so so so nice to little Zil. 'You need some help with that math homework there, Zilly?'

Zilly. Rhyming with silly. Silly Zilly. And Zane the Brain.

Well, where are you now, Zane? Zil wondered. Not here, that's for sure. Zane was sixteen. He had poofed on that first day, that first minute.

Good riddance, big brother, Zil thought.

'So we take out the dangerous freaks,' Turk prattled on. 'Take them out. A few we keep around basically as slaves. Like Lana. Yeah, we keep Lana. Only maybe keep her tied up or whatever so she doesn't get away. And then the others, man, they have to find some other place to go. Simple as that. Out of Sperry Beach.'

Zil sighed. That was Turk's latest idea: to rename the town Sperry Beach. Make it clear for everyone that Perdido Beach now belonged to the Human Crew.

'Humans only. Freaks out,' Turk said. 'We're going to rule. Can you believe Sam didn't come after us? They're all scared.'

Turk could carry on like this forever, talking to himself. It was like he had to go over everything ten times. Like he was arguing with someone who wasn't answering back.

The last part of the trip was the long trudge across the rutted fields. When they reached it there would be nice, clear, clean water, at least, even if there wasn't any food. Emily and Brother had their own well. Not enough water to take a shower or anything because the power was off to the pump, so everything had to be pumped up by hand. But you could drink all you wanted. That was rare in dry and hungry Perdido Beach.

Sperry Beach.

Maybe. Why not?

Zil led the way up the stairs. 'Emily,' he called out. 'It's us.'

He knocked on the door. This was surprising because every other time Emily had seen them coming she'd pulled her usual pop-up-behind-you freak trick. Sometimes she played with them, disappearing the house and letting them wander around like fools.

Freak. She'd get hers eventually. When Zil was done with her.

Emily opened the door.

Zil's instincts screamed danger.

He backed away, but something stopped him. Like some invisible giant had wrapped a hand around him.

The invisible hand lifted him slightly off his feet, just enough so that his toes dragged as he levitated inside, past Emily, who stepped aside with a rueful look.

'Let me go!' Zil cried. But now he could see who had him. He fell silent. Caine sat on the couch, barely moving his hand but utterly controlling Zil.

Zil's heart pounded. If there was any freak as dangerous as Sam, it was Caine. More dangerous. There were things Sam wouldn't do. There was nothing Caine wouldn't do.

'Let me go!'

Caine set Zil down gently.

'Stop yelling, huh?' Caine said wearily. 'I have a headache and I'm not here to hurt you.'

'Freak!' Zil spat.

'Why, yes. Yes, I am,' Caine said. 'I'm the freak who can smack you against the ceiling until you're nothing but a skin sack full of goo.'

Zil glared hatred. Freak. Filthy, mutant freak.

'Tell your boys to come on in,' Caine said.

'What do you want, freak?'

'A conversation,' Caine said. He spread his hands, placating.

'Look, you little creep, if I wanted you dead, you'd be dead. You and your little crew of losers.'

Caine had changed since the first time Zil had seen him. Gone was the smart Coates blazer, the expensive haircut, the tan, and the gym-rat body. Caine looked like a scarecrow version of himself.

'Hank. Turk. Lance. 'Toine,' Zil yelled. 'Come on in.'

'Have a seat.' Caine indicated the La-Z-Boy.

Zil sat.

'So,' Caine said conversationally, 'I hear you're not a big fan of my brother, Sam.'

'The FAYZ is for humans,' Zil muttered. 'Not freaks.'

'Yeah, whatever,' Caine said. For a moment he seemed to fade, to draw in on himself. Weak from hunger. Or from something else. But then the freak pulled himself together and, with visible effort, plastered on his cocky expression.

'I have a plan,' Caine said. 'It involves you.'

Turk, showing more nerve than Zil would have expected, said, 'The Leader makes the plans.'

'Uh-huh. Well, *Leader Zil*,' Caine said with only minimal sarcasm. 'You're going to like this plan. It ends with you being in total control of Perdido Beach.'

Zil sat back in the recliner. He tried to recover some of his dignity. 'OK. I'm listening.'

'Good,' Caine said. 'I need some boats.'

'Boats?' Zil repeated cautiously. 'Why?'

'I kind of feel like taking an ocean cruise,' Caine said.

Sam went home for lunch. Home being Astrid's house. He still thought of it that way, as hers not his.

Actually her own house had been burned to the ground by Drake Merwin. But she seemed to take ownership of whatever house she was in. This house was home to Astrid and her brother, Little Pete, Mary and her brother, John Terrafino, and Sam. But in everybody's mind it was Astrid's house.

Astrid was in the backyard when he got there. Little Pete sat on the deck steps playing with a dead handheld game player. Batteries were in very short supply. At first Astrid and Sam, both of whom knew the truth about Little Pete, were scared. No one knew what Little Pete might do if he went into a complete meltdown, and one of the few things that kept Little Pete pacified was his game.

But to Sam's surprise, the strange little boy had adapted in the oddest way imaginable: he just kept playing. Sam had looked over his shoulder and seen a blank, black screen. But there was no knowing what Little Pete saw there.

Little Pete was severely autistic. He lived in a world of his own imagining, unresponsive, only rarely speaking.

He was also far and away the most powerful person in the

FAYZ. This fact was a secret, more or less. Some suspected a part of the truth. But only a few – Sam, Astrid, Edilio – really grasped the fact that Little Pete had, to some degree, at least, created the FAYZ.

Astrid was stoking a small fire in a hibachi set atop a picnic table. She had a fire extinguisher close at hand. One of the very few that had survived – kids had found them a lot of fun to play with in the early weeks of the FAYZ.

From the smell, Sam concluded she was cooking a fish.

Astrid heard him but did not look up as he approached. 'I don't want to have a fight,' she said.

'Me neither,' he said.

She poked at the fish with a fork. It smelled delicious, although it didn't look too good.

'Get a plate,' Astrid said. 'Have some fish.'

'That's OK, I'm –'

'I can't believe you lied to me,' she snapped, still poking at the fish.

'I thought you didn't want a fight?'

Astrid shovelled the mostly cooked fish on to a serving dish and set it aside. 'You weren't going to tell us about Orsay?'

'I didn't say I –'

'You don't get to decide that, Sam. You're not the only one in charge any more. OK?'

Astrid had an icy sort of anger. A cold fury that manifested itself in tight lips and blazing eyes and short, carefully enunciated sentences.

'But it's OK for all of us to lie to everyone in Perdido Beach?' Sam shot back.

'We're trying to keep kids from killing themselves,' Astrid said. 'That's a little different from you just deciding not to tell the council that there's a crazy girl *telling* people to kill themselves.'

'So not telling *you* something is a major sin, but lying to a couple of hundred people and trashing Orsay at the same time, that's fine?'

'I don't think you really want to have this debate with me, Sam,' Astrid warned.

'Yeah, because I'm just a dumb surfer who shouldn't even be questioning Astrid the Genius.'

'You know what, Sam? We created the council to take pressure off you. Because you were falling apart.'

Sam just stared at her. Not quite believing she'd said it. And Astrid seemed shocked herself. Shocked at the venom behind her own words.

'I didn't mean . . .' she started lamely, but then couldn't find her way to explaining just what it was she didn't mean.

Sam shook his head. 'You know, even now, as long as we've been together it still surprises me that you can be so ruthless.'

'Ruthless? Me?'

'You will use anyone to get what you want. Say anything to get your way. Why was I ever even in charge?' He stabbed an accusing finger at her. 'Because of you! Because you manipulated me into it. Why? So I would protect you and Little Pete. That's all you cared about.'

'That's a lie!' she said hotly.

'You know it's the truth. And now you don't have to bother manipulating me, you can just give me orders. Embarrass me. Undercut me. But as soon as some problem hits, guess what? It'll be, oh, please, Sam, save us.'

'Anything I do, I do for everyone's good,' Astrid said.

'Yeah, so you're not just a genius now, you're a saint.'

'You are being irrational,' Astrid said coldly.

'Yeah, that's because I'm crazy,' Sam snapped. 'That's me, crazy Sam. I've been shot, beaten, whipped, and I'm crazy because I don't like you ordering me around like your servant.'

'You're really a jerk, you know that?'

'Jerk?' Sam shrilled. 'That's all you've got? I was sure you'd have something with more syllables.'

'I have plenty of syllables for you,' Astrid said, 'but I'm trying not to use language I shouldn't.'

She made a show of calming herself down. 'Now, listen to me, without interrupting. OK? You're a hero. I get that. I believe it. But we're trying to make the transition to having a normal society. Laws and rights and juries and police. Not one person making all the important decisions and then enforcing his will by shooting killer light beams at anyone who annoys him.'

Sam started to reply, but he didn't trust himself. Didn't trust himself not to say something he shouldn't, something he might not be able to take back.

'I'm getting my stuff,' he said, and bolted for the steps.

'You don't have to move out,' Astrid called after him.

Sam stopped halfway up the steps. 'Oh, I'm sorry. Is that the voice of the council telling me where I can go?'

'There's no point having a town council if you think you don't have to listen to it,' Astrid said. She was using her patient voice, trying to calm the situation. 'Sam, if you ignore us, *no one* will pay attention.'

'Guess what, Astrid, they're already ignoring you. The only reason anyone pays any attention to you and the others is because they're scared of Edilio's soldiers.' He thumped his chest. 'And even more scared of me.'

He stormed up the stairs, grimly pleased with her silence.

Justin got lost once on his way home. He ended up at the school, though, and that was OK, because he knew how to get to his house from there.

Three-oh-one Sherman. He had memorised it a long time ago. He used to know his phone number, too. He had forgotten that. But he had not forgotten 301 Sherman.

His house looked kind of funny when he saw it. The grass was way too tall. And there was a black bag all split open on the sidewalk. Old milk cartons and cans and bottles. That was all supposed to go in recycling. It sure wasn't supposed to be on the sidewalk. His daddy would go crazy if he ever saw that.

Here's what Daddy would say: *Excuse ME? Can someone KINDLY explain how GARBAGE is on the SIDEwalk? In what universe is THAT OK?*

That's how Daddy talked when he got mad.

Justin walked around the trash and almost tripped over his old tricycle. He'd left it there on the front walk a long time ago. He hadn't even put it away like he should.

Up the stairs to the door. His door. It didn't feel like his door, really.

He pushed the lever on the heavy brass doorknob. It was stiff. He almost couldn't do it. But then it clicked and the door opened.

He pushed it and went inside quickly, feeling guilty, like he was doing something he shouldn't be.

The hallway was dark, but he was used to that. Everything was dark all the time now. If you wanted light, you had to go out and play in the plaza. Which was where he was supposed to be. Mother Mary would be wondering where he was.

He went into the kitchen. Usually Daddy would be in the kitchen; he was the one who mostly did the cooking.

Mommy did the cleaning and laundry, and Daddy did the cooking. Fried chicken. Chilli. Casserole. Beef Burgundy, but they called it Beef Burpundy after one time when Justin was eating some and burped really loud.

The memory made him smile and be sad at the same time.

No one was in the kitchen. The refrigerator door was open. Nothing was inside except an orange box with some white powder inside. He tasted some and spit it out. It tasted like salt or something.

He went upstairs. He wanted to make sure his room was still there. His footsteps sounded really loud on the stairs and it made him creep slowly, like he was sneaking.

His room was on the right. Mommy and Daddy's room was on the left. But Justin didn't go in either direction, because he noticed right then that he wasn't the only person in the house. There was a big kid in the guest room where Meemaw slept when she came to visit at Christmas.

The big kid was a boy, Justin thought, even though his hair was really long and he was turned away. He was sitting in a chair, reading a book, with his feet up on the bed.

The walls of the room had been covered with drawings and colourings that someone had taped up.

Justin froze in the doorway.

Then he slid backwards, turned, and went to his room. The big kid hadn't seen him.

His room was not the same as it used to be. For one thing, there were no sheets or blankets or anything on his bed. Someone had taken his favourite blanket. The nubby blue one.

'Hey.'

Justin jumped. He spun around, flushed and nervous.

The big kid was looking at him with a kind of puzzled look on his face.

'Hey, little dude, take it easy.'

Justin stared at him. He didn't seem mean. There were lots of mean big kids, but this one seemed OK.

'You lost?' the big kid asked.

Justin shook his head.

'Oh. I get it. Is this your house?'

Justin nodded.

'Right. Oh. Sorry, little dude, I just needed a place to stay and no one was living here.' The big kid looked around. 'It's a nice house, you know? It has a nice feeling.'

Justin nodded, and for some reason started to cry.

'It's cool, it's cool, don't cry. I can move out. One thing we have plenty of is houses, right?'

Justin stopped crying. He pointed. 'That's my room.'

'Yeah. No prob.'

'I don't know where my blanket is.'

'Huh. OK, well, we'll find you a blanket.'

They stared at each other for a minute. Then the big kid said, 'Oh yeah, my name is Roger.'

'My name is Justin.'

'Cool. People call me the Artful Roger. Because I like to draw and paint. You know, from the Artful Dodger in *Oliver Twist.*'

Justin stared.

'It's a book. About this kid who's an orphan.' He waited like he expected Justin to say something. 'OK. OK, you don't read a lot of books.'

'Sometimes.'

'I'll read it to you, maybe. That way, I'd be paying you back for living in your house.'

Justin didn't know what to say to that. So he said nothing.

'Right,' Roger said. 'OK. I'm . . . um, going to go back to my room.'

Justin nodded fervently.

'If it's OK with you, I mean.'

'It's OK.'

TEN

51 HOURS 50 MINUTES

'THAT'S THE LAST of the fuel,' Virtue reported mournfully. 'We can run the generator for another two, three days at most. Then no more electricity.'

Sanjit sighed. 'I guess it's good we finished off the ice cream last month. It'd melt otherwise.'

'Look, *Wisdom*, it's time.'

'How many times have I told you: Don't call me Wisdom.'

It was a tired old joke between them. Virtue would call Sanjit Wisdom to provoke him, when he thought Sanjit wasn't being serious.

For a part of his life, Sanjit Brattle-Chance had been called Wisdom by just about everyone. But that part of his life had ended seven months earlier.

Sanjit Brattle-Chance was now fourteen years old. He was tall, thin, slightly stooped, with black hair down to his shoulders, laughing black eyes, and skin the colour of caramel.

He had been an eight-year-old orphan, a Hindu street kid in

Buddhist Bangkok, Thailand, when his very famous, very rich, very beautiful 'parents', Jennifer Brattle and Todd Chance, had kidnapped him.

They called it adoption.

They named him Wisdom. But they, and every other adult on San Francisco de Sales Island, were gone. The Irish nanny? Gone. The ancient Japanese gardener and the three Mexican groundskeepers? Gone. The Scottish butler and the six Polish maids? Gone. The Catalan chef and his two Basque assistants? Gone. The pool guy/handyman from Arizona, and the carpenter from Florida who was working on an ornate balustrade, and the artist-in-residence from New Mexico who painted on warped sheets of steel? Gone, gone, and gone.

Who was left? The kids.

There were five children all together. In addition to Sanjit, they were: Virtue, who Sanjit had nicknamed 'Choo', Peace, Bowie and Pixie. None of them had started their lives with those names. All were orphans. They came from the Congo, Sri Lanka, Ukraine and China respectively.

But only Sanjit had insisted on fighting for his birth name. *Sanjit* meant 'invincible' in Hindi. Sanjit figured he was closer to being invincible than he was to being wise.

But for the last seven months he'd had to step up and at least try to make smart decisions. Fortunately he had Virtue, who was just twelve but a smart, responsible twelve. The two of them were the 'big kids', as opposed to Peace, Bowie and Pixie who were seven, five, and three and mostly concerned with watching DVDs, sneaking candy from the storeroom, and playing too close to the edge of the cliff.

Sanjit and Virtue were at the edge of the cliff themselves now, gazing down at the crumpled, half-sunk, sluggish yacht a hundred feet below.

'There are hundreds of gallons of fuel down there,' Sanjit observed. 'Tons of it.'

'We've been over this about a million times, Sanjit. Even if we could get that fuel up the cliff without blowing ourselves up, we would just be delaying the inevitable.'

'When you think about it, Choo, isn't all of life really just delaying the inevitable?'

Virtue sighed.

He was short and round where Sanjit was angular. Virtue was black. Not African-*American* black, African black. His head was shaved bald – not his usual look, but he hadn't liked the way his hair looked after three months without a haircut, and the best Sanjit could do for him was a buzz cut with the electric clippers.

But the two of them balanced each other perfectly: tall and short, thin and beefy, glib and pessimistic, charismatic and dutiful, a little crazy and utterly sane.

'We are about to lose electricity, Sanjit. We have enough

food, but even that won't last forever. We need to get off this island,' Virtue said firmly.

The swagger seemed to go out of Sanjit. 'Brother, I don't know how to do it. I cannot fly a helicopter. I'll get us all killed.'

Virtue didn't answer for a while. There was no point in denying the truth. The small, bubble-canopied helicopter perched on the stern of the yacht was a flimsy-looking thing, like a rickety dragonfly. It could lift the five of them off the island and to the mainland. Or crash into the cliff and burn. Or crash into the sea and drown them. Or just spin out of control and chop them up like they'd been dropped into a giant food processor.

'Bowie is not getting better, Sanjit. He needs a doctor.'

Sanjit jerked his chin towards the mainland. 'What makes you think there are doctors there? Every single adult disappeared off this island and off the yacht. And the phones and the satellite TV and everything stopped working. And there's never a plane in the sky, and no one comes here to find out what's going on.'

'Yes, I noticed all that,' Virtue said dryly. 'We've seen boats off towards town.'

'They might just be drifting. Like the yacht. What if there are no adults over there, either? Or what if . . . I don't know . . .' Sanjit grinned suddenly, 'maybe it's nothing but man-eating dinosaurs over there.'

'Dinosaurs? You're going with dinosaurs?'

Peace was coming across what had once been a perfectly manicured lawn and was now on its way to becoming a jungle. She had a distinctive walk, knees together, feet taking too many short steps. She had glossy black hair and worried brown eyes.

Sanjit steeled himself. Peace had been watching over Bowie.

'Can I give Bowie another Tylenol? His temperature is going up again,' Peace said.

'How high?' Virtue asked.

'A hundred and two. Point two.'

'A hundred point two or a hundred and two point two?' Virtue asked a bit impatiently.

'That one. The second one.'

Virtue shot a look at Sanjit, who stared down at the grass. 'It's too early for another pill,' Virtue said. 'Put a wet washcloth on his forehead. One of us will be in soon.'

'It's been two weeks,' Sanjit said. 'It's not just the flu, is it?'

Virtue said, 'I don't know what it is. According to the book, the flu doesn't last this long. It could be . . . I don't know, like a million things.'

'Like what?'

'Read the stupid book yourself, Sanjit,' Virtue snapped. 'Fever? Chills? It could be fifty different things. For all I know, it could be leprosy. Or leukemia.'

Sanjit noticed the way his brother winced after he said that last word. 'Jeez, Choo. Leukemia? That's, like, serious, right?'

'Look, all I can go by is the book. I can't even pronounce most of it. And it goes on and on, maybe this, could be that, I mean, I don't see how anyone understands it.'

'Leukemia,' Sanjit said.

'Hey, don't act like that's what I said, OK? It was just one possibility. I probably just thought of it because I can actually pronounce it. That's all.'

They both fell silent. Sanjit stared down at the yacht and more specifically at the helicopter.

'We could try to patch the lifeboat from the yacht,' Sanjit said, although he knew Virtue's answer already. They'd tried to launch the lifeboat. A rope had snagged, and the lifeboat had landed on a spur of rock. The wooden hull had been punctured, the boat had sunk and was now sloshing in between two rocks that slowly, gradually widened the extent of the damage. The lifeboat was a pile of sticks.

'It's the helicopter or nothing,' Virtue said. He was not a touchy-feely kid, Virtue, but he squeezed Sanjit's thin bicep and said, 'Man, I know it scares you. It scares me, too. But you're Sanjit, invincible, right? You're not that smart, but you have amazing luck.'

'*I'm* not that smart?' Sanjit said. 'You'd be flying with me. So how smart are you?'

*

Astrid settled Little Pete in a corner of her office at town hall. He kept his eyes focused on the long-dead handheld and continued pushing buttons, as if the game were still on. And maybe in Little Pete's head, it still was.

It was the office the mayor had used back in the old pre-FAYZ days. The office Sam had used for a while.

She was still seething from the fight with Sam. They had argued before. They were both strong-willed people. Arguments were inevitable, she supposed.

Plus, they were supposedly in love and sometimes that brought its own set of disagreements.

And they were roommates, and sometimes that caused problems.

But they had never, either of them, fought like this.

Sam had taken his few things and moved out. She supposed he would find an unoccupied house – there were plenty of those.

'I shouldn't have said that to him,' she muttered under her breath as she scanned the giant list of things to do. The things that needed doing to keep Perdido Beach functioning.

The door opened. Astrid looked up, hoping and fearing that it was Sam.

It wasn't. It was Taylor.

'I didn't think you walked through doorways, Taylor,'

Astrid said. She regretted the edgy tone in her voice. By now the news that Sam had moved out would have spread throughout the town. Juicy personal gossip moved at the speed of light in Perdido Beach. And there was no bigger item of gossip than a breakup between the first couple of the FAYZ.

'I know how cranky you get when I pop in,' Taylor said.

'It is a little unsettling,' Astrid said.

Taylor spread her hands placatingly. 'See? That's why I walked in.'

'Next you could work on knocking.'

Astrid and Taylor didn't like each other much. But Taylor was an extremely valuable person to have around. She had the ability to instantly transport herself from place to place. To 'bounce', as she called it.

The enmity between them went back to Astrid's belief that Taylor had a crush of major proportions on Sam. No doubt Taylor would figure she had a golden opportunity now.

Not Sam's type, Astrid told herself. Taylor was pretty but a bit younger, and not nearly tough enough for Sam, who, despite what he might be thinking right now, liked strong, independent girls.

Brianna would be more Sam's style, probably. Or maybe Dekka, if she were straight.

Astrid shoved the list away irritably. Why was she torturing herself like this? Sam was a jerk. But he would come around. He would realise sooner or later that Astrid was right. He would apologise. And he'd move back in.

'What is it you want, Taylor?'

'Is Sam here?'

'I'm head of the council, and you've just come bursting in and interrupting my work, so if you have something to say, why don't you just say it to me?'

'Meeooow,' Taylor mocked her. 'Cranky much?'

'Taylor.'

'Kid says he saw Whip Hand.'

Astrid's eyes narrowed. 'What?'

'You know Frankie?'

'Which one?'

'The one who's a boy. He says he saw Drake Merwin walking along the beach.'

Astrid stared at her. The mere mention of Drake Merwin gave Astrid chills. Drake was – had been – a boy who proved all by himself that you didn't have to be an adult to be evil. Drake had been Caine's number one henchman. He had kidnapped Astrid. Forced her with threats, with sheer terror, to ridicule her own brother to his face.

He had burned down Astrid's house.

He had also whipped Sam so badly that Sam had almost died.

Astrid did not believe in hate. She believed in forgiveness.

But she had not forgiven Drake. Even with him dead, she had not forgiven him.

She hoped there was a hell. A real hell, not some metaphorical one, so that Drake could be there now, burning for all eternity.

'Drake's dead,' Astrid said evenly.

'Yeah,' Taylor agreed. 'I'm just telling you what Frankie is saying. He's saying he saw him, whip hand and all, walking down the beach, covered with mud and dirt and wearing clothes that didn't fit.'

Astrid sighed. 'This is what happens when little kids get into the alcohol.'

'He seemed sober,' Taylor said. She shrugged. 'I don't know if he was drunk or crazy or just making trouble, Astrid, so don't blame me. This is supposed to be my job, right? I keep my eyes open and come tell Sam – or you – what's up.'

'Well, thanks,' Astrid said.

'I'll tell Sam when I see him,' Taylor said.

Asrid knew Taylor was trying to provoke her, and yet it worked: she was provoked. 'Tell him anything you want, it's still a free . . .' She had started to say *country*. 'You're free to say whatever you like to Sam.'

But Taylor had already bounced away, and Astrid was talking to air.

ELEVEN

47 HOURS 53 MINUTES

THE PERDIDO BEACH Anomaly, that's what they called it on the news. The Anomaly. Or the Dome.

Not the FAYZ. Although they knew that's what the kids inside the Anomaly called it.

The parents, the family members, all the other pilgrims who gathered in a special 'viewing area' at the southern end of the Dome tended to call it the fishbowl. Sometimes just the bowl. That's what it was to the ones who camped out there in tents and sleeping bags and 'dreamed' of their children on the other side: a fishbowl. They knew a little of what was in the bowl, but the little fish, their children, did not know what was outside in the great big world beyond.

Construction was going on in the area. The state of California was rushing through a bypass for the highway. The old road disappeared into the bowl and reappeared on the other side, twenty miles away. It made a mess for the businesses on the coastal route.

And other businesses were springing up on the south side of the bowl. The tourists had to be fed, after all. Carl's Jr. was building a restaurant. So was Del Taco.

A Courtyard by Marriott was being thrown together at startling speed. Next to it a Holiday Inn Express had broken ground.

In her more cynical moments Connie Temple thought every construction company in the state of California saw the bowl as nothing but a huge opportunity to make money.

The politicians were enjoying it all a bit too much, too. The governor had been there half a dozen times, accompanied by hundreds of reporters. Satellite trucks were packed like sardines all up the beach.

But each day Connie noticed the number of reporters and satellite trucks was just a bit smaller than the day before. The world had gone from stunned disbelief to giddy exploitation to the mundane grind of turning a tragedy into a tourist trap.

Connie Temple – Nurse Temple, as she was inevitably called by the media – had become one of two spokespersons for the families.

That was the shorthand for all those who had children locked inside the bowl: *the families.*

Connie Temple and Abana Baidoo.

It was easier before they could know what was happening inside the bowl. At first all anyone had known was that a terrifying thing had happened. An impenetrable energy field had created a dome twenty miles across. They figured out very quickly that the nuclear power plant was at the epicentre.

There were dozens of theories about what it was, that dome. Every scientist in the world, it seemed, had made a pilgrimage to the site. Tests had been conducted, measurements taken.

They had tried drilling through it. Under it. Had flown over it. Had dug beneath it. Had approached it by submarine.

Nothing worked.

Every species of doomsayer from Luddite to End Times nut had had his say. It was a judgment. On America's technological obsession, on America's moral failure. This. That. Something else.

Then the twins had popped out. Just like that. First Emma. Then, a few minutes later, Anna. Alive and well at the exact moment of their fifteenth birthday.

They told tales of life inside the bowl. What they called the FAYZ.

Connie Temple's heart had swelled with pride for what she had learned of her son, Sam. And crashed into despair with tales of her other son, her unacknowledged child, Caine.

Then, nothing. No other kids arrived for a while.

Black despair settled over the families as they realised that it would be only these two. Months passed. Many lost faith. How could kids survive alone?

But then, the Prophetess had reached into their dreams.

One night Connie Temple had a lurid, incredible dream. She'd never had such a detailed dream. It was terrifying. The power of it took her breath away. There was a girl in that dream.

This girl spoke to her in the dream. *It's a dream*, the girl said.

Yes, just a dream, Connie had answered.

Not just a dream. Never say 'just' a dream, the girl had corrected. *A dream is a window to another reality.*

Who are you? Connie had asked.

My name is Orsay. I know your son.

Connie had been about to say, *Which one?* But some instinct stopped her. The girl did not look dangerous. She looked hungry.

Do you have a message for Sam? the girl asked.

Yes, Connie said. *Tell him to let them go.*

Let them go.

Let them go off into the red sunset.

Orsay woke with a start. She kept her eyes closed because she could feel the close presence of another person. She wanted to stay asleep and private and alone for just another moment.

But the other person, the girl, would not let her.

Nerezza said, 'I know you're awake, Prophetess.'

Orsay opened her eyes. Nerezza was close, very close. Orsay could feel her breath on her face.

She looked into Nerezza's eyes. 'I don't understand,' Orsay said. 'I already had that dream. A dream of a woman dreaming.' She frowned with the effort of remembering. It was all so strange and wispy and unreal. Like grabbing on to fog.

'It must be a very important dream,' Nerezza said.

'The first time, I was at the FAYZ wall. Now I'm seeing the same thing when I sleep. But I've already told Sam the message. Why am I seeing the same thing again?'

'There's a difference between you *delivering* a message and Sam *getting* the message, Prophetess.'

Orsay sat up. Nerezza was bothering her. More and more she found herself wondering about Nerezza. But she had become dependent on the girl to guide her and shield her and take care of her.

'You think I need to repeat the message to Sam?'

Nerezza shrugged and made a modest smile. 'I'm not the Prophetess. That's for you to decide.'

'She said to let the kids go. Into the red sunset.'

'Your vision of the great escape from the FAYZ,' Nerezza said. 'The red sunset.'

Orsay shook her head. 'This wasn't a dream I reached for. I wasn't at the FAYZ wall, I was here, asleep.'

'Your powers are expanding,' Nerezza suggested.

'I don't like it. It's like . . . I don't know. Like they're coming from somewhere. Like I'm being pushed. Manipulated.'

'No one can push you or control your dreams,' Nerezza said. 'But . . .'

'But?'

'Maybe it's very important that Sam hear you. Maybe it's very, very important that he not stand in the way of truth.'

'I'm not a prophet,' Orsay said wearily. 'I just dream. I don't know if any of it is even real. I mean, sometimes it seems real, but other times it seems crazy.'

Nerezza took her hand. Orsay found her touch strong and cool. It sent a shiver up Orsay's arm.

'They're all telling lies about you, Prophetess,' Nerezza said. 'You must not doubt yourself because they are busy, even now, attacking you.'

'What are you talking about?'

'They fear you. They fear your truth. They are spreading lies that you are a false prophet.'

'I don't . . . What are you . . . I . . .'

Nerezza put her finger on Orsay's mouth, shushing her. 'No. You must be sure. You must *believe.* You must be the Prophetess. Otherwise, their lies will pursue you.'

Orsay lay still as a terrified mouse.

'The fate of false prophets is death,' Nerezza said. 'But you are the true Prophetess. And you will be protected by your faith. Believe, and you will be safe. Make others believe, and you will live.'

Orsay stared in horror. What was Nerezza talking about? What was she saying? Who were these people who were telling lies about her? And who would threaten her? She wasn't doing anything wrong.

Was she?

Nerezza called out in a loud voice tinged with impatience. 'Jill! Jill! Come in here.'

The girl came in a few seconds later. She was still carrying her doll, holding on to it for all it was worth.

'Sing for the Prophetess,' Nerezza ordered.

'What song should I sing?'

'It doesn't really matter, does it?' Nerezza asked.

So, the Siren sang:

Sunny days . . .

And Orsay stopped thinking of anything but sunny, sunny days.

45 HOURS 36 MINUTES

HUNTER HAD BECOME a creature of the night. It was the only way. Animals hid during the day and came out at night. Opossums, rabbits, raccoons, mice and the biggest prize of all: deer. The coyotes hunted at night, and Hunter had learned from them.

Squirrels and birds you had to go after in the daytime. But night was the time for Hunter to truly live up to his name.

Hunter's range was wide, from the edge of town, where raccoons and deer came to look for ways into people's backyard gardens, to the dry lands, where snakes and mice and other rodents were to be found. Along the shoreline he could kill birds, gulls, and terns. And once, he had bagged a lost sea lion.

He had responsibilities, Hunter did. He wasn't just Hunter, he was *the* hunter.

He knew the two words were the same, although he could no longer spell the word.

Hunter's head didn't work the way it used to. He knew that. He could feel it. He had murky memories of himself living a very different life. He had memories of himself raising his hand in a classroom to answer a hard question.

Hunter would not have those answers now. The answers he did have, he couldn't really explain with words. There were things he knew, things about the way you could tell if a rabbit was going to run or stand still. Whether a deer could smell you or hear you or not.

But if he tried to explain . . . words didn't come out right.

One side of his face wasn't right. It kind of didn't have any feeling in it. Like that side wasn't anything but a slab of dead meat. And sometimes it felt as if that same dead-meat thing spread into his brain. But the strange mutant power, the ability to direct killing heat wherever he wanted, that remained.

He couldn't talk very well, or think very well, or form a real smile, but he could hunt. He had learned to walk quiet. He had learned to keep the breeze in his face. And he knew that in the night, in the darkest hours, the deer would head towards the cabbage field, drawn there despite the killer worms, the zekes that would kill anything that stepped foot in one of their home fields without permission.

The deer, they weren't that smart. Not even as smart as Hunter.

He walked carefully, treading on the balls of his feet, feeling through his worn boots for the twig or loose rock that would give him away. He moved as quietly as a coyote.

The doe was ahead, moving through the scrub brush, indifferent to the thorns, intent on leading her baby towards the smell of green ahead.

Close. Closer. The breeze blowing from the deer to Hunter, so that they didn't smell him.

A few more feet and he'd be close enough. First the doe. He'd kill her first. The baby wouldn't know how to react. She would hesitate. And he'd take her.

So much meat. Albert would be very excited. There hadn't been many deer lately.

Hunter heard the noise and saw the deer bolt.

They were gone before he could so much as raise his hands, let alone send the invisible killing heat.

Gone. The whole night stalking and tracking and just seconds away from a good kill, and now they were bounding away through the brush.

The noise was people, Hunter knew that right away. Talking and jostling and rattling and tripping and complaining.

Hunter was angry but also philosophical. Hunting was like that: a lot of the time you ended up wasting your time. But . . .

Hunter frowned.

That voice.

He crouched in the brush and quieted his breathing. He strained to hear. More than one person. Boys.

They were coming in his direction, skirting the zeke field.

He could see them now, dark silhouettes. Four of them. He could see them through stalks of weed and tangles of bramble. Stumbling around because they didn't know how to move like Hunter. Stumbling under the weight of heavy packs.

And that voice . . .

'. . . what he wants. That's the problem with mutant freaks like him, you can never trust a word they say.'

That voice . . .

Hunter had heard that voice before. He'd heard that voice crying out to a bloodthirsty mob.

This mutant, this nonhuman scum here, this freak Hunter, this chud deliberately murdered my best friend, Harry.

He's a killer!

Take him! Take him, the murdering mutant scum!

That voice . . .

Hunter touched his neck, feeling again the scrape of the rough rope.

He'd been hurt so bad. Head beaten. Blood running in his eyes. And his words not working . . .

Mind not . . .

Brain confused . . . so afraid . . .

Grab on to the rope!

That voice had urged, pitch rising, bellowing, the mob of kids shrieking and giddy, and the rope had tightened around Hunter's neck and pulled and pulled and he couldn't breathe, Oh God, gasping for air but no air . . .

Grab on to the rope!

They had. They had grabbed on to the rope and pulled and Hunter's neck had stretched and his feet lifted, kicking in the air, kicking and wanting to scream and his head pounding and pounding and eyes going dark . . .

Zil!

Zil and his friends.

And here they were. They didn't even know Hunter was there. They didn't see him. They weren't hunters.

Hunter crept closer. Moving to intersect their path. His powers didn't usually reach more than fifty paces or so. He had to be closer.

'. . . think you're right, Leader,' one of the others was saying.

'Can we take a rest?' a third voice whined. 'This stuff weighs a ton.'

'We should have gone back when it was still light so we could see,' Antoine griped.

'Idiot. We waited until dark for a reason,' Zil snapped. 'You want Sam or Brianna to catch us out in the open?'

'We have guns now.'

'Which we will use when the time is right,' Zil said. 'Not in some open fight with Sam and Dekka and Brianna where they'll take us out.'

'When the time is right,' one of them echoed.

They had guns, Hunter thought. Sneaking with guns.

'Leader will decide,' another voice said.

'Yeah, but . . .' someone began. Then, 'Shh! Hey! I think I just saw a coyote. Or maybe it was a deer.'

'Better not be a coyote.'

BLAM! BLAM!

Hunter dived face down in the dirt.

'What are you shooting at?' Zil demanded.

'I think it was a coyote!'

'Turk, you idiot!' Zil raged. 'Blasting away like a moron!'

'The sound carries, Turk,' Hank said.

'Give that gun to Hank,' Zil snapped. 'Idiot.'

'Sorry. I thought . . . it looked like a coyote.'

It wasn't a coyote. It was Hunter's deer.

They were moving on now. Still grumping at one another. Still complaining.

Hunter knew he could move faster and more quietly than they did. He could get close enough . . .

He could stretch out his hands and bring the killing heat to Zil's brain. Cook it. Cook it inside his skull.

Like he had Harry . . .

'An accident,' Hunter moaned softly to himself. 'Didn't mean to . . .'

But he had.

Tears filled his eyes. He wiped at them, but more came.

He'd been defending himself from Zil. So long ago. They'd been roommates, Zil and Harry and Hunter. A stupid argument; Hunter no longer remembered what had started it. He only remembered that Zil had threatened him with a fireplace poker. Hunter had been scared. He'd reacted. But Harry had moved between them, trying to separate them, trying to stop the fight.

And Harry had cried out. Grabbed his head.

Hunter remembered his eyes . . . the way they had turned milky . . . the light going out . . .

Hunter had seen that same dying light in the eyes of many animals since then. He was Hunter the hunter.

Of animals. Not of boys. Not even bad boys like Zil.

Taylor bounced.

Sam's house. Night-time. Astrid asleep, Little Pete asleep, Mary out at the day care working the night shift, John asleep.

Sam's bedroom empty.

There was still trouble in paradise, Taylor thought with some satisfaction. Sam and Astrid had not made up.

She wondered if it was permanent. Sam was way hot. If Sam

and Astrid had broken up for good, hey, maybe there was an opportunity.

She could wake Astrid. That would probably be the proper thing to do. But her instinct said no, especially after Astrid had chilled her earlier.

Boy, was Astrid going to freak when she found out Taylor had gone to Sam first. But this was the kind of thing you took to Sam right away. Too big for Astrid.

Well, too big for anyone, really.

Taylor thought of the fire station. On occasion Sam had stayed there. But all she found there was a sleeping Ellen, the fire chief – the fire chief with no water to spray. Ellen grumbled in her sleep.

Not for the first time Taylor considered the fact that she could be the world's greatest thief. All she had to do was think of a place and, *pop*! There she was. No sound – unless she happened to bang into something once she had materialised. In and out – no sound, no sign – and even if someone was awake, she could bounce right back out before they so much as breathed.

Yep, she could be a great thief. If there had been anything to steal. And only as long as it was small. She couldn't move anything much more than the clothes on her back when she bounced.

She bounced from the fire station to Edilio's place. Edilio now ran a sort of barracks, or whatever you called it. He had occupied a big seven-bedroom house. He had one bedroom to himself, and the other six were used to sleep two guys each. It was his quick reaction force. Half the boys and girls had automatic weapons within easy reach of their beds. One boy was awake. He jumped when he noticed Taylor.

'Go back to sleep; you're dreaming,' she said with a wink. 'And, dude: smiley face boxers? Really?'

For Taylor it was like changing channels on the TV. It didn't feel like she was moving as she bounced, more like the world was moving around her. It made the world seem unreal. Like a hologram or something. An illusion.

She thought of a place and, like tapping a button on the remote control, suddenly she was there.

The day care.

The beach.

Clifftop – but not Lana's room. The word was out that the Healer was extremely cranky since she'd been practically sucked into the gaiaphage. And no one in her right mind wanted to piss off the Healer.

Finally, it occurred to Taylor where Sam might go to crash on a couch if he was fighting with Astrid.

Quinn was awake, getting dressed in the dark. He seemed strangely unperturbed by Taylor popping in.

'He's here,' Quinn said without preamble. 'The bedroom at the top of the stairs.'

'You're up early,' Taylor said.

'Four a.m. Fishing is a job for early risers. Which I am. Now.'

'Well, good luck. Get a tuna or something.'

'Hey, you talking to Sam? Is this some kind of life-and-death emergency? I need to know if I'm going to get killed on my way down to the marina,' Quinn said.

'No.' Taylor waved a dismissive hand. 'Not life and death. More like death and life.'

She bounced to the top of the stairs and then, with unusual consideration, knocked on the door.

No answer.

'Oh, well.'

She bounced. Sam, asleep, tangled in a mess of sheets and blankets, face down in a pillow like he was trying to dig his way through the bed and escape the room.

She grabbed an exposed heel and shook his leg.

'Unh?'

He rolled over fast, hand raised, palm out, ready for trouble.

Taylor was not too worried. She'd done this many times before. At least half the time Sam woke up ready to fire.

'Chill, big boy,' Taylor said.

Sam sighed and rubbed his hand over his face, trying to banish sleep. Definitely nice chest and shoulders. And arms. A little skinnier than he used to be, and not as tan as he'd been back when he was a serious beach rat.

But, oh yeah, Taylor thought: *he'd do.*

'What is it?' Sam asked.

'Oh, nothing too big,' Taylor said. She examined her nails, having fun with the moment. 'I was just out spreading the word. You know, talking to kids who were heading out to see Orsay. It's all way nocturnal, you know?'

'And?'

'Oh, a little something came up that I thought might be more important than trashing Orsay for Astrid.'

'You mind just telling me what's going on?' Sam grated.

So much, Sam, Taylor thought. *Sooo much.* But there was no point complicating things by recounting some crazy kid's story about Drake. It could only distract from the excellence of her main piece of news.

'Remember Brittney?'

His head snapped up. 'What about her?'

'She's sitting in Howard and Orc's living room.'

THIRTEEN

45 HOURS 16 MINUTES

ORC HAD ENDED up crushing every couch or bed Howard had ever found for him. Not immediately, not as soon as he sat down, but within a few days.

That had never stopped Howard. He just kept on trying. The current arrangement was more bed than couch or chair. Three king-size mattresses piled one atop the other and pushed into a corner so that Orc could sit up if he chose by leaning against the walls. A plastic tarp went over the top of the mattress pile. Orc liked to drink. And sometimes when Orc had enough to drink, he might wet the bed. Sometimes he vomited all over it. And then Howard would gather the corners of the tarp and drag it into the backyard to join the pile of similar fouled sheets, broken furniture, puke-reeking mattress pads, and so on that covered most of the yard.

No one had any real idea how much Orc weighed, but he was not light, that was for sure. But not fat, either.

Orc had suffered one of the strangest and most disturbing

of mutations. He'd been attacked and very badly hurt by coyotes. Very badly. Large portions of him had been eaten by the ravenous wild beasts.

But he had not died. The torn, mangled, massacred portions of his body had been replaced by a substance that looked like damp gravel. It made a soft slurry sound when he moved.

All that was left of Orc's own skin was a patch around his mouth and one cheek. It seemed unbearably delicate to Howard. Howard could see it, pink flesh turned putty-coloured in the unnatural green light.

Orc was awake but just barely. And only because Howard had lied to him and told him he was out of booze.

Orc watched balefully from his perch in the corner as the girl sat in the chair Howard had dragged in from the kitchen.

'You want some water?' Howard asked her.

'Yes, please,' the girl said.

Howard, hands shaking, filled a glass from the gallon jug. He handed it to her. She took it with both dirt-caked hands and raised it to her puffy lips.

She drank it all.

Normal. Perfectly normal except for the fact that there was absolutely nothing normal about this.

'You want more?' Howard asked her.

Brittney handed the glass back. 'No, thank you.'

Howard steadied his breath and shaking fingers and took it.

Almost dropped it. Set it down and then it did topple off the edge of the table. It didn't smash, it bounced on the wood, but the sound seemed very loud, anyway. Howard flinched.

The knock at the door was comforting by contrast.

'Thank God,' Howard muttered, and ran to answer it.

Sam, with Taylor. Sam looking grim. Well, that was normal enough. Poor Sammy had lost some of his happy-go-lucky surfer boy sparkle.

'Howard,' Sam said in that voice he used when he was trying to hide his contempt.

But there was more going on with Sam. Even shaking with fear, Howard saw it. Something strange about the way he was reacting.

'Hey, thanks for stopping by,' Howard said. 'I'd offer you some tea and cookies, but all we have is boiled mole and artichokes. Plus, we kind of have a dead girl in the living room.'

'A dead girl?' Sam said, and there it was again. The wrong reaction. Sam was too calm and too grim.

Of course Taylor had told him. Duh. Of course. That's why Sam wasn't surprised. Except there was something still off about Sam's reaction. Howard had maintained his position by being able to read people pretty well. He'd kept on Orc's good side for a long time, and managed, despite everything, to wrangle a place on the town council. Despite the fact that Sam surely suspected Howard was the one selling most of the illegal substances in Perdido Beach.

Sam stood there looking at Brittney. Who looked right back at him. Like maybe Sam was a teacher getting ready to ask her a question.

Brittney, can you explain the significance of the Missouri Compromise?

No? Well, then, young lady, you need to go back and reread the assignment.

Oh, and by the way: why are you not dead?

'Hello, Brittney,' Sam said.

'Hi, Sam,' Brittney said.

There was mud even in her braces, Howard noticed. Washed out only a little by the water. He could see a tiny piece of gravel wedged between chrome wires next to Brittney's left canine.

Weird thing to notice, Howard thought.

Yeah, that's what's weird. Not that she's sitting here chatting.

'How did you get here?' Sam asked.

Brittney shrugged. 'I guess I walked. I don't remember.'

Orc spoke for the first time in his low grumble. 'She was standing on the porch when I stepped out to take a whiz.'

Sam glanced at Howard, who nodded.

'Do you know where you are?' Sam asked her.

'Sure. I'm . . .' Brittney began. She frowned. Then the frown line disappeared. 'I'm here.'

'You know all of us?'

She nodded slowly. 'Sam. Howard. Taylor. Orc. Tanner.'

'Tanner?' Taylor blurted.

That rocked Sam back on his heels. Howard was perplexed. 'Who is Tanner?'

'One of the littles who . . .' Taylor began, then bit her lip. 'He's her little brother. He was at the day care when . . .'

The pieces fell into place for Howard. He'd forgotten the name. Tanner, one of the preschoolers killed at what people called the Thanksgiving Battle, or the Battle of Perdido Beach. Coyotes mad with fear. Undisciplined gunfire. Drake and Caine and Sam using all their powers.

'Where is Tanner?' Sam asked softly.

Brittney smiled at a space between Howard and Taylor. 'Right where he always is.'

'Brittney, do you know what's happened?' Sam obviously didn't know quite how to ask the question. 'Brittney, do you remember being at the power plant? Caine and Drake came –'

Her scream made everyone jump, even Orc.

A wild shriek, a shocking loud sound, full of something that could only be hatred.

'The demon!' she screamed. An animal howl followed, a sound that rose and lifted the hairs on the back of Howard's neck and made his insides feel watery.

Suddenly she was silent.

She held up one arm. She stared at it. Like it wasn't part of her, like it was there and she couldn't understand why. Her forehead creased in puzzlement.

In the shocked quiet, Sam said, 'Brittney, can you tell us –'

'I think I'm sleepy,' Brittney said, dropping her arm back down to her side.

'OK,' Sam said. 'I'll, um . . . we'll find someplace for you to stay the night.' He looked at Taylor. 'Bounce over to Brianna's. Tell her we're coming.'

Howard almost laughed. Brianna would not be thrilled by this. But Sam was reaching out to someone who was unquestioningly loyal to him.

'This doesn't leave this room,' Sam said.

'More secrets, Sammy?' Howard said.

Sam winced. But he held his ground. 'People are scared enough,' he said.

'You're asking a lot, Sammy boy,' Howard said. 'After all, I'm on the council. You're asking me to keep this from my fellow council members. I don't need Astrid mad at me.'

'I know about your little booze-and-drug operation,' Sam said. 'I'll mess up your life.'

'Ah,' Howard said smoothly.

'Yeah. I need some time to figure this all out,' Sam said. 'I don't need people talking about . . . about anything.'

Howard laughed. 'You mean . . .'

'Don't,' Sam snapped. 'Don't even say it.'

Howard laughed and crossed his heart. 'I swear. I won't be the first to use the "Z" word.' Then in a stage whisper he said, 'Zom – beee.'

'She's not a zombie, Howard. Don't be an idiot. 'She obviously has some kind of power that lets her regenerate. If you think about it, it's not that different from what Lana does. After all, she's physically back together, and she was torn up when we buried her.'

Howard laughed. 'Uh-huh. Except somehow I don't remember Lana ever crawling her way up out of a grave.'

Sam headed towards Brianna's house. Brittney walked along behind him. *Perfectly normal*, Howard thought, watching them go. *Just another stroll with a dead person.*

Little Pete woke up.

Dark. Dark was good. Light filled his brain with too much.

It was quiet. Good. Sounds made his head hurt.

He had to be quiet himself or someone would come and bring light and noise and touching and pain and panic and it would all come at him like a tidal wave a million feet high, spinning him, crushing him, smothering him.

Then he would have to shut down. He would have to turn it all off. Hide from it. Go back to the game, back to the game, because inside the game, it was dark and quiet.

But for now, with no light and no sound and no touch,

he could hold on, for just a moment, to . . . himself.

Hold on to . . . to nothing.

He knew where the game was. Just there, on the nightstand, waiting. Calling to him so softly so as not to upset him.

Nemesis, it called him.

Nemesis.

Lana had not slept. She had read and read, trying to lose herself in the book. She had a small candle, not much, but a rare thing in the FAYZ.

She lit a cigarette in the candle and sucked the smoke into her lungs. Amazing, really, how quickly she had become addicted.

Cigarettes and vodka. The bottle was half empty, sitting there on the floor beside her bed. It hadn't worked, hadn't helped her sleep.

Lana searched her mind for the gaiaphage. But it was not with her. For the first time since she had crawled up out of that mineshaft.

It was done with her, for now, at least.

That fact should have given her peace. But Lana knew it would return when it needed her, that it would still be able to use her. She would never be free.

'What did you do, evil old troll?' Lana asked dreamily. 'What did you do with my power?'

She told herself that the monster, the gaiaphage . . . the

Darkness . . . could only use the Healer to heal, and that no evil could come from that.

But she knew better. The Darkness did not reach out through the back doors of time and space and siphon off her power for no reason.

For days it had been inside her mind, using her to heal.

To heal *who*?

She dropped her hand to the vodka bottle, raised it to her lips, and swallowed the liquid fire.

To heal *what*?

FOURTEEN

30 HOURS 25 MINUTES

ON THE FIRST day of the disappearance – or, as Sanjit secretly thought of it, the deliverance – he and his brothers and sisters had searched the entire estate.

Not one single adult had been found. No nanny, no cook, no groundskeepers – which was a relief because one of the assistant groundskeepers seemed like kind of a perv – and no maids.

They stayed together as a group, Sanjit cracking jokes to keep everyone's spirits up.

'Are we sure we want to find anyone?' he'd asked.

'We need grown-ups,' Virtue had argued in his pedantic way.

'For what, Choo?'

'For . . .' This had stumped Virtue.

'What if someone gets sick?' Peace had asked.

'You feel OK?' Sanjit asked her.

'I guess so.'

'See? We're fine.'

Despite the undeniable creepiness of the situation, Sanjit had been more relieved than worried. He didn't like having to respond to the name 'Wisdom'. He didn't like being told what to do just about every minute of the day. He didn't like rules. And then, suddenly, no rules.

He'd had no answer to the repeated questions from the others as to what had happened. All that seemed clear was that all the adults were gone. And the radio and phones and satellite TV were dead.

Sanjit figured he could live with that.

But the little kids, Peace, Bowie and Pixie, had been scared from the beginning. Even Choo, whom Sanjit had never seen upset, had been creeped out.

The simple silence of the empty island was oppressive. The huge house, with some rooms the kids had never even seen, rooms no one had ever used, seemed as big and as dead as a museum. And searching through the butler's home, through Nanny's upstairs suite, through the bungalows and dorms, left them feeling like burglars.

But everyone's mood had improved when they returned to the main house and opened the walk-in freezer in search of a long-overdue dinner that first evening.

'They *do* have ice cream!' Bowie accused. 'They've had ice cream all along. They lied to us. They have tons of ice cream.'

There were twelve big five-gallon tubs of ice cream. Sixty gallons of ice cream.

Sanjit had patted Bowie on the shoulder. 'Are you really surprised, little guy? Cook weighs three hundred pounds, and Annette isn't far behind.' Annette was the maid who cleaned the children's rooms.

'Can we have some?'

Sanjit was surprised to be asked for permission that first time. He was the oldest, but it had not really occurred to him that he was in charge.

'You're asking me?'

Bowie shrugged. 'I guess you're the grown-up for now.'

Sanjit smiled. 'Then, as temporary adult, I decree that we have ice cream for dinner. Grab one of those tubs and five spoons and we don't stop till we hit the bottom.'

That had kept everyone happy for a while. But at last Peace raised her hand, like she was in school.

'You don't have to raise your hand,' Sanjit said. 'What's up?'

'What's going to happen?'

Sanjit had considered this for a few seconds. He was not normally a thoughtful person, he knew that. He was normally a joker. Not a clown, but not someone who took life too seriously. Taking life seriously was Virtue's job.

Back in the days when he'd lived on the Bangkok streets and alleyways there were endless dangers: sweatshop bosses who would try to kidnap you and put you to work fourteen hours a day, cops who would beat you, shopkeepers who would chase you away from their fruit displays with bamboo sticks, and always the pimps who would turn you over to strange foreign men for their own purposes.

But Sanjit had always tried to laugh and not cry. No matter how hungry, how scared, how sick, he'd never given up like some of the kids he saw. He hadn't become brutal, though he surely had survived by stealing. And as he aged on those wondrously exciting, terrifying, never-dull streets he'd nurtured a certain swagger, a certain attitude that made him stand out. He had learned to live each day, not to worry too much about the next. If he had food for the day, if he had a box to sleep in, if the rags on his back weren't crawling with too many lice, he was happy.

'Well, we have plenty of food,' Sanjit said, as four faces looked to him for guidance. 'So, I guess what we do is just kind of hang out. Right?'

And that was answer enough for that first day. They were all weirded out. But they had always pretty much taken care of one another, not relying too much on the indifferent adults around them. So they had brushed teeth and tucked each other into bed that first night; Sanjit the last to go to his room.

Pixie had come in and slept with him. Then Peace had come, holding a blanket to tearful eyes. And later Bowie, too.

When morning came they woke on schedule. They met for breakfast, which consisted largely of toast with lots of forbidden butter and forbidden jelly and thick slatherings of forbidden Nutella.

They went outside afterwards, and that's when they noticed the strange grinding noise.

They had rushed to the cliff's edge. A hundred feet down they saw the yacht. The yacht – a huge, beautiful, sleek white boat so big, it had its own helicopter – had run aground. The knife-sharp prow was crumpled, wedged between huge boulders. Each slight swell lifted the ship and then let it grind slowly back down.

The yacht belonged to their parents. They hadn't even known it was coming, hadn't known their parents were nearby.

'What happened?' Peace asked in a tremulous voice.

Virtue answered, 'It ran into the island. It must have been on its way . . . and then . . . then it just ran into the island.'

'Why didn't Captain Rocky stop it?'

'Because he is gone,' Sanjit had said. 'Just like all the other grown-ups.'

Somehow at that moment it had hit Sanjit. He'd never had much affection for the two actors who called themselves his mother and father, but seeing their yacht smashed heedlessly against the rocks had brought it home.

They were alone on the island. Maybe alone in the whole world.

'Someone will come for us,' Sanjit had said, not quite sure he believed it.

So they had waited. Days. And then weeks.

And then they had begun to ration food. There was still plenty of that left. The island was stocked for parties that sometimes included a hundred guests, all coming in by helicopter or private jet.

Sanjit had seen some of the parties. Lights strewn everywhere, all kinds of famous people in fancy clothes drinking and eating and laughing too loud while the kids were kept in their rooms, occasionally hauled out to say good evening and listen to people talk about how great it was that their parents had been so generous, rescuing 'these kids'.

Sanjit had never considered himself rescued.

There was still a lot of food left. But the diesel fuel that ran the generator was running out despite all their efforts to conserve.

And now there was Bowie. Sanjit could usually manage to sidestep responsibility. But he couldn't let Bowie die.

There were only two ways on or off the island. By small boat – and they had no boat. Or helicopter. And that they had. Sort of.

The time had come to seriously examine the most impossible option.

Sanjit and Virtue found rope in the groundskeeper's shed. Sanjit anchored one end of the rope around the not-very-secure trunk of a sapling. He hurled the other end out into the void.

'Probably pull the tree down on our heads, huh?' He laughed.

Sanjit and Virtue went down. The rest were told to stay put, stay away from the cliff, and wait.

Twice Sanjit lost his footing and slid down on his butt till he managed to stop by digging his heel into a shrub or rock outcropping. The rope ended up being no use at all for the descent. It lay off to the right of the path, far out of reach.

The boat, the *Fly Boy Two,* was still there, battered, rusting, algae sliming around the waterline. It wallowed in the gentle swell, its bow seemingly hanging on for dear life to the rocks it had hit months earlier.

'How do we get on to the boat?' Virtue asked when they had reached the bottom.

'That's a really good question, Choo.'

'I thought you were invincible, Sanjit.'

'Invincible, not fearless,' Sanjit said.

Virtue made his wry smile. 'If we climb up on that rock, we can maybe grab the guardrail on the bow and pull ourselves up.'

From down here the boat was far larger. And the gentle motion that rocked the crumpled bow back and forth looked a lot more dangerous.

'OK, little brother, I'm going to do this, OK?' Sanjit said.

'I'm a better climber than you are.'

Sanjit put his hand on his shoulder. 'Choo, my brother, there aren't going to be a lot of times when I'm brave and self-sacrificing. Enjoy this one. It may be the last you ever see.'

To forestall further argument Sanjit climbed up on to the rock spur and made his way carefully, cautiously, to the end, sneakers slipping on rock coated with algae and salt spray. He leaned with one hand against the white hull. He was at eye level with the deck.

He grabbed the frail-looking stainless-steel rail with both hands and pulled himself up until his elbows were at ninety-degree angles. The danger zone was just below him and if he let go, he'd be lucky to survive with just a crushed foot.

His scramble aboard the boat wasn't pretty, but he made it with only a scraped elbow and a bruised thigh. He lay panting, face down on the teak deck for a few seconds.

'Do you see anything?' Virtue called up.

'I saw my life flashing before my eyes, does that count?'

Sanjit stood up, bending his knees to roll with the boat. No sound of human activity. No sign of anyone. Not exactly a surprise, but in some dark corner of his mind, Sanjit had almost expected to see bodies.

He placed his hands on the rails, looked down at Virtue's anxious face, and said, 'Ahoy there, matey.'

'Go look around,' Virtue said.

'That's "Go look around, Captain," to you.'

Sanjit strolled with false nonchalance to the first door he found. He'd been on the yacht twice before, back when Todd and Jennifer were still around, so he knew the layout.

It was the same eerie feeling he'd had that first day of the big disappearance: he was going into places he didn't belong, and there was no one to stop him.

Silence. Except for the groan of the hull.

Creepy. A ghost ship. Like something out of *Pirates of the Caribbean.* But very posh. Very nice crystal glasses. Little statues stuck in alcoves. Framed movie posters. Photos of Todd and Jennifer with some kind of famous old actor.

'Hello?' he called, and instantly felt like an idiot.

He went back to the bow. 'No one home, Choo.'

'It's been months,' Virtue said. 'What did you think? They were all down here playing cards and eating potato chips?'

Sanjit found a ladder and hung it over the side. 'Come aboard,' he said.

Virtue climbed up carefully and instantly Sanjit felt a little better. Shielding his eyes he could see Peace up at the top of the cliff, looking down anxiously. He waved to show everything was OK.

'So, I don't suppose you've found a manual for the helicopter lying around?'

'*Helicopters for Dummies?*' Sanjit joked. 'No. Not exactly.'

'We should look.'

'Yeah. That would be great,' Sanjit said, momentarily losing his jaunty sense of humour as he looked up at Peace on the cliff. 'Because just between you and me, Choo, the idea of trying to fly a helicopter up out of here scares the pee out of me.'

Six rowboats set out from the marina under bright stars. Three kids in each boat. Two pulling oars, one at the tiller. The oars stirred phosphorescence with each stroke.

Quinn's fleet. Quinn's armada. The Mighty Quinn Navy.

Quinn didn't have to take a turn at the oars; after all, he was the boss of the whole fishing operation, but he found he kind of liked it.

They used to just motor out and drop their lines and trail their nets. But gasoline, like everything else in the FAYZ, was in short supply. They had a few hundred gallons of marine fuel left at the marina. That would have to be saved for emergencies, not for daily work like fishing.

So it was oars and sore backs. A long, long day that started long before dawn. It took an hour to get everything ready in the morning, the nets stowed after they'd been dried, the bait, hooks, lines, poles, the boats themselves, the day's food supply, water, life jackets. Then it took another hour of working the oars to get out far enough.

Six boats, three armed with poles and lines, and three dragging nets. They took turns because everyone hated the nets. It was more rowing, dragging the nets back and forth slowly across the water. Then hauling the nets up into the boat and picking fish and crabs and assorted debris out of the cords. Hard work.

Later, in the afternoon, a second batch of boats would go out to fish mostly for the blue water bats. The water bats were a mutated species that lived in caves during the night and flew out into the water during daylight. The only use for the bats was to feed the zekes, the killer worms that lived in the vegetable fields. The bats were the tribute kids paid the zekes. The economy of Perdido Beach was doubly dependent on Quinn's efforts.

Today Quinn was with a net boat. He'd let himself go for a long time, getting more and more out of shape in the first months after FAYZ fall. Now he was kind of enjoying the fact that his legs and arms, shoulders, and back were getting stronger. It helped, of course, that he had a better supply of protein than most people.

Quinn worked a long morning, him and Big Goof and Katrina, the three of them having a pretty good day of it. They hauled up a number of small fish and one huge one.

'I thought for sure that was the net being snagged,' Big Goof said. He stared happily at the almost-five-foot-long fish in the bottom of the boat. 'I believe that's the biggest fish we ever landed.'

'I think it's a tuna,' Katrina opined.

None of them really knew what some of the fish were. They were either edible or not, either had a lot of bones or didn't. This fish, slowly gasping his last, looked very edible.

'Maybe so,' Quinn said mildly. 'Big, anyway.'

'Took all three of us to haul him aboard,' Katrina said, laughing happily at the memory of the three of them slipping, sliding, and cursing.

'Good morning's work,' Quinn said. 'So, guys. You think it's about time for brunch?' It was an old joke by now. By mid-morning everyone was starving. They'd come to call it brunch.

Quinn dug out the silver coach's whistle he used to communicate across his scattered fleet. He blew three long blasts.

The other boats all dug in their oars and began heading towards Quinn's boat. Everyone found new energy when it was time to assemble for brunch.

There were no waves, no storms, even here, a mile offshore; it was like lolling in the middle of a placid mountain lake. From this far out it was possible to believe that Perdido Beach looked normal. From this far out it was a lovely little beach town sparkling in the sun.

They broke out the hibachi and the wood they'd kept dry, and Katrina, who had amazing skill with these things, started a fire going. One of the girls in another boat cut off the tail section of the tuna, scaled it, and sliced it into purple-pink steaks.

In addition to the fish they had three cabbages and some cold, boiled artichokes. The smell of the fish cooking was like a drug. No one could really think of anything else until it had been eaten.

Then they sat back, with the boats loosely roped together, and talked, taking a break before they spent another hour fishing and then faced the long row back into town.

'I bet that was tuna,' a boy said.

'I don't know what it was, but it was good. I wouldn't mind eating another few slices of that.'

'Hey, we have plenty of octopus,' someone joked. Octopi weren't something you had to catch; they sort of caught themselves, a lot of the time. And no one liked them very much. But everyone had eaten them on more than one occasion.

'Octopus this,' someone said, accompanying it with a rude gesture.

Quinn found himself staring off to the north. Perdido Beach was at the extreme southern end of the FAYZ, snuggled right up against the barrier. Quinn had been with Sam when in the first days of the FAYZ they'd fled Perdido Beach and headed up the coast looking for a way out.

Sam's plan had originally been to follow the barrier all

the way. Foot by foot, over water and land, looking for an escape hatch.

That had not quite happened. Other events had intervened.

'You know what we should have done?' Quinn said, barely realising that he was speaking out loud. 'We should have explored all that area up there. Back when we still had plenty of gas.'

Big Goof said, 'Explore what? You mean, looking for fish?'

Quinn shrugged. 'It's not like we've exactly run out of fish down here. We almost always seem to catch some. But don't you ever kind of wonder if there's better fishing farther north?'

Big Goof considered it carefully. He was not the sharpest pencil in the box; strong and sweet, but not very curious. 'That's a long row.'

'Yeah, it would be,' Quinn acknowledged. 'But I'm saying, if we still had gas.'

He pulled the visor of his floppy hat low and considered taking just a brief snooze. But no, that wouldn't do. He was in charge. For the first time in his life, Quinn had responsibility. He wasn't going to screw that up.

'There are islands up there,' Katrina said.

'Yep.' Quinn yawned. 'I wish we'd checked all that out. But Goof is right: it's a long, long row.'

29 HOURS 51 MINUTES

BRIANNA TOOK BRITTNEY in, as Sam asked. She gave her a room.

Sam had instructed her not to tell anyone. She was fine with that.

Brianna respected Astrid and Albert and the others on the council, but she and Sam, hey, they had been in battle together many times. He had saved her life. She had saved his.

Jack was also at Brianna's, but she didn't think that was really Sam's business, or anyone's. Jack was doing a little better. The flu seemed to have a short shelf life, just one of those twenty-four-hour things. Jack had stopped coughing quite so spectacularly. The walls and floor were safe again. Besides, one of Jack's charming quirks was that if it wasn't on a computer screen, he pretty much didn't see it. So she doubted he would notice their new roomie unless she came with a USB port in her head.

Sam had also asked Brianna not to do anything other than feed Brittney, maybe help her wash up a little, though the closest thing to a shower now was walking into the surf.

'Don't ask her questions,' Sam had said quite clearly.

'Why not?'

'Because we may not want to hear the answers,' he had muttered. Then, he amended that. 'Look, we don't want to stress her, OK? Something very weird has happened. We don't know if this is some kind of freak thing or something else. Either way, she's been through a lot.'

'You think?' Brianna had said. 'What with being dead and buried and all?'

Sam sighed, but tolerantly. 'If anyone's going to question her, it probably shouldn't be me. And definitely not you.'

Brianna knew what he was saying. Despite keeping Brittney under wraps, Sam probably figured it would all have to come out soon enough. And he probably figured if anyone was going to question Brittney, it should probably be Astrid.

Well . . .

'So, Brittney, how are you?' Brianna asked. She had been up for a few minutes, which was a long time for Brianna. In a few minutes she had been able to run down to the shore, fill a gallon jug with salt water, and run back to the house.

Brittney was still in the room where Brianna had put her. Still on the bed. Still lying there, eyes open. Brianna wondered if she'd slept at all.

Did zombies sleep?

Brittney sat up in the bed. Brianna set the water down on the nightstand.

'You want to wash up?'

The sheets were smeared with mud, which wasn't much dirtier than they usually were. It was amazingly hard to get things clean by swooshing them around in the ocean, even when you could swoosh at super speed like Brianna.

Things still came out kind of dirty. And crusty with salt. And scratchy. And they gave you rashes.

Brittney sort of smiled, showing her dirty braces. But she showed no interest in cleaning up.

'OK, let me help out.' Brianna took a dirty old T-shirt off the floor and dipped it in the water. She rubbed at some mud on Brittney's shoulder.

The mud came off.

But Brittney's skin did not come clean.

Brianna rubbed some more. More mud came off. No clean skin showed through.

Brianna felt a chill. Brianna wasn't scared of much. She had grown accustomed to the fact that her super speed rendered her almost invulnerable, unstoppable. She had gone toe-to-toe with Caine and walked away laughing. But this was just plain disturbing.

Brianna swallowed hard. She wiped again. And again, the same thing.

'OK,' Brianna said softly. 'Brittney, I think maybe it's, like, time for you to tell me what's going on with you. Because I'd like to know whether you're sitting there thinking you'd like to eat my brain.'

'Your brain?' Brittney asked.

'Yeah. I mean, come on, Brittney. You're a zombie. Let's face it. I'm not supposed to use that word, but someone who rises from the dead and climbs up out of their grave and walks among us: that's a zombie.'

'I'm not a zombie,' Brittney said calmly. 'I'm an angel.'

'Ah.'

'I called upon the Lord in my tribulation and he heard me. Tanner went to Him and asked Him to save me.'

Brianna considered that for a moment. 'Well, I guess it's better than being a zombie.'

'Give me your hand,' Brittney said.

Brianna hesitated. But she told herself if Brittney tried to bite it, she could snatch it back before she sank her teeth in.

Brianna extended her hand. Brittney took it. She pulled it towards her, but not towards her mouth. Instead, she placed Brianna's hand against her chest.

'Do you feel it?'

'Feel what?' Brianna asked.

'The quiet. I have no heartbeat.'

Brianna felt cold. But not as cold as Brittney. Brianna kept her hand in place. She felt no vibration.

No heartbeat.

'I don't breathe, either,' Brittney said.

'No?' Brianna whispered.

'God saved me,' Brittney said earnestly. 'He heard my prayers and He saved me to do His will.'

'Brittney, you're . . . you were down there in the ground for a long time.'

'Very long,' Brittney said. She frowned. The frown made creases in the mud that smeared her face. The mud that could not be cleaned off.

'So, you must be hungry, right?' Brianna asked, returning to her primary concern.

'I don't need to eat. Before, I took water. I swallowed it, but I didn't feel it go down. And I realised . . .'

'What?'

'That I didn't need it.'

'OK.'

Brittney smiled her metal smile again. 'So, I don't want to eat your brain, Brianna.'

'That's good,' Brianna said. 'So . . . what *do* you want to do?'

'The end is coming, Brianna,' Brittney said. 'It's why my prayers were answered. It's why Tanner and I came back.'

'You and . . . OK. When you say "the end", what's that mean?'

'The prophet is already among us. She will lead us from this place. She will lead us to our Lord, out of bondage.'

'Good,' Brianna said dryly. 'I just hope the food's better there.'

'Oh, it is,' Brittney said enthusiastically. 'It's cake and cheeseburgers and everything you would ever want.'

'So you're the prophet?'

'No, no,' Brittney said with modestly downcast eyes. 'I am not the prophet. I am an angel of the Lord. I am the avenger of the Lord, come to destroy the evil one.'

'Which evil one? We have a few. Are we talking pitchforks?'

Brittney smiled, but this time her braces did not show. It was a cool, wintry smile, a secret smile. 'This demon does not have a pitchfork, Brianna. The evil one comes with a whip.'

Brianna considered this for several seconds.

'I have someplace I have to be,' Brianna said. She left as quickly as only she could.

'What do you want for your birthday?' John asked Mary.

Mary shook poop from a napkin that was doubling as a diaper. The faeces dropped into a plastic trash can that would be taken out later and buried in a trench dug by Edilio's backhoe.

'I'd like to not do this, that would be a great birthday,' Mary said.

'I'm serious,' John said reproachfully.

Mary smiled and inclined her head towards his, forehead to forehead. It was their version of a hug. A private thing between the two members of the Terrafino family. 'I'm serious, too.'

'You should definitely take the day off,' John said. 'I mean, you have to get through the whole poof thing. People say it's kind of intense.'

'Sounds like it,' Mary said vaguely. She dropped the diaper into a second bucket, this one half filled with water. The water smelled of bleach. The bucket rested in a little red wagon so that it could be hauled to the beach. There, laundry workers would do an indifferent job of washing it in the ocean and send it back still stained and itchy with sand and salt.

'You're ready for it, right?' John asked.

Mary glanced at the watch. Francis's watch. She'd taken it off while she was washing. How many hours left? How many minutes until the big One-Five?

Mary nodded. 'I read the instructions. I talked to a person who'd been through it. I did everything I was supposed to.'

'OK,' John said unhappily. Out of nowhere, John said, 'You know Orsay is lying, right?'

'I know she cost me Francis,' Mary snapped. 'That's all I need to know.'

'Yeah! See? Look what happened from him listening to her.'

'I wonder how Jill is doing with them,' Mary wondered aloud.

She was on to the next diaper. With Francis gone and no one entirely trained to take over for him, Mary had even more work than usual. And not the best work, either.

'She's probably OK,' John said.

'Yeah, but if Orsay is this big liar, maybe I shouldn't have let her take Jill,' Mary said.

John seemed baffled by that, not sure how to respond. He blushed and looked down.

'I'm sure she's fine,' Mary said quickly, interpreting his look as concern for Jill.

'Yeah. Just because Orsay is, like, lying, that doesn't mean she'd be bad to Jill,' John said.

'Maybe I'll go check on her,' Mary said. 'In my spare time.' She laughed. It was a running joke that had long since stopped being funny.

'You probably should just stay away from Orsay,' John said.

'Yeah?'

'I mean, I don't know. I just know Astrid says Orsay's making everything up.'

'If Astrid said it, it must be true,' Mary said.

John did not answer, just looked pained.

'OK,' Mary said, 'this load can go down to the beach.'

John seemed relieved to have a chance to get away. Mary heard him leave, wagon wheels squeaking. She glanced into the main room. Three helpers there, only one of them really motivated or trained. But they could handle things for a few minutes.

Mary washed her hands as well as she could and dried them by wiping them on her loose-fitting jeans.

Where would Orsay be at this time of day?

Mary stepped outside and took a deep breath of air that didn't smell like pee or poop. She closed her eyes, enjoying the sensation. When she opened them again she was surprised to find Nerezza walking quickly towards her as though they'd arranged to meet right now and Nerezza was a bit late. 'You're –' Mary began.

'Nerezza,' the girl reminded her.

'Yeah. That's right. It's weird, but I don't remember having really met you before the other day when you came and got Jill.'

'Oh, you've seen me around,' Nerezza said. 'But I'm no one important. Everyone knows you, though, Mary. Mother Mary.'

'I was just coming to look for Orsay,' Mary said.

'Why?'

'I wanted to check on Jill.'

'That's not why,' Nerezza said, almost smiling.

Mary's expression hardened. 'OK. Francis, that's why. I don't know what Orsay told him, but you must know what he did. I can't believe that's what Orsay wanted. But you need to stop it, not let it happen again.'

'Stop what from happening?'

'Francis stepped out. He killed himself.'

Nerezza's dark eyebrows climbed. 'He did? No. No, Mary. He went to his mother.'

'That's stupid,' Mary said. 'No one knows what happens if you step out during the poof.'

Nerezza put her hand on Mary's arm. It was a surprising gesture. Mary wasn't sure she liked it, but she didn't shake it off. 'Mary: the Prophetess does know what happens. She sees it. Every night.'

'Oh? Because I've heard she's lying. Making it all up.'

'I know what you've heard,' Nerezza said in a pitying voice. 'Astrid says the Prophetess is lying. But you must know that Astrid is a very religious person, and very, very proud. She thinks she knows all the truth there is to know. She can't stand the idea that someone else might be chosen to reveal the truth.'

'I've known Astrid a long time,' Mary said. She was about to deny what Nerezza had said. But it was true, wasn't it? Astrid *was* proud. She had very definite beliefs.

'Listen to the words of the Prophetess,' Nerezza said, as though imparting a secret. 'The Prophetess has seen that we will all suffer a time of terrible tribulation. This will come very soon. And then, Mary, *then* will come the demon and the angel. And in a red sunset we will be delivered.'

Mary held her breath, mesmerised. She wanted to say

something snarky, something dismissive. But Nerezza spoke with absolute conviction.

'Come tonight, Mary, in the hours before dawn. Come and the Prophetess will speak to you herself, I can promise that. And then, I believe, you will see the truth and goodness inside her.' She smiled and crossed her arms over her chest. 'She's like you, Mary: strong and good, and filled with love.'

16 HOURS 42 MINUTES

IN THE HOURS of darkest night, Orsay climbed on to the rock. She had done it many times, so she knew where to place her feet, where to grab on with her hands. It was slick in places and she sometimes worried that she would fall into the water.

She wondered if she would drown. It wasn't very deep, but what if she hit her head on the way down. Unconscious in the water, with the foam filling her mouth.

Little Jill, wearing a fresh dress and no longer clutching her doll quite so tightly, climbed behind her. She was surprisingly nimble.

Nerezza was right behind her as she climbed, spotting her, keeping an eagle eye on her.

'Careful, Prophetess,' Nerezza murmured. 'You too, Jill.'

Nerezza was a pretty girl. Much prettier than Orsay. Orsay was pale and thin and seemed almost concave, like she was hollowed out, caving in on herself. Nerezza was healthy and strong, with flawless olive skin and lustrous black hair. Her eyes were incongruously bright, an amazing shade of green. Sometimes it seemed to Orsay that her eyes almost glowed in the dark.

She was fierce in defending Orsay. A small knot of kids was just at the base of the rock, already waiting. Nerezza had turned back to speak to them. 'Lies are being spread by the council because they don't want anyone to know the truth.'

The supplicants gazed up with faces full of hope and expectation. They wanted to believe that Orsay was the true prophet. But they had heard things . . .

'But why wouldn't they want us to know?' someone asked.

Nerezza made a pitying expression. 'People who have power usually like to hold on to it.' Her tone of knowing cynicism seemed to be effective. Kids nodded, mimicking Nerezza's older, cooler, wiser expression.

Orsay could almost not remember what life had been like before Nerezza became her friend and protector. She'd never even noticed Nerezza around town. Which was weird because she wasn't the kind of girl you overlooked.

Then again, Orsay herself was relatively new in town. She'd been living with her park ranger father in the Stefano Rey National Park and only came down to town long after the coming of the FAYZ.

Orsay had developed her powers before the FAYZ, though. At first she hadn't known what was going on, where the bizarre images in her head were coming from. But eventually she figured it out. She was inhabiting other people's dreams. Walking around inside their sleeping fantasies. Seeing what they saw, feeling what they felt.

Not always a great thing to experience. She'd been inside Drake's head, for example, and that was a snake pit no one wanted to witness.

Over time her powers seemed to have expanded, developed. She'd been asked to try to touch the mind of the monster in the mineshaft. The thing they called the gaiaphage. Or just the Darkness.

It had torn her mind open. Like scalpel blades had sliced through all the barriers of security and privacy in her brain. And after that, nothing had been quite the same. After that contact, her powers had risen to a new level. An unwelcome level.

When she touched the barrier she could see dreams from the other side. From those out there.

Those out there . . .

She could feel their presence even now as she climbed the rock and neared the barrier. She could feel them but not yet hear them, not yet step into their dreams.

She could do that only when she touched the barrier. For on the other side, outside the barrier, on the other side of that grey, implacable barrier, they touched it, too. Orsay saw the barrier as thin but impenetrable. A sheet of milky glass just a few millimetres thick. That's what she believed, what she felt.

Out there, on the other side, back in the world, parents and friends came as pilgrims to touch the barrier and try to reach the one mind capable of hearing their cries and bearing their loss.

They reached out for Orsay.

She felt them. Most of the time. She'd had doubts at first, still did at times. But it was too vivid not to be real. That's what Nerezza had told her:

Things that feel real are real. Stop doubting yourself, Prophetess.

Sometimes she doubted Nerezza. But she never told Nerezza that. There was something forceful about Nerezza. She was strong, a person with depths Orsay couldn't quite see but could sense.

Sometimes Orsay was almost afraid of Nerezza's certainty.

Orsay reached the top of her rock. She was surprised to realise that there were now dozens and dozens of kids gathering on the beach, or even ascending the base of the rock itself.

Nerezza stood just below Orsay, acting as guard, keeping the kids back.

'Look how many have come,' Nerezza said to her.

'Yes,' Orsay said. 'Too many. I can't . . .'

'You must only do what you *can* do,' Nerezza said. 'No one

expects you to suffer more than you can bear. But be certain to speak with Mary. If you do nothing else, prophesy for Mary.'

'It hurts,' Orsay admitted. She felt bad admitting it. All these anxious, hopeful, desperate faces turned towards her. And all she had to do was endure the pain in order to ease their fears.

'See! They come despite Astrid's lies.'

'Astrid?' Orsay frowned. She'd heard Nerezza saying something about Astrid before. But most of Orsay's thoughts were elsewhere. She was only partly aware of what went on around her in this world. Since that day when she had touched the Darkness she had felt as if the whole world was just a little bleached of colour, the sounds muffled. The things she touched she seemed to touch through gauze bandages.

'Yes, Astrid the Genius is telling these lies about you. She is the font of lies.'

Orsay shook her head. 'You must be wrong. Astrid? She's a very honest girl.'

'It's definitely Astrid. She's using Taylor and Howard and a few others. Lies travel quickly. By now everyone has heard. And yet, look how many have come.'

'Maybe I should stop doing this,' Orsay said.

'You can't let lies bother you, Prophetess. We have nothing to fear from Astrid, the genius who never sees what's right under her nose.'

Nerezza smiled her mysterious smile, then seemed to shake

herself out of a daydream. Before Orsay could ask her what she meant, Nerezza said, 'Let's let the Siren sing.'

Orsay had only heard Jill sing twice. Both times had been like mystical religious experiences. It didn't matter what the song was, really, although some songs almost made you feel like you should do more than just stand there listening.

'Jill,' Nerezza said. 'Get ready.' Then, in a louder voice, she addressed those on the beach. 'Everyone. We have a really special experience for you. Inspired by the Prophetess, our little Jill has a song for you. I think you'll all really enjoy it.'

Jill sang the first lines of a song that Orsay didn't recognise.

Hushaby, don't you cry,
go to sleep little baby . . .

The world closed in around Orsay like a soft, warm blanket. Her own mother, her real mother, had never been the kind for singing lullabies. But in her mind it was a different mother, the mother she'd wished she had.

When you awake, you shall have
all the pretty little ponies . . .

And now Orsay could see, in her mind's eye, the blacks and the bays, the dapples and greys, all dancing through her imagination.

And with them a life she had never had, a world she'd never known, a mother who would sing . . .

Hushaby . . .

Jill fell silent. Orsay blinked, a sleepwalker waking. She saw her followers, the children, all so close together now, they seemed almost to meld into one. They had shuffled ever closer to Jill and now pressed against the rock.

But their eyes were not on Jill, or even on Orsay. They were on that angel-decorated sunset and their own mothers' faces.

'Now it's time,' Nerezza said to Orsay.

'OK,' Orsay said. 'Yes.'

She pressed her hand against the barrier. The electric jolt burned her fingertips. The pain was still stunning, even after so many times. She had to fight the compelling urge to pull back.

But she pressed her hand against the barrier, and the pain fired every nerve in her hand, travelled up her arm, searing, burning.

Orsay closed her eyes.

'It's . . . is there . . . is Mary here?'

A voice gasped.

Orsay opened her tear-filled eyes and saw Mary Terrafino towards the back. Poor Mary, so burdened.

Mary, so terribly thin now. Starvation made so much worse by anorexia.

'Do you mean me?' Mary asked.

Orsay closed her eyes. 'Your mother . . . I see her dreams of you, Mary.' Orsay felt the images wash over her, comforting, disturbing, blessedly distracting from the pain.

'Mary six years old . . . Your mother misses you . . . She dreams of when you were little and you were so upset when your little brother got a toy for Christmas that you wanted.'

'The skateboard,' Mary whispered.

'Your mother dreams that you will come to her soon,' Orsay said. 'It's your birthday again, so soon, Mary. So grown up now.

'Your mother says that you have done enough, Mary. Others will take over your work.'

'I can't . . .' Mary said. She sounded stricken. 'I can't leave those kids alone.'

'Your birthday falls on Mother's Day, Mother Mary,' Orsay whispered, finding her own words strange.

'Yes,' Mary admitted. 'How did you –'

'On that day, Mother Mary, you will free your children so that you can be Mary the child again,' Orsay said.

'I can't leave them behind –'

'You won't, Mary. As the sun sets, you will lead them with you to freedom,' Orsay whispered. 'As the sun sets in a red sky . . .'

*

Sanjit had spent the evening watching a movie starring his adoptive father. *Fly Boy Too*. He'd seen it before. They'd all seen every single one of Todd Chance's movies. And most of Jennifer Brattle's movies. Just not the ones with nudity.

But *Fly Boy Too* was of particular interest for a twelve-second clip that showed an actor – or maybe it was an actual pilot, who could tell – flying a helicopter. In this case he was flying a helicopter while trying to machine-gun John Gage – played by Todd Chance – while Gage leaped from car to car of a speeding freight train.

Sanjit had replayed that same twelve-second clip a hundred times, till his brain was swimming and his eyes were glazed over.

Now, with all the others in bed, Sanjit took the late, late shift with Bowie. Or maybe it was the early, early shift.

He sat down in the deep armchair by Bowie's bed.

There was a goosenecked floor lamp that arched over his shoulder and shone a small circle of light on the book he opened. It was a war novel. About Vietnam, which was a country next to Thailand, where he'd been born. Evidently there had been a war there a long time ago, and Americans had been in that war. That wasn't what interested him. What interested him was that they used a lot of helicopters and this particular novel focused on a soldier who flew a helicopter.

It wasn't much, but it was all he had. The author must have done some research, at least. His descriptions sounded good. Sounded like they weren't just made up.

This was not the way to learn how to fly a helicopter.

Bowie flopped his head angrily to one side, as if he was having a bad dream. Sanjit was close enough to put his hand on Bowie's forehead. The skin was hot and damp.

He was a good-looking kid, Bowie was, with watery blue eyes and goofy teeth. So pale that sometimes he looked like one of the white marble gods Sanjit had seen in his long-lost childhood.

Those were cool to the touch. Bowie, not.

Leukemia. No, surely not. But it wasn't a cold or flu, either. This had gone on way too long for it to be the flu. Plus, no one else had gotten sick. So it probably wasn't that kind of thing. A catching thing.

Sanjit really did not want to have to see this little boy die. He had seen people die. An old beggar man with no legs. A woman who had died in a Bangkok alleyway after having a baby. A man who'd been stabbed by a pimp.

And a boy named Sunan.

Sanjit had taken Sunan under his wing. Sunan's mother was a prostitute. She'd disappeared one day; no one knew if she was alive or dead. And Sunan had found himself on the streets. He didn't know much. Sanjit had taught him what he could.

How to steal food. How to escape when you were caught stealing food. How to get tourists to give you money for carrying their bags. How to get shop owners to pay you for guiding rich foreign tourists to the shop.

How to survive. But not how to swim.

Sanjit had pulled him out of the Chao Phraya River, too late. He'd taken his eyes off the boy for just a minute. When he turned back . . . too late. By the time he'd fished him out of the silty water it was too late.

Sanjit sat back down. He turned back to the book. His hands were shaking.

Peace came in wearing footie pajamas and rubbing sleep out of her eyes.

'I forgot Noo Noo,' she said.

'Ah.' Sanjit spotted the doll on the floor, picked it up, and handed it to her. 'Hard to sleep without Noo Noo, huh?'

Peace took the doll and cradled it to her. 'Is Bowie going to be all right?'

'Well, I hope so,' Sanjit said.

'Are you learning how to fly the helicopter?'

'Sure,' Sanjit said. 'Nothing to it. There's some pedals for your feet. This stick thing called a collective. And another stick called . . . something else. I forget. But don't worry.'

'I always worry, don't I?'

'Yeah, you kind of do.' Sanjit smiled at her. 'But that's OK, because the stuff you worry about almost never happens, does it?'

'No,' Peace admitted. 'But the stuff I hope for doesn't happen, either.'

Sanjit sighed. 'Yeah. Well, I'm going to do my best.'

Peace came and hugged him. Then she took her doll and left.

Sanjit returned to the story, something about a firefight with 'Charlie'. He skimmed along, trying to glean enough clues to figure out how to fly a helicopter. Off a boat. Next to a cliff.

Loaded with everyone he cared about.

15 HOURS 59 MINUTES

'MOTHER MARY? CAN I get up and be with you?'

'No, hon. Go back to sleep.'

'But I'm not tired.'

Mary put her hand on the four-year-old's shoulder. She led him back to the main room. Cots on the floor. Filthy sheets. Not much she could do about that any more.

Your mother says that you have done enough, Mary.

Mother Mary, they called her. Like she was the Virgin Mary. Kids always professed admiration for her. They admired her all to pieces. Big deal. Not really very helpful as Mary trudged through the daily, nightly, daily, nightly grind.

Sullen 'volunteers'. Endless battles between the kids over toys. Older siblings constantly trying to dump their brothers or sisters off on the day care. Scratches, scrapes, sniffles, bloody noses, loose teeth, and ear infections. Kids who just wandered off, like Justin, the latest. And endless, endless series of questions to be answered. A demand for attention that never let up, ever, not even for a second.

Mary kept a calendar. She'd had to make her own, carefully drawing it out on a big piece of butcher paper. She needed big spaces to write endless reminders and notes. Every child's birthday. When a kid first complained of an ear infection. Reminders to get more cloth for diapers. To get a new broom. Things she needed to tell John or one of the other workers.

She stared at the calendar now. Stared at a note she'd made to give Francis a day off in honour of three months' worth of great work.

Francis had given himself his own time off.

On the schedule a note from weeks earlier to find 'P'. That was code for Prozac. She hadn't found any Prozac. Dahra Baidoo's medicine cabinet was just about empty. Dahra had given Mary a couple of different antidepressants, but they were having side effects. Vivid, absurd dreams that left Mary feeling unsettled all day long and made her dread sleep.

She was eating what she was supposed to.

But she had started vomiting again. Not every time. Just some of the time. Sometimes it came to a choice between not eating and allowing herself to stick her finger down her throat. Sometimes she couldn't control both impulses, so she had to choose one.

And then sobbing, filled with hatred for her own mind, for

the little cancers that seemed to eat at her soul day and night and night and day.

Your mother misses you . . .

On the calendar, Mother's Day was a mark in red, '15th b'day!' She twisted Francis's watch around and checked the time. Could it really be that late? Sixteen hours now. Sixteen hours until she would be fifteen years old.

Not long. Had to be ready for that, the big fifteen.

Had to be ready to fight the temptation that came to each kid in the FAYZ as they reached that deadly date.

Everyone knew by now what happened. Time would seem to freeze. And while you hung in a sort of limbo, a tempter would come to you. The one person you wanted most to please. The one you wanted most to be reunited with. And they would offer you escape. They would beg you to come across with them, to step out of the FAYZ.

There were a hundred theories on why it happened. Mary had heard numerological theories, conspiracy theories, astrological theories, every variation on aliens, government scientists . . .

Astrid's explanation, the 'official explanation', was that the FAYZ was a freak of nature, an anomaly no one could understand, with rules the kids inside the FAYZ should try to discover and understand.

The weird psychological effect of the big fifteen was just a distortion in the mind. There was no reality to the 'tempter' and no reality to the demon that followed it.

'Just your mind's way of dramatising a choice between life and death,' Astrid had explained with her usual slightly superior tone.

Mostly kids didn't think about it. To a ten- or a twelve-year-old, age fifteen seemed a long way off. When your fifteenth started getting closer you started thinking about it, but Astrid – back when they still had electricity and printers – had actually printed up a handy little instruction sheet called 'Surviving 15'.

Mary didn't think Astrid would ever deliberately lie. No matter what Nerezza said. But she didn't think Astrid was infallible, either.

Mostly Mary didn't have time to waste on philosophical inquiries. To put it mildly. Mostly she was up to her neck in child-related crises.

But the date kept drawing closer. And then . . . Francis.

And now, Orsay.

On that day you will free your children so that you can be Mary the child again . . .

Mary could feel the depression closing in on her. It was a patient stalker. It watched and waited. And when it sensed the slightest weakness, it moved closer.

She had forced herself to eat.

And then she had forced herself to throw up.

She was not stupid. She was not unaware. She knew she was unravelling. Again.

Coming apart at the seams.

And soon she would be in that frozen, timeless stasis that Astrid's helpful booklet had talked about. And she would see her mother's face calling to her . . .

Lay down the burden, Mary . . .

And go to her . . .

Mary closed her eyes tight. When she opened them, Ashley stood before her. The little girl was crying. She'd had a nightmare and needed a hug.

A kid named Consuela, one of Edilio's soldiers, had seen it first.

She had run to find Edilio. She was one of the late-night shift that kept an eye out during the wee hours. She'd come across it, screamed, and gone running for Edilio. That's what she was supposed to do.

And now Edilio was standing over it. Wondering what he was supposed to do. He knew the correct answer: report it to the council. He'd given Sam grief for failing to do that earlier.

But this . . .

'What should I do?' Consuela whispered.

'Don't tell anyone.'

'Should I get Astrid? Or Sam?'

Perfectly reasonable questions. Edilio wished he had a perfectly reasonable answer. 'Take off,' Edilio said. 'Good job. Sucks you had to see this.'

She left, grateful to get away. And Edilio stared down balefully at the thing . . . the person . . . the body . . . that would be like a dagger in Sam's heart.

In the months since the death of Drake Merwin, the defeat of the gaiaphage and the deal with the zekes, a tenuous order and calm had come to the FAYZ.

Edilio felt that tenuous structure, the system Edilio had worked so hard to build, the system he had just started to believe might last, coming apart in his hands now, like tissue paper in a rainstorm.

It had never been real. The FAYZ would always win.

Sam stood over the body. The sight of it rocked him. He took a stagger-step back.

Edilio grabbed him.

Sam felt panic welling up inside him. He wanted to run. He couldn't breathe. His heart was pounding in his chest. His veins filled with ice water.

He knew what had happened.

'Hey, Boss,' Edilio said. 'You OK, man?'

Sam couldn't answer. He took air in little gasps. Like a toddler on the edge of tears.

'Sam,' Edilio said. 'Come on, man.'

Edilio looked from the mutilated body to his friend and back again.

He had been there. Sam knew the terrible wounds he was seeing. The body of a twelve-year-old boy named Leonard bore marks Sam knew and would never forget.

The marks of a whip.

The street was quiet. No one in sight. No one who could have borne witness.

'Drake,' Sam said in a whisper.

'No, man: Drake's dead and gone.'

Sam, suddenly furious, grabbed Edilio's shirt. 'Don't tell me what I'm seeing, Edilio. It's him,' Sam yelled.

Edilio patiently pried Sam's fingers off. 'Listen, Sam, I know what it looks like. I saw you. I saw what you looked like that day. So, I know, all right? But man, it makes no sense. Drake is dead and buried under tons of rock in a mineshaft.'

'It's Drake,' Sam said flatly.

'OK, that's enough, Sam,' Edilio snapped. 'You're freaking out.'

Sam closed his eyes and felt again the pain . . . pain like nothing he'd imagined could exist outside of hell. Pain like being burned alive.

The blows of Drake's whip hand. Each one tearing strips of flesh . . .

'You don't . . . You don't know what it was like . . .'

'Sam . . .'

'Even after Brianna shot me full of morphine . . . you don't know . . . you don't know . . . All right? You don't know. Pray to God you don't ever know.'

Taylor chose that moment to bounce in. She took a look at the body and yelped. She covered her mouth and looked away.

'He's back,' Sam said.

'Taylor, get Sam out of here. Take him to Astrid,' Edilio ordered.

'But Sam and Astrid are –'

'Just do it!' Edilio roared. 'And then haul your butt around and get the other members of the council over there. They want to know what's going on? Fine. Then they can get up out of their beds.'

'It doesn't go away,' Sam said through gritted teeth. 'You know that, Edilio? It doesn't go away. It's always with me. It's always with me.'

'Take him,' Edilio ordered Taylor. 'And tell Astrid we need to talk.'

EIGHTEEN

15 HOURS 57 MINUTES

'**WE** GO TONIGHT,' Caine said. Weak. So weak in every muscle. Sore. Panting just from climbing the stairs to the dining hall. Like he'd run a marathon.

Starvation. It did that to you.

He tried to count the exhausted, gaunt faces that turned towards him. But he couldn't keep the number in his head. Fifteen? Seventeen? No more than that, certainly.

The last candle flickered on the table that had once been piled high with turkey loaf and pizza, Jell-O and limp salad, cartons of milk, all the usual school lunchroom fare.

This room had once been full of kids. All so healthy looking. Some thin, some fat, none as gaunt and hideous as what was left here now.

Coates Academy, the fashionable place for the well-off to send their troublesome kids. Kids who started fires. Bullies. Skanks. Druggies. Kids with psychological problems. Or just kids who talked back once too often. Or kids whose parents wanted them gone from their lives.

The difficult, the losers, the rejects. The unloved. Coates Academy, where you could dump your kids and not be bothered by them any more.

Well, that was certainly working out well for all concerned.

Now, the desperate remnants of Coates. The ones mean enough or lucky enough to survive. Only four of them known to be mutants: Caine himself, a four bar; Diana, whose only power was the ability to gauge another mutant's powers; Bug, with his ability to almost disappear; and Penny, who had developed an extremely useful power of illusion: she could make a person believe they were being attacked by monsters or stabbed with knives or on fire.

She had demonstrated it on a kid named Barry. Barry had been made to believe he was being chased around the room by spears. It had been funny watching him run in terror.

That was it. Four mutants, only two of which, Caine and Penny, were any good in a fight. Bug had his uses. And Diana was Diana. The only face he wanted to see now.

But she had her head down, resting it on her hands with elbows on her knees.

The others looked to him. They didn't love him or even like him, but they still feared him.

'I called everyone here tonight because we are leaving,' Caine said.

'Do you have any food?' a voice cried pitifully.

Caine said, 'We're going to get food. We know a place. It's an island.'

'How are we going to get to an island?'

'Shut up, Jason. It's an island. Used to be owned by two famous actors you probably remember. Todd Chance and Jennifer Brattle. It's a huge mansion on a private island. The kind of place they'd have stocked with lots of food.'

'The only way to get there is on a boat,' Jason whined. 'How can we do that?'

'We're going to take some boats,' Caine said with far more confidence than he felt.

Bug sneezed. He became almost visible when he sneezed.

'Bug knows about this place,' Caine said. 'It's famous.'

'So why didn't we hear about it earlier?' Diana asked, mumbling at the floor.

'Because Bug is an idiot and it didn't occur to him,' Caine snapped. 'But the island is there. It's called San Francisco de Sales. It's on the map.'

He pulled a torn and crumpled paper from his pocket and unfolded it. It was taken from an atlas in the school's library. 'See?' He held it up and was gratified to see flickers of actual interest.

'We're going to get boats,' Caine said. 'We're going to get them in Perdido Beach.'

That killed whatever faint enthusiasm there had been. 'They got all kinds of freaks and guns and all,' a girl nicknamed Pampers said.

'Yeah, they do,' Caine admitted wearily. 'But they're all going to be too busy to deal with us. And if any of them get in our way, I'll take care of them. Me or Penny.'

Kids glanced at Penny. She was twelve years old. She'd probably been pretty once. A pretty little Chinese-American girl with a tiny nose and surprised eyebrows. Now she looked like a scarecrow, brittle hair, gums red from malnutrition, with a rash that covered her neck and arms in a lacy pink pattern.

Jason said, 'I think you're nuts. Go through Perdido Beach? Half of us can't even walk that far, let alone fight. We're starving, man. Unless you have some food to give us, we'll fall out before we reach the highway.'

'Listen to me,' Caine said softly. 'We're definitely going to need some food. Soon.'

Diana looked up, dreading what Caine might do next.

'The only food we're going to get is on that island. We reach it, or we find someone else to eat.'

NINETEEN

15 HOURS 27 MINUTES

IT WAS WEIRD, Zil thought. Weird how it had come to this. Weird how scared he was, how rattly his insides were, but he couldn't let on. Because he was in charge. Because they were all looking to him.

The Leader. Capital 'T', capital 'L', when Turk said it.

Turk, a creepy little toady with his bad leg and his rat face.

And Hank. Hank was scary. Probably crazy as a loon. OK, not probably, definitely. Hank was always the one pushing, provoking, demanding.

The others. Twenty-three of them. Antoine, the fat druggie. Max. Rudy. Lisa. Trent. Others Zil barely knew. The only one Zil really even liked was Lance. Lance was cool. Lance was the good-looking, smart one who made Zil feel like maybe this was all OK, like maybe Zil really did deserve to be The Leader, capital 'T', capital 'L'.

Anyway, too late to turn back now. He'd made his deal with Caine. The deal was very simple: there were two people in the

FAYZ who Zil had to fear above all others – Sam and Caine. Caine had offered Zil a chance to discredit one and wave goodbye to the other.

The time was now or never.

First things first. Gasoline. And after that it would be too late for second thoughts.

The declaration of total war against the freaks was a minute away.

Twenty-three of them filtered through the dark streets in ones and twos, guns and clubs hidden beneath hoodies and coats. Swaggering, some of them, others creeping along scared like mice. The great fear was that Sam might see them early. Try to stop them before they could start the party.

Zil laughed, not meaning to.

Turk was with him. Neither of them carrying a weapon, nothing that would give Sam an excuse if he stopped them.

'See, that's a Leader,' Turk said in his greasy way. 'You laugh despite everything.'

Zil said nothing. His stomach was in his throat.

So much could go wrong. Brianna. Dekka. Taylor. Edilio. Even Orc. Freaks and freak supporters, traitors. Any one of them could bring this to a sudden halt.

Zil felt as if he was standing at the edge of a cliff.

One step at a time. First, the gas station.

It had to be tonight.

Now.

And the whole town had to burn.

Out of that fire the Human Crew would gather the survivors under Zil's leadership. Then he'd be the Leader, not just of this little crew of losers, but of everyone.

Brittney did not know where she'd been. Or what she'd done since leaving Brianna's house. She had flashes, like single frames pulled out of a movie. A flash of a crawl space under a house. Of lying in the dirt again, of feeling it cold on her back. Of spiderwebbed wooden beams above her, a comforting coffin lid.

Other flashes showed rocks at the beach. Sand that made it hard to walk.

She remembered seeing kids. Two, at a distance. They ran away when they saw her. But maybe they weren't real. Maybe they were just ghosts because Brittney wasn't totally sure that anyone she saw was real. They looked real on the surface – their eyes and hair and lips were all familiar to her. But at times they seemed to have lights coming out of them in wrong places.

It was hard to know what was real and what was not. All she could know was that Tanner appeared sometimes, just beside her. And he was real.

The voice in her head was real, too, the voice that told her to serve him, to obey, to follow the path of truth and goodness.

Then Brittney remembered feeling that the evil one was close. Very close. She could feel his presence.

Oh, yes: *he* had been here.

But where had she been? She asked her brother, Tanner. Tanner was looking a bit messy, his wounds all too visible.

'Where am I, Tanner? How did I get here?'

'You rose, an avenging angel,' Tanner said.

'Yes,' Brittney said. 'But where was I? Just now? Just before. Where was I?'

There was a noise at the end of the block. Two people walking. Sam and Taylor.

Sam was good. Taylor was good. Neither was allied with the evil one. They didn't seem to see her. They trailed blurs of ultraviolet light behind them, like a slime trail.

'Did you see him, Tanner?'

'Who?'

'The evil one. Did you see the demon?'

Tanner didn't answer. He was bleeding from the awful wounds that had killed him.

Brittney let it go. Indeed she'd already forgotten that she'd asked a question.

'I have to find the Prophet,' she said. 'I must save her from the evil one.'

'Yes.' Tanner had assumed his other guise, his angelic

raiment. He glowed beautifully, like a golden star. 'Follow me, sister. We have good works to perform.'

'Praise Jesus,' Brittney said.

Her brother stared at her, and for just a moment it seemed he was smiling. His teeth were bare, his eyes red with an inner fire. 'Yes,' Tanner said. 'Praise.'

TWENTY

15 HOURS 12 MINUTES

THE GAS STATION was dark. Everything was dark.

Zil looked up at that sky. Stars shone. Amazingly bright and sharp. Black night, brilliant, eye-piercing white stars.

Zil was no poet, but he could understand why people got sort of mesmerised by stars. Lots of great, important people must have looked up at the stars when they were on the edge, getting ready to do the things that would mark them forever as great.

Too bad these weren't real stars.

Hank appeared, like a ghost. He was with Antoine. Zil saw others in the darkness beside the highway, already gathered. Milling together, scared, nervous, most ready to run like rabbits probably.

'Leader,' Hank said in an intense whisper.

'Hank,' Zil answered, his voice reassuringly calm.

'The Human Crew awaits your orders.'

A murmur of many voices. Scared sheep bleating

together, trying to keep their courage up.

Lance was there. 'I checked it out. Four of Edilio's soldiers. Two of them asleep. No freaks, as far as I could see.'

'Good,' Zil said. 'If we move fast and get the element of surprise I doubt we'll even have to hurt anyone.'

'Don't count on it,' Hank said.

'Whatever happens, it's meant to be,' Turk said.

'Fate.'

Zil swallowed hard. If he showed any weakness it would be over. 'This is the beginning of the end for the freaks,' he said. 'Tonight we take Perdido Beach back for humans.'

'You heard the Leader,' Turk said.

'Let's go,' Hank said. He had a shotgun as big as he was hanging on his shoulder. He slipped it off and ostentatiously clicked the safety to 'off'.

And then, they were on the move. Walking fast. Zil in the lead with Hank on one side and Lance on the other and Antoine waddling along with Turk in the second row.

No one spotted them as they emerged up on to the highway. Or as they marched in quick-step past the battered old sign showing gas prices.

Past the first pump before a voice cried out, 'Hey!'

They kept moving, breaking now into an exhilarating run.

'Hey! Hey!' the voice cried again.

A boy, Zil didn't know his name, was yelling and then a

second voice was shouting, 'What's happening?'

BLAM!

The sound was deafening. A dagger of yellow fire from the blast.

Hank's shotgun.

The first boy fell back hard.

Zil almost cried out. Almost yelled 'Stop'. Almost said 'You don't need to . . .'

But it was too late for that. Too late.

The second soldier raised his own gun, but hesitated. Hank did not.

BLAM!

The second soldier turned and ran. He threw his gun down and ran.

More voices yelling in fear and confusion. Gunfire. Here. There. Wild blasting, everyone who could, explosions of light in the dark.

'Cease fire!' Hank yelled.

The firing continued. But it was all coming from Zil's own side now.

'Knock it off!' Zil shouted.

The explosions stopped.

Zil's ears rang. From far off a pitiful voice cried. Cried like a baby.

For a long moment no one said or did anything. The boy who

lay on his back made no sound. Zil did not take a closer look.

'OK, follow the plan,' Hank said, as calmly as if all this was just a video game he'd put on pause.

Kids who had been tasked with bringing bottles began to unload them. Lance went to the hand-pump that brought gasoline up from the underground storage. He began to work it and fill glass bottles held by shaking hands.

'I can't believe it,' someone said.

'We did it!' one exulted.

'Not yet,' Zil growled. 'But it's beginning.'

Hank said, 'Remember: Stuff the rags far down into the bottle like I told you. And keep your lighters dry.'

They found a wheelbarrow in the weeds behind the station. It didn't roll very well – the wheel was lopsided – but it worked to hold the bottles.

The smell of gasoline was thick in Zil's throat. He was stressing, waiting for the counterattack. Waiting to see Sam striding up, hands blazing.

That would end it all.

But no matter how hard he peered into the black night, Zil did not see the one freak who would stop him.

Little Pete made a grunting sound as he pushed the buttons and worked the trackpad of his handheld.

Sam sat silent, withdrawn. He had said nothing since Taylor

had hauled him through the door and woken Astrid from a fretful sleep.

It was stupid, Astrid realised, not talking to Sam. When Taylor had awakened her, she'd imagined somehow, in her sleepy confusion, that Sam had come running back, all forgiven.

But then Taylor had said she'd be back with the rest of the council and Astrid knew something had gone wrong.

Now they were all there. Well, most of them. Word was Dekka was sick with whatever was going around. But Albert was there, and really, Astrid admitted to herself, so long as Albert and Astrid were there, the important members of the council were present.

Unfortunately, Howard had also come. No one wanted to drag John out into the night. He could hear about it all later.

They had enough. Astrid, Albert, Howard, and Sam. Five out of seven. And, Astrid couldn't help but note, any vote would be more likely to go in her favour.

They were at the table beneath an eerie Sammy Sun.

'OK, Taylor, since Sam doesn't exactly seem talkative,' Astrid said, 'why are we all here?'

'A kid got murdered tonight,' Taylor said.

A hundred questions popped into Astrid's head, but she asked the most important one first. 'Who was it?'

'Edilio says he thinks it's Juanito. Or Leonard.'

'He thinks?'

'Kind of hard to tell,' Taylor said, not quite smirking.

'What happened?' Albert asked.

Taylor looked at Sam. Sam said nothing. He stared. First at his own light, hovering in the air. Then at Taylor. He looked pale and almost frail. Like he was suddenly a much, much older person.

'Kid was whipped,' Taylor said. 'It looked like what happened to Sam.'

Sam lowered his head and wrapped his hands behind his neck. He seemed to be trying to hold on to his head, pressing it hard like it might explode.

'Drake's dead,' Albert said. Sounding like a guy who really, really hoped it was true. 'He's dead. He's been dead.'

'Yeah, well . . .' Taylor said.

'Yeah well, what?' Astrid asked, instantly hearing the change in her tone of voice, the evasion.

Taylor shifted uncomfortably. 'Look, Edilio told me to bring Sam here and get you guys together. I think Sam is kind of, you know, flashing on stuff that happened.'

'That boy was whipped. Just like I was,' Sam said to the floor. 'I know the marks. I . . .'

'It doesn't mean it was Drake,' Albert said.

'Drake's dead,' Astrid said. 'Dead people don't come back. Let's not be ridiculous.'

Howard made a derisive snort. 'OK. That's as far as I go with you on this, Sammy boy.' He made a hand-washing gesture.

Astrid slammed her palm on the table, surprising even herself. 'Somebody better tell me what all these back-and-forth looks are about.'

'Brittney,' Howard said, spitting the name out like it was poison. 'She came back. Sam had her and stuck her with Brianna, and told me not to talk about it.'

'Brittney?' Astrid said, confused.

Howard said, 'Yeah. You know, like dead-girl Brittney? Way dead? Dead a long time and buried a long time and suddenly she's sitting in my house chatting? That Brittney.'

'I'm still not . . .'

'Well, Astrid,' Howard said, 'I guess we just found the limits of your big old genius brain. Point is that someone who was very seriously dead is suddenly not so dead any more.'

'But . . .' Astrid started. 'But Drake . . .'

'As dead as Brittney,' Howard said. 'Which might be a slight problem, since Brittney isn't exactly dead herself.'

Astrid felt sick to her stomach. No. Surely not. Impossible. Insane. Not even here, not even in the FAYZ.

But Howard wasn't lying. Taylor's expression confirmed that. And Sam wasn't jumping up to dispute it, either.

Astrid stood up. She stared hard at Sam. She could feel a throbbing in her head. 'You didn't tell me? This is happening and you didn't tell the council?'

Sam barely glanced up.

'He didn't tell *you*, Astrid,' Howard said, obviously enjoying the moment.

A part of Astrid felt sorry for Sam. She knew he was still a long way from being over the beating he had taken from Drake. One look at him now, head hung, looking small and scared, was proof of that.

But he wasn't the only one to be terrorised by Drake. Drake had come after her, early on. If she thought about it, she could still almost feel the sting of his slap on her face.

He'd made her . . .

He'd bullied her into calling Little Pete a retard. He'd terrorised her into betraying the person she loved most in the world.

She had managed to put it out of her mind. Why couldn't Sam do the same?

Howard laughed. 'Sammy didn't want people using the "Z" word.'

'The what?' Astrid snapped.

'Zombie.' Howard made a booga-booga face and stretched his hands out like a sleepwalker.

'Taylor, get out of here,' Astrid said.

'Hey, I –'

'This is council business now,' Astrid said, putting all the frost she could command into her voice.

Taylor hesitated, looked to Sam for guidance. He didn't look up or stir. Taylor took a second to give Astrid a middle-finger salute and then popped out of the room.

'Sam, I know you're upset over what happened with you and Drake,' Astrid began.

'Upset?' Sam echoed the word with an ironic smirk.

'But that's no excuse for you keeping secrets from us.'

'Yeah,' Howard said, 'Don't you know only Astrid is allowed to keep secrets?'

'Shut up, Howard,' Astrid snapped.

'Yeah, we get to lie because we're the smart ones,' Howard said. 'Not like all those idiots out there.'

Astrid turned her attention back to Sam. 'This is not OK, Sam. The council has the responsibility. Not you alone.'

Sam looked like he could not care less about what she was saying. He looked almost beyond reach, indifferent to what was going on around him.

'Hey,' Astrid said. 'We're talking to you.'

That did it. His jaw clenched. His head snapped up. His eyes blazed. 'Don't push me. That wasn't *you* with your skin whipped off and covered in blood. That was *me*. That was me who went down into that mineshaft to try to fight the gaiaphage.'

Astrid blinked. 'No one is minimising what you've done, Sam. You're a hero. But at the same time –'

Sam was on his feet. 'At the same time? At the same time you were here in town. Edilio had a bullet in his chest. Dekka was torn to pieces. I was trying not to scream from the . . . You and Albert and Howard, you weren't there, were you?'

'I was busy standing up to Zil, trying to save Hunter's life,' Astrid yelled.

'But it wasn't you and your big words, was it? It was Orc who stopped Zil. And he was there because I sent him to rescue you. Me!' He stabbed a finger at his own chest, actually making what looked like painful impact. 'Me! Me and Brianna and Dekka and Edilio! And poor Duck.'

Suddenly, there was Taylor again. 'Hey! One of Edilio's soldiers just came staggering in from the gas station. He says someone attacked, took the place over.'

That silenced the argument.

Sam, with exquisite contempt, turned to his girlfriend and said, 'You want to go deal with it, Astrid?'

Astrid flushed red.

'No? I didn't think so. Guess it will be up to me then.'

He left silence in his wake.

'Maybe we better pass some laws real quick so Sam can save our butts legally,' Howard said.

'Howard, go get Orc,' Albert said.

'Now *you're* giving me orders, Albert?' Howard shook his head. 'I don't think so. Not you or her,' he said, jerking a thumb at Astrid. 'You may not think much of me, you two, but at least I know who saves our butts. And if I got to take orders from someone, it'll be the someone who just walked out of here.'

TWENTY ONE

14 HOURS 44 MINUTES

'FIND EDILIO AND Dekka and Brianna,' Sam told Taylor. 'Edilio and Dekka to the gas station. Brianna on the streets. We're going to deal with Zil.'

For once, Taylor did not argue. She bounced away.

He took a deep breath of cold night air and tried to get his head together. Zil. Had to stop him.

But all he could see was Drake. Drake in the shadows. Drake behind bushes and trees. Drake with his whip hand.

Drake, not Zil.

He squeezed his eyes shut. It would be different this time. Back then he'd had no choice but to let Drake take him. No choice but to stand there and endure . . . and endure . . .

He noticed Howard coming up behind him. It surprised him a little, until he realised Howard would see it as an opportunity to use Orc for profit.

'Howard? What kind of shape is Orc in?'

Howard shrugged. 'Passed out, dead drunk.'

Sam cursed under his breath. 'See if you can get him up.'

He tossed out the orders on automatic. Not needing to think about it. But he still felt like he was in a dream. Not quite focusing.

Drake. Somehow that animal was back. Somehow he was alive.

How was he supposed to fight something that could not be killed? Zil he could handle. But Drake? A Drake who could return from the dead?

I'll burn him, Sam told himself. I'll burn him inch by inch. I'll turn him into a piece of charcoal. I'll reduce him to ashes.

And scatter the ashes over a mile of sea and land.

Kill him. Destroy him. Destroy the remains of the remains of the remains.

Let him come back from that.

'If I get Orc up, it will cost you,' Howard said. 'He's fought Drake before.'

'I'll burn him down,' Sam muttered to himself. 'I'll kill him myself.'

Howard seemed to think this was directed at either Orc or him, and scuttled off as quickly as he could without another word.

It wasn't far to the gas station. Just a few blocks.

Sam walked down the middle of the street. No lights. Silence. His footsteps echoed.

He walked on legs stiff with fear.

He had forgotten to tell Taylor to get Lana. Lana would be needed. Taylor would figure it out, though. Smart girl, Taylor.

He remembered Lana's healing touch that day as the last effects of the morphine wore off and the pain, like a tidal wave of fire, consumed him. Her touch, and the wave had slowly receded.

He had screamed. He was sure of that.

He had screamed until his throat was raw. And in nightmares since that day.

'Ashes,' Sam said.

Alone on the dark street. Walking towards the thing he feared most in the world.

Astrid was shaking. Every type of emotion. Fear. Fury. Even hate.

And love.

'Albert, I don't know how long we can keep Sam involved at all,' she said.

'You're upset,' Albert replied.

'Yes, I'm upset. But that's not the point. Sam is out of control. If we're ever going to have a working system we may have to find someone else to play the role of saviour.'

Albert sighed. 'Astrid, we don't know what's out there in the night. And maybe you're right that Sam is out of control. But me? I'm really glad it's him out there getting ready to face whatever it is.'

Albert picked up his omnipresent notebook and left.

To a now empty, silent room, Astrid said, 'Don't die, Sam. Don't die.'

Taylor found Edilio already en route to the gas station. He had just one soldier with him, a girl named Elizabeth. Both were carrying machine pistols, part of the armoury they'd found long ago at the power plant.

Elizabeth spun and almost sprayed Taylor when she popped in.

'Whoa!' Taylor yelled.

'Sorry. I thought . . . We heard gunfire.'

'Gas station. Sam's on his way, told me to get you going in that direction.'

Edilio nodded. 'Yeah, we're on our way.'

Taylor grabbed him and pulled him aside so Elizabeth wouldn't overhear. 'Sam is fighting with Astrid.'

'Great. That's just what we need: the two of them at each other.' Edilio ran his hand back over his brush-cut hair. He still kept it short unlike most kids, who had given up on personal grooming. 'I haven't heard anyone shooting in the last few minutes. Probably just some drunk fool got hold of a gun.'

'That's not what your guy said,' Taylor corrected him, talking fast. 'He said the station was being attacked.'

'Caine?' Edilio mused.

'Or Drake. Or Caine *and* Drake.'

'Drake's dead,' Edilio said flatly. Then he made the sign of the cross over his chest. 'At least I sure hope so. Where is Brianna? Where's Dekka?'

'Next on my list,' Taylor said and bounced to the house where Dekka was staying. The house was dark but for a Sammy Sun burning grimly in the living room.

'Dekka?' Taylor yelled.

She heard a stirring coming from upstairs. Taylor bounced to the bedroom to find Dekka sitting up and swinging her legs over the side of the bed.

'Sam sent me. Said you should haul butt to the gas station. Someone's shooting the place up.'

Dekka coughed. Covered her mouth and coughed again. 'Sorry. I guess I have a –' She coughed again, more violently. 'I'm OK,' she managed to say.

'Whatever you've got, don't give it to me,' Taylor said, backing away. 'Hey, do you know where Brianna is?'

Dekka's already gloomy expression darkened further. 'She's at her place. With Jack, in case you're looking for him, too.'

'Jack?' Taylor said, momentarily distracted by the possibility of good gossip. 'She's with Computer Jack?'

'Yeah, Computer Jack. Nerdy kid, glasses, does stupid things like turn off the power plant? That Jack. He's sick and she's taking care of him.'

'OK. Bouncing . . . Wait. I forgot. You might want to keep an eye out for Drake.'

Dekka's eyebrows shot up. 'Say what?'

'Welcome to the FAYZ,' Taylor said, and changed the channel. Dekka's dark bedroom became Brianna's.

Jack had set up a cot in the corner of Brianna's bedroom, but he wasn't lying on it. Jack was in a big office chair, feet up on a side table with a blanket wrapped around him. He was snoring. His glasses were on the floor. Brianna was in her bed.

'Wake up!' Taylor yelled.

Jack didn't stir. But Brianna was up and off of the cot in less time than it took for Taylor's shout to echo.

Brianna said, 'What are you –' and then she started coughing.

It was a strange thing to witness because Brianna coughed fast. She did everything fast. It used to be it was only when she ran – something she could do at about the speed of sound. But more and more lately that speed had translated to the rest of her movements, too. So now she coughed much faster than a normal person would cough.

And then she sat down as suddenly as she'd stood up.

Jack's eyes fluttered open. 'Huh,' he muttered. He blinked a couple of times and fished around for his fallen glasses. 'What?'

'Trouble,' Taylor said.

'I'm coming,' Brianna said. She stood up again and sat back down again.

'She's sick,' Jack said. 'Like the flu or whatever. What I had.'

'What do you mean she's sick?' Taylor demanded. 'Dekka told me *you* were sick.'

'I was,' Jack grumbled. 'I still am, a little, but I'm getting better. Now Brianna's got it.'

'Interesting,' Taylor said with a leer.

'What's . . .' Brianna began, and then started coughing again.

'What's happening?' Jack asked, completing Brianna's thought.

'You don't even want to know,' Taylor said. 'Take care of the Breeze. Sam can probably handle whatever this is by himself.'

'Handle what?' Brianna managed.

Taylor shook her head slowly, side to side. 'If I said Drake Merwin, what would you say?'

'I'd say he's dead,' Jack said.

'Yeah,' Taylor said, and bounced out of the room.

*

Sam reached the station. Edilio was already there. Alone.

Edilio didn't waste any time. 'I got here a minute ago,' he said. 'Me and Elizabeth. No one here but Marty and he'd been wounded. Shot in the hand. I sent him to Clifftop with Elizabeth to have Lana fix him.'

'What's going on, can you tell?' Sam asked.

'Marty says a whole crowd was here. Shooting, yelling, "Death to freaks".'

Sam frowned. 'Zil? That's what this is? I thought . . .'

'Yeah, I know what you're thinking, man. This isn't a Drake kind of thing,' Edilio said. 'Drake shows up, you know it's him, right? He makes sure you know it's him.'

'Where are your other soldiers?'

'Run off.' Edilio sounded disgusted.

'They're just kids,' Sam said. 'People shooting at them. In the dark. All of a sudden. Almost anyone would run off.'

'Yeah,' Edilio said curtly. But Sam knew he was embarrassed. The army was Edilio's responsibility. He picked the kids and trained them and motivated them as well as he could. But twelve- thirteen- fourteen-year-old kids were not supposed to be dealing with this kind of craziness. Not even now.

Never.

'You smell that?' Edilio asked.

'Gas. So Zil stole some gas? You think that's it? He wanted to be able to use a car?'

In the pitch black Sam couldn't see Edilio's face but he could feel his friend's doubt. 'I don't know, Sam. What's he going to do with a car? Why's he need it so bad, he's going to do this? Zil's a creep but he's not totally stupid. He's got to know this is over the line and we'll go after him.'

Sam nodded. 'Yeah.'

'You OK, man?'

Sam didn't answer. He peered into the darkness. Searched the shadows. Clenched. Ready.

Finally, he forced his fists to relax. Forced himself to take a breath. 'I've never set out to hurt anyone,' Sam said.

Edilio waited.

'I never set out thinking I'm going to kill someone. I go into a fight and I think, maybe I'll have to hurt someone. Yeah. I think that. And I have. You know: you've been there.'

'Yeah, I've been there,' Edilio said.

'If it's him, though, I mean if Drake is somehow back . . . it's not going to be about just doing what I have to do. You know?'

Edilio did not answer.

'I've done what I had to do. To save people. Or to save myself. This won't be like that. If it's him, I mean.'

'Dude, it's Zil. Zil and the Human Crew did this.'

Sam shook his head. 'Yeah. Zil. But I know he's out there, Edilio. I know Drake is out there. I feel it.'

'Sam . . .'

'If I see him, I'll kill him,' Sam said. 'Not self-defence. I'm not waiting until he attacks. I see him, I burn him.'

Edilio grabbed him by both shoulders and got in his face. 'Hey! Listen to me, Sam. You're getting freaked out here. The problem is Zil. OK? We have real problems, we don't need nightmares. And, anyway, we don't do cold-blooded murder. Not even if it is Drake.'

Sam firmly pried Edilio's hands off his shoulders. 'If it's Drake, I'm burning him down. If you and Astrid and the rest of the council want to arrest me for doing it, fine. But I'm not sharing my life with Drake Merwin.'

'Well, you do what you got to do, Sam, and I will, too. Right now what we got to do is figure out what Zil is up to. So, I'm going to go and do that. You want to come? Or do you want to stand here in the dark talking about murder?'

Edilio stomped away, swinging his machine pistol down into firing position.

For the first time, Sam followed Edilio.

TWENTY TWO

14 HOURS 17 MINUTES

DOWN THE ACCESS road they marched, the station lost behind them in the night.

Their numbers had diminished a little. Kids, the weak and scared ones, had peeled off unnoticed, slinking home once they'd had a taste of violence.

Weaklings, Zil thought. *Cowards.*

Just a dozen of them now, the hard core, pushing a wheelbarrow loaded with softly clinking bottles, trailing the smell of gasoline.

Left at the school. Past the gloomy, darkened buildings. So alien now. So long ago, all of that.

Zil couldn't make out individual windows in the edifice, but he could see approximately where his old home room had been. He imagined himself back then. Imagined himself sitting, bored during morning announcements.

And now here he was at the head of an army. A small army. But dedicated. All together in a great cause. Perdido

Beach for humans. Death to freaks. Death to mutants.

On stiff legs he led the march. The march to freedom and power.

Right at Golding. Golding and Sherman, off the north-west corner of the school, that was the target zone, as agreed with Caine. No idea why. Caine had only said that they should start at Golding and Sherman. And move along Sherman towards the water. Burn all they could till they reached Ocean Boulevard. Then, if they still had any left, they could go along Ocean towards town. Not towards the marina.

'If I see you nitwits heading towards the marina, our little agreement is over,' Caine had warned.

Nitwits. Zil seethed at the memory. Caine's casual arrogance, his contempt for anyone who wasn't a freak like him. His time would come, Zil vowed.

'We're here,' Zil said. But that wasn't a very historic thing to say. And this, make no mistake, was history happening in the FAYZ. The beginning of the end for the freaks. The beginning of Zil being in control.

Zil turned to faces he knew were expectant, giddy, excited. He could hear it in their whispered conversation.

'Tonight we strike a blow for humans,' Zil said. That was the line Turk had come up with. Something everyone would be able to quote. 'Tonight we strike a blow for humans!' Zil cried, raising his voice, no longer afraid.

'Death to freaks!' Turk shouted.

'Light up!' Hank cried.

Lighters and matches flicked. Tiny yellow pinpoints in the black night, casting eerie shadows on wild eyes and mouths pulled back in grimaces of fear and rage.

Zil took the first of the bottles – Molotov cocktails, Hank said they were called. The spark of the lighter caught the gasoline-saturated wick.

Zil turned and heaved the bottle towards the closest house.

It arced like a meteor, spinning.

It crashed on to the brick steps and burst. Flames spread over several square feet of porch.

No one moved. All eyes were fixed. Faces fascinated.

The spilled gasoline burned blue. For a while it seemed it would do nothing but burn itself out on the porch.

But then a wicker rocking chair caught fire.

And then the decorative lattice.

And suddenly the flames were licking up the pillars that supported the porch roof.

A wild cheer went up.

More bottles were lit. More wild arcs of twirling fire.

A second house. A garage. A parked car sitting on deflated tyres.

Cries of shock and horror came from inside the first house.

Zil didn't let himself hear them.

'Onwards!' he cried. 'Burn it all down!'

Down through the dark they shuffled and stumbled, Caine's starved and starving remnants.

'Look!' Bug cried. No one could see him, of course, or his outstretched pointing hand. But they looked, anyway.

An orange glow lit the horizon.

'Huh. The stupid punk actually did it,' Caine said. 'We have to hurry. Anyone falls out, they are on their own.'

Orsay climbed to the top of the cliff, weary but propelled by Nerezza's helping hand.

'Come on, Prophetess, we're almost there.'

'Don't call me that,' Orsay said.

'It's what you are,' Nerezza said softly but insistently.

The others had all gone ahead. Nerezza always insisted that the supplicants leave the beach first. Orsay suspected it had to do with Nerezza not wanting anyone to see Orsay struggling and scraping her knees on rocks. Nerezza seemed to think it was important for kids to see Orsay as above all that normal stuff.

A prophet.

'I'm not a prophet,' Orsay said. 'I'm just a person who hears dreams.'

'You are helping people,' Nerezza said as they rounded a

buried boulder that always gave Orsay trouble. 'You are telling them the truth. Showing them a path.'

'I can't even find my own path,' Orsay said as she slipped and landed on her palms. They were scraped, but not too badly.

'You show them the way,' Nerezza said. 'They need to be shown a way out of this place.'

Orsay stopped, panting from exertion. She turned to Nerezza, whose face was just two faintly glowing eyes, like a cat's eyes. 'You know, I'm not totally sure. You know that. Maybe I'm . . . maybe it's . . .' She didn't have the word for what she felt at times like this, times of doubt. Times when a small voice down deep inside her seemed to be whispering warnings in her ear.

'You need to trust me,' Nerezza said firmly. 'You are the Prophetess.'

Orsay topped the cliff. She stared. 'I must not be much of a prophet. I didn't foresee this.'

'What?' Nerezza called up from just below.

'The town is burning.'

'Look, Tanner,' Brittney said. She raised one arm and pointed.

Her brother, now glowing a dark green, like a billion little nodules of radioactivity, but still Tanner, said, 'Yes. It is time.'

Brittney hesitated. 'Why, Tanner?'

He gave no answer.

'Are we doing the Lord's will, Tanner?'

Tanner did not answer.

'I am doing what's right. Aren't I?'

'Go towards the flames, sister. All your answers are there.'

Brittney lowered her arm to her side. It seemed strange, somehow. All of it. All of it so very strange.

She had burrowed up through the wet dirt. How long? Forever and ever. She had burrowed like a mole. Blind. Like a mole. No. Like an earthworm.

Tanner began chanting in a sing-song voice. An eerie poem that Brittney remembered from so very long ago. A class assignment, a thing memorised and quickly forgotten.

But it was still buried in her memory. And now it came from Tanner's mouth, his dead mouth gaping with black-edge fire dribbling like magma.

But see, amid the mimic rout
A crawling shape intrude!
A blood-red thing that writhes from out
The scenic solitude!
It writhes! – it writhes! – with mortal pangs
The mimes become its food,
And seraphs sob at vermin fangs . . .

Tanner smiled a ghastly smile and said, '*In human gore imbued.*'

'Why are you saying that? You're scaring me, Tanner.'

'Not for long, sister,' Tanner said. Soon you will understand the Lord's will.'

Justin woke suddenly. He immediately rolled to one side and felt the spot where he'd been sleeping. Dry!

See? He'd been right all along. He didn't wet *this* bed.

But just to be safe he should run out to the backyard and pee because he could feel a little pressure. He was wearing his same old pajamas; they'd been in his same old drawer. They were so soft because they were still from the old days. His mommy had washed these pyjamas and made them all soft.

The floor was cold under his bare feet. He hadn't been able to find his old slippers. Roger had even helped him look. The Artful Roger was nice. The only new thing in this room was a picture Roger had coloured for him. It showed a happy Justin with his mommy and daddy and a ham with sweet potatoes and cookies. It was taped on Justin's wall.

Roger had also found the picture album for him. It was downstairs in the cupboard in the dining room. It was full of pictures of Justin and his family and his old friends.

Now it was under Justin's bed. It made him feel pretty sad looking at it.

Justin crept down the stairs so he wouldn't wake up Roger.

The old toilets didn't work any more. People all peed and did number twos in holes in their backyards. No big deal. But it was scary going out at night. Justin was scared the coyotes would come back.

It was easier than usual to find the hole. It was kind of light out, a flickery orange light.

And it wasn't quiet like it usually was. He could hear kids yelling. And it sounded like someone dropped a glass and broke it. And then he heard someone screaming, so he ran back in the house.

He stopped, amazed. The living room was burning.

He could feel the heat. Smoke was pouring out of the living room, swooping up the stairs.

Justin didn't know what to do. He remembered he was supposed to stop, drop, and roll if he ever caught on fire. But he wasn't on fire – the house was.

'Call 911,' he said aloud. But that probably wouldn't work. Nothing worked any more.

Suddenly a loud beeping noise. Really loud. It was upstairs. Justin covered his ears but he could still hear it.

'Justin!' It was Roger yelling from upstairs.

Then he appeared at the top of the stairs. He was choking from the smoke.

'I'm down here!' Justin yelled.

'Hang on, I'm –' Roger started coughing then. He tripped

and went falling down the stairs. He fell all the way on his face. Roger hit the bottom and stopped.

Justin waited for him to get up.

'Roger. Wake up. There's a fire!' Justin said.

The fire was coming out of the living room now. It was like it was eating the carpet and the walls. It was so hot. Hotter than an oven.

Justin started choking from the smoke. He wanted to run away.

'Roger, wake up! Wake up!'

Justin ran to Roger and tugged on his shirt. 'Wake up!'

He couldn't move Roger, and Roger did not wake up. Roger made a moaning sound and kind of moved, but then he fell back asleep.

Justin pulled and pulled and cried and the fire must have seen him there crying and pulling because the fire was coming to get him.

TWENTY THREE

14 HOURS 7 MINUTES

TAYLOR WAS STARTING to worry by the time she popped into the hallway outside Lana's Clifftop home.

She would never bounce straight into Lana's room. Everyone knew that Lana had been through an unspeakable hell. And no one believed she was totally over it.

But more than concern for Lana's possible delicacy was deep respect and affection for her. There were far too many kids buried in the plaza. But without Lana the number would have been four or five times as high.

Taylor knocked and earned an instant barrage of loud barks from Patrick.

'It's me, Taylor,' she called through the door.

A voice that betrayed no sleepiness said, 'Come in.'

Taylor bounced in, ignoring the door.

Lana was on the balcony, back turned to her.

'I'm awake,' Lana said unnecessarily. 'There's some trouble.'

'You know about it?'

'I can see it,' Lana said.

Taylor stepped out beside her. Off to the north, up the coast, the orange glow of fire.

'Some idiot burning down their house with a candle again?' Taylor suggested.

'I don't think so. This is no accident,' Lana said.

'Who would start fires deliberately?' Taylor wondered. 'I mean, what does it accomplish?'

'Fear. Pain. Despair,' Lana said. 'Chaos. It accomplishes chaos. Evil things love chaos.'

Taylor shrugged. 'Probably just Zil.'

'Nothing in the FAYZ is ever *just* anything, Taylor. This is a very complicated place.'

'No offence, Healer, but you're getting weirder all the time,' Taylor said.

Lana smiled. 'You have no idea.'

Quinn's little flotilla set out to sea. Dark as always. Too early. Sleep still crunchy in everyone's eyes. But that was normal. Routine.

They were a tight little group, Quinn thought. It made him feel good. As much as he had screwed up in his life, he had done this well.

Quinn's fishing fleet. Feeding the FAYZ.

As they cleared the marina and headed out to sea Quinn felt

an unusual joy welling up inside him. *What did I do when the FAYZ happened?* he asked himself. *I fed people.*

Not a bad thing. A bad start, yes. He had freaked out. He had at one point betrayed Sam to Caine. And he had never gotten over the memory of that awful battle against Caine and Drake and the coyotes.

So many vivid, indelible memories. He wished he could cut them out of his brain. But other times he realised no, that was foolish. It was all those things that had made him this new person.

He wasn't Quinn the coward any more. Or Quinn the turncoat. He was Quinn the fisherman.

He pulled on the oars, enjoying the healthy burn in his shoulders. He was facing Perdido Beach.

So he saw the first small flower of flame. An orange pinpoint in the darkness.

'Fire,' he said calmly. He was in a pole-fishing boat with two other guys.

The others stirred and looked.

From a nearby boat a shout. 'Hey, Quinn, you see that?'

'Yeah. Keep pulling. We're not the fire department.'

They set to their oars again and the boats edged farther from shore. Far enough out that they could soon drop hooks and spread nets.

But every eye was on the town now.

'It's spreading,' someone said.

'It's jumping from house to house.'

'No,' Quinn said. 'I don't think it's spreading. I think . . . I think someone is setting those fires.'

He felt his stomach churn. His muscles, warm from rowing felt suddenly stiff and cold.

'The town is burning,' a voice said.

They watched in silence as the orange flames spread and billowed up into the sky. The town was no longer dark.

'We're fishermen, not fighters,' Quinn said.

Oars splashed. Oarlocks creaked. The boats pushed water aside with a soft shushing sound.

Sam and Edilio broke into a run. Across the highway on to the access road. Past the rusting hulks of cars that had crashed into one another or into storefronts or simply stalled in the middle of the highway on that fateful day when every driver disappeared.

They ran down Sheridan, passing the school on their right. At least it wasn't on fire. Once they reached the cross-street at Golding the smoke was much thicker. It billowed towards them, impossible to avoid. Sam and Edilio choked and slowed down.

Sam pulled off his T-shirt and bunched it over his mouth, but it didn't do much good. His eyes stung.

He crouched low, hoping the smoke would pass overhead. That didn't work, either.

Sam grabbed Edilio's arm and pulled him along. They crossed Golding and in the lee of houses on Sheridan they found the air was clearer but still reeking. The houses on the west side of Sheridan were black silhouettes cut out of the sheet of flame that soared and danced and curled towards heaven from Sherman Avenue.

They started running again, down the street and around the corner on Alameda, trying to stay on the sweet side of the very slight breeze. The smoke was still thick but no longer blowing towards them.

Fire was everywhere along Sherman. A roaring, ravenous, living thing. It was more intense north of Alameda, but it was moving fast south towards the water down the rest of Sherman.

'Why is the fire moving against the breeze?' Edilio asked.

'Because someone's setting new fires,' Sam said grimly.

Sam glanced left. Right. At least six houses burning to their right. The rest of that block would go up, no stopping it, not a thing they could do.

'There are kids in some of these houses,' Edilio said, choking from emotion as much as smoke.

At least three fires burned to their left. As they watched, Sam saw a twirling firework, a spinning Roman candle that soared and arced downward and crashed into the front of a house far down the block. He couldn't hear the Molotov cocktail smash over the roar of fire around him.

'Come on!' Sam yelled, and ran towards the newest fire.

He wished he had Brianna with him, or Dekka. Where were they? Both could have helped save lives.

Sam barely missed ploughing into a group of kids, some as young as three, all huddled together in the middle of the street, faces lit by fire, eyes wide with fear.

'It's Sam!'

'Thank God, Sam is here! Sam is here!'

'Sam, our house is burning down!'

'I think my little brother is in there!'

Sam pushed past them, but one girl grabbed his arm. 'You have to help us!'

'I'm trying,' he said grimly, and tore himself free. 'Come on, Edilio!'

Zil's mob was backlit by a sheet of orange that consumed the front of a colonial-style house. They danced and cavorted and ran with burning Molotov cocktails.

'Don't waste them!' Hank shouted. 'One Molotov, one house!'

Antoine screamed as he waved a lit bottle. 'Aaaaarrrggh! Aaaaarrrgh!' Almost as if he were the one burning. He threw the bottle high and hard, and it soared straight through an upper floor window of an older wood house.

Immediately there were cries of terror from inside. And Antoine screamed back, an echo of their horror, twisted into savage glee.

Kids came pouring out of the door of the house as flames licked the curtains.

Sam did not hesitate. He raised his hand, palm out. A beam of brilliant green light drew a line to Antoine's body.

Antoine's berserk cries ended instantly. He clutched once at the three-inch-wide hole just above his belt. Then he sat down in the street.

'It's Sam!' one of Zil's thugs cried.

As one they turned and ran, dropping gas-filled bottles behind. The gasoline spread from the shattered bottles and caught fire instantly.

Sam tore after them in pursuit, racing to leap the patches of burning gasoline.

'Sam, no!' Edilio shouted. Edilio tripped over the body of Antoine, who lay now on his back, gasping like a fish, eyes staring up in horror.

Sam had not noticed Edilio fall. But he heard Edilio's single shouted warning. 'Ambush!'

Sam heard the word, knew it was true, and without thinking dropped and rolled. He stopped just inches away from rolling into burning gasoline.

At least three guns were firing. But Zil's thugs had had no

practice with weapons. They were firing wild, bullets flying in every direction.

Sam hugged the pavement, shaking from the close call.

Where were Dekka and Brianna?

Another weapon was firing now. Edilio's rapid bam-bam-bam, short bursts from his machine gun. There was a big difference between Edilio with a gun and some punk like Turk with a gun. Edilio practiced. Edilio trained.

There was a loud shriek of pain, and the ambush was over.

Sam pried himself up a few inches, enough to see one of Zil's gunmen. The kid was running away, a wraith in the smoke.

Too late, Sam thought. He aimed, straight for the boy's back. The beam of burning light caught the gunman in the back of his calf. He screamed. The gun flew from his hand and clattered on the sidewalk.

Hank ran back to grab it. Sam fired and missed. Hank snarled at him, a face like a wild animal. Hank raced away as Edilio's bullets chased him, ploughing a furrow in the hot blacktop.

Sam jumped to his feet. Edilio ran up, panting.

'They're running for it,' Edilio said.

'I'm not letting them get away,' Sam said. 'I'm tired of having to fight the same people again and again. It's time to finish it.'

'What are you saying, man?'

'I'm killing Zil. Clear enough? I'm putting him down.'

'Whoa, man,' Edilio said. 'That's not what we do. We're the good guys, right?'

'There has to be an end to it, Edilio.' He wiped soot from his face with the back of his hand, but smoke had filled his eyes with tears. 'I can't keep doing it and never reaching the end.'

'It's not your call any more,' Edilio said.

Sam turned a steely glare on him. 'You too? Now you're siding with Astrid?'

'Man, there have to be limits,' Edilio said.

Sam stood staring down the street. The fire was out of control. All of Sherman was burning, from one end to the other. If they were lucky it wouldn't jump to another street. But one way or the other, Sherman was lost.

'We should be looking to save any kids that are trapped,' Edilio said.

Sam didn't answer.

'Sam,' Edilio pleaded.

'I begged Him to let me die, Edilio. I prayed to the God who Astrid likes so much and I said, God, if You're there, kill me. Don't let me feel this pain any more.'

Edilio said nothing.

'You don't understand, Edilio,' Sam said so softly, he doubted Edilio could hear him over the roar and crackle of the fire raging all around them. 'You can't do anything else with people like this. You have to kill them all. Zil. Caine. Drake.

You just have to kill them. So right now, I'm starting with Zil and his crew,' Sam said. 'You can come with me or not.'

He started walking in the direction of the fleeing Hank.

Edilio did not move.

TWENTY FOUR

14 HOURS 5 MINUTES

DEKKA COULDN'T JUST lie there. She couldn't. Not when there was a fight. Not when Sam might be walking into danger.

Half the girls in the FAYZ had a crush on Sam, but it wasn't like that for Dekka. What she felt for Sam was different. They were soldiers, the two of them. Sam, Edilio, and Dekka – more than anyone else in Perdido Beach, they were the tip of the spear. When there was trouble, it was the three of them in the middle of it.

Well, the three of them plus Brianna.

Best not to think about Brianna too much. That way lay sadness and misery and loneliness. Brianna was what she was. Wanted what she wanted. Which was not what Dekka wanted.

Almost surely not what Dekka wanted. Although, Dekka had never asked, never said anything.

She doubled over with a fit of coughing as she rose from her bed.

She should probably get dressed at least. Put on some clothes, not stagger out into the street wearing flannel pyjama bottoms and a purple hoodie. But another round of strangled coughing left her feeling weak. She had to save her strength.

Shoes. Definitely needed shoes. That was the minimum. She shuffled out of her slippers and searched around under the bed for her sneakers. Found them after more hacking and almost lost the will at that point. Sam didn't need her. Whatever was going on . . .

Then she noticed the orange glow from the window. She pushed back the curtains. The sky was orange. She saw sparks, like fireflies. She pushed the window open and almost gagged on the smoke.

The town was on fire.

Dekka got her shoes on. She found a scarf and her bucket of fresh water. She drank deeply of the water. It was going to be a thirsty night. Then she plunged the scarf into the rest of the water, soaked it, and tied the soggy mess over her mouth and nose. She looked like a pyjama-wearing bandit.

Out on to the street. An amazing, awful, unreal scene. Kids were coming past, alone or in small groups, glancing back over their shoulders. Carrying a few pitiful possessions in their arms.

A girl loaded down with a big bundle of dresses staggered past. 'Hey! What's going on?' Dekka rasped.

'Everything's burning up,' the girl said, and kept moving.

Dekka let her go because now she spotted a boy she knew. 'Jonas! What is this?'

Jonas shook his head, scared. Scared and something else.

'Hey, don't walk off, I'm talking to you!' Dekka snapped.

'I'm not talking to you, freak. I'm done with all of you. It's because of you this is happening.'

'What are you talking about?' But she'd already guessed. 'Is it Zil doing all this?'

Jonas snarled at her, his face transformed by rage. 'Death to freaks!'

'Hey, fool, you're a soldier.'

'Not any more,' Jonas said, and took off at a run.

Dekka wobbled. She was so weak. So unlike her usual self. But there was no doubt about what she had to do. If kids were running away in one direction she had to head in the other. Into the smoke. Towards the bright orange glow that sent up sudden flares of fire, like fingers reaching for the heavens.

Diana stumbled as she raced to keep up. Caine was pushing the pace. The haggard band of Coates kids trotted along, terrified of being left behind.

She had enough strength to keep up, but barely. And she hated herself for having that strength. And hated Caine for giving it to her. For what he had done. For where he had led them to.

But like the others she raced to keep up the punishing pace.

Across the highway. Smooth concrete under foot. Across the access road, and pelting across the school yard. So bizarre, Diana thought. The school yard where the town kids used to play soccer and try out for cheerleader, and now they were running like no one before had ever run on this overgrown field.

The fire was in the east, a wall of flames down Sherman. Their path lay down Brace Road, just two blocks from the fire. It was a straight shot down Brace to the marina.

'What about Sam?' someone asked. 'What if we run into him?'

'Idiot,' Caine muttered. 'You think this fire is a coincidence? It's all part of my plan. Sherman cuts off the western end of town. Kids will run towards the plaza, on the other side of Sherman, or down to the beach. Either way, it's away from us. And Sam will be there with them.'

'Who's that?' Diana said. She stopped. Caine and the rest stopped as well. Someone walked straight down the middle of Brace. It was impossible to tell at first whether he was walking towards them or away. But Caine knew the silhouette instantly.

The hair on the back of his neck stood on end. No one else looked like that.

No one.

'No,' he whispered.

'Do we keep going?' Penny asked.

Caine ignored her. He turned to Diana. 'Am I . . . am I crazy?'

Diana said nothing. Her horrified expression gave Caine his answer.

'He's moving away,' Caine whispered.

Smoke swirled and the apparition was gone.

'Optical illusion,' Caine said.

'So we keep going straight?'

Caine shook his head. 'No. Change of plans. We'll cut through town. Head for the beach, then make our way back.'

Diana pointed a shaking finger at the burning street beyond. 'Go through the fire? Or go down streets that are going to be filled with Sam's people?'

'I have another way,' Caine said. He crossed quickly to a fence around the backyard of the closest house. 'We'll make our own street.'

He raised a hand and the fence bulged inward. With a rending, tearing sound the fence gave way.

'Backyard to backyard,' he said. 'Let's move.'

'We did it, Leader! We did it!' Hank said. He had to shout to be heard over the roar of the flames.

Antoine lay on the ground, crying loudly. He had pulled off

his shirt to see the wound in his side. He lay there, fat and jiggly, as he cried about the pain.

'Man up,' Hank said harshly.

'Are you crazy?' Antoine cried. 'I have a hole in me! I have a hole in me! Oh, God. It hurts so bad!'

Perdido Beach was burning. At least a big part of it was. Zil climbed atop a Winnebago in the beach parking lot. He could see much of the town from there.

Sherman was ablaze. It looked like a volcano had erupted in the middle of town. And now the flames were advancing towards the centre of town along Alameda.

His doing, all of this. His creation. And now they would all know that he was serious. Now they would all know that you didn't mess with Zil Sperry.

'Take me to Lana,' Antoine moaned. 'You guys have to take me to Lana!'

The sun wasn't up yet, so it wasn't possible to see the smoke plume, but Zil sensed that it was huge. There was not a star to be seen in the sky.

'Think we got Sam?' Lance asked.

No one answered.

'Should we go back and get more gas?' Turk asked. He, like everyone else, was ignoring Antoine.

Zil couldn't answer. A part of him wanted to burn it all down. Every last house. Every vacant, useless store. Burn it all down and dance up here atop the Winnebago while it burned.

The plan was to create chaos. And to help the freak Caine to escape.

'Leader, we need to know what to do,' Turk urged.

'Help me,' Antoine moaned. 'We gotta stick together, don't we? Don't we?'

Hank said, 'Antoine, shut up or I'll shut you up.'

'He burned a hole in me. Look at it! Look at it!'

Hank glanced up at Zil. Zil turned away. He didn't have an answer to the problem of Antoine.

The truth was, Zil hated seeing wounds of any kind. He'd always been squeamish about blood. And the one quick glance he'd stolen at Antoine's injury had made him sick to his stomach.

Which probably didn't help Antoine much.

Hank said, 'Come on, Antoine. Come with me.'

'What? What are you . . . I'll be good, it's just that it hurts, man, it hurts so much.'

'Dude, come on,' Hank said. 'I'll get you to Lana. Come on.'

Hank bent low and propped Antoine up as he struggled on to his feet. Antoine shrieked in pain.

Zil climbed down the ladder that was bolted to the back of the Winnebago.

'What do you think, Lance?' Handsome Lance. Tall, cool,

smart Lance. If only, Zil thought for not the first time, all Human Crew could look like Lance. Lance reflected well on Zil. Whereas fat, drunken Antoine, Turk with his dragging foot, and Hank with his nasty ferret's face made it seem that he was surrounded by losers.

Lance looked thoughtful. 'Kids are spread all over the place. All confused. What do we do if they decide we were responsible for burning the town and decide to come after us?'

Turk laughed derisively. 'Like the Leader hasn't thought of that? We tell people it was Sam.'

Zil was surprised by the suggestion. He'd given it no thought, but obviously Turk had.

'Not Sam,' Zil corrected, thinking on the fly. 'We blame Caine. Kids won't believe it was Sam. We say it was Caine and everyone will believe us.'

'Kids saw us throwing Molotov cocktails,' Lance argued.

Turk snorted. 'Man, don't you know? People believe all kinds of stuff if you tell them it's true. People will believe in flying saucers and stuff.'

'It was Caine,' Zil said, making it up as he went along and liking it more with each word he spoke. 'Caine can make people do what he wants, right? So he used his powers to force some of us to do it.'

'Yeah,' Turk said. His eyes lit up. 'Yeah, because he wanted to make us look bad. He wanted it to be on us because he's a freak and we fight the freaks.'

Hank reappeared. He took a position behind Lance. The contrast between the two was all the more clear when they were close together.

'Where's 'Toine?' Turk asked.

'Dumped him down the beach,' Hank said. 'He's not going to make it. Not with that hole in him. He'd just slow us down.'

'Then he'll be the first to give his life for the Human Crew,' Turk said solemnly. 'That's major. That's hard core. Murdered by Sam.'

Zil reached a sudden realisation. 'If people are going to believe Caine is responsible for all this, we have to fight Caine.'

'Fight Caine?' Turk said blankly. He took an unconscious step back.

Zil grinned. 'We don't have to win. We just have to make it look real.'

Turk nodded. 'That's really smart, Leader. Everyone will think Caine used us and then we managed to chase him off.'

Zil doubted everyone would believe that. But some would. And that doubt would slow down Sam's reaction as the council tried to make sense of everything.

Each hour of chaos would leave Zil stronger.

Would his big brother, Zane, have figured it all out this well?

And would he have had the nerve to pull it off? Not likely. Zane would have been on Sam's side.

It was almost a pity he wasn't here.

TWENTY FIVE

14 HOURS 2 MINUTES

EDILIO HAD WATCHED Sam go with a feeling of doom. What chance was there if Sam had lost it? What chance did Edilio have to fix anything?

'Like I could,' he muttered. 'Like anyone could.'

It was very hard for him to see what was happening around him. He heard screams. He heard shouts. He heard laughter. He saw only smoke and flame.

Gunshots rang out. From where, he couldn't say.

He glimpsed kids running. So brightly lit, they looked like they were burning. Then they were obscured by the smoke.

'What do I do?' Edilio asked himself.

'Too bad we don't have marshmallows. This is an amazing fire.'

Howard emerged through the smoke behind Edilio. Orc was with him.

'This sucks,' the monster growled. 'Burning everything up.'

Ellen, the fire chief, showed up with two other kids.

And Edilio began to realise that they were all looking to him for answers. 'Fire chief' was a mostly empty title now. There was no water in the hydrants. But at least she had a clue, which was more than Edilio had.

'I think the fire is moving towards the centre of town. Lot of kids live between here and there,' Ellen said. 'We need to make sure kids get out of the way.'

Yeah,' Edilio agreed, grateful for any useful suggestion.

'And we got to see if anyone is still inside any of these houses that are already burning. Anyone that we can save.'

'Right. Right,' Edilio said. He took a deep breath. 'OK, good, Ellen. You and your guys run ahead of the fire, get people out. Tell them either go towards the beach or cross the highway.'

'Right,' Ellen agreed.

'Orc and Howard and I'll see if we can save anyone.'

Edilio didn't bother to ask Howard or Orc's opinion on that. He just started moving. Straight back down Sherman. He didn't look back to see if they were following. Either they were, or they weren't. If they weren't, well, he couldn't really blame them.

Down the burning street.

The fire was on both sides now. It made a sound like a tornado. The roar rose and fell and rose again. There came a loud crash as a roof collapsed and sparks like an eruption of fireflies billowed into the sky.

The heat reminded Edilio of sticking his face into his mother's oven when she was baking. A blast of burning air first from one side and then the other, buffeting him back and forth.

Glancing back, Edilio saw Howard lose his balance and fall. Orc grabbed him and propped him back up.

Smoke filled the air, scalding Edilio's throat, seeming to shrivel his lungs. He breathed in pints, then cups, then teaspoons of air.

He stopped walking. Through the pall he could see an endless vista of flame and smoke ahead. Parked cars burned in driveways. Overgrown, unwatered lawns burned with almost explosive force.

Glass shattered. Beams collapsed. The blacktop street bubbled at the edges, liquified.

'Can't,' Edilio gasped.

He turned again to see that Howard was already retreating. Orc stood stolidly, unmoving.

Edilio put a hand on his pebbled shoulder. Unable to speak, choking and crying, Edilio guided him back away from the flames.

Roger did not wake up. The Artful Roger did not wake up.

Justin had to run. He ran into the backyard.

But he couldn't just do that, he couldn't, he couldn't.

So he ran back inside. And he heard Roger coughing

like crazy. He was awake! But it was like he couldn't see, his eyes were closed, all the smoke, and Roger ran but he hit a wall.

'Roger!'

Justin ran to him and grabbed his shirt tail. 'It's this way!'

He pulled Roger towards the kitchen, towards the back door.

Roger stumbled along with him. But it wasn't right because the fire and the smoke were in front of him now. The fire had circled around and filled the kitchen.

The dining room. It made him think about the picture album upstairs under his bed. Maybe he could go and grab it really fast.

Maybe, but probably not. There was no door from the dining room into the backyard. But there was a big window, and Justin led Roger to it.

'I'm –' Justin started to say he was going to open the window, but the smoke was everywhere now stinging his eyes, so he had to shut them and choking his throat so he couldn't talk.

He felt blindly for the window handles.

Caine kept pushing the pace. Push over a fence and move through. Backyards choked with weeds. Stinking swimming pools that had been turned into toilets. Garbage strewn everywhere.

In the dark they stumbled over fence posts and forgotten toys.

They banged into rusting swing sets and barbecues.

They were making a lot of noise. Off the street, but noisy. Kids yelled down at them from dark windows: 'Hey, who is that? Get out of my yard.'

Caine ignored them. Keep moving, that was the key. Keep moving, get to the beach.

They had one chance, one chance only. They had to reach the marina within minutes. Sam and his people would be confused by the destruction, running around like crazy trying to figure it out. But sooner or later it would occur to someone, Astrid if not Sam, that it was all a diversion.

Or Sam would take Zil and squeeze him. Then the little punk would give Caine up. In a heartbeat.

Caine did not want to reach the marina to find Sam waiting for him. Caine was holding on by his fingernails, desperate. He couldn't take Sam on. Not now. Not this night.

Even here, blocks from the fire, the air reeked. The smell of burning was everywhere. Almost enough to cover the smell of human waste.

They reached another street. No alternative but to cross it, as they had earlier streets. But there were too many kids here to easily avoid them. No way around, nothing to do but bluff and keep moving.

They pushed past terrified refugees.

'Keep moving, keep moving,' Caine yelled as some of his

people peeled off in a vain attempt to beg food from two traumatised, soot-covered five-year-olds.

Then, just down the street, wreathed in smoke, a shape.

'Down!' Caine hissed. 'Stop!'

He peered through blurry eyes. Was it? No. Of course not. Madness.

The shape resolved into a kid, a regular kid, with regular hands and arms and nothing at all like that other form he had seen in the smoke.

Caine stood up, feeling foolish for having been spooked. 'Move on, move on,' he yelled.

He raised his hands and used his power to shove the group forwards. Half of them stumbled and fell.

He cursed them. 'Move!'

The earlier form in the smoke. That tall, lean body. The arm that went on and on. Impossible. An illusion, just like this one. Imagination fed by exhaustion and fear and hunger.

'Penny, are you doing anything?' Caine demanded.

Penny rasped, 'What do you mean?'

'I thought I saw something,' Caine said. Then he amended. 'Someone. Before.'

'It wasn't me,' Penny said. 'I would never use my powers on you, Caine.'

'No,' Caine agreed. 'You wouldn't.' His confidence was draining away. His mind was playing tricks on him. The others would sense it soon. Diana already did. But then she'd had the same hallucination, hadn't she?

'This is too slow,' Caine said. 'We have to go straight down the street. Penny, either you or me, one of us takes down anyone that gets in our way. Right?'

He plunged down the street, aiming for the beach. He had to fight the urge to look over his shoulder for the boy who could not possibly be there.

They made it safely as far as the beach. But there they ran into a group of maybe twenty kids, all milling around gaping at the fire, crying, giggling, encouraging one another. Half like they were watching a show, half like they were personally burning in those flames.

At first the gaggle of kids didn't notice Caine's group, but then one glanced over and his eyes widened as he saw Diana. And then, Caine.

'It's Caine!'

'Out of my way,' Caine warned. The last thing he wanted was a stupid, pointless, and time-wasting fight. He was in a hurry.

'You!' another kid cried. 'You started the fire!'

'What? Moron.' Caine pushed past, using his actual hands, not his powers, not looking for trouble right now. But the cry was being taken up by others and now a dozen furious, terrified kids were in his face, yelling and crying and then one threw a punch.

'Enough,' Caine yelled. He raised a hand, and the nearest kid went flying. He landed with a sickening crunch twenty feet away.

Caine never even saw the person who brained him with a crowbar. The blow seemed to come out of nowhere. He was on his knees, too confused to be scared.

He saw the crowbar just before it hit the second time. A weaker blow, and badly aimed, but shockingly painful on the bone of his left shoulder. It sent a numbing electricity all the way down to his fingertips.

He wasn't going to wait for a third blow. He raised his right hand, but before he could pulverise the little boy, Penny made her move.

The boy leaped back, almost as far as if Caine had thrown him.

He screamed and swung his crowbar wildly around him. When the crowbar flew from his fear-weakened grip, he began punching and clawing the air, eyes wild.

'What's he seeing?' Caine asked.

'Very large spiders,' Penny answered. 'Really large. And they jump really fast.'

'Thanks,' Caine grunted. He stood up and rubbed his numbed arm. 'Hope they give him a heart attack. Come on,' he yelled. 'It's not far now. Hang in with me, everyone, by morning you'll be eating.'

*

Mary didn't have the energy to go home. Not much point, really . . . no shower . . . no . . .

She sagged on to the chair in the cramped office. She tried to lift her legs, rest her feet on a cardboard box, but even that required too much energy.

She rattled the pill bottle on her desk. She pried the top off and looked at what she had. She didn't even recognise the pill, but it must be some kind of antidepressant. That's all she ever got from Dahra.

She downed it dry.

When had she last taken a pill? She needed to keep track of them.

Two kids down with some kind of flu.

What was she supposed to . . .

What might have been dreams melded seamlessly with memory and Mary wandered for a while in a place filled with sick children and the smell of pee and her mother making peanut butter and jelly sandwiches in giant stacks for some event at school and Mary wrapping the sandwiches in Ziploc bags, counting them into recycled plastic Ralph's bags.

'Did you wet yourself?' her mother asked.

'I guess so. It smells like it.' She wasn't embarrassed, just annoyed, wishing her mother wouldn't make an issue out of it.

And then the door was opened and a little girl came and crawled on to Mary's lap but Mary couldn't move her arms to hug because her arms were made out of lead.

'I'm so tired,' Mary told her mother.

'Well, we've made eight thousand sandwiches,' her mother explained, and Mary saw from the stacks and stacks that teetered comically like something from a Dr. Seuss book, that it was true.

'You look sickly.'

'I'm fine,' Mary said.

'I want my mommy,' the little girl said in her ear, and warm tears rolled on to Mary's neck.

'You should come home now,' Mary's mother said.

'I have to do the laundry first,' Mary said.

'Someone else will do it.'

Mary felt a sudden sharp sadness. She felt herself sinking into the tile floor, shrinking as her mother watched, no longer making sandwiches.

Her mother held the knife covered with peanut butter and raspberry preserves. Globules of red, red fruit dripped from the edge of the knife, which was awfully large for making sandwiches.

'It won't hurt,' her mother said. She held the knife out for Mary.

Mary jerked awake.

The girl on her lap had fallen asleep and peed. Mary was soaked by it.

'Oh!' she cried. 'Oh, get off me! Get off me!' she yelled, still half in her dream, still seeing that knife floating, handle towards her, dripping.

The girl fell to the floor and, stunned, began to cry.

'Hey!' someone yelled from the main room.

'I'm sorry,' Mary mumbled, and tried to stand up. Her legs gave way and she sat down again, too suddenly. As she fell she reached for the knife but it wasn't real, though the little girl's cry was, and so was the voice yelling, 'Hey, you can't come in here!'

On the next try Mary managed to stand up. She staggered out. Three kids, faces dull with terror.

Not her age group. Too old.

'What are you doing here?' Mary asked.

The whole room was waking up, kids asking what was going on. Zadie, the helper who'd been yelling, said, 'I think something's wrong, Mary.'

Two more kids pushed through the front door. They smelled of something that wasn't pee.

A boy ran in, shrieking. He had a livid burn all over the back of his hand.

'What's going on?'

'Help us, help us!' a boy cried, and now it was all chaos, more kids streaming in the door. Mary recognised the smell now, the smell of smoke.

She pushed none too gently past the new arrivals. Outside, she coughed as she drew a lungful of smoke.

Smoke was everywhere, swirling, hanging ghostly in the air, and an orange glow reflected from the shattered glass of town hall.

Off to the west a tongue of fire suddenly shot into the sky and was swallowed by its own smoke.

No one else was in the plaza. No one but one girl.

Mary rubbed the sleep from her eyes, stared at her. Not possible, not possible, not real, some leftover fragment of dream.

But the girl was still there, face in shadow, a glint of chrome steel glinting from her braces.

'Have you seen him?' the girl asked.

Mary felt something die inside her, dread and horror like the impact of an explosion in her mind.

'Have you seen the demon?' Brittney asked.

Mary couldn't answer. She could only stare as Brittney's arm began to elongate, to change shape.

Brittney winked. Cold, dead blue eyes.

Mary ran into the day care. She slammed the door behind her and leaned back against it.

TWENTY SIX

13 HOURS 43 MINUTES

THE SMOKE ALTERED the familiar streetscape for Sam. He turned around, unsure for a moment of where he was or which direction was which. He stopped, heard footsteps running behind him, and spun around, hands up, palms out.

But the footsteps headed away.

Sam cursed in frustration. The town was burning down and the smoke made it all but impossible to find the enemy.

He had to do this now, during the heat of battle, before Astrid intervened and forced him once again to sit helpless, waiting for her to invent some system they'd never be able to put in place.

This was the night. This was the time to do what he should have done a month before: finish off Zil and his insanity.

But he would have to find them first.

He forced himself to think. What was Zil up to, aside from the obvious? Why would he decide to burn the town down? It seemed bold for Zil. It seemed insane: Zil lived there, too.

But Sam's thoughts were fractured by the recurring image in his mind of Drake. Out there somewhere. Drake who had somehow come back from the dead.

Of course they'd never seen his body, had they?

'Focus,' Sam ordered himself. The problem right now was that the town was burning down. Edilio would be doing whatever he could to save those who needed saving. Sam's job was to stop the terror now.

But where was Zil?

And was he with Drake?

Could the timing all be coincidence? No. Sam didn't believe in coincidence.

Again, a movement glimpsed through a veil of smoke. Again Sam raced towards it. This time the figure did not disappear.

'Don't . . .' a young voice cried out, and then choked and hacked. A boy who looked to be maybe six years old.

'Get out of here,' Sam snapped. 'Go to the beach.'

He ran on, faltered, turned to his right. Where was Drake? No, Zil. Where was Zil? Zil was real.

And all at once he was at the beach wall. He practically tripped over it. He had sent the six-year-old off in the wrong direction. Too late to do anything about that. The kid wasn't the only lost one tonight.

Where were Dekka and Brianna and Taylor? Where were Edilio's soldiers?

What was going on?

Sam saw a group of kids rushing along the sand in the direction of the marina. And for a moment he almost thought he saw Caine. He was hallucinating. Imagining things.

'Freaks out!'

Sam heard it clearly. It seemed very close. Maybe a trick of acoustics.

He tried to penetrate the dark and the smoke but he saw nothing now, not even the hallucinated Caine.

BLAM!

A shotgun blast. He saw the bright flash.

He ran. His feet hit something soft but heavy. He flew and landed face down. Mouth gritty with sand he climbed to his feet. A body, someone in the sand.

No time for that.

It was time to see who was who and what was what. Sam raised his hands high and a ball of cold brilliant light formed in the air.

In the eerie half-light Sam saw a dozen of Zil's thugs, half armed.

A mob was running away from them.

Another group, smaller, and looking oddly like doddering old people, kicked through the surf towards the distant marina.

Zil and his crew knew immediately who was responsible for the revellatory light. It could only be . . .

'Sam!'

'It's Sam!'

'Run!'

'Shoot him! Shoot him!'

Three shotgun blasts in rapid succession. BLAM! BLAM! BLAM!

Sam fired back. Pencils of blistering green light scoured the sand. A cry of pain.

'Don't run away!'

'Cowards!'

BLAM! BLAM!

Someone firing methodically now, working the shotgun pump.

Sam felt a sharp sting in the meat of his shoulder. He hit the dirt, knocking the wind from his lungs.

People running past. He rolled on to his back, hands at the ready.

BLAM!

The pellets hit the sand near enough for Sam to hear the impact.

He rolled away, over and over.

BLAM! BLAM!

Then a click. A curse. More feet running, pummelling the sand.

He leaped up, aimed and fired. The killing green light drew

a scream of pain or fear, but the retreating figure didn't stop.

Sand was in Sam's shirt, his mouth, his ears. In his eyes. Smoke and sand and his eyes were streaming. He saw nothing but blurs.

Now the light was working against him, making him an easy target. He waved and the tiny sun blinked out. The beach was dark again, though a faint hint of grey pearled the sky over the ocean.

He spat, trying to get the sand out of his mouth. Rubbed his eyes gently, trying to dislodge the grit.

Someone behind him!

The pain was like fire. A lash that cut through his shirt and tore his flesh.

Sam spun from the impact.

A dark shape.

A razor-sharp whistling sound and Sam, too stunned to move, felt the lash on his shoulder.

'Hey there, Sammy. Long time, huh?'

'No,' Sam gasped.

'Oh, yes,' the voice snarled. The voice Sam knew. The voice he dreaded. The voice that had laughed and crowed as he lay on the polished floor of the power plant, screaming in agony.

Sam blinked, struggled to open one eye, to see what could not possibly be real. He raised his hands and fired blind.

The whistling, whooshing sound. Sam ducked instinctively and the blow went harmlessly by.

'The demon!' a girl's voice cried.

But it came from behind Sam because he had turned and run.

He ran. Ran blindly down the sand.

Ran and fell and jumped up to run again.

He didn't stop until he hit the concrete beach wall, smashing his calves. He landed face down on the ground and lay there, panting.

Quinn had turned the boats to shore, dreading what he would find when they reached land.

The fire had spread and now seemed to cover half the town, although there were no new explosions. The smoke had reached them out at sea. Quinn's eyes stung. His heart was in his throat.

Not another massacre, not another atrocity. Enough! He just wanted to fish.

The rowers were silenced by the awful spectacle of their homes burning.

They reached the first of the piers and saw a group of kids staggering on to it, no doubt panicked kids running away, thinking the marina would be safe.

Quinn called out to them.

No answer.

His boat touched the bumper that sloshed in the water. His moves were automatic from long practice. He tossed a rope loop over the piling and pulled his boat closer. Oars were shipped. Big Goof jumped on to the pier and secured the second line.

The staggering gaggle of kids on shore ignored them and kept moving. They moved strangely. Like frail old people.

Something strange about them . . .

And familiar.

The dawn was still an hour away. The only light was from the fire. The false stars were blotted by the pall of smoke.

Quinn jumped on to the pier.

'Hey there! Hey!' he yelled. Quinn was responsible for the boats. The marina was his.

The kids kept moving, like they were deaf. They headed down a parallel pier towards the two boats that were kept fuelled for rescues: a bass boat and an inflatable Zodiac.

'Hey!' Quinn yelled.

The foremost of the kids turned to face him. They were separated by fifty feet of water, but even in the faint fire glow Quinn recognised the shape of shoulders and head.

And he recognised the voice.

'Penny,' Caine said. 'Keep our friend Quinn busy.'

From the water a monster erupted in a tremendous geyser.

Quinn bellowed in terror.

The monster rose, taller and taller. It had a head like a tortured, deformed elephant. Two black, dead eyes. Curved teeth. The jaw gaped open to reveal a long, pointed tongue.

It roared then, a sound like a hundred massive cellos played with garbage cans for bows. Hollow. Tortured.

Quinn fell back. He fell from the pier. His back hit the edge of his boat. The impact knocked the air out of his lungs and he fell head-down into the water.

Panicked, he breathed. Salt water filled his throat. He gagged and coughed and strained with all his might not to breathe again.

Quinn knew the water. He'd been a good surfer and a very good swimmer. This was not his first experience of being upside down and turned around underwater.

He grabbed on to his fear and kicked hard to bring himself around. The surface, the barrier between water and air, death and life, was ten feet up. One foot kicked dirt. The water was not deep here.

He began to rise.

But the monster was reaching beneath the pier. Insanely long arms, with impossible clawlike hands.

The arms reached for him and he backpedalled away. Panicky, kicking, pushing at the water, lungs burning.

Too slow. One gigantic hand closed around him.

The fingers went through.

No pain.

No contact or sensation at all.

The second claw swiped through the water. It would disembowel him.

But it passed through him.

Illusion!

With the last of his strength Quinn reached the surface. He gagged on air and vomited seawater from his stomach. The monster was gone.

Big Goof hauled him like dead weight into the boat. Quinn lay on the bottom of the boat, uncomfortable atop the oars.

'You OK?'

Quinn couldn't answer. If he tried he knew he would retch again. His voice was not yet back. He still felt as if he were breathing through a straw. But he was alive.

And now it all fell into place. That monster. The sound it made. He knew them.

Cloverfield.

It was the monster from the movie. The *exact* monster, the *exact* sound.

He sat up and coughed.

Then he stood up in the rocking boat and saw Caine and his crew climbing aboard the two motorboats.

Caine caught sight of him and sent him a wintry, ironic smile. There was a strange girl with him. She, too, stared at him, but she did not smile. Instead, she bared crooked teeth at him in a grimace that was far more threat than smile.

An engine started, throaty and rough. Then a second.

Quinn stayed where he was. No chance he could take on Caine. Caine could kill him with a gesture.

The two motorboats chugged slowly, cautiously, away from the pier.

There came the sound of running feet. A rush of kids, some armed. Quinn recognised Lance, then Hank. Finally Zil, hanging back, letting the other two get out in front.

They reached the end of the pier. Hank stopped, aimed, and fired.

The shot hit the Zodiac. The air blew out in a sudden exhale. The boat's motor chugged beneath the water as the stern collapsed and sank.

Quinn climbed halfway up on to the pier to see. His jaw dropped.

Caine, wet and furious, rose and levitated above the sinking Zodiac.

He yanked Hank and his gun up into the air. Hank soared, twisting, crying out in terror, helpless. Up and up and up, and all the while Caine floated as his companions foundered.

A hundred feet in the air, Hank came to a stop. And then, down he came. But not falling. Too fast to be a fall. Too fast for it to be mere gravity.

Caine hurled Hank down from the greying sky. Like a meteor. Impossibly fast, a blur.

Hank hit the water. A huge spout went up, like someone had fired off a depth charge.

Quinn knew the waters of the marina. It was no more than eight feet deep where Hank hit. The bottom was sand and shell.

There was not the slightest chance that Hank would come bobbing back up to the surface.

Caine floated as Zil looked on in helpless horror.

'Now that,' Caine shouted, 'was a mistake, Zil.'

Zil and his crew turned tail and ran. Caine laughed and lowered himself into the second boat. Five of his people were still in the water, calling out and waving and then cursing and raging as the motorboat roared away.

TWENTY SEVEN

13 HOURS 32 MINUTES

'GET UP,' PEACE whispered. She shook Sanjit's shoulder.

Sanjit had long been accustomed to being awakened at odd hours. That part of being the oldest kid in the Brattle-Chance family had long since lost its charm.

'Is it Bowie?' he said.

Peace shook her head. 'No. I think the world is burning.'

Sanjit raised a sceptical eyebrow. 'That seems kind of extreme, Peace.'

'Just come.'

Sanjit groaned and rolled out of bed. 'What time is it?'

'It's almost morning.'

'The key word being "almost",' Sanjit complained. 'You know what's a better time to get up? Actual morning. Much better than "almost" morning.'

But he followed her down the hall to the room she shared with Bowie and Pixie. The house had twenty-two bedrooms, but only Sanjit and Virtue had chosen to sleep by themselves.

Pixie was asleep. Bowie tossed and turned, still under attack from the fever that would not go away.

'The window,' Peace whispered.

Sanjit went to the window. It was almost floor-to-ceiling, a stunning view during the day. He stood there gazing towards the far-distant town of Perdido Beach.

'Go get Choo,' he said after a moment.

She came back with a poisonously cranky Virtue, rubbing sleep from his eyes and muttering.

'Look,' Sanjit said.

Virtue stared, just as Sanjit had done. 'It's a fire.'

'You think?' Sanjit shook his head, awestruck. 'The whole town must be on fire.'

Red and orange flames were a bright dot on the horizon. In the grey predawn light he saw a massive pillar of black smoke. The scale seemed ridiculous. The bright fire was a dot, but the smoke seemed to be miles high, shaped like a twisted funnel.

'So that's where I'm supposed to fly the helicopter?' Sanjit said.

Virtue left and returned a few moments later. He was carrying a small telescope. It wasn't very powerful. They'd used it at times to try to see details in the town or on the wooded shore closest to the island. It had never shown much. It showed no more now, but even slightly magnified the fire looked terrifying.

Sanjit looked at Bowie, who was whimpering in his sleep.

'I'm getting a very bad feeling,' Virtue said.

'It's not like the fire can spread here,' Sanjit said, trying to sound nonchalant and failing.

Virtue didn't say anything. He just stared. And it dawned on Sanjit that his brother was seeing more than just the fire.

'What is it, Choo?'

Virtue sighed, 'You never ask me about where I came from.'

Sanjit was surprised by the turn in the conversation. 'Africa. I know you come from Africa.'

'Africa's a continent, not a country,' Virtue said with a faint echo of his normal pedantry. 'Congo. That's where I'm from.'

'OK.'

'That doesn't mean anything to you, does it?'

Sanjit shrugged. 'Lions and giraffes and all?'

Virtue didn't even bother to sneer. 'There's been war there for, like, ever. People killing one another. Stuff you don't even want to know about, brother.'

'Yeah?'

'I wasn't in an orphanage when Jennifer and Todd adopted me. I was four years old. In a refugee camp. All I remember is being hungry all the time. And no one taking care of me.'

'Where were your real mom and dad?'

Virtue didn't answer for a long time, and some instinct warned Sanjit not to push him.

Finally, Virtue said, 'They came and started burning down our village. I don't know why. I was just a little kid. I just know my mother – my birth mom – told me to run and hide in the bush.

'I . . .' Virtue took a deep, shuddering breath. In a strained, unnatural voice he said, 'You know what? I can't tell you. I can't use words for it. I don't want the words to come out of my mouth.'

Sanjit stared at him, feeling as if he was looking at a stranger. Virtue had never talked about his early childhood. Sanjit berated himself for being so self-centred, he'd never asked.

'I see that fire and I just have a bad feeling, Sanjit. I have a bad feeling it's getting ready to happen again.'

Taylor found Edilio with Orc, Howard, Ellen and a few others. They were retreating from the worst of the fire.

Voices cried pitifully from the upper floors of a house that burned like a match head. Taylor saw Edilio press his hands to his ears.

Taylor grabbed his hand and pulled it away. 'There are kids in that house!'

'Yeah?' Edilio said savagely. 'Do you think?'

It was so unlike Edilio, it shocked Taylor. The others looked at her like she was an idiot. They all heard the cries. 'I can do it,' Taylor said. 'I can pop in and out before the fire gets me.'

Edilio's furious glare softened just a little. 'You're a brave girl, Taylor. But what are you going to do? You can bounce, but you can't carry anyone out with you.'

Taylor stared at the house. It was half a block away and even from this distance the heat was like a furnace.

'Maybe I can . . .' She faltered.

'What's happening in there? You can't stop it. And you don't want to bounce in there just to see it. Believe me,' Edilio said. 'You don't want to see it.'

The cries were not heard again. A few minutes later the roof collapsed inward.

'The fire is spreading on its own now. We should try to make a fire break,' Ellen said.

'A what?' Edilio asked.

'A fire break. It's what they do in forest fires. They knock down the trees that are in the path of the fire. It stops the fire from moving from tree to tree.'

'You talking about knocking down houses?' Howard said. 'You talking about Orc knocking down houses. That's going to –'

'Shut up, Howard,' Orc said. Not mean, but definite.

Howard shrugged. 'OK, big guy, if you want to get all altruistic.'

'Whatever,' Orc said.

Dekka ran into Edilio. Literally. She was obviously half blinded by smoke.

'Dekka!' Edilio cried. 'Have you seen Sam?'

Dekka tried to answer, choked, coughed, and ended up shaking her head.

'OK. Come with us. The fire is still spreading.'

'What are you –?' she managed to ask.

'We're going to make a fire break,' Edilio said. 'The fire is jumping house to house. We're going to knock some houses down and push them back.'

'Get Jack, too,' Dekka said, squeezing the words out and biting off the racking cough that followed.

'Good idea,' Edilio said. 'Taylor?'

Taylor disappeared.

'Come on, guys,' Edilio said, trying to rally his sick, dispirited group. 'We can maybe still save a lot of the town.'

He led the way and the others followed.

Where was Sam? Usually it would be Sam leading the way. Sam handing out orders.

Was Sam OK? Had he caught up with Zil? Had he done what he threatened to do? Had he killed Zil?

Edilio could still hear echoes of the cries from the burning house. He knew he would be hearing them in his dreams for a long time to come. He wasn't going to manage too much sympathy for Zil if Sam had carried out his threat.

But even now it didn't sit well with Edilio. It was just another symptom of a world gone crazy.

Taylor bounced back as they reached Sheridan Avenue. There was smoke everywhere. The fire was moving across backyards from Sherman to the west side of Sheridan.

'Jack's on his way. Breeze tried to get up but she took like three steps and folded.'

'Is she OK?' Dekka asked.

'Flu and super speed don't go too well together, I think,' Taylor said. 'She'll live.'

Edilio tried to make sense of the lay of the land. Fire raged to the west. There was no normal wind, there never was in the FAYZ, but it seemed as if the fire was making its own wind. Blowtorch heat blew. No question the fire would follow that wind.

'It's coming this way,' Ellen said.

'Yeah.' The fires on Sherman made silhouettes out of the row of houses on the west side of Sheridan.

Suddenly, out of a swirl of smoke came a small boy pulling a larger one behind him.

'Hey, little man,' Edilio said. 'Get straight out of here.'

The little boy, Edilio recognised him now, was Justin. Mary had asked him to keep an eye out for Justin. And Roger. Roger was in a bad way, unable to speak or even open his eyes.

'Don't try to talk,' Edilio said. 'Justin: get to the plaza, OK? Both of you. Lana will be there, probably. Go to her or go to Dahra Baidoo, OK? Right now! Get out of here!'

The two soot-covered kids took off, choking, staggering, Justin still pulling Roger behind him.

'I don't think we can save the houses on that side,' Ellen said. 'But the street's pretty wide here. And if we can knock the east-side houses down, push them back, maybe that'll be enough.'

Jack came down the street, looking stunned and cautious.

'Thanks for coming, Jack,' Edilio said.

Jack shot a dirty look at Taylor, who smiled blandly. Something had gone on there, but now wasn't the time to worry about it. Taylor had convinced Jack, that was all Edilio needed to know.

'OK,' Edilio said. 'We're going to take that house down. Taylor, check inside. Dekka, I guess we'll have you weaken it first. Then Orc and Jack can go at it.'

Orc and Jack looked each other over. Orc revelled in his strength. Jack was almost embarrassed by his. But that didn't mean he was prepared to be shown up by Orc.

'You take the left side,' Orc said.

Taylor popped back. 'No one home. I checked every room.'

Dekka raised her hands high. Edilio wondered if her being sick would weaken her power. But the porch furniture was rising, weightless, smashing into the overhang. A long-disused bike floated up and into the sky.

The house groaned and creaked. Dirt and garbage rose in a sort of slow-motion, reverse rain.

Then, suddenly Dekka dropped her hands. The bike and furniture and garbage all crashed back to earth. The house complained loudly. A part of the roof fell in.

Orc and Jack moved in.

Orc slammed his fist through a wall near a corner. He hooked his arm through and pulled on the support beams. It was hard work, he strained, but all at once the corner broke. Siding splintered outwards, wooden studs cracked and protruded like bones in a compound fracture. The corner of the house sagged.

Jack tore a light pole from its cement base, handed it off to Orc and then grabbed a second metal streetlight for himself. Once the house was reduced to sticks and slabs and broken pipes Dekka raised the whole mess off the ground.

There followed an awkward, dangerous sort of dance. Orc and Jack used the long lamp poles to shove the weightless debris back from the street. But it wasn't an easy thing to manage because Dekka had to keep adjusting gravity to keep the debris from rising skyward, and Orc and Jack had to fight the differing gravity levels that at times made the light poles almost weightless, and at other times returned them to their full weight.

Eventually, the crumpled, shattered home was shoved into the parking spaces behind the buildings that fronted San Pablo and the town plaza. As they finished that first house the fire jumped to the home to their west. But there was now at least a chance that it would be stopped from crossing Sheridan.

Throughout the morning they worked. They slogged up and down three blocks of Sheridan, taking down the most directly endangered houses. Edilio and Howard searched each house, shuttled kids away from the danger, and ran behind Dekka, Orc and Jack, stomping out embers that landed on the east side of the street, smothering smoldering grass with trash can lids and shovels.

The sound of it all, the tearing, ripping and sudden crashes, joined the snapping and crackling and whoosh of the fire that ate its way down the west side of the street.

The sounds of Perdido Beach dying.

TWENTY EIGHT

13 HOURS 12 MINUTES

THE BOAT CHUGGED away from Perdido Beach.

There were only seven of them now. Caine. Diana. Penny. Tyrell. Jasmine. Bug. And Paint. Paint had gotten his nickname from huffing paint out of a sock. His mouth was invariably whatever colour of paint he'd found most recently. It was red at the moment, Caine noted. Like Paint had gone vampire.

Of the seven, only two had useful powers: Penny and Bug. Diana still had the ability to gauge powers accurately, but how useful would that be?

The other three were here only because they'd had the good luck not to be in the Zodiac. Although maybe that was bad luck: those who had fallen in at the marina were probably being fed by Sam's people.

'Where we going, man?' Paint asked for about the tenth time since they'd set out.

'Bug's island,' Caine said. He was feeling patient. He'd gotten this far, proven that he could still hurt Sam, proven that he could still carry out a plan. As weak as he was, he had succeeded in moving himself and his followers from Coates right through the heart of enemy country.

The motor chugged reassuringly. The tiller vibrated in Caine's hand. A memory of the long ago world filled with machines and electronics and food.

It was cramped in the boat. It wasn't much of a craft. A bass boat, shallow-draft, flat-bottomed, low sided. Dirty white fibreglass. Or maybe it was aluminium. Caine didn't care.

There were three life jackets on the boat, just three. Tyrell, Bug and Penny had them on, strapped with varying degrees of effectiveness. A lifeboat full of starved refugees.

Diana didn't take a life jacket. Caine knew why. She didn't care any more whether she lived. It had been hours since she had spoken.

It was as if Diana had finally given up. Caine could look at her openly now without having to pretend he wasn't. She would no longer lash out with some mean-funny remark.

She was the wreck of Diana. She was what was left if you took Diana's beauty and wit and toughness away. A crispy-haired, trembling, sullen, sallow-fleshed skeleton.

'I see more than one island,' Penny commented.

'Yeah,' Caine said.

'Which one is it?'

Not a time to admit that he didn't know. And a bad time,

probably, to admit that if they guessed wrong and managed to climb off on to the wrong island they'd probably die there. Not enough strength left in any of them to go island hopping.

'There's food there?' Tyrrell asked hopefully.

'Yes,' Caine said.

'It's like these totally rich people, these actors,' Bug said. A voice from a faint shadow of a boy sitting in the bow.

'Is there enough gas to get there?' Tyrrell asked.

'I guess we'll find out,' Caine said.

'What if we run out?' Paint asked. 'I mean, what do we do if we run out of gas?'

Caine was tired now of playing the confident leader. 'We'll float around helpless and die out here on the deep blue sea,' he said.

That shut everyone up. Everyone knew what would happen before they just let themselves starve out here, becalmed.

'You saw him,' Diana said to Caine. She didn't even have enough energy to look at him.

He could lie. But what was the point? 'Yes,' Caine said. 'I saw him.'

'He's not dead,' Diana said.

'I guess not.'

He deeply disliked the idea that Drake might be alive. Not just because Drake would blame Caine for his death. Not just because Drake would never forgive, never forget, never stop.

Caine hated the idea of Drake alive because he really hoped that death at least was real. He could face dying, if he had to. He could not face dying and then living again.

Jasmine stood up, shaky.

Caine glanced at her, indifferent really, but hoping she wouldn't capsize the boat.

Without a word, Jasmine toppled over the side. She hit the water with a splash.

'Hey,' Diana said wanly.

Caine kept his hand on the tiller. Jasmine did not surface. A white lace doily of disturbed water marked where she had sunk gratefully into the deep.

And then there were six, Caine thought dully.

Hank dead.

Antoine gone, lost somewhere in the madness, maybe dead too, as bad as he was hurt.

Zil sat trembling. Home in his stupid little compound, with his stupid little girlfriend, Lisa, staring at him like a cow, with stupid Turk mumbling in the corner, trying to make up some kind of explanation of how all this was really a good thing.

Sam would come for him now. Zil was sure of that. Sam would come for him. The freaks would triumph. If they could kill Hank and maybe Antoine, too, oh God, then it was just a matter of time.

Caine could just as easily have smashed Zil himself into the water that way. If Zil had been the one shooting, Caine would have killed him as easily as he did Hank. Him! The Leader!

It wasn't in the plan. Zil was supposed to use the confusion of the fire to rally as many normals as he could and take over town hall. Make Astrid a prisoner, hold her as a hostage so Sam wouldn't . . .

A stupid plan. Caine's plan. How was he ever going to rally kids in all that chaos? In all the smoke and panic and confusion, with Sam blasting Antoine and then Hank.

Stupid, stupid, stupid.

And then, attacking Caine to make it look good. Stupider, still. He couldn't fight the freaks head-on.

Zil could still see the look on Hank's face as he soared into the air. The scream that tore his throat as he came hurtling back down. The stretched-out quality of time as they waited for Hank to come back up, knowing he wouldn't. Knowing that there was no way to survive that fall.

Like diving off a building into a cereal bowl of water, Lance had said. Hank was deep in the submarine mud. And it could have been Zil. It could have been him with his head buried in wet mud, maybe still alive for just long enough to try to take a breath . . .

'Good thing is, kids will totally believe us now,' Turk was saying as he chewed his fingernails.

'What?' Zil snapped.

'With Hank killed by Caine,' Turk explained. 'I mean, no one's going to think we had a deal with Caine.'

Zil nodded absently.

'That's true,' Lance said. He didn't quite grin, but almost. And for a second Zil saw something different in Lance. Something that didn't match his handsome face and cool demeanor.

'Maybe we should just stop it.'

Lisa. Zil was surprised to hear the sound of her voice. She didn't usually say anything. Mostly she just sat there like a bump on a log. Like a stupid cow. Mostly he hated her, and right now he hated her a lot, because she was seeing the truth, that Zil had lost.

'Just stop what?' Lance asked. He clearly didn't like Lisa, either. Zil knew one thing for sure: Lisa wasn't pretty enough that Lance would ever be interested in her. No, she was just the best Zil could get. At least, so far.

'I mean . . .' Lisa began, but she ended with a shrug and fell silent again.

'The thing we need to do,' Turk said, 'is keep telling people how it was all Caine. We keep telling people Caine burned the town.'

'Yes,' Zil said without conviction. He dropped his head and looked down at the floor, the dirty, ratty rug. 'The freaks.'

'Right,' Turk said.

'It was the freaks,' Lance said. 'I mean, it *was*. Who pushed us into it? Caine.'

'Exactly,' Turk said.

'We need some more people, is all,' Lance said. 'I mean, Antoine was mostly just a stupid druggie. But Hank . . .'

Zil lifted his head. Maybe there was still hope. He nodded at Lance. 'Yeah. That's it. We need more kids.'

'If kids know we were trying to stop Caine, we'll get plenty more kids,' Turk said.

Lance smiled faintly. 'We tried to stop Caine burning down the town.'

'Hank died trying,' Zil said.

He said it. And he knew that Turk already half believed it. In fact, he half believed it himself.

'Lance, kids will listen to you. You and Turk, the two of you, and you too, Lisa: Go out there. Spread the word.'

No one moved.

'You have to do what I say,' Zil said, trying to sound strong, not like he was pleading. 'I'm the Leader.'

'Yeah,' Turk agreed. 'Only . . . I mean, kids may not believe us.'

'Are you scared?' Zil demanded.

'I'm not,' Lisa said. 'I'll do it. I'll go around and tell all our friends the truth.'

Zil peered suspiciously at her. Why was she being brave all of a sudden?

'Cool, Lisa,' he said. 'I mean, that would be heroic.'

Lance sighed. 'I guess if she can do it, so can I.'

Only Turk kept his seat. He glanced furtively at Zil. 'Someone better stay here to protect you, Leader.'

Zil laughed mirthlessly. 'Yeah, if Sam comes I'm sure you'll stop him, Turk.'

'It's the tribulation,' Nerezza said.

Orsay didn't say anything. She'd heard that word before. Had she actually used it herself?

As if she'd guessed, Nerezza explained. 'Tribulation. A time of trouble. When people look for a prophet to tell them what to do. You prophesied that this would happen.'

'Did I? I don't remember.' Her memory was a cramped attic full of broken toys and damaged furniture. It was getting harder and harder to be sure where she was. Or when. And she had given up asking why.

They stood on the edge of the burned area, in the middle of Sheridan. The destruction was awful and eerie in the morning light. Smoke still rose from a dozen or more houses. Tongues of flame could still be seen here and there, peeking out from charred windows.

Some houses stood untouched, surrounded by devastation.

Like they'd been spared by divine intervention. Some houses were only half burned. Some, you could tell, had been gutted but the exteriors seemed almost intact, aside from soot stain around blackened windows.

A house close by had only its roof gone, burned and fallen in. The cheerful green-painted siding was barely soot smudged, but the top of the house was gone, just a few blackened sticks poking up at the sky. Peering in the windows Orsay could see what was left of roof tiles and timbers, jumbled and black. Like someone had come along, ripped the roof off and used the house as a trash can to dump ashes.

On the other side of the street a different sort of devastation. It looked as if a tornado had come through and shoved an entire street's worth of houses off their foundations.

'I don't know what to do,' Orsay said. 'How would I tell anyone else?'

'It's a judgment,' Nerezza said. 'You can see that. Everyone can see it. It's a judgment. A tribulation sent to remind people that they aren't doing right.'

'But . . .'

'What have your dreams told you, Prophetess?'

Orsay knew what her dreams had told her. Dreams of all those on the outside, all those who saw a girl named Orsay walking inside their sleeping minds. The girl who carried messages to their children and in return showed the parents startling visions of life inside the FAYZ. Visions of their children trapped and burning.

Trapped and dying.

Yes, the dreams of all those good people were anguished, knowing what was happening inside. And they were so frustrated, because they knew – those good people, those grown-ups, those parents – that there *was* a way out for their terrified children.

Orsay's dreams had shown her that. They had shown her that Francis had emerged safe and sound, welcomed by his parents with tears of gratitude after he took the poof.

That had made Orsay happy. Taking the poof when you reached fifteen let you go free of the FAYZ. It was something she could look forward to herself. Escape, when the time came.

But lately there were different images. These came to her not at the FAYZ wall, not even when she was asleep. They weren't dreams, exactly. Visions. Revelations. They snuck in behind other thoughts. Like burglars creeping inside her brain.

She felt she no longer had any control over what happened inside her head. Like she'd left a door unlocked and now there was no holding back a flood of dreams, visions, vague terrible imaginings.

These new visions showed her not just those who had escaped the FAYZ by reaching the magic age. These new images were of children who had died. And yet, who now held their mothers tight on the outside.

She had seen images of those who had perished last night in the fire. Agony followed by death followed by escape into the loving arms of their parents.

Even Hank. Hank's father, not there waiting at the Dome, but notified by the California Highway Patrol. They'd called him on the phone. Reached him at a bowling alley in Irvine where he was drinking draught beer and flirting with the bartender. He'd had to press one hand over his ear to hear over the sound of rolling balls and crashing pins.

'What?'

'Your son, Hank. He's out!' the CHP had said.

Orsay saw the images, knew what they meant, and felt sick inside from knowing.

'What are your dreams telling you, Prophetess?' Nerezza pressed.

But Orsay couldn't tell her. She couldn't tell her that death itself, not just the poof, not just the big fifteen, was a way out.

Oh, God. If she told people that . . .

'Tell me,' Nerezza urged. 'I know your powers are growing. I know you are seeing more than ever before.'

Nerezza's face was close to Orsay's. Her arm squeezed Orsay's arm. Nerezza pressed Orsay with all the force of her will. Orsay could feel it – that will, that need, that hunger – pushing her.

'Nothing,' Orsay whispered.

Nerezza drew back. For a moment a snarl flashed on her face. Like an animal.

Nerezza glared at her. Then, with a will, she softened her expression. 'You're the Prophetess, Orsay,' she said.

'I don't feel well,' Orsay said. 'I want to go home.'

'The dreams,' Nerezza said. 'They don't let you sleep very well, do they? Yes, you should get back to your bed.'

'I don't want to dream any more,' Orsay said.

TWENTY NINE

11 HOURS 24 MINUTES

HUNTER HAD SIX birds in his bag. Three of them were crows, which didn't have much meat on them. One was an owl. Owls tasted pretty bad, but they had more meat. But two were the kind of birds that had colourful feathers and were juicy. Hunter didn't know what they were called, but he always looked for them because they were tasty and Albert would be very happy to get some of those.

He was high on the far side of the ridge, north of town, hauling the sack of dead birds up. Hard work. He carried them slung over one shoulder in a pouch that mothers used to use to carry babies.

Hunter had a backpack with his sleeping bag and his pan and his cup and extra socks and an extra knife. Knives broke sometimes, although the knife he had in his belt had lasted a long time so far.

Hunter was on the trail of two deer. He had tracked them through the night. If he caught them he would kill them.

Then he would use his knife and clean them like he had learned to do, spilling their insides out. He wouldn't be able to carry both deer down at the same time. He would have to gut one of them and then hang it from a tree, come back for it later.

Hunter sniffed. He had learned that he could actually smell the animals he was hunting. Deer had a smell, so did raccoons and opossums. He sniffed, but now what reached his nose was the smell of fire.

Hunter's brow creased in concentration. Had he recently made camp near this spot? Or was someone else up here lighting campfires?

He was in a deep cleft, dark trees all around and overhead. He hesitated. The fire smell wasn't right for a campfire. It wasn't just burning wood and brush.

He was standing there, unprepared, when a big deer with a full rack of antlers appeared out of nowhere. It didn't see him. It was running, not in panic but at a steady pace, bounding nimbly along over fallen logs and skirting the thicker thorn bushes.

He aimed both hands at the deer. There was no flash of light. Nothing at all that you could see or hear.

The deer took two more steps and fell forwards.

Hunter raced to it. The deer was hurt but not dead.

'Don't worry,' Hunter whispered. 'It won't hurt.'

He held his palm towards the deer's head. The deer's

eyes turned milky. And it stopped breathing.

Hunter slid off his pack and his bird bag and drew his knife.

He was excited. This was the biggest deer he'd ever bagged. No way he could carry it. He would have to cut it into pieces. It was going to be a lot of work.

He took a long drink from his canteen and sat down, contemplating the job ahead of him.

Hunter hadn't slept in quite a while, chasing the two other deer. He was sleepy now. And there was no longer any need to keep going. Between the birds and this buck he had two days of butchering and hauling ahead of him just to get it all to town.

There were some shallow caves not far from this spot, but some of them had flying snakes in them. Better not to go near those things. Better to stay out here in the open.

He lay his head on a soft rotted log and fell instantly to sleep.

How long he slept he couldn't know, he had no watch, but the sun was overhead when he woke to the sound of clumsy movement. Someone trying to be sneaky and not doing a very good job of it.

'Hi, Sam,' Hunter said.

Sam froze.

Hunter sat up. 'What are you doing here?'

Sam looked around like he was searching for an answer. He seemed weird to Hunter. He didn't look like Sam usually looked. He looked like animals sometimes looked when

Hunter had them cornered and they knew it was the end.

'I'm just . . . um . . . walking,' Sam said.

'Are you running away?' Hunter asked.

Sam looked startled. 'No.'

'I smell fire.'

'Yeah. There's been a fire. In town,' Sam said. 'So. Is that a deer?'

It seemed like a stupid question to Hunter. 'Yes.'

'I was getting hungry,' Sam confessed.

Hunter smiled his lopsided smile. Half of his mouth didn't work quite right. 'I can cook us a bird. But I have to give the deer to Albert.'

'Some bird would be great,' Sam said.

He sat down cross-legged on the pine-needle carpet. He'd been hurt. There was blood on his shirt and he moved his shoulder stiffly.

'I can cook it with my hands. But it tastes better if I cook it with fire.'

Hunter gathered dried needles, small branches, and a couple of larger chunks of wood. Soon he had a fire going. He cleaned one of the colourful birds, burned off the pinfeathers, and cut it into smaller pieces. These he skewered with a wire clothes hanger he carried in his backpack and propped them over the coals at the edge of the fire.

He split the meat with scrupulous fairness. Sam ate greedily.

'This isn't a bad life you have up here,' Sam said.

'Except when there are mosquitoes. Or fleas,' Hunter said.

'Yeah, well everyone's getting fleas since most of the dogs and cats are . . . um . . . gone.'

Hunter nodded. Then he said, 'I don't have much talking.'

When Sam looked puzzled, Hunter explained. 'Sometimes my head doesn't want to give me words.'

Lana had healed him as well as she could, but the skull had never grown back all the way right. She'd fixed his brain well enough that he didn't pee in his pants like he did for a while after the beating. And when he talked he could mostly make himself understood. But Lana had been unable to return him all the way to normal.

'It's OK,' Hunter said, not realising that he hadn't said any of this out loud. 'I'm just different now.'

'You're important,' Sam said. 'You're a lifeline for kids. Do the coyotes ever bother you?'

Hunter shook his head and gulped some more of the hot bird meat. 'We made a deal. I don't go where they're hunting. And I don't hunt coyotes. So they don't bother me.'

For a while neither of them said anything. The fire burned down. The last of the bird was consumed. Hunter pushed dirt on to the fire, smothering it.

'Maybe I could work with you,' Sam said. He held up his own hand. 'I can hunt, too, I guess.'

Hunter frowned. This was confusing. 'But you're Sam and I'm Hunter.'

'You could teach me what you know,' Sam said. 'You know. About animals. And how to find them. And how to cut them up and all.'

Hunter thought about it, but then the idea slipped out of his brain. And he realised he'd forgotten what Sam was talking about.

'If I go back I'm going to do things,' Sam said. He looked down at the ashes of the near-dead fire.

'You're good at doing things,' Hunter said.

Sam looked angry. Then his face softened until he looked sad. 'Yeah. Only I don't always want to do those things.'

'I'm Hunter. So I hunt.'

'My real name is Samuel. He was this prophet in the Bible.'

Hunter didn't know what 'prophet' meant. Or 'Bible.'

'He was the guy who picked out the first king of Israel.'

Hunter nodded, mystified.

'You believe in God, Hunter?' Sam asked.

Hunter felt a sudden stab of guilt. He hung his head. 'I almost killed those boys.'

'What boys?'

'Zil. And his friends. The ones who hurt me. I was hunting a doe, and I saw them. And I could have.'

'Could have killed them.'

Hunter nodded.

'To tell you the truth, Hunter, I wish you had.'

'I'm Hunter,' he said, and grinned because it struck him as funny. 'I'm not Boy Killer.' He laughed. It was a joke.

Sam didn't laugh. In fact, it looked like he wanted to cry.

'You know Drake, Hunter?'

'No.'

'He's a boy with a kind of snake for an arm. A snake. Or a whip. So he's not really a boy. So if you ever saw him, you could hunt him.'

'OK,' Hunter said doubtfully.

Sam bit his lip. He looked like he wanted to say something else. He stood up, knees popping after sitting so long. 'Thanks for the meat, Hunter.'

Hunter watched him go. A boy with a snake arm? No. He'd never seen anything like that. That would be something. That would be even weirder than the snakes he'd seen in the caves. The ones with wings.

That reminded Hunter. He pushed up his sleeve to examine the spot where the snake had spit on him. It hurt. There was a little sore, a sort of hole. The hole had scabbed over, like any of the endless number of scrapes Hunter had suffered tearing through brush.

But as he looked at the scab Hunter was disturbed to see that it was a strange colour. Not reddish like most scabs. This was green.

He rolled his sleeve back down. And forgot about it again.

Sanjit stood at the edge of the cliff. The binoculars didn't show much detail. But it wasn't hard to see the plume of smoke. It was like a massive, twisted exclamation point over Perdido Beach.

He tilted the glasses upwards. Far up in the sky the smoke seemed to spread out horizontally. Like it was running into a glass ceiling. But that had to be an illusion.

He turned to his right and focused on the yacht. His view travelled from the bow to the stern. The helicopter.

Choo was trying to fly a kite for Pixie. The kite wasn't really taking off. It never did, but Pixie kept hoping and Choo kept trying. Because, Sanjit reflected, as grumpy as Virtue was, he was a good person. Something Sanjit wasn't sure he could say about himself.

Peace was inside, keeping watch over Bowie. His fever had stopped spiking. But Sanjit knew better than to think this was a permanent improvement. They'd been up and down like this for a long time.

He stared at the helicopter. Not a chance he could fly it. He was going to have to convince Choo of that. Because if Sanjit tried to fly the chopper he'd get all of them killed.

And if he didn't then Bowie might die.

He was too lost in his dark thoughts to notice that Virtue was running towards him.

'Hey, there's a boat coming.'

'What?'

Virtue pointed at the sea. 'Right there.'

'What? I don't see anything.'

Virtue rolled his eyes. 'You really can't see that?'

'Hey, I didn't grow up searching the savannah for lions.'

'Lions. That's right. That's what I spent most of my time doing: looking for lions.'

Sanjit thought he could almost make out a spot that might be a boat. He aimed the binoculars. It took a while to pick out the boat and he found it by first locating its wake.

'It is a boat!'

'They don't call you Wisdom for nothing,' Virtue said dryly.

'There are people in it,' Sanjit said. He handed the binoculars to Virtue.

'It looks like maybe a half dozen people,' Virtue said. 'I can't see them very well. I can't even tell for sure if they're heading in this direction. They might be aiming for one of the other islands. Or they might just be fishing.'

'The town burns up and suddenly we have a boatload of

people on their way here?' Sanjit said sceptically. 'I'm going to guess they aren't fishing.'

'They're escaping from Perdido Beach,' Virtue agreed. 'Running from something.'

'The fire.'

But Virtue shook his head dolefully. 'No, brother. Think about it. There's a fire, so do you jump in a boat and head for an island? No. You just go where there's no fire. Like to the next town.'

Sanjit fell silent. He was a little embarrassed. Now that he thought of it, it was obvious. Choo was right. Whatever they were doing in that boat it wasn't about getting away from a fire.

'What do we do if they come here?' Virtue asked.

Sanjit had no easy answer. He stalled. 'They'll have a hard time landing. Even with no surf they'll never get off that boat and up the cliffs.'

'Unless we help them,' Virtue said.

'What they'll do is come around and try to get in by the yacht. If they go the right direction, they'll come around and see it. Pretty good chance they'll end up drowning if they try that. Crushed in between the yacht and the rocks. Even with no surf. It's too tight.'

'If we helped them they could make it,' Virtue said cautiously. 'It'll take them a while to get here. That's not exactly a fast boat.

And they're still a long way off.' He looked again through the binoculars. 'I don't know,' he said.

'Don't know what?'

Virtue shrugged. 'It's not good to just decide you don't like people, not even give them a chance.'

Sanjit felt the hairs on his neck tingle. 'What are you saying, Choo?'

'I don't know. I'm not saying anything. They're probably fine.'

'Do they look fine?'

Virtue didn't answer. Sanjit noticed that his jaw was tight. Brow furrowed. Lips pressed into a thin line.

'Do they look, fine, Choo?' Sanjit repeated.

'They could be like, refugees, you know?' Virtue said. 'What are we going to do? Turn them away?'

'Choo. I'm asking you. Do they look fine to you? Crazy as it sounds, I kind of trust your feelings on things.'

'They don't look anything like the men who came out of the jungle to our village,' Choo said. 'But they *feel* like them.'

'Where are we supposed to land?' Diana asked.

The islands, which she'd been watching for what felt like days now, were finally within reach. The motorboat wallowed before bare cliffs that might have been one hundred feet high.

'There has to be something, like a dock or whatever,'

Bug said. He was nervous, Diana knew. If his story about this island turned out to be a fantasy, Caine would make him wish he were dead.

'We are about out of gas,' Tyrell said. 'Maybe, like a gallon or whatever. I can hear it sloshing around, you know?'

'In which case the boat doesn't matter,' Caine said. 'We survive here, on the island, or we die.' He cast a reptilian look at Bug. 'Some of us sooner than others.'

'Which way do we go?' Penny wondered aloud. 'Right or left?'

'Anyone have a coin we can flip?' Diana asked.

Caine stood up. He shaded his eyes and looked left. Then right. 'The cliffs look lower to the right.'

'Can't you just go all magic powers and levitate us up to the top of the cliff?' Paint asked and then giggled nervously, slobbering down his red-stained lips.

'I've been wondering just that,' Caine said thoughtfully. 'It's a long way up. I don't know.' He looked down at the kids in the boat. Diana knew what was coming next. She wondered idly who would get the honour.

'Let's go, Paint,' Caine said. 'You're about useless, might as well be you.'

'What?' Paint's alarm was comical. Diana would have felt sorry for him another time. But this was life and death and right now.

And Caine was right: Paint didn't exactly contribute anything vital. He had no powers. He was no good in a fight. He was a druggie moron who had long since fried whatever brain he'd had.

Caine raised his hands and Paint floated up from his seat. It was as if Caine was lifting him from the middle of his body because Paint's feet dangled and kicked and his arms waved. His long, ratty brown hair drifted and swirled as if he was in a slow-moving tornado.

'No, no, no,' he moaned.

Paint floated out over the water.

'If you lowered him a little it would be like he was walking on water,' Penny said.

Paint moved closer to the cliff, still just a few feet above the water, now twenty or thirty feet away from the boat.

'You know, Penny,' Diana said, 'it's not all that funny. If it works we'll all be going up the same way.'

Somehow that fact had not occurred to Penny. Diana felt a distant sort of satisfaction at the way sadistic pleasure turned to worry on the girl's face.

'OK, now for the altitude,' Caine said. Paint began to rise again, up the cliff face. It was almost bare, hard-packed soil dotted with extrusions of rock and a few scattered bushes that looked like they'd chosen a very precarious spot to grow.

Paint rose. Diana held her breath.

'No, no, no!' Paint's voice floated back down, ignored. He was no longer kicking. Instead he was trying to twist around to face the cliff, arms straining outward, looking for something – anything – to grab.

Halfway up, the height of a five-storey building, Paint's ascent slowed noticeably. Caine took a deep breath. He didn't seem to be straining physically. His muscles were not taut; the power he had was not about muscles. But his expression was grim and Diana knew that in some unfathomable way he was exerting all his power.

Paint rose, but more slowly.

And then he slipped. Fell.

Paint screamed.

He came to rest just ten feet in the air.

'Let's go get him,' Caine said. Tyrell lowered the outboard into the water and the boat moved towards the screaming, wailing boy.

Caine dropped him into the boat. He landed hard, fell on to his rear end and began sobbing.

'Well, that didn't work,' Diana said.

Caine shook his head. 'No. I guess it's too far. I could throw him that far. I've thrown cars that far. But I can't levitate him.'

No one suggested throwing Paint. Diana's warning that whatever worked would be done to each of them in turn kept them quiet. Diana mentally measured the distance Paint had travelled. Maybe seventy, eighty feet in all. So. Now she knew how far Caine could reach. The day might come when it would be very good to know that.

THIRTY

10 HOURS 28 MINUTES

SAM HAD NO idea what he was doing, or even why.

He had run in blind panic from Perdido Beach. That shameful fact filled his mind, driving out even hunger.

He had seen Drake and he had panicked.

Freaked.

Lost it.

After bumming a free meal off Hunter Sam had headed towards the power plant. The power plant was where it had happened.

The beating, the whipping, had been so bad that Brianna had found morphine in the medical supplies at the plant and jabbed the needle into him and even then, even after the painkiller flooded him, the pain was too awful to endure.

But he had endured. And he'd lived through the next nightmarish hours, the morphine hallucinations, the staggering, stumbling, needing-to-scream hours.

He had fought Drake again, but it was Caine who had finally

killed the psychopath. Caine had thrown Drake down a mineshaft that then collapsed on Drake's head. Nothing could have survived.

And yet, Drake was alive.

He'd coped since that day by knowing that Drake was dead, buried under tons of rock, dead, gone, never to be faced again. That fact had let him cope.

But if Drake was unkillable . . .

Immortal . . .

Would Drake always be a part of life in the FAYZ?

Sam sat on the edge of the cliff, just half a mile from the power plant. He had found a bike on the way there and ridden it until the tyre blew out. Then he had walked down the winding coast road intending to return to the power plant, to that room where it had happened. The place where Drake had broken him.

That was the thing of it, Sam thought, as he looked out over the empty, sparkling sea: Drake had broken something inside him. Sam had tried to put it back together. He'd tried to go back to being Sam. The Sam everyone expected him to be.

Astrid had been a part of it. Love and all. It was so corny, but love had kept him from despair. Love and the cold comfort of knowing that Drake had died while Sam had survived.

Love and revenge. Nice combination.

And responsibility, he realised suddenly. That had helped in a strange way, knowing that kids needed him. Knowing that he was necessary.

Now Astrid was telling him he was not so necessary. And, by the way, not so loved. And the comfort of thoughts of Drake's broken body lying under the ground? Gone.

Sam took off his shirt. The wound in his shoulder didn't look like much. When he probed it with his finger he could feel something hard and round just below the skin.

He squeezed the wound with his fingers, wincing at the pain, squeezed some more and the dull lead ball came out along with a little blood.

He looked at the ball. A shotgun pellet. About the size of a BB. He tossed it away. A Band-Aid would have been nice, but he would have to content himself with washing the wound.

He started climbing down the cliff, needing something to do, and hoping he might find something to eat down in the tidal pools in the rocks.

It was a tough climb. He wasn't sure he'd be able to get back up once he was down. But physical movement seemed necessary to him.

I could jump in the water and swim, he told himself.

I could swim until I can't swim any more.

He wasn't afraid of the ocean. You couldn't be a surfer and be afraid of the ocean. He could start swimming, straight out. From here it was ten miles to the distant FAYZ wall. Couldn't see it from here, couldn't usually see it at all until you were up close to it. It had a grey, satiny, pseudo-reflective character that fooled the eye. As far as they knew, it was a complete sphere, a dome, though it looked like the sky, and at night it looked like stars.

He wondered if he could reach the wall. Probably not. He wasn't in as good a shape as he'd been back in the old days.

He'd probably wear out after a mile. If he swam hard, maybe a mile, maybe a mile and a half. And then, if he let it, the ocean would take him down, swallow him up. Not the first person to be taken by the Pacific. There were human bones scattered across the ocean floor, from here to China.

He reached the rocks and bent over awkwardly to rinse the shotgun wound in salt water.

Then he began poking around in the tidal pools. Darting little fish. Some molluscs too tiny to bother opening. But after half an hour he had collected a couple handfuls of mussels, three small crabs, and a seven-inch-long sea cucumber. He placed them all in a small tidal pool. Then he aimed one palm at the pool and blasted it with enough light to set the salt water boiling.

He sat on slick rocks and ate the seafood stew, gingerly picking pieces out of the hot broth. It was delicious. A little salty, which would be bad later unless he found fresh water, but delicious.

It improved his mood, eating. Sitting by the water. Being alone with himself. No one demanding anything of him.

No terrible threat to rush off and handle. No nagging details.

Suddenly, to his own amazement, he laughed out loud.

How long had it been since he'd sat by himself, no one in his face?

'I'm on vacation,' he said to no one.

'Yes, I'll be taking some time off. No, no, I won't be answering my phone or even checking my BlackBerry. Also, I won't be burning holes in anyone. Or getting the crap beaten out of me.'

An outcropping hid Perdido Beach from view, which was just fine. He could make out the nearest of the small islands and looking north he could see the spit of land that jutted out from the power plant.

'Nice place,' Sam said, looking around at his rocky perch. 'If only I had a cooler of sodas I'd be set.'

His mind drifted to Perdido Beach. How were they doing in the aftermath of the fire? How were they dealing with Zil?

What was Astrid doing right now? Probably bossing everyone around with her usual confidence.

Picturing Astrid was not helpful. There were two pictures in his mind, vying for dominance. Astrid in her nightgown, the one that was modest and sensible until she happened to step in front of a light source and then . . .

Sam shook that off. Not helpful.

He pictured the other Astrid with the haughty, cold, contemptuous expression she wore in the council meetings.

He loved the first Astrid. The Astrid who occupied his daydreams and sometimes his night dreams.

He couldn't stand the other Astrid.

Both Astrids frustrated him, although in very different ways.

It wasn't like there weren't other pretty girls in the FAYZ, ready to more or less throw themselves at Sam. Girls who maybe wouldn't be quite so moral, or quite so superior in their attitude.

It seemed to Sam that, if anything, Astrid was getting more and more that way. She was becoming less the Astrid of his daydreams and more the Astrid who had to control everything.

Well, she *was* head of the council. And Sam had agreed that he couldn't run things all by himself. And he'd never wanted to run anything to begin with. He had resisted, in fact. It had been Astrid who manipulated him into taking on the responsibility.

And then she had taken it away from him.

He wasn't being fair. He knew that. He was being self-pitying. He knew that, too.

But the bottom line with Astrid was that the answer from her was always 'No'. No to any number of things. But when things went wrong, suddenly it was his responsibility.

Well, no more.

He was done being played. If Astrid and Albert wanted to keep Sam in some little box, where they could take him out and use him whenever they wanted, and then not even let him do his job – they could forget it.

And if Astrid wanted to think of herself and Little Pete and Sam as being some kind of family, only Sam never got to, well . . . she could forget that, too.

You didn't run away because of any of that, a cruel voice in his head said. *You didn't run away because Astrid won't sleep with you. Or because she is bossy. You ran away from Drake.*

'Whatever,' Sam said aloud.

And then, a thought occurred to Sam that rocked him. He'd become a big hero because of Astrid. And when he seemed to have lost her, he stopped being that guy.

Was that possible? Was it possible that arrogant, frustrating, manipulative Astrid was the reason he could play Sam the Hero?

He had shown some courage before, the actions that earned him the nickname School Bus Sam. But he had immediately walked away from that image, done his best to disappear back into anonymity. He'd been allergic to responsibility. When the FAYZ came he'd been just another kid. And even after the FAYZ came he'd done his best to avoid the role that others wanted to force on him.

But then there had been Astrid. He had done it for her. For her he'd been the hero.

'Yeah, well,' he said to the rocks and the surf, 'In that case, I'm fine being regular old Sam.'

He felt comforted by that thought. For a while. Until the image of Whip Hand bubbled to the surface again.

'It's just an excuse,' Sam admitted to the ocean. 'Whatever's going on with Astrid, you still have to do it.'

He still, no matter what, had to face Drake.

'I'm glad you saw that, too, Choo,' Sanjit whispered. 'Because otherwise I'd be sure I was crazy.'

'It was that kid, that boy. He did it. Somehow,' Virtue said.

The two of them were in the rocks atop the cliff. There was scarcely an inch of the island they hadn't explored both before the big disappearance and after. Much of the island had been denuded of trees dating back to a time when someone had raised sheep and goats on the island. But at the fringes there was still virgin forest of scrub oak, mahogany and cypress trees, and dozens of flowering bushes. The island foxes still hunted in these woods.

In other places palm trees swayed high above tumbled rocks. But there were no beaches on San Francisco De Sales Island. No convenient inlets. In the days of sheep ranching the shepherds had lowered the animals in wicker baskets. Sanjit had seen the tumbled remains of that apparatus, had considered trying to swing out over the water for the sheer fun of it, had decided it was crazy when he noticed that the support beams were eaten by ants and termites.

The island was almost impregnable, which was why his adopted parents had bought it. It was one place the paparazzi couldn't reach. In the interior of the island was a short airstrip large enough to accommodate private jets. And at the compound was the helipad.

'They're going east,' Sanjit commented.

'How did he do that?' Virtue asked.

Sanjit knew already that Virtue was not quick to adapt to new and unexpected circumstances. Sanjit had grown up on the streets with con men, pickpockets, magicians and others who specialised in illusion. He didn't think what he had just witnessed was an illusion, he believed it was real. But he was ready to accept that and move on.

'It's impossible,' Virtue said.

The boat was definitely under way again, heading east, which was good. It was the long way around the island. It would take hours and hours for them to get to where the beached yacht lay.

'It's not possible,' Virtue said again.

'Choo. Every single adult disappears in a heartbeat, there's no TV or radio, no planes in the sky, no boats sailing by. Have you not figured out we're not exactly in the land of possible? New world, new rules.'

Virtue blinked once. Twice. He nodded. So, what do we do?'

'Whatever we have to do to survive,' Sanjit said.

And then the old familiar Virtue was back. 'That's a nice

line, *Wisdom.* Like something out of a movie. Unfortunately it's kind of meaningless.'

'Yes. Yes, it is,' Sanjit admitted with a grin. He slapped Virtue on the shoulder. 'Coming up with something more meaningful is your thing.'

'Can you guys handle things for a few minutes?' Mary asked. John glanced at the three helpers, three kids who had either been scheduled or, in the case of one, was a homeless fugitive who had come to the day care looking for shelter and been put to work.

During the night and morning the population of the day care more than doubled. Now the numbers were starting to decline a little as kids drifted off in ones or twos, looking for siblings or friends. Or homes that, from all that Mary had heard, might no longer exist.

Mary knew she probably should not let anyone leave. Not until they were sure it was safe.

'But when would that be?' she muttered. She blinked a couple of times, trying to focus. Her vision was weird. More than just sleepiness. A blur that turned edges to neon when she moved her head too fast.

She searched for and found her pill bottle. When she shook it, it made no sound. 'No, no way.' She opened it and looked inside. She upended it. Still empty.

When had she finished it off? She couldn't remember.

The depression beast must have come for her and she must have fought it off with the last of the meds.

At some point. Before. Must have.

'Yeah,' she said aloud, voice slurred.

'What?' John asked, frowning like it was all he could do to pay attention.

'Nothing. Talking to myself. I have to go find Sam or Astrid or someone, whoever is in charge. We're out of water. We need twice the usual amount of food. And I need someone to . . . you know . . .' She lost her train of thought, but John didn't seem to notice.

'Use some of the emergency food to feed them until I get back,' Mary said. She walked away before John could ask how he was supposed to stretch four cans of mixed vegetables and a vacuum-pack of spicy dried peas to cover thirty or forty hungry kids.

Near the plaza things didn't look much different to usual. They smelled different – smoke and the acrid stench of melted plastic. But the only evidence of the disaster at first was the pall of brown haze that hovered above the town. That and a pile of debris peeking out from behind the McDonald's.

Mary stopped at town hall, thinking maybe she would find the council hard at work making decisions, organising, planning. John had gone on a tour with them earlier, but if he was back they should be, too.

She needed to talk to Dahra. See what meds she had available. Get something before the depression swallowed her up again. Before she . . . something.

No one was home in the offices, but Mary could hear moans of pain coming from the basement infirmary. She didn't want to think about what was going on down there. No, not now, Dahra would kick her out.

Even though it would really only take Dahra a few seconds to grab a Prozac or whatever she had.

Mary almost ran smack into Lana who was sitting outside on the town hall steps smoking a cigarette.

Her hands were stained red. No one had water to waste on washing off blood.

Lana glanced up at her. 'So. How was your night?'

'Me? Oh, not great.'

Lana nodded. 'Burns. They take a long time to heal. Bad night. Bad, bad night.'

'Where's Patrick?' Mary asked.

'Inside. He helps kids stay calm,' Lana said. 'You should get a dog for the day care. Helps kids . . . Helps them, you know, not notice that their fingers are burned off.'

Something she was supposed to check on. No, not meds. Something else. Oh, of course. 'I hate to ask, I know you've had a hard night,' Mary said. 'But one of my kids, Justin, came in crying about his friend Roger.'

Lana almost smiled. 'The Artful Roger? He'll live, probably. But all I had time to do was keep him from dying right away. I'll have to spend a lot more time with him before he's going to be drawing any more pictures.'

'Z'anyone know what happened?' Mary's lips and tongue felt thick.

Lana shrugged. She lit a second cigarette from the butt of the first. It was a sign of wealth, in a way. Cigarettes were in short supply in the FAYZ. Of course the Healer could have whatever she wanted. Who was going to say no?

'Well, it depends on who you believe,' Lana said. 'Some kids are saying it was Zil and his idiots. Others are saying it was Caine.'

'Caine? That's crazy, isn't it?'

'Not so crazy. I heard crazier from kids.' Lana laughed humourlessly.

Mary waited for Lana to add something. She didn't want to ask, but she had to. 'Crazier?'

'Remember Brittney? Girl who died in the big fight at the power plant? Buried right over there?' Lana pointed with her cigarette. 'I have kids saying they saw her walking around.'

Mary started to speak, but her clumsy mouth was dry.

'And even crazier stuff than that,' Lana said.

Mary felt a chill deep inside her.

'Brittney?' Mary said.

'Dead things don't always stay dead, I guess,' Lana said.

'Lana . . . what do you know?' Mary asked.

'Me? What do I know? I'm not the one with a brother on the council.'

'John?' Mary was surprised. 'What are you talking about?'

There was a loud groan of pain from the basement. Lana didn't flinch. But she noticed Mary's concerned expression. 'He'll live.'

'What are you getting at, Lana? Are you, um, saying something?'

'This kid tells me Astrid told him to spread the word that Orsay is full of crap. Then, same kid says, a couple hours later, Howard tells him to spread the word that anyone who sees anything crazy is full of crap. So the kid says to Howard, what are you talking about "crazy"? Because everything is crazy in the FAYZ.'

Mary wondered if she was supposed to laugh. She couldn't. Her heart was pounding and her head was banging, banging.

'Meanwhile, guess what Sam's doing a couple of days ago? He's over at Clifftop asking me if I happen to have gotten a telephone call from the gaiaphage.'

Mary stood very still. She wanted desperately for Lana to explain what she meant about Orsay. Focus, Mary, she told herself.

Lana went on after a moment. 'See, what Sam really wanted,

was to know whether it's dead. The gaiaphage. Whether it's really gone. And guess what?'

'I don't know, Lana.'

'Well, it's not. You know? It's not gone. It's not dead.' Lana took a deep breath and stared at the blood dried on her hands like it was the first time she'd noticed. She peeled some off with a thumbnail.

'I don't understand . . .'

'Me neither,' Lana said. 'It was there with me. In my mind. I could feel it . . . using . . . me.' She looked ashamed. Embarrassed. And then her eyes flashed angrily. 'Ask your brother, he's in with all of them, Sam and Astrid and Albert. At the same time Sam is asking me whether the gaiaphage is still its old lovable self and council kids are asking other kids to run around dissing Orsay and making sure no one thinks anything's wrong.'

'John would never lie to me,' Mary said, but with a lack of conviction even she could hear.

'Uh-huh. Something's going wrong. Something's going really, really wrong,' Lana said. 'And now? The town is half burned and Caine's stealing a boat and heading out to sea. What does that tell you?'

Mary sighed. 'I'm too tired for guessing games, Lana.'

Lana stood up. She flicked her cigarette away. 'Just remember: the FAYZ is working out fine for some people. You ever think about what would happen if the walls came down tomorrow?

That would be good news for you. Good for most people. But would it be good for Sam and Astrid and Albert? Here they're big deals. Back in the world they're just kids.'

Lana waited, watching Mary closely. Like she was waiting for her to say something or react. Or deny. Something.

All Mary could think to do was say, 'John is on the council.'

'Exactly. So, maybe you should ask him what's really going on. Because, me? I don't know.'

Mary had no answer to that.

Lana squared her shoulders and headed back towards the hell of the basement. She turned halfway down and said, 'One other thing I almost forgot: this one kid? He said Brittney wasn't the only officially dead person walking around in the fire.'

Mary waited. She tried not to show anything, but Lana had already seen it in her eyes.

'Ah,' Lana said. 'So you saw him, too.'

Lana nodded once and was gone down the stairs.

The Darkness. Mary had only heard of it from others. Like stories of a boogeyman. Lana said it had used her.

Did Lana not see? Or did she simply refuse to see? If it were true that Brittney was somehow alive, that Drake was alive, too, then Mary could guess just how the gaiaphage had used Lana's power.

THIRTY ONE

9 HOURS 17 MINUTES

ASTRID HAD WAITED all night for Sam to come back.

Waited all morning.

Smelling the stink of smoke.

From the office in town hall she saw the fire spread the length of Sherman, down the west side of Sheridan, down the single block of Grant Street and two blocks of Pacific Boulevard.

It seemed certain to reach the plaza. But finally the fire's march stalled.

Now the flames were mostly out, but a plume of smoke continued to rise.

Little Pete was asleep in the corner, curled into a ball with a ratty blanket thrown over him. His game player was on the floor beside him.

Astrid felt a towering wave of disgust. She was furious with Sam. Furious with Little Pete. Mad at the whole world around her. Sickened by everyone and everything.

And mostly, she admitted, sick of herself.

So desperately sick of being Astrid the Genius.

'Some genius,' she muttered. The town council, headed by that blonde girl, what was her name? Oh right: Astrid. Astrid the Genius. Head of the town council that had let half the town burn to the ground.

Down in the basement of town hall Dahra Baidoo handed out scarce ibuprofen and expired Tylenol to kids with burns, like that would pretty much fix anything, as they waited for Lana to go one by one, healing with her touch.

Astrid could hear the cries of pain. There were several floors between her and the makeshift hospital. Not enough floors.

Edilio staggered in. He was barely recognisable. He was black with soot, dirty, dusty, with ragged scratches and scrapes and clothing hanging in shreds.

'I think we got it,' he said, and lay straight down on the floor.

Astrid knelt by his head. 'You have it contained?'

But Edilio was beyond answering. He was unconscious. Done in.

Howard appeared next, in only slightly better shape. Some time during the night and morning he'd lost his smirk. He glanced at Edilio, nodded like it made perfect sense, and sank heavily into a chair.

'I don't know what you pay that boy, but it's not enough,' Howard said, jerking his chin at Edilio.

'He doesn't do it for pay,' Astrid said.

'Yeah, well, he's the reason the whole town didn't burn. Him and Dekka and Orc and Jack. And Ellen, it was her idea.'

Astrid didn't want to ask, but she couldn't stop herself. 'Sam?'

Howard shook his head. 'Didn't see him.'

Astrid found a jacket in the closet, probably still there from the real mayor. It was a loud plaid thing. She draped it over Edilio. She went to the conference room and came back with a chair cushion which she slipped under Edilio's head.

'Was it Zil?' Astrid asked Howard.

Howard barked a laugh. 'Of course it was Zil.'

Astrid clenched her hands into fists. Sam had demanded a free hand to go after Zil. He'd wanted to deal with Human Crew.

Astrid had stopped him.

And the town had burned.

And now the basement was full of hurt kids.

And the ones who were *just* hurt were the lucky ones.

Astrid twisted her hands into a knot, an anguished, prayerful gesture. She had a powerful urge to drop to her knees and demand some kind of explanation from God. Why? Why?

Her gaze fell on Little Pete, sitting quietly, playing his dead game.

'And that ain't all of it,' Howard said. 'You have some water?'

'I'll get you some,' a voice said. Albert had entered the room unnoticed. He found the water jar and poured a glass for Howard, who drained it in one long swallow.

'Thanks. Thirsty work,' Howard said.

Albert took the seat Astrid had vacated. 'What's the rest of it?'

Howard sighed. 'All night kids were coming by, right? Crazy stories. Man, I don't know what's true and what's not.'

'Tell us some stories,' Albert urged quietly.

Edilio snored softly. Something about the sound made Astrid want to weep.

'OK. Well, you've got kids saying they saw Satan. Seriously, devil horns and all. And others kept it a little more real, saying Caine, but skinny and acting crazy.'

'Caine?' Astrid's eyes narrowed. 'Caine? Here? In Perdido Beach? That's crazy.'

Albert cleared his throat and shifted in his seat. 'No. It's not crazy. Quinn saw him, too. Up close. Caine stole the two emergency boats late last night or early this morning. Depending on how you see it.'

'What?' The shrill exclamation made Edilio stir.

'Yeah. No question it was Caine,' Albert said in a forced calm voice. 'He came though while the fire was at its worst and everything was confused. Quinn and his people were just coming back in, wanting to help, and there was Caine and maybe a dozen kids with him.'

As Albert laid out the details Astrid grew cold inside. Not a coincidence. It couldn't be a coincidence. It was planned. Somehow in the back of her mind she had pictured Zil just losing it, acting out, maybe losing control of a situation that got out of hand. But that wasn't it. Not if Caine was involved. Caine didn't lose it. Caine planned.

'Zil and Caine?' Astrid said, feeling stupid even thinking it.

'Zil's whole thing is hating freaks,' Howard said. 'And Caine? Let's face it: he's kind of the Prince of Wales of freaks.'

Albert cocked an eyebrow.

'You know, Sammy being the king,' Howard explained. 'OK, the joke's no good if I have to explain it.'

'Caine and Zil,' Astrid said. It felt better somehow putting the names in that order. Zil was a thug. An evil, twisted little creep who exploited the differences between freaks and normals. But smart he was not. Maybe cunning. But not smart.

No. Caine was smart. And in Astrid's mind it was impossible that the stupider of the two would be in control. No, it had to be Caine behind all this.

'Also . . .' Albert said.

At the same time, Howard said, 'Plus . . .'

Edilio woke up suddenly. He seemed surprised and confused to find himself on the floor. He looked around at the others and scrubbed his face with his hands.

'You missed a little,' Howard said. 'Caine and Zil worked together on this.'

Edilio blinked like an owl. He started to get up, then sighed, gave up, and leaned his back against the desk.

'Also,' Albert said before Howard could continue, 'there must have been some kind of falling-out. Because Zil's guys started shooting at Caine as he was pulling away. They got one of the boats. Quinn pulled a couple of Caine's kids out of the water.'

'What did you do with them?'

Albert shrugged. 'We left them. They weren't going anywhere. They're starved. And Quinn says he thinks maybe they've gone a little crazy.'

Albert picked fastidiously at a spot of something on his pants. 'Caine took out Hank. Hank was the one shooting.'

'Jesus,' Astrid said. She crossed herself quickly, hoping that doing so would turn the word from blasphemy to blessing. 'How many kids died last night?'

Edilio answered. 'Who knows. Two that we know of in the fires. Probably others. Probably we won't ever know for sure.' A huge sob escaped from him. He wiped at his eyes. 'Sorry. I'm just tired.'

He wept silently after that.

'I guess I might as well get this out there, too,' Howard said. 'A couple of kids are saying they saw Drake. And a lot have seen Brittney.'

Silence stretched after that. Astrid found a chair and sat down.

If Drake was alive . . . If Caine was working with Zil . . .

'Where's Sam?' Edilio asked suddenly, as though he'd just noticed.

No one answered.

'Where's Dekka?' Astrid asked.

'In the basement,' Edilio said. 'She kept going for a long time. Her and Orc and Jack. But she's sick. Tired and sick. And she got a bad burn on one hand. That was it for her. I made her go to Dahra. Lana will . . . you know, when she's done with . . . Man, I'm sorry,' he said as he began crying again. 'I can't be digging graves. Someone else has to do that, OK? I can't do that any more.'

Astrid realised that Albert and Howard were both staring at her, one with intense curiosity, the other with a weary smirk.

'What?' Astrid snapped. 'You're both on the council, too. Don't look at me like it's all up to me.'

Howard laughed grimly. 'Maybe we better get John here, huh? He's on the council, too. Sammy's missing, Dekka's out of it, Edilio's losing it and he should be losing it, the night he had.'

'Yes. We should get John here,' Astrid said. It felt wrong bringing the little kid into this, but he was on the council.

Howard laughed, loud and long. 'Yeah, let's get John here. That way we can stall for a while longer. We can keep on doing nothing for just a little while longer.'

Albert said, 'Take it easy, Howard.'

'Take it easy?' Howard jumped to his feet. 'Yeah? Where were you last night, Albert? Huh? Because I didn't see you out there on the street listening to kids screaming, seeing kids running around hurt and scared and choking, and Edilio and Orc struggling, and Dekka hacking up her lungs and Jack crying and . . .

'You know who couldn't even take it?' Howard raged. 'You know who couldn't even take what was happening? Orc. *Orc,* who's not scared of anything. Orc, who everyone thinks is some kind of monster. He couldn't take it. He couldn't . . . but he did. And where were you, Albert? Counting your money? How about you, Astrid? Praying to Jesus?'

Astrid's throat tightened. She couldn't breathe. For a moment panic threatened to overwhelm her. She wanted to run from the room, run away and never look back.

Edilio got to his feet and put an arm around Howard. Howard allowed it, and then he did something Astrid never thought she would see. Howard buried his face in Edilio's shoulder and cried, racking sobs.

'We're falling apart,' Astrid whispered for herself alone.

But there was no easy escape. Everything Howard had said was true. She could see the truth reflected in Albert's stunned expression. The two of them, the smart ones, the clever ones, the great defenders of truth and fairness and justice, had done nothing while others had worked themselves to exhaustion.

Astrid had figured her job was to bring order out of chaos when the night of horror was finally over. And now was the time for her to step up. Now was the time for her to show that she could do what needed doing.

Where was Sam?

It hit her full force then, the shocking realisation. Was this how Sam felt? Was this how he'd been feeling since the beginning? All eyes on him? Everyone waiting for a decision? Even as people doubted and criticised and attacked?

She wanted to be sick. She had been there for so much of it. But she hadn't been *the one.* She hadn't been the one making those choices.

And now . . . she was.

'I don't know what to do,' Astrid said. 'I don't know.'

Diana leaned far out over the side of the boat and dipped her head into the water. She kept her eyes closed at first, intending to come straight back up once her hair was wet.

But the flow of cool water around her ears and scalp was so very pleasant that she wanted to stay there. She opened her eyes. The salt water stung. But the pain was a new pain and she welcomed it.

The water was green foam, swirling down the side of the boat.

She wondered idly if Jasmine would come floating up towards her, face bloated, pale . . .

But no, of course not. That was a long time ago. Hours. Hours like weeks when you're hungry and sunburned and now thirst is screaming at you to drink, drink the lovely green water like punch, like Mountain Dew, like refreshing mint tea, so cold all around your head.

All she had to do was let go. Slip into the water. She wouldn't last long. She was too weak to swim very long and then she would slide down into the water like Jasmine had done.

Or maybe she could just hold her head down here and take a deep breath of water. Would that do it? Or would she just end up choking and puking?

Caine wouldn't let her drown, of course. Then Caine would be all alone. He would raise her up out of the water. She couldn't drown until Caine was gone, and then she might as well because, as sad as it was to realise, he was all she had.

The two of them. Sick puppies. Twisted, arrogant, cruel and cold, both of them. How could she love someone like that? How could he? Process of elimination? Neither of them could find anyone else?

Even the nastiest, ugliest species found mates. Flies found mates. Worms, well, who knew? Probably. The point being . . .

Sudden panic! She yanked her head back up and gasped at the air. Choked, gasped, and started crying with her face in her hands, sobbing without tears because you needed something inside you to produce tears. The water running down from her hair felt like tears.

No one noticed. No one cared.

Caine was watching the shore of the island as it passed on their left.

Tyrell was checking the gas gauge nervously every two seconds. 'Dude, we're on empty. I mean, we are way in the red.'

The cliffs were sheer and impossible. The sun beat down on Diana's head and if someone had magically appeared beside her and said, here, Diana, press this button and . . . oblivion . . .

No. No, that's what was amazing as she thought about it. No. She still wouldn't. She would still choose to live. Even this life. Even though it meant spending her days and nights with herself.

'Hey!' Penny said. 'Look at that. Isn't that, like, an opening?'

Caine shielded his eyes and stared hard. 'Tyrell. In there.'

The boat turned lazily towards the cliff. Diana wondered if they were going to just ram the wall. Maybe. Nothing she could do about it.

But then, she saw it, too, nothing more than a dark space in the buff, sun-blasted rock. An opening.

'Probably just a cave,' Tyrell said.

They weren't far out from the cliff and it didn't take long for them to see that what at first looked like a cave was actually a gash in the rock face. At some point a part of the cliff had collapsed in on itself, creating a narrow inlet, no more than twenty feet wide at the base, but five times that wide at the top. But the base of the inlet was choked with rock. There was no sandy beach awaiting them, no place to land the boat.

And yet, if a boat could be landed, a person could climb up the back of that rock slide to the top of the cliff.

The engine caught and missed several strokes, sending a shudder through the hull.

Tyrell cursed furiously and said, 'I knew it, I knew it!'

The boat kept moving towards the gap. The engine died. The boat lost way.

It drifted and the opening fell slowly away.

Only twenty feet. So close.

Then thirty feet.

Forty.

Caine turned cold eyes on his little crew. He stretched out his hand and Penny rose from her place in the boat. He flung her towards shore. She flew, tumbling and yelling through the air and landed with a splash just feet from the nearest of the tumbled boulders.

No time to see whether she made it. Caine reached and threw Bug, who disappeared halfway through his flight but created a splash so close to the rocks Diana wondered if he had smashed his head.

The boat kept drifting.

What was Caine's range for throwing a fifty- or seventy-five- or one-hundred-pound person with any accuracy? Diana wondered. That must be close to his limit.

Diana's eyes met Caine's.

'Protect your head,' he warned.

Diana locked her fingers together behind her neck and squeezed her arms in tight, covering her temples.

Diana felt a giant, invisible hand squeeze her tight and then she was hurtling through the air.

She didn't cry out. Not even as the rocks rushed towards her. She would hit them head on, no way would she survive. But then gravity had its way and her straight line became a down-turned arc.

The rocks, the foamy water, all in the same blink of an eye, and the plunge. Deep and cold, the water filled her mouth with salt.

There was a hard sharp pain as her shoulder hit rock. She kicked her legs and her knees scraped against an almost-vertical wet slurry of gravel.

Her clothing weighed her down, wrapped tight around her, seized her arms and legs. Diana struggled, surprised by how hard she struggled, how much she wanted to reach the bright, sunlit surface, which was a hundred million miles away.

She came up, was caught by the soft swell, and tossed like a doll against a lichen-slicked boulder. She scrabbled with both hands as she choked. Fingernails on rock. Feet ploughing crumbling pebbles beneath her.

Suddenly she was up and out of the water from the waist up. On a little shelf of rock, gasping for air.

She waited there for a moment, catching her breath. Then, she pushed on, oblivious to scrapes and rips, to a drier spot. She stopped there, all energy spent.

Caine had already reached shore. He slumped, exhausted, wet, but at the same time, triumphant.

Diana heard voices crying his name.

She blinked water and tried to focus on the boat. It was already so far away. Tyrell and Paint, standing up in it and yelling, 'Get me! Get me!'

'Caine, you can't leave us out here!'

'Can you reach them?' Diana asked in a hoarse croak.

Caine shook his head. 'Too far. Anyway . . .'

Diana knew the 'anyway'. Tyrell and Paint had no powers. They would do nothing useful for Caine. They were just two more mouths to feed, two more whiny voices to heed.

'We better start climbing,' Caine said. 'I can help at the rough spots. We'll make it.'

'And there will be food and everything up there?' Penny asked, gazing wistfully up the cliff.

'We had better hope there is,' Diana said. 'We have nowhere else to go. And no way to get there.'

THIRTY TWO

8 HOURS 11 MINUTES

ASTRID HAD GONE to look at the burn zone. Doing the right thing.

Kids had yelled at her. Demanded to know why she had let it happen. Demanded to know where Sam was. Deluged her with complaints and worries and crazy theories until she had retreated.

She'd hidden out after that. She'd refused to answer the door when kids knocked. She had not gone to her office. It would be the same there.

But through the day it had eaten at her. This feeling of uselessness. A feeling of uselessness made so much worse by the growing realisation that she needed Sam. Not because they were up against some threat. The threat was mostly past now.

She needed Sam because no one had any respect for her. There was only one person right now who could get a crowd of anxious kids to settle down and do what needed to be done.

She had wanted to believe that she could do that. But she had tried. And they hadn't listened.

But Sam was still nowhere to be seen. So despite everything it was still on her shoulders. The thought of it made her sick. It made her want to scream.

'We have to go out, Petey. Walkie, walkie. Let's go,' Astrid said.

Little Pete did not respond or react.

'Petey. Walkie, walkie. Come with me.'

Little Pete looked at her like she might be there and might not. Then he went back to his game.

'Petey. Listen to me!'

Nothing.

Astrid took two steps, grabbed Little Pete by the shoulders, and shook him.

The game player went flying across the carpet.

Little Pete looked up. Now he was sure she was there. Now he was paying attention.

'Oh, my God, Petey, I'm sorry, I'm so sorry,' Astrid cried and reached to draw him close. She had never, ever shaken him before. It had happened so suddenly, like some animal in her brain had seized control of her and suddenly she was moving and suddenly she'd grabbed him.

'Ahhh ahhhh ahhhh ahhhh!' Little Pete began shrieking.

'No, no, no, Petey, I'm so sorry, I didn't mean to do it.'

She wrapped her arms around him but she could not touch him. Some force kept her arms from making physical contact.

'Petey, no, you have to let me –'

'Ahhh ahhh ahhhh ahhh!'

'It was an accident! I just lost control, it's just, I just, I can't, Petey, stop it, stop it!'

She ran to retrieve his game. It was warm. Strange. She carried it back to Little Pete, but for just a moment her step faltered. The room seemed to warp and wobble around her.

Little Pete's frantic shrieks snapped her back.

'Ahhhh ahhh ahhhh ahhh!'

'Shut up!' Astrid screamed, as confused and unsettled as she was furious. 'Shut up! Shut up! Here! Take your stupid toy!'

She stepped back, stepped away, not trusting herself to be near him. Hating him at that moment. Terrified that the enraged thing inside her head would lash out at him again. A voice inside her rationalised it even now. He is a brat. He does these things deliberately.

It was all his fault.

'Ahhh ahhh ahhh ahhh!'

'I do everything for you!' she cried.

'Ahhh ahhh ahhh ahhh!'

'I feed you and I clean you and I watch over you and I protect you. Stop it! Stop it! I can't stand it any more. I can't stand it!'

Little Pete did not stop. Would not stop, she knew, until he chose to, until whatever crazy loop that was in his head had played itself out.

She sank into a kitchen chair. Astrid sat with her head in her hands running through the list of her failures. Before the FAYZ there hadn't been very many. She'd gotten a B+ once when she should have gotten an A. She'd inadvertently been cruel to people on a couple of occasions, memories that still bothered her, even now. She'd never learned to play an instrument . . . Wasn't as good as she would like to be with Spanish pronunciations . . .

'Ahhh ahhh ahhh ahhh!'

Before the FAYZ the ratio of success to failure in her life had been hundreds to one. Even in coping with her little brother, back then she'd been as successful as anyone could be.

But since the FAYZ the ratio had reversed. On the positive side she was still alive, and so was her brother. On the negative side there were too many failures to list, though she could recall them all, each and every one in painful detail.

'Ahhh ahhhh ahhh ahhh!'

She had intended to do so many good things. She had wanted to restart therapy and lessons for Little Pete. Failure. She had wanted to get the church fixed up and find some way for kids to attend on Sunday mornings. Failure. She had wanted to write a constitution for the FAYZ, create a government. Failure.

She had tried to stop Albert from making everything about money. She had failed. And just as bad, Albert had succeeded.

He'd been right, she had been wrong. It was Albert feeding Perdido Beach now, not her.

She'd wanted to find a way to stop Howard from selling booze and cigarettes to kids. Wanted to reason with Zil, get him to act like a decent human being. Failure and failure.

Even her relationship with Sam had come apart. And now, he'd run away, abandoned her. Had enough, she supposed. Had enough of her and Little Pete and all of it.

Someone had heard it from someone else that Hunter had seen him leaving town. Leaving. Going where? The gossip machine had no answer to that. But the gossip machine was sure who was to blame: Astrid.

She had wanted to be brave and strong and smart and right.

And now she was hiding out in her home because she knew if she went out, they would all look to her for answers she didn't have. She was the head of the town council in a town that had come close to burning to the ground.

It had been saved. But not by Astrid.

Little Pete fell silent at last. His blank eyes were focused on the game again. Like nothing had happened.

She wondered if he even remembered her loss of control. She wondered if he knew how terrified she was, how hopeless and defeated. She knew he didn't care.

No one cared.

'OK, Petey,' she said, her voice shaky. 'We still have to go out.

Walkie, walkie. Time to go and talk to my many friends,' she said sardonically.

This time he followed her meekly.

She'd meant to visit the burn zone again. To visit the basement hospital. To find Albert and find out how soon he would have food.

But out on the street she was surrounded within minutes, just as she'd known she would be. Kids came to her. More and more kids, until there were dozens of them, trailing her as she tried to make her way back to the burn zone. They yelled, demanded, insulted, pleaded, begged. Threatened.

'Why won't you talk to us?'

'Why don't you answer?'

Because she didn't have any answers.

'OK,' she said finally. 'OK! OK!' She shoved at a boy who was in her face yelling about his big sister being missing, about her going to visit a friend. Over on Sherman.

'OK,' Astrid said. 'We'll have a town meeting.'

'When?'

'Right now.' She pushed through the crowd, which surged around her as she led the way to the church.

Oh, Sam would get a good laugh out of seeing this. More than once he'd stood up at the altar trying to pacify a bunch of terrified kids. And she, Astrid, had watched, and judged his performance. And when the pressure of it finally got to be too much she had formed the council and tried to push him aside.

Well, Sam, she thought as she stepped on to that ruined altar, *you can have this job back any time you like.*

The crucifix that long ago Caine had used to crush a boy named Cookie had been propped up and fallen and propped up again. It now lay on a pile of debris. It hurt Astrid to see it there. She considered asking for volunteers to lift it again, but this was not the time. No, not the time for her to ask anything of anyone.

Edilio came in with Albert, but neither rushed to the front to stand in solidarity with her.

'If you guys will all sit down and stop trying to talk at once, we can have a town meeting,' Astrid said.

The response was loud and derisive. A wave of bitter words washed over her.

'Hey, the mall is closed, there's no food!'

'No one brought any water down, we're thirsty!'

'Hurt . . .'

'Sick . . .'

'Scared . . .'

And again and again, where is Sam? Where is Sam? Things like this happen, Sam should be around. Is he dead?

'As far as I know, Sam is fine,' Astrid said calmly.

'Yeah, and we can totally trust you, right?'

'Yes,' Astrid said without conviction. 'You can trust me.'

That drew laughter and more insults.

Someone yelled, 'Let her talk, she's the only one even trying.'

'All Astrid does is lie and do nothing,' a voice shot back.

Astrid knew the voice. Howard.

'All Astrid can do is talk,' Howard said. 'Blah blah blah. And most of it lies.'

The mob of kids was silent now, watching as Howard stood up slowly, stiffly, and turned to face the kids.

'Sit down, Howard,' Astrid said. Even she could hear the defeat in her tone.

'Did you write some kind of law that made you boss of everyone? Because I thought you were all about laws.'

Astrid fought the urge to walk out. Like Sam had apparently done, just leave town. No loss to anyone.

'We need to figure out how we're going to organise and deal, Howard,' Astrid said. 'People need food.'

'Got that right,' a voice said.

'How are you going to make that happen?' Howard demanded.

'OK, well, tomorrow everyone will work their regular job,' Astrid said. 'It will be bad for a couple of days, but we'll get food and water going again. The crops are still in the fields. The fish are still in the ocean.'

That had a calming effect. Astrid could feel it. It helped to remind the kids that not everything had been lost in the fire. Yes, maybe she could reach them after all.

'Tell us about the zombie,' Howard said.

Astrid's face and neck flushed red, betraying her guilt.

'And then maybe you can explain why you stopped Sam from taking Zil out before Zil burned down the town.'

Astrid managed a wry smile. 'Don't you lecture me, Howard. You're a lowlife drug dealer.'

She could see that the insult hit home.

'If people want to buy things, I make sure they can,' Howard said. 'Just like Albert. Anyway, I never put myself up on a pedestal and said I was some big deal. Me and Orc, we do what we do to get by. We're not the ones being so perfect and mighty and above it all.'

'No, you're beneath it all,' Astrid said.

Part of her knew that as long as she kept this personal between her and Howard, the others wouldn't jump in. But that would get them nowhere. Accomplish nothing.

'You still haven't explained anything, Astrid,' Howard said, as though reading her mind. 'Forget me. I'm just *me.* What about a girl who was dead and isn't dead any more? And what about kids saying they've seen Drake walking the streets? You got any answers, Astrid?'

She considered bluffing. Another time, another day, she would have found a way to heap frosty scorn on Howard and shut him down. But she couldn't seem to find that inside herself. Not now.

'You know, Howard,' Astrid began in a wry voice, 'I've made a lot of mistakes lately and –'

'And what about the Prophetess?' a different voice broke in. 'What about Orsay?'

'Mary?' Astrid couldn't believe it. Mary Terrafino, her face red with anger, her voice crackling.

'I just talked to my brother. My brother, who never in his whole life ever lied to me,' Mary said.

She walked down the aisle of the church. The crowd parted for her. Mother Mary.

'He admitted it to me, Astrid,' Mary said. 'He lied. He lied because you told him to.'

Astrid wanted to deny it. The words of denial were on the tip of her tongue. But she couldn't make them come out.

'Mary's right, everyone,' Howard said. 'Astrid told us all to lie. About Brittney and about Orsay.'

'Orsay is a fake,' Astrid said weakly.

'Maybe,' Howard said. 'But you don't know that. None of us *know* that.'

'Orsay's no fake. She told me something only I knew,' Mary said. 'And she prophesied that a tribulation was coming soon.'

'Mary, that's an old trick,' Astrid said. 'This is the FAYZ: a tribulation is always coming, in case you haven't noticed.

We're up to our necks in tribulation. She's manipulating you.'

'Yeah, unlike you,' Howard said, his voice dripping sarcasm.

Every eye was on her. Disbelieving. Angry. Accusing. Scared.

'Orsay says we can step out on our fifteenth,' Mary said. 'She told me to lay down my burden. That was what my mom said in her dream. Put down my burden.'

'Mary, you must know better than that,' Astrid said.

'No. I don't know better,' Mary said so quietly, Astrid almost didn't hear her. 'And neither do you.'

'Mary, those kids need you,' Astrid pleaded.

Suddenly, unexpectedly, this had become life and death. What Mary was talking about was suicide. Astrid was sure of that much. Logic told her this was probably true. But her faith told her even more certainly: giving up, surrendering, accepting something that at the very least looked and felt like suicide could never be good. That was a joke that God would not play.

'Maybe not,' Mary said softly. 'Maybe what they need is a way out of here, those kids. Maybe their moms and dads are waiting for them and we're the ones keeping them apart.'

And there it was: the thing Astrid had feared from the first time she heard of Orsay's so-called prophecies.

The silence in the church was nearly absolute.

'None of the littles are anywhere near their fifteenth,' Astrid said.

'And they won't make it to their fifteenth in this horrible

place,' Mary said. Her voice broke. Astrid recognised the desperation: she'd felt it herself as she endured Little Pete's meltdown. She'd felt it so many times since the coming of the FAYZ.

'We're in hell, Astrid,' Mary said, almost pleading with her to understand. 'This. *This* is hell.'

Astrid could imagine what Mary's life was like. The constant work. The constant responsibility. The unbelievable stress. The depression. The fear. All of it so much worse for Mary than for just about anyone else.

But this couldn't go on. This had to be stopped. Even if it meant hurting Mary.

'Mary, you've been one of the most important, necessary people in the FAYZ,' Astrid said carefully. 'But I know it's been hard on you.'

Astrid had a sick feeling inside, knowing what she was going to say, what she had to say. Knowing that it was a betrayal.

'Mary, look, I know you're not able to find the meds you need to take. I know you've been taking a lot of drugs, trying to control the things in your head.'

The silence was total in the church. Kids stared at Mary, then at Astrid. It had turned into a test of who they would believe. Astrid knew the answer to that.

'Mary, I know you're dealing with depression and anorexia. Anyone looking at you knows that.'

The crowd hung on each word.

'I know that you've been battling some demons, Mary.'

Mary barked a disbelieving laugh. 'Are you calling me crazy?'

'Of course not,' Astrid said, but in such a way that it was clear even to the youngest or dumbest in the room that she was alleging exactly that. 'But you do have a couple of mental . . . issues . . . that are possibly distorting your thinking.'

Mary flinched as if someone had hit her. She looked around the room, looking for a friendly face, looking for signs that not everyone was agreeing with Astrid.

Astrid saw those same faces. They had turned stony and suspicious. But all of that suspicion was aimed at Astrid, not at Mary.

'I think you need to stay home for a while,' Astrid said. 'We'll get someone else to run the day care, while you pull yourself together.'

Howard's jaw was hanging open. 'You're firing Mary? And *she's* the one who's nuts?'

Even Edilio seemed amazed. 'I don't think Astrid's talking about Mary not running the day care,' he said quickly, with a warning look at Astrid.

'That's exactly what I'm talking about, Edilio. Mary has fallen for Orsay's lies. It's dangerous. Dangerous to Mary if she decides to step out. And dangerous to the kids if Mary keeps listening to Orsay.'

Mary covered her mouth with one hand, aghast. The hand touched her lips, then went to her hair. Then she smoothed the front of her blouse. 'You think I would ever hurt one of my kids?'

'Mary,' Astrid said, finding a pitiless tone, 'you're a troubled, depressed person off her meds who is talking about how maybe it would be best if those kids died and went to their parents.'

'That's not what I . . .' Mary began. She took a couple of quick, shallow breaths. 'You know what? I'm going back to work. I have things to do.'

'No, Mary,' Astrid said forcefully. 'Go *home*.' Then, to Edilio she said, 'If she tries to enter the day care, stop her.'

Astrid expected Edilio to agree, or at least to do as he'd been told. But when she glanced his way, she knew better.

'I can't do that, Astrid,' Edilio said. 'You keep saying we need laws and all, and you know what? You're right. We got no law says I have a right to stop Mary. And you know what else we need? We need laws to keep you from trying stuff like this.'

Mary walked from the room followed by loud applause.

'She could hurt those kids,' Astrid said shrilly.

'Yeah, and Zil burned down the town because you said we couldn't stop him,' Edilio shot back.

'I'm the head of the council,' Astrid pleaded.

'You want us to vote on that?' Howard asked. 'Because we can vote right now.'

Astrid froze. She looked out at a sea of faces, not one of which belonged to someone who was on her side.

'Petey. Come on,' Astrid said.

She held her head up high as she walked through the crowd and out of the church.

Another failure. The only comfort was that it would be her last as the head of the council.

THIRTY THREE

7 HOURS 51 MINUTES

'I DON'T SEE any big mansion,' Diana said. 'I see trees.'

'Bug,' Caine called.

'Good luck finding him,' Diana said. Bug had been clearly visible during the climb up from the water. Caine had caught him once as he fell.

But as they topped the cliff they faced a line of trees, not a fabulous Hollywood hideaway. Trees and more trees.

Penny lost it then. She started yelling, 'Where is it? Where is it?' and running into the forest.

'Bug!' Caine shouted. No answer.

'Yeah,' Diana said, 'We trusted Bug. And here we are.' She turned and saw the boat. It was drifting farther and farther away. On its way to the distant power plant maybe. Maybe they would survive somehow. Maybe they would be better off than Diana was.

'Sheep!' Penny's voice from some distance away.

Diana exchanged a look with Caine. Was Penny crazy?

Maybe so, but was she hallucinating sheep?

The two of them started forwards into the woods. Soon they saw that the trees were just a narrow belt and that beyond them lay a sunny meadow of knee-high grass.

Penny was at the edge of the meadow, staring and pointing and wobbling like she might topple over at any moment.

'They're real, right?' Penny asked.

Diana shaded her eyes and, yes, they were real. Three dirty-white cotton balls with black faces, almost within reach. The sheep turned and stared at them with stupid eyes.

Caine acted quickly. He raised his hand and snatched one of the sheep off the ground. It flew through the air and smacked with sickening force into a large tree. It fell to the ground, white wool marked with red.

They were on it like tigers. Bug, suddenly visible right there next to them, tearing at the wool, desperate to expose the flesh. But with bare hands and brittle fingernails, even with their dull loose teeth, they couldn't reach the meat.

'We need something sharp,' Caine said.

Penny found a sharp-edged rock. Too big for her to carry, but not too heavy for Caine. The rock rose in the air and came down like a cleaver.

It was messy. But it worked. And the four of them ripped and tore at chunks of raw mutton.

'Kind of hungry, huh?'

Two kids were standing there like they had appeared out of thin air. The taller one had spoken. His eyes were intelligent, mocking and wary. The other kid's face was impassive, expressionless.

Both were dressed in bandages. Bandages wrapped around their hands. The shorter kid had a bandana around his lower face.

The silence stretched as Caine, Diana, Penny, and Bug stared and were stared back at.

'What are you supposed to be, mummies?' Diana asked. She wiped sheep's blood from her mouth and then realised that it had saturated her shirt and that there would be no wiping it away.

'We're lepers,' the tall kid said.

Diana felt her heart skip several beats.

'My name is Sanjit,' the tall boy said, and extended a hand that seemed to be stumps of fingers bound with gauze. 'This is Choo.'

'Stay back!' Caine snapped.

'Oh, don't worry,' Sanjit said. 'It's not always contagious. I mean, sure, sometimes. But not always.'

He dropped his hand to his side.

'You have leprosy?' Caine demanded.

'Like at Sunday school?' Bug said.

Sanjit nodded. 'It's not that bad. It doesn't hurt. I mean, if your finger falls off, you kind of don't even feel it.'

'I felt it when my penis fell off, but it didn't hurt that bad,' the one called Choo said.

Penny yelped. Caine shifted uncomfortably. Bug faded from view as he backpedalled away.

'But people are scared of leprosy, anyway,' Sanjit said. 'Silly. Kind of.'

'What are you doing here?' Caine asked warily. He had put down his food, keeping his hands ready.

'Hey, I should ask you that,' Sanjit said. Not harsh but definitely not willing to be pushed around by Caine, either. 'We live here. You just got here.'

'Plus, you killed one of our sheep,' Choo said.

'This is the San Francisco de Sales leper colony,' Sanjit said. 'Didn't you know?'

Diana began to laugh. 'A leper colony? That's where we are? That's what we half killed ourselves getting to?'

'Shut up, Diana,' Caine snapped.

'You guys want to come back to the hospital with us?' Sanjit offered hopefully. 'All the adult patients and the nurses and doctors are gone, they just disappeared one day. We're all by ourselves.'

'We heard there was some movie star's mansion out here.'

Sanjit's dark eyes narrowed. He glanced right, as if trying to make sense of what she was saying. Then he said, 'Oh, I know what you're thinking of. Todd Chance and Jennifer Brattle pay for this place. It's, like, their charity.'

Diana couldn't stop giggling. A leper colony. That's what Bug had read about. A leper colony paid for by two rich movie stars. Their charity thing.

'I think Bug may have gotten just a few of the details wrong,' she managed to say between dry, racking laughs that were indistinguishable from sobs.

'You can have the sheep,' Choo said.

Diana stopped laughing. Caine's eyes narrowed.

Sanjit quickly said, 'But we'd rather just have you come back with us. I mean, we're kind of lonely.'

Caine stared at Choo. Choo stared back, then looked away. 'He doesn't seem to want us to come to this hospital,' Caine said, indicating Choo.

Diana saw fear in the younger boy's eyes.

'Have them take off their bandages,' Diana said. All urge to laugh was gone now. Both boys had bright eyes. The visible parts of them seemed healthy. Their hair wasn't brittle and broken like hers.

'You heard her,' Caine said.

'No,' Sanjit said. 'It's not good for our leprosy to be exposed.'

Caine took a deep breath. 'I'm going to count to three and then I'm going to throw your little lying friend there straight into a tree. Just like I did with this sheep.'

'He'll do it,' Diana warned. 'Don't believe he won't.'

Sanjit hung his head.

'Sorry,' Choo said. 'I screwed it up.'

Sanjit began unwinding the gauze from his perfectly healthy fingers. 'OK, you got us. So, allow me to welcome you to San Francisco de Sales Island.'

'Thanks,' Caine said dryly.

'And yes, we do have some food. Maybe you'd like to join us? Unless you want to stick with your sheep sushi.'

Throughout the morning and early afternoon, the shell-shocked kids of Perdido Beach milled around, lost and confused.

But Albert was neither lost nor confused. Throughout the day kids came to his office in the McDonald's. He had a booth there, in a corner by the window so he could look out on the plaza and see what passed by.

'Hunter came in with a deer,' a kid reported. 'And some birds. About seventy-five pounds of usable meat.'

'Good,' Albert said.

Quinn came in, looking tired and smelling of fish. He sagged into the seat across from Albert. 'We went back out. We didn't do very well since we got started late. But we have maybe fifty pounds usable.'

'That's good work,' Albert said. He calculated in his head.

'We have about six ounces a head of meat. Nothing from the fields.' He tapped the table, thinking. 'It's not worth opening the mall. We'll do a cookout in the plaza. Roast up the meat, make a stew out of the fish. Charge a 'Berto a head.'

Quinn shook his head. 'Man, you really want to get all these kids together in one place? Freaks and normals? As crazed as everyone is?'

Albert thought that over. 'We don't have time to open the mall and we need to get this product out there.'

Quinn made a half smile. 'Product.' He shook his head. 'Dude, the one guy I'm not worried about when the FAYZ ends – or even if it doesn't – is you, Albert.'

Albert nodded in agreement, accepting the flattery as a simple statement of fact. 'I keep my focus.'

'Yes. You do,' Quinn agreed in a tone that made Albert wonder just what he meant.

'Hey, by the way, one of my guys thinks he saw Sam. Up on the rocks, just down from the power plant,' Quinn said.

'Sam's not back here yet?'

Quinn shook his head. 'The number one question I keep hearing: where is Sam?'

Albert curled his lip. 'I think Sam's having some kind of breakdown.'

'Well, he's got a right, doesn't he?' Quinn said.

'Maybe,' Albert allowed. 'But mostly I think he's just pouting.

He's mad because he's not the only person in charge any more.'

Quinn shifted uncomfortably. 'He's the one who goes right into the danger when most of us are sitting on our butts or hiding under a table.'

'Yeah. But that's his job, isn't it? I mean, the council pays him twenty 'Bertos a week, which is twice what most people make.'

Quinn didn't look as if he liked that explanation very much. 'Doesn't change the fact that he could get killed. And, you know, it's still not fair pay or anything. My guys make ten 'Bertos a week to fish, and it's hard work, but dude, a lot of people could do that job. Only one guy can do Sam's job.'

'Yes. The only single person. But what we need is more people doing it. With less power.'

'You're not getting anti-freak, are you?'

Albert pushed the idea away. 'Don't accuse me of being an idiot, OK?' It irritated him, Quinn standing up for Sam. He had nothing against Sam. Sam had kept them safe from Caine and that creep Drake and Pack Leader, Albert understood that. But the time for heroes was on its way out. Or at least he hoped it was. They needed to build an actual society with laws and rules and rights.

This was Perdido Beach, after all, not Sam's Beach.

'Heard another kid, this is like the fourth, say he saw Drake Merwin during the fire,' Quinn said.

Albert snorted. 'There's a lot of bull going around.'

Quinn looked at him long enough that it almost made Albert uncomfortable. Then, Quinn said, 'I guess if it turns out to be true we better hope Sam decides to come back.'

'Orc could take care of Drake. And he'd do it for a pint of vodka,' Albert said dismissively.

Quinn sighed and got up to leave. 'Sometimes I worry about you, man.'

'Hey, I'm feeding people in case you didn't notice,' Albert said. 'Astrid talks and Sam pouts, and I get the job done. Me. Why? Because I don't talk, I just do.'

Quinn sat back down. He leaned forwards, elbows on knees. 'Man, don't you remember taking tests in school? Multiple choice: A, B, C, D, or E, all of the above.'

'Yeah?'

'Dude, sometimes the answer is "all of the above". This place needs you. And it needs Astrid. And it needs Sam. It's all of the above, Albert.'

Albert blinked.

'I mean, no offence,' Quinn said quickly. 'But it's like Astrid's yapping away about how we need some kind of system, and you're counting your money, and Sam's acting like we should all just shut up and get out of his way and let him fry whoever messes with him. And the three of you aren't really stepping up. You aren't working together, which is what all of us regular people need you to do. Because, and really, I'm not trying to be a jerk or whatever, but duh: we do need a system, and we do need you and your 'Bertos, and sometimes we need Sam to just come along and kick some ass.'

Albert said nothing. His brain was clicking away, but it occurred to him after a minute that he hadn't said anything and that Quinn was waiting for an answer, and cringing a little like he expected Albert to lash out.

Quinn stood up again, shook his head ruefully, and said, 'OK, I get it. I'll stick to fishing.'

Albert met his eyes. 'Cookout in the plaza tonight. Spread the word, OK?'

THIRTY FOUR

7 HOURS 2 MINUTES

DIANA STARTED TO cry when Sanjit put the bowl of Cheerios in front of her. He poured from a carton of shelf-stable milk and the milk was so white and the cereal so fragrant, so wonderfully noisy as it sloshed around in the blue bowl.

She reached for it with her fingers. Then she noticed the spoon. It was clean. Bright.

With trembling fingers she dipped the spoon into the cereal and raised it to her lips. The rest of the world disappeared then, for just a few moments. Caine and Penny wolfed from their own bowls, Bug completely visible as he did likewise. But all she noticed, all she felt, was the cool crunch, the rush of sugar, the shock of recognition.

Yes, this was food.

Diana's tears ran down her face into the spoon, adding a touch of salt to her second bite.

She blinked and saw Sanjit staring at her. He held the

industrial-size box of cereal at the ready in one hand, the carton of milk in the other.

Penny laughed and spilled cereal and milk from her lips.

'Food,' Caine said.

'Food,' Bug agreed.

'What else do you have?' Caine asked.

'You have to take it slow,' Sanjit said.

'Don't tell me how to take it.'

Sanjit did not back down. 'You aren't the first starving people I've seen.'

'Someone else from Perdido Beach?' Caine demanded sharply.

Sanjit exchanged a look with the younger boy, Virtue. He'd told Diana that was his real name.

'So it's pretty bad on the mainland,' Sanjit said.

Caine finished his cereal. 'More.'

'A starving person eats too much all at once, he gets sick,' Sanjit said. 'You end up puking it all up.'

'More,' Caine said with unmistakable threat in his voice.

Sanjit poured him a refill, then did the same for the rest of them. 'Sorry we don't have any Cap'n Crunch or Froot Loops,' Sanjit said. 'Jennifer and Todd are into nutrition. I guess it wouldn't do for them to be photographed with fat children.'

Diana noted the sardonic tone. And as she gulped the second

bowl she noted, too, that her stomach was cramping. She made herself stop.

'There's plenty of food,' Sanjit said gently just to her. 'Take your time. Give your body time to adjust.'

Diana nodded. 'Where did you see starving people?'

'Where I grew up. Beggars. Maybe they'd get too sick to beg sometimes, or just have a run of bad luck, and then they'd get pretty hungry.'

'Thanks for the food,' Diana said. She wiped away tears and tried to smile. But she remembered that her gums were swollen and red and her smile wasn't too attractive.

'I also saw scurvy sometimes,' Sanjit said. 'You have it. I'll get you each some vitamins. You'll be better in a few days.'

'Scurvy,' Diana said. It seemed ridiculous. Scurvy was from pirate movies.

Caine was looking around the room, appraising. They were at a massive wooden table just beyond the kitchen. It could have seated thirty people on the long benches.

'Nice,' Caine said, waving his spoon to indicate the room.

'It's the staff table,' Virtue said. 'But we eat here because the family table is kind of uncomfortable. And the formal dining room . . .' He petered out, fearing he'd said something he shouldn't.

'So, you're like super-rich,' Penny said.

'Our parents are,' Virtue said.

'Our step-parents,' Sanjit corrected.

'Jennifer and Todd, right?' Caine said.

'Right,' Sanjit said, holding his gaze.

'So. How much food do you have?' Caine asked bluntly, not liking that Sanjit wasn't quivering with fear.

It had been a long time since anyone had faced Caine without fear, Diana realised. Sanjit had no idea what he was dealing with.

Well, Sanjit would learn soon enough.

'Choo? How much food do we have?'

Virtue shrugged. 'When I figured it out, it was enough for the two of us to last maybe six months,' he said.

'There's just the two of you?' Diana asked.

'I thought there were, like, ten of you or whatever,' Bug said.

'Five,' Sanjit said. 'But we weren't all here on the island.'

Diana didn't believe it. Right then, as soon as the words were out of Sanjit's mouth, she didn't believe it. But she kept silent.

'Diana,' Caine said. 'Have you read our two friends here?'

To Sanjit, Diana said, 'I need to hold your hand. For just a moment.'

'Why?' Virtue demanded, defending his brother.

'I can tell whether you have any strange . . . mutations,' Diana said.

'Like him,' Sanjit said, nodding towards Caine.

'Let's hope not,' Diana said. Her stomach was settling down enough and now she really, really wanted to know what else was behind the pantry doors.

Sanjit gave her his hand. Palm up. Like he was making a gesture of peace. Open-handed. Trusting. But his eyes were not.

Diana held his hand. His hand was still. Hers was shaking.

She closed her eyes and concentrated. It had been some time since she had done this. She tried to remember the last time, but memories were scattered fragments, too tiring to make sense of.

She felt it work. She squeezed her eyes tight, both relieved and afraid at the same time.

'He's a zero,' Diana said. Then, to Sanjit, 'Sorry. I don't mean it that way.'

'I didn't think you did,' Sanjit said.

'You next,' Diana said to Virtue.

Virtue held his hand out like he was shaking hands. Fingers curled in as if he was thinking of making a fist. Diana took his hand. There was something there. Not a two bar, not quite. She wondered what his power was, and whether he was even aware of it.

The mutations occurred in different degrees, at different times. Most kids seemed never to develop powers. Some developed powers that were pointless. Only twice had Diana ever read a four bar: Caine and Sam.

'He's a one,' she told Caine.

Caine nodded. 'Well, that's both bad and good. Bad because if you did have serious powers you might be useful to me. Good because since you don't, I have very little reason to worry about you.'

'That sounds kind of stupid,' Sanjit said.

Bug and Penny stared in disbelief.

'I mean, it sounds good, but then if you think about it, it doesn't make any sense,' Sanjit said. 'If I did have these powers you're talking about, I'd be a threat. I don't, so I'm not as useful as I'd be if I did. Useful and threatening are actually the same thing here.' But as he said it he smiled a huge, innocent-seeming smile.

Caine returned the smile. But it was a shark smiling at Nemo.

No, that was wrong. Sanjit's smile was slyer than that. Like he knew what he was doing was dangerous.

Not many people held their own with Caine. Diana did. But she had long known that was part of her appeal to him: Caine needed someone who wasn't intimidated.

But that wasn't going to work for Sanjit. She wondered if there was some way she could warn him that he wasn't dealing with a garden variety schoolyard bully who would give him a wedgie.

She saw the dangerous light in Caine's eyes. She felt the way everyone held their breath. So must Sanjit. But he held

Caine's gaze and kept that infectious smile in place.

'Get me something else to eat,' Caine said at last.

'Absolutely,' Sanjit said. Virtue followed him out of the room.

'He's lying about something,' Caine said in a low voice to Diana.

'Most people lie,' Diana said.

'But not you, Diana. Not to me.'

'Of course not.'

'He's hiding something,' Caine said. But then Sanjit and Virtue came back carrying a serving tray loaded with cans of peaches, and a box of graham crackers with big tubs of jelly and peanut butter. Unimaginable luxuries, worth so much more than gold.

Whatever Sanjit was hiding, Diana thought, it was nowhere near as important as what he was giving them.

They ate and ate and ate. Not caring that their stomachs cramped. Not caring that their heads pounded.

Not even caring when weariness and exhaustion caught up with them and one by one their eyes drooped.

Penny slid from her chair, like a passed-out drunk. Diana glanced blearily at Caine to see if he was going to react. But Caine just put his head down on the table.

Bug was snoring.

Diana looked at Sanjit, her eyes barely able to focus. He winked at her.

'Oh,' Diana said, and then crossed her arms on the table and lay her head down.

'It's going to be really bad when they wake up,' Virtue said. 'Maybe we should kill them.'

Sanjit grabbed his brother and pulled him close for a quick hug. 'Yeah. Right. We're a pair of desperate killers.'

'Caine may be, though. When he wakes up . . .'

'The Ambien I gave them should keep them asleep for a while at least. And when they wake, they'll be tied up. And we'll be gone,' Sanjit said. 'At least, I hope. The way it sounds, we'd better take some time to get food stowed away first. Which means a lot of climbing up and down and up and down.'

Virtue swallowed. 'You're actually going to do it?'

Sanjit's smile was gone. 'I'm going to try, Choo. That's all I can do.'

THIRTY FIVE

1 HOUR 27 MINUTES

SAM WAS FINALLY where he'd known all along he would end up. It had taken him all day to get there. The sun was already sinking towards the false horizon.

The Perdido Beach nuclear power plant was eerily silent. In the old days it had kept up a constant roar. Not from the actual nuclear reactor, but from the giant turbines that turned superheated steam into electricity.

Things were as he'd left them. A hole burned into the control room wall. Cars smashed here and there by Caine or by Dekka. All the evidence of the battle that had taken place a few short months ago.

He went in through the turbine room. The machines were big as houses, hunched, coiled metal monsters turned to so much scrap.

The control room, too, as Caine and he had left it. The door ripped from its hinges by Jack. Dried blood – Brittney's, most of it – formed a flaky brown crust on the polished floor.

The ancient computers were blank. The warning lights and indicator lights were all dead, except for a fading pool of illumination cast by a single functioning emergency beam. The battery would be exhausted soon.

No wonder Jack had refused to come back to this place. It wasn't fear of radiation. It was fear of ghosts. It hurt Jack deep down inside, Sam thought, to see machines rendered useless.

Sam's steps echoed softly as he walked. He knew where he was going, where he had to go.

There was a badge on a desk, one of the warning badges that changed colour when radiation levels were high. Sam picked it up, looked at it, not sure whether he cared.

Safe or not, he was going to the reactor.

Sunlight shone through the hole Caine had blown in the concrete containment vessel. But it was faint: sunset reflected off the mountains.

Sam raised his hand and formed a ball of light. It didn't reveal anything but shadows.

He reached the spot. Right here Drake had shown Sam that he could cause a chain reaction and kill every living thing in the FAYZ.

Right here Drake had named the price.

This was the floor where Sam had laid down and taken the beating.

Sam saw the wrapper of the morphine syringe that Brianna

had stuck into him. Here, too, the floor was coated in a flaky brown scum.

A noise! He spun, raised his hands and shot brilliant beams of light.

Something cracked. He fired again and swept the killing beam from left to right, slowly around the room, burning anything it touched.

A catwalk ladder crashed to the floor. A computer monitor exploded like a burned-out lightbulb.

Sam crouched, ready. Listening.

'If someone's there you'd better tell me,' he said to the shadows. 'Because I'll kill you.'

No voice spoke.

Sam formed a second light and tossed it high overhead. Now shadows crossed each other, cast by two competing lights.

Another light and another and another. He formed them with his will and hung them in the air like Japanese lanterns. He saw no one.

His beams had cut cables and melted instrument panels. But there were no bodies lying on the floor.

'A rat, probably,' he said.

He was shaking. The lights were still not enough, it was still too dark. And even if it were light, something could be hiding anywhere. Too many nooks and crannies, too many awkward machines providing possible concealment.

'A rat,' he said, without any conviction. 'Something.'

But not Drake.

No, Drake was in Perdido Beach, if in fact he was anywhere outside of Sam's overworked imagination.

The reactor chamber was only fractionally lighter than when he'd come in. He'd found nothing. He'd learned nothing.

'I blew the crap out of the place though,' he said.

And accomplished? Nothing.

Sam stuck one hand in the neck of his T-shirt. He touched the skin of his shoulder. He reached under his shirt and touched his chest and stomach. Reached around with both hands to run his fingers along his sides and back. New wounds, the still-fresh marks of Drake's whip. But worse was the memory of old wounds.

He was here. He was alive. He was hurt, yes, but his skin was not hanging in tatters.

And he was very definitely alive.

'Well,' Sam said. 'There's that.'

He had needed to come back to this place because this place filled him with terror. He had needed to take possession of this place. This very place where he had begged to die.

But had not died.

One by one he extinguished the Sammy Suns, until only the faint, indirect rays of sunset lit the room.

He stood for a moment, hoping he was saying goodbye to this place.

Sam turned and walked away, heading towards home.

Brittney woke up face down in the sand. For a terrible moment she thought she was underground again.

The Lord might ask anything of her, but please God, not that. Not that.

She rolled over, blinked her eyes and was surprised to see that the sun was still in the sky.

She was above the tide line, several body lengths from the thin lace of surf. Something, a soggy lump the size of a person, was between her and the water. Half in the surf, legs stretched on to dry land, like he'd been running into the ocean, tripped, and had drowned.

Brittney stood up. She brushed damp sand from her arms, but it stuck to the grey mud that coated her from head to toe.

'Tanner?'

Her brother was not near. She was alone. And now fear began to make her shake. Fear for the first time since she had emerged from the ground. It was a dark, soul-eating monster, this fear.

'What am I?' she asked.

She could not tear her gaze away from the body. She could not stop her feet from moving her closer. She had to see, even though she knew, deep inside knew, that what she would see would destroy her.

Brittney stood over the body. Looked down at it. Shirt torn to ribbons. Puffy lacerated flesh. The marks of a whip.

A terrible animal noise strangled Brittney's throat. She had been there, on the sand, unconscious when it happened. She'd been right there, just a few feet away when the demon had struck this poor boy.

'The demon,' Tanner said, appearing beside her.

'I have not stopped him, Tanner. I failed.'

Tanner said nothing and Brittney looked at him, pleading. 'What is happening to me, Tanner? What am I?'

'You are Brittney. An angel of the Lord.'

'What aren't you telling me? I know there's something. I can feel it. I know you're not telling me everything.'

Tanner did not smile. He did not answer.

'You're not real, Tanner. You're dead and buried. I'm imagining you.'

She looked at the damp sand. Two sets of footprints came to this place. Hers. And the poor boy in the surf. But there was a third set as well, not hers, not the boy's. And this set of footprints did not stretch back across the beach. It was only here. As if it belonged to someone who had materialised out of thin air and then disappeared.

When Tanner still said nothing, Brittney pleaded with him.

'Tell me the truth, Tanner. Tell me the truth.' Then, in a trembling whisper, 'Did I do this?'

'You are here to fight the demon,' Tanner said.

'How can I fight a demon when I don't know who or what he is, and when I don't even know what I am?'

'Be Brittney,' Tanner said. 'Brittney was good and brave and faithful. Brittney called on her saviour when she felt herself weaken.'

'Brittney was . . . You said Brittney *was*,' Brittney said.

'You asked for the truth.'

'I'm still dead, aren't I?' Brittney said.

'Brittney's soul is in heaven,' Tanner said. 'But you are here. And you will resist the demon.'

'I'm talking to an echo of my own mind,' Brittney said, not to Tanner, to herself. She knelt and put her hand on the wet, tousled head. 'Bless you, poor boy.'

She stood up. Faced the town. She would go there. She knew the demon would go there too.

Mary worked on the next week's schedule in her cramped little office. John stood in the doorway.

In the plaza they were starting to cook food. Mary smelled it, even through the omnipresent stink of pee and poop and finger paint and paste and filth.

Charred, crisping meat. She would need to gag some of it

down and do it publicly. Or everyone would look at her and point and whisper 'anorexic'.

Crazy. Unstable.

Mary's losing it.

No longer Mother Mary. Crazy Mary. Off-her-meds Mary. Or on-too-many-meds Mary. Everyone knew now, thanks to Astrid. They all knew. They all could picture it in their heads, Mary searching for Prozac and Zoloft like Gollum chasing the ring. Mary sticking her finger down her throat to vomit up food even while normal people were reduced to eating bugs.

And now they thought she'd been tricked by some fraud. Made a fool of by Orsay.

They thought she was suicidal. Or worse.

'Mary,' John said. 'Are you ready?'

He was so sweet, her little brother. Her lying little brother, so sweet and so concerned. Of course he was. He didn't want to get stuck taking care of all these kids alone.

'That food smells good, huh?' John asked.

It smelled like rancid grease. It smelled sickening.

'Yes,' Mary said.

'Mary.'

'What?' Mary snapped. 'What do you want from me?'

'I'm . . . Look, I'm sorry I lied. About Orsay.'

'The Prophetess, you mean.'

'I don't think she's a prophet,' John said, head hung down.

'Why, because she doesn't agree with Astrid? Because she doesn't think we just have to be trapped here?'

John moved closer. He put his hand on Mary's arm. She shook him off.

'You promised me, Mary,' John pleaded.

'And you lied to me,' Mary shot back.

There were tears in her brother's eyes. 'Your birthday, Mary. In an hour. You shouldn't be wasting time on the schedule, you should be getting ready. You have to promise me you won't leave me or these kids.'

'I already promised you,' Mary said. 'Are you calling me a liar?'

'Mary . . .' John pleaded, having run out of words.

'Get the kids ready to go outside,' Mary said. 'There's food being cooked. We have to get our share for the littles.'

THIRTY SIX

47 MINUTES

WORD HAD GONE out about the cookout. But it wasn't really necessary. The smell of food cooking was all that was necessary. Albert had arranged it all with his usual efficiency.

Astrid sat on the town hall steps. Little Pete sat a few steps behind her, playing his dead game like he was playing for his life.

Astrid swallowed, nervous. She smoothed the two sheets of paper in her hands. She kept crumpling them unconsciously and then, realising what she had done, straightening them out. She pulled a pen out of her back pocket, scratched out some words, rewrote them, scratched them out, and started the whole crumple and uncrumple pattern again.

Albert was nearby, watching the whole place, arms folded over his chest. He was, as usual, the neatest, cleanest, calmest, most focused person there. Astrid envied that about Albert: he set a goal and never seemed to suffer any doubt about it. Astrid was almost, but not quite, resentful of the way he had come to her and ordered her to quit feeling sorry for herself and get her act together.

But it had worked. She'd finally done what she needed to do. She hoped. She hadn't shown the results to anyone yet. People might just decide she was crazy. But she hoped not, because even after all the self-doubt, after all the abuse she'd endured, she still thought she was right. The FAYZ couldn't just be Albert making money and Sam kicking butts. The FAYZ needed rules and laws and rights.

People were coming, drawn by the smell of meat. Not a lot of it per person, Albert had made that clear, but in the aftermath of the fire, with many kids having lost their limited stocks of food, and with nothing coming in from the fields, the prospect of any food at all made stomachs rumble and mouths water.

Albert had guards ready, four of his own people armed with baseball bats, the default weapon of the FAYZ. And two of Edilio's guys, and Edilio himself, walked with guns slung over their shoulders.

The strange thing was how it no longer seemed strange to Astrid. A nine-year-old dressed in rags, sharing a bottle of Scotch with an eleven-year-old with a shaved head and a cape made out of an olive green bed sheet. Kids with sunken eyes. Kids with open sores, untreated, barely noticed. Boys wearing nothing but boxer shorts and boots. Girls wearing their mother's glittery formal gowns, shortened with rough scissor hacks.

A girl who had tried to remove her own braces with pliers and now couldn't close her mouth because of the jagged wire sticking through her front teeth.

And the weapons. Everywhere weapons. Knives, ranging from big chef's knives stuck in belts, to hunting knives in ornate leather sheaths. Crowbars. Pieces of pipe with taped handles and lanyards. Some had been even more creative. Astrid saw a seven-year-old carrying a wooden table leg to which he had glued big slivers of broken glass.

And it had all become normal.

In this plaza coyotes had attacked screaming, defenceless children. That had changed a lot of people's attitudes towards weapons.

But at the same time, girls carried dolls. Boys crammed action figures into their back pockets. Stained, torn, ratty comic books still stuck out of waistbands or were clutched in hands with nails as long and filthy as a wolf's. Kids pushed baby strollers loaded with their few possessions.

The kids of Perdido Beach were a mess at the best of times. But it was so much worse now in the aftermath of the fire. Kids were still black with soot or grey with ash.

Coughing was the background noise. The flu that had been going around was sure to spread through this crowd, Astrid thought grimly. Lungs damaged by smoke inhalation would be especially vulnerable.

But they were still alive, Astrid told herself. Against all the odds, more than ninety per cent of the kids first trapped in the FAYZ were still alive.

Mary led the preschoolers out of the day care into the plaza. Astrid looked closely. Mary seemed her normal self. She grabbed a little girl who was about to step in front of a boy on a skateboard.

Had she been wrong about Mary? Mary would never forgive her.

'Well, so what?' Astrid muttered wearily. 'It's not like I was ever popular.'

Then, Zil and a half dozen of his crew swaggered into the plaza from the far side. Astrid clenched her jaw. Would the crowd turn on them? She almost hoped so. People thought because she wouldn't let Sam go after Zil she must not really despise the Human Crew's Leader. That was wrong. She hated Zil. Hated everything he had done and everything he had tried to do.

Edilio moved quickly between Zil and a few of the boys who had started towards him, sticks and knives at the ready.

Zil's kids were armed with knives and bats, and so were those who wanted to take them on. Edilio was armed with an assault rifle.

Astrid hated that this was what life so often came down to: my weapon is bigger than your weapon.

If Sam were here it would be about his hands. Everyone had either seen what Sam could do, or heard the stories retold in vivid detail. No one challenged Sam.

'It's what makes him dangerous,' Astrid muttered to herself.

But it was also what had kept her alive on more than one occasion. Her and Little Pete.

She hated Sam for doing this, for just withdrawing like this. Disappearing. It was passive aggressive. Unworthy of him.

But another part was glad he was gone. If he were here it would be all about him. If Sam were here then every word Astrid spoke would be conditioned on what Sam would say or do. The kids would be watching his face for clues, waiting to see whether he nodded or laughed or smirked or gave them that cool, steely warning look he'd acquired over these last months.

Orc made his way into the crowd. People parted to let him pass. Astrid spotted Dekka, as always left alone by other kids so that she seemed to have a force field around her. The one person Astrid didn't see was Brianna. Brianna wasn't someone you missed or overlooked. She must still be too sick to go out.

'It's time,' Albert said over his shoulder.

'Now?' Astrid was surprised.

'Once we feed them they'll go off in separate directions. I got them here and behaving themselves because of food. Once the food is gone . . .'

'OK.' Astrid's heart was in her throat. She clenched her papers again and stood up too suddenly.

'Like Moses, huh?' Albert said.

'What?'

'Like Moses coming down off the mountain with the Ten Commandments,' Albert said.

'Those were written by God,' Astrid said. 'This wasn't.'

She tripped a little walking down the steps but caught herself. No one was paying particular attention as she entered the crowd. One or two kids called out greetings. Many more made rude or hostile remarks. Mostly kids were focused on the small fires, where venison and chunks of fish browned on skewers made of wire clothes hangers.

She reached the fountain, which was close enough to the cook fires that kids noticed when she climbed up and unfolded her papers.

'Everyone . . .' she began.

'Oh, puh-leeze, not some speech,' a voice heckled.

'I . . . I just have a few things to say. Before you can eat,' Astrid said.

A groan went up. One kid picked up a piece of dirt and tossed it with poor aim – and not too much commitment – at Astrid. Orc took two steps, brushing aside a couple of kids in the process, and made a low growling noise with his scary face right up against the kid's nose. That signalled the end of dirt throwing.

'Go ahead, Astrid,' Orc rumbled.

Astrid noticed Edilio hiding a smile. Back a million years ago, back in the old life, Astrid had tutored Orc.

'OK,' Astrid began. She took a deep breath, trying to calm herself down. 'I . . . OK. When the FAYZ came, all our lives changed. And ever since then all we've tried to do is get by, day to day. We've been lucky because some people worked very hard and took big risks to help us all make it.'

'Can we eat now?' a younger kid cried.

'And we've all been focused on getting by and focused on what we've lost. Now it's time to start working on the future. Because we're going to be here for a while. Maybe for the rest of our lives.'

That drew some very harsh words, but Astrid kept going.

'We need rules and laws and rights and all,' Astrid said. 'Because we need to have some justice and some peace.'

'I just want food,' a voice cried.

Astrid ploughed ahead. 'So, you'll all get to vote on this. But I've written down a list of laws. I kept it simple.'

'Yeah, because we're too stupid,' Howard said, suddenly just in front of her.

'No, Howard. If anyone was stupid, I was. I kept looking for some perfect system, something that wouldn't involve compromising anything.'

That got the attention of a few more kids.

'Well, there is no perfect system. So I wrote down an imperfect set of laws.'

'Rule number one: Each of us has the right to be free and to do whatever we want as long as nothing we do hurts anyone else.'

She waited. No heckling. Not even from Howard.

'Two: No one can hurt another person except in self-defence.'

Grudging attention was being paid. Not everyone. But some, and more as she continued.

'Three. No one can take another person's possessions.'

'Not that we have anything much to take,' Howard said, but was shushed.

'Four. We're all equal and have exactly the same rights. Freak or normal.'

Astrid saw the glint of anger on Zil's face. He was looking around himself, seeming to take the temperature of the crowd. She wondered if he would make a move now or wait for another opportunity.

'Five. Anyone who commits a crime – stealing or hurting someone – will be accused and then tried by a jury of six kids.'

Some of the crowd were losing interest again and beginning to cast sidelong glances at the food. But others waited patiently. Even respectfully.

'Six: lying to the jury is a crime. Seven: penalties can be

anything from a fine to getting locked up in a jail for a period of a month or more, to permanent exile from Perdido Beach.'

The crowd mostly liked this. There was some clowning around, kids pointing at each other, some shoving, mostly good-natured.

'Eight. We'll elect a new town council every six months. But the council cannot change these first nine rules.'

'Are we done, yet?' Howard asked.

'One more. The ninth rule,' Astrid said. 'And this is the one I have the most doubt about. I kind of hate the idea of this rule. But I can't see any way around it.' She glanced at Albert and then nodded at Quinn, who frowned and looked confused.

This, finally, got everyone's attention.

Astrid folded the paper and stuffed it into her pocket. 'Everyone has to live by these laws. Normal or freak. Regular citizen or member of the council. Except . . .'

'Except Sammy?' Howard supplied.

'No!' Astrid snapped. Then, more calmly, refusing to be provoked, 'No, not except Sam. Except in the event of an emergency. The council will have the right to suspend all other rules for a period of twenty-four hours if there's a major emergency. In that case the council can appoint a person, or several people, to act as Town Defenders.'

'Sammy,' Howard said. He laughed cynically.

Astrid ignored him and instead focused on Zil. 'And if you

think that's directed at you, Zil, you're welcome to think so.'

In a louder voice Astrid cried, 'You'll all get a chance to vote, but for now, temporarily, these rules will be the law as soon as a majority on the council says so.'

'I vote yes,' Albert said quickly.

'Me, too,' Edilio called out from somewhere in the crowd.

Howard rolled his eyes. He looked at Orc, who nodded his head yes. Howard sighed theatrically. 'Yeah, whatever.'

'OK, then,' Astrid said. 'With my vote that's four out of seven. So. These are the laws of Perdido Beach. The laws of the FAYZ.'

'Can we eat now?' Howard asked.

'One last thing,' Astrid said. 'I lied to people. And I got other people to lie. That's not against any of these rules, but it's still wrong. The result is that kids won't really trust me in the future. So I'm quitting the town council. Effective right now.'

Howard began an ironic slow clapping. Astrid laughed. It didn't even bother her. In fact, she felt like joining in herself. Like she could finally stand outside herself, see herself as shrill and controlling and faintly ridiculous.

Strangely, it made her feel better.

'Now, let's eat,' Astrid said. She hopped down from the fountain and actually felt lighter when she landed. Like she'd weighed five hundred pounds a minute ago and was now as light and nimble as a gymnast. She patted Howard on the shoulder and went to Albert, who was shaking his head slowly.

'Nice,' Albert said. 'You get to quit.'

'Yep. So now I guess I need a job, Albert,' Astrid said. 'You have any openings?'

THIRTY SEVEN

33 MINUTES

'I DIDN'T WET my bed or anything,' Justin said. 'At my house I mean.'

Mary ignored him. Instead she watched Astrid's performance. It made her bitter. Of course Astrid had found a way out of the hole she'd dug for herself. Smart, beautiful Astrid. It must be great to be Astrid. It must be great to have so much confidence that you could just stand up there handing out a set of rules and then blithely walk away, with your pretty blonde head held high.

'Can I go see Roger after we eat?'

'Whatever,' Mary said. She'd be out of it all soon. Done with this awful place and these awful people. She'd sit outside with her mother and tell her stories about it.

Astrid was lining up now for barbecue. Astrid and Little Pete together. Kids were clapping her on the back. Grinning at her. Liking her more than they had in the past. Why? Because she had admitted she had screwed up and then she'd quit and left them with a new set of rules to follow.

In her own way Astrid had taken the poof, Mary thought.

How many minutes left until Mary had her own chance at escape? She pulled Francis's watch from her pocket. Half an hour.

After all the worry and anticipation it still seemed to rush up at her, the time.

John was looking at her now, even as he herded the kids towards the front of the food line. Looking at her. Expecting something from her. Just like everyone else.

Mary should go stand in the food line herself, of course, show Astrid up as a liar for calling her anorexic.

But really, what did Mary have to prove to anyone?

She ignored John's wave, ignored kids around her, and headed back into the day care.

It was quiet and empty.

This place had been her whole life since the FAYZ. Her whole life. This messy, stinking, gloomy hole. She stared at it. Hated it. Hated herself for letting this define her.

She didn't hear anyone behind her. But she felt it.

The back of her neck tingled.

Mary turned. There. Behind the milky translucent plastic that covered the jagged hole between the day care and the hardware. A shape. A form.

Mary's mouth was dry. Her heart pounded.

'Where are they, Mary?' Drake asked. 'Where are the snot-nosed little monsters?'

'No,' Mary whispered.

Drake looked at the edges of the cinderblock with detached interest. 'This was clever, the way Sam did this. Burned right through the wall. I didn't see it coming.'

'You're dead,' Mary said.

Drake snapped his whip hand. The plastic was sliced from top to bottom.

He stepped through. Into the room where he and the coyotes had threatened to kill the children.

Drake. No one else. No one else had those eyes. No one else had that python arm the colour of dried blood.

He was dirty, that was the only difference. His face was smeared with mud. Mud was in his hair. Mud was on his clothes.

The whip writhed and curled like it had a life of its own.

'Get out of here,' Mary whispered.

What happened if she died here in the FAYZ? No. She had to get away. And she had to save the children.

Had to. No other choice. She'd been a fool even to think of any other choice.

'I think I'll wait for the kiddies to come back,' Drake said. He grinned his wolf's grin and Mary could see mud in his teeth. 'I think it's time to finish what I started.'

Mary wet herself then. She could feel it. But she could not stop it.

'Go,' Drake said. 'Go get them. Bring them here.'

Mary shook her head slowly, her muscles watery and weak.

'Go!' Drake roared.

The whip hand lashed out. The tip drew a line of fire on her cheek and she ran from the room.

Zil was frozen with indecision. Astrid had directly threatened him. The Ninth Law? She hadn't even pretended it wasn't about him. She had turned her icy blue eyes on him and threatened him. Astrid! That treasonous, freak-loving girl!

And now? Astrid had laid down the law and laid out her threat and now everyone was eating fish and venison and actually talking about Astrid's laws.

Yesterday Zil had burned down a big piece of the town. The result was supposed to be chaos. But now Albert was dishing out meat and Astrid was dishing out laws and it was as if Zil had done nothing, as if he was not someone to be feared and respected.

Like he was nobody.

Threatened! And once Sam decided to reappear . . .

'Leader, maybe we'd better get back to the compound,' Lance suggested.

Zil stared at him in amazement. Lance was suggesting they

slink away? Things must be as bad as Zil feared if even Lance was scared.

'No,' Turk argued, but not very loudly, or very forcibly. 'If we run away, we're done for. We'll just be waiting there for Sam to come around and finish us off.'

'He's right,' a girl's voice said.

Zil spun around and saw a dark-haired girl, a pretty girl, but not someone he knew. Not Human Crew. The thing to do was tell her to take off, stop presuming to speak to him. He was the Leader. But there was something about her . . .

'Who are you?' Zil asked, eyes narrowed, suspicious.

'My name is Nerezza,' she said.

'Weird name,' Turk commented.

'Yes, it is,' Nerezza allowed. She smiled. 'It's Italian. It means darkness.'

Lisa was standing behind Nerezza. Zil could see them both. The contrast did not work to Lisa's benefit. Nerezza was more beautiful the longer you looked at her.

'Darkness,' Zil said.

'We have that in common,' Nerezza said.

'You know what Zil means?' Zil asked, amazed.

'I know what darkness is,' Nerezza said. 'And I know that its time is coming.'

Zil remembered to breathe. 'I don't understand.'

'It will begin very soon,' Nerezza said. 'Send this one' –

she nodded at Lance – 'to bring your weapons.'

'Go,' Zil ordered Lance.

Nerezza tilted her head a little and looked at Zil curiously. 'Are you ready to do what has to be done?'

'What has to be done?' Zil asked.

'Killing,' Nerezza said. 'There must be killing. It's not enough to build a fire. The bodies must be fed into the flame.'

'Only the freaks,' Zil said.

Nerezza laughed. 'Tell yourself whatever makes you happy,' she said. 'The game is chaos and destruction, Zil. Play it to win.'

Edilio saw Nerezza with Zil. He couldn't hear what they were saying. But he could read body language.

Something was wrong there.

Zil rapt. Nerezza flirting just a little.

Where was Orsay? He'd never seen Nerezza without Orsay. They'd been inseparable.

Lance went tearing off in the direction of Zil's compound.

Edilio glanced at Astrid, but she was paying no attention. Her little brother had a piece of fish in one hand and his game player in the other.

Little Pete stared at him, as if he'd never seen Edilio before and was surprised by what he saw now. Little Pete blinked once. He frowned. He dropped the last of his fish and went instantly back to his game.

There was a scream. It cut through the chatter and drone of a crowd of kids eating.

Edilio's head snapped around.

Mary was running from the day care. Screaming a word, a name.

'Drake! Drake!'

She tripped and sprawled face down on the concrete. She rose to her knees and held up scraped, bloody palms.

Edilio raced towards her, none-too-gently pushing wandering kids out of the way.

There was a bright red line on Mary's face. Magic marker? Paint?

Blood.

'Drake! He's in the day care!' Mary screamed as Edilio reached her. He didn't even slow down but leaped past her, swinging his gun into firing position as he ran.

Someone coming out of the day care. Edilio slowed, raised his weapon, aimed. He would give Drake one chance to surrender. He'd give him to the count of three. And then he would squeeze the trigger.

Brittney!

Edilio lowered the gun. Stared in confusion. Had Mary just lost it? Mistaken a dead girl for a dead monster?

'Is Drake inside there?' Edilio demanded.

Brittney frowned in confusion.

'Is Drake in there? Is he in there? Tell me!'

'The demon is not in there,' Brittney said. 'But he is near. I can feel him.'

Edilio shuddered. Her braces were still flecked with mud and tiny fragments of gravel.

He pushed past her and stopped at the day care door. He heard two of his soldiers rushing up behind him.

'Stay back unless I call you,' Edilio said. He shouldered through the doorway and swung the barrel of the gun left and right.

Nothing. Empty.

Mary had seen a ghost. Or more likely she was losing it, just like Astrid had said. Too much stress, too many problems, no relief.

Losing it.

Edilio let go of a shaky breath. He lowered the weapon. His finger was trembling on the trigger. Carefully he unclenched and rested his finger against the trigger guard.

Then he saw the plastic sheet, sliced straight down the middle.

'Mary,' Nerezza said. 'Terrible things will happen here, and soon.'

Mary stared past her. Eyes searching the crowd. She saw Edilio emerge from the day care. He looked like he'd seen a ghost.

'The demon is coming,' Nerezza said insistently. 'All will burn. All will be destroyed. You must take the children to safety!'

Mary shook her head helplessly. 'I only have . . . I'm almost out of time.'

Nerezza put a hand on her shoulder. 'Mary. You will soon be free. You will be in the loving arms of your mother.'

'Please,' Mary pleaded.

'But you have one last great service left to perform. Mary: you must not leave the children behind to the madness that is coming!'

'What am I supposed to do?'

'Lead them now to the Prophetess. She waits in her place. Take the children there. To the cliff above the beach.'

Mary hesitated. 'But . . . I have no food for them there. I won't have diapers . . . I won't . . .'

'Everything you need will be there. Trust the Prophetess, Mary. Believe in her.'

Mary heard a terrible scream. A wailing sound of terror that shifted to agony. From the far side of the plaza, out of view.

Children were running. Panicked.

'The FAYZ for humans!' Zil shouted.

A gun went off. Mary could see the littles cowering, terrified.

'Children!' Mary commanded. 'Come with me. Follow me!'

Children who had lost parents and grandparents, who had

lost friends and school and church. Who had been abandoned, neglected, starved, and terrorised had learned to trust only one voice: Mother Mary.

'Come with me, children!'

The children rushed to her. And Mary, a stumbling shepherd, led them away from the plaza towards the beach.

Brittney had come to the plaza, drawn there not by the smell of food, or by the crowd, but by a force she didn't understand.

Now she saw children running and screaming.

'Is it the demon?' she asked her angel brother.

'Yes,' Tanner answered. 'You are.'

Brittney saw children running. Running. From her?

She saw Edilio, his face a mask of dread, coming out of the day care, coming towards her. He was staring at her, eyes wide, the whites visible all around.

She did not understand why he should be afraid of her. She was an angel of the Lord. She had been sent to fight the demon.

But now she found herself unable to move. Unable to will her limbs to walk where she wanted, unable to look where she wanted to look. It was so like being dead, she thought, memories of cold earth in her ears and mouth.

Edilio took aim at her.

No, she wanted to say. No. But the word would not come.

'Drake,' Edilio said.

He was going to shoot her. Would it hurt? Would she die? Again?

But a mob of fleeing children rushed between them. Edilio raised the gun skyward.

'Run,' Tanner urged her.

She ran. But it was hard to run when her arm was growing so long and her consciousness was shrivelling as another mind shoved hers aside.

Astrid saw and heard the panic.

Saw the littles running with Mary, a panicky gaggle of stumbling, screaming preschoolers, babies in the arms of Mary's helpers, all racing from the square towards the beach.

In a flash too many images to process.

Zil, with a shotgun in his hands, aiming it in the air.

Edilio just emerging from the day care.

Nerezza smiling calmly.

And Brittney, from behind, facing away from Astrid.

Little Pete playing his game with feverish intensity. Fingers frantic. Like he had never played before.

And then, Nerezza moving quickly, straight towards Astrid, determined. She had something in her hand, a crowbar.

Was Nerezza going to attack her?

Insane!

Nerezza raised the crowbar and brought it down with sudden, shocking force.

Little Pete toppled forwards on to his game without making a sound.

Nerezza bent over and yanked Little Pete on to his back.

Astrid cried, 'No!' But Nerezza didn't seem to hear her. She raised the crowbar again, this time aiming the pointed end at Little Pete.

Astrid stuck out a hand, too slow, too clumsy. The crowbar came down hard on Astrid's wrist.

The pain was shocking. Astrid screamed in pain and fury. But Nerezza had no interest in her, pushed at her with her free hand like she was a minor irritation. And once again aimed the crowbar at Little Pete. But this time Nerezza was off-balance and her blow went wild. The crowbar stabbed the dirt beside Little Pete's head.

Astrid was up and shoved Nerezza back a step.

'Stop it!' Astrid cried.

But Nerezza wasn't going to stop. And she wasn't going to be distracted. She was after Little Pete with fanatic focus.

Astrid punched her as hard as she could. Her fist connected with Nerezza's collar bone, not her face. Not enough to hurt the dark girl, but enough to once again throw off her aim.

Now at last Nerezza turned with icy rage on Astrid.

'Fine. You want to go first?' Nerezza slashed horizontally with the crowbar and hit Astrid in the stomach. Astrid doubled over but rushed at Nerezza, head down like a bull, blinded by pain.

She hit Nerezza squarely and knocked her on her back. The crowbar flew from Nerezza's grip and landed in the trampled grass.

Nerezza, quick, squirmed to grab it. Astrid punched her in the back of the head. Then again and again, but Nerezza's hand was nevertheless just inches from the crowbar.

Astrid hauled herself along Nerezza's back, her weight slowing the girl down. Astrid did all she could think to do: she bit Nerezza's ear.

Nerezza's howl of pain was the most satisfying thing Astrid had ever heard.

She clamped her jaw together as hard as she could, yanked her head back and forth, ripping at the ear, tasting blood in her mouth and pounding with her fists at the back of Nerezza's head.

Nerezza's hand closed on the crowbar, but she couldn't reach behind herself to get Astrid. She stabbed blindly with the edged end of the tool, grazing Astrid's forehead, but not dislodging her.

Astrid wrapped her fingers around Nerezza's throat and squeezed, now releasing the ear, spitting something squirmy out of her mouth, and put all her strength into squeezing Nerezza's windpipe.

She felt the pulse in Nerezza's neck.

And she squeezed.

THIRTY EIGHT

32 MINUTES

SANJIT AND VIRTUE carried Bowie on a makeshift stretcher that was nothing but a sheet stretched between them.

'What are we doing?' Peace asked, twisting her hands together anxiously.

'We are fleeing,' Sanjit said.

'What's that?'

'Fleeing? Oh, it's something I've done a few times in my life,' Sanjit said. 'It's all about fighting or fleeing. You don't want to fight, do you?'

'I'm scared,' Peace moaned.

'No reason to be scared,' Sanjit said as he struggled to hold the sheet ends in his fingers while walking backwardss towards the cliff. 'Look at Choo. He doesn't look scared, does he?'

Actually Virtue looked scared to death. But Sanjit didn't need Peace losing her head. The scary part was still ahead. Scary had only just begun.

'No?' Peace said doubtfully.

'Are we running away?' Pixie asked. She had a plastic bag of Lego in her hand, no idea why, but she seemed determined to hold on to them.

'Well, we're hoping to fly away, actually,' Sanjit said brightly.

'We're going on the helichopper?' Pixie asked.

Sanjit exchanged a look with Virtue, who was struggling along much like Sanjit, legs wobbly, feet tripping in the long grass.

'Why are we running?' Bowie moaned.

'He's awake,' Sanjit said.

'You think?' Virtue snapped between gasps for air.

'How do you feel, little dude?' Sanjit asked him.

'My head hurts,' Bowie said. 'And I want some water.'

'Good timing,' Sanjit muttered.

They had reached the edge of the cliff. The rope was still where he and Virtue had left it the other day. 'OK, Choo, you go down first. I'll lower the kids down to you one by one.'

'I'm scared,' Peace said.

Sanjit lowered Bowie to the ground and flexed his cramped fingers. 'OK, listen up, all of you.'

They did. Somewhat to Sanjit's surprise. 'Listen: we're all scared, OK? So no one needs to keep reminding me. You're scared, I'm scared, we're all scared.'

'You're scared, too?' Peace asked him.

'Peeless,' Sanjit said. 'But sometimes life gets tough and

scary, OK? We've all been scary places before. But here we are, right? We're all still here.'

'I want to stay here,' Pixie said. 'I can't leave my dolls.'

'We'll come back for them another time,' Sanjit said.

He knelt down, wasting precious seconds, waiting for the cold-eyed mutant creep Caine to step out of the house any moment. 'Kids. We are a family, right? And we stick together, right?'

No one seemed too sure of that.

'And we survive together, right?' Sanjit pressed.

Long silence. Long stares.

'That's right,' Virtue said at last. 'Don't worry, you guys. It's going to be OK.'

He almost seemed to believe it.

Sanjit wished he did.

Astrid could feel the arteries and veins and tendons in Nerezza's neck. She could feel the way the blood hammered trying to reach Nerezza's brain. The way the muscles twisted.

She felt Nerezza's windpipe convulsing. Her entire body was jerking now, a wild spasm, organs frantic for oxygen, nerves twitching as Nerezza's brain sent out frantic panic signals.

Astrid's hands squeezed. Her fingers dug in, like she was trying to form fists and Nerezza's neck was just kind of in the way and if she just squeezed hard enough –

'No!' Astrid gasped.

She released. She stood up fast, backed away, stared in horror at Nerezza as the girl choked and sucked air.

They were almost alone in the plaza. Mary had led the littles away at a run, and it had signalled a full-fledged panic that drew almost everyone in her wake. Everyone was pelting towards the beach. Astrid saw their backs as they ran.

And then she saw the unmistakable silhouette that sauntered after them.

He might almost have been anyone, any tall, thin boy. If not for the whip that curled in the air and wrapped caressingly around his body and uncurled to snap and crack.

Drake laughed.

Nerezza sucked air. Little Pete stirred.

Gunfire, a single loud round.

The sun was setting out over the water. A red sunset.

Astrid stepped over Nerezza and turned her brother over. He moaned. His eyes fluttered open. His hand was already reaching for the game player.

Astrid picked it up. It was warm in her hand. A pleasurable sensation tingled her arm.

Astrid grabbed the front of Little Pete's shirt in her sore fist.

'What is the game, Petey?' she demanded.

She could see his eyes glaze over. The veil that separated Little Pete from the world around him.

'No!' she screamed, her face inches from his. 'Not this time. Tell me. Tell me!'

Little Pete looked at her and met her gaze. Aware. But still, he said nothing.

A waste of time demanding Little Pete use words. Words were her tool, not his. Astrid lowered her voice. 'Petey. Show me. I know you have the power. *Show* me.'

Little Pete's eyes widened. Something clicked beneath that blank stare.

The ground split open beneath Astrid. The dirt was a mouth. She cried out and fell, spinning downwards, down a tunnel in mud lit by neon screams.

Diana opened one eye. What she saw before her was a wooden surface. A spilled Cheerio was the closest recognisable object.

Where was she?

She closed her eye and asked herself that question again. Where am I?

She'd had a horrible dream, full of gruesome detail. Violence. Starvation. Despair. In the dream she had done things she would never, ever do in real life.

She opened her eyes again and tried to stand up. She fell backwards a very, very long way. She barely felt the floor when it smacked her in the back of the head.

Now she saw legs. Table legs, chair legs, the legs of a boy

wearing frayed jeans and beyond the splayed, scarred legs of a girl in shorts. Both sets of legs were tied with rope.

Someone was snoring. Someone too close. A snore from an unseen source.

Bug. The name came to her. And with it the shock of knowing that she was not dreaming, had not dreamed.

Better to close her eyes and pretend.

But the girl, Penny, her legs strained against their ropes. Diana heard a moan.

With clumsy hands Diana grabbed the chair and pulled herself up into a seated position. The urge to lie back down was almost irresistible. But hand over hand, and then numb foot over numb foot, Diana pulled herself back up and into the chair.

Caine slept. Bug snored loudly and invisibly on the floor.

Penny blinked at her. 'They drugged us,' Penny said. She yawned.

'Yeah,' Diana agreed.

'They tied us up,' Penny said. 'How did you get free?'

Diana rubbed her wrists, as though she had been tied up. Why hadn't Sanjit tied her? 'Loose knots.'

Penny's head wobbled a little. Her eyes wouldn't quite focus. 'Caine's going to kill 'em.'

Diana nodded. She tried to think. Not easy in a brain still slowed by whatever drug Sanjit had slipped her.

'They could have killed us,' Diana said.

Penny nodded. 'Too scared,' she said.

Or maybe they just aren't killers, Diana thought. Maybe they just weren't the kind of people who could take advantage of a sleeping foe. Maybe Sanjit wasn't the kind of kid who could cut a sleeping person's throat.

'They're running,' Diana said. 'They're trying to get away.'

'Never hide on this island,' Penny said. 'Not for long. We'll find them. Cut me loose.'

Penny was right, of course. Even drugged Diana knew it was true. Caine would find them eventually. And he *was* the kind who killed.

Her true love. He was not the beast Drake was, but something worse. Caine wouldn't kill them in some psychotic rage. He'd kill them in cold blood. Diana staggered out of the room, moving like a drunk, slamming into a doorway, absorbing the pain, moving on. Windows. Big windows in a room so huge it made the furniture arranged here and there in separate pods look like doll's house toys.

'Hey, untie me!' Penny demanded.

She spotted Sanjit immediately. He was in profile against a red sky, standing at the edge of the cliff. There was a little girl with him. Not Virtue, some girl Diana had not seen before.

That's what Sanjit had been hiding: there were other kids here on the island.

Sanjit looped a rope around the girl in a sort of web.

He hugged her. Leaned down to speak to her face-to-face.

No, not the killing kind, Sanjit.

Then he began to lower the clearly terrified girl out of sight. Over the cliff.

There was a shout from the other room. Bug. He yelled, 'Ah ah ah ah! Get them off me!'

Bug was awake. Penny had used her power to give Bug a nice shot of fear adrenalin.

As Diana watched, Sanjit himself climbed over the side. He faced the house as he did so. Did he see Diana standing there, watching?

Diana heard Penny coming into the room, at least as wobbly as Diana herself.

'You stupid witch,' Penny snarled. 'Why didn't you untie me?'

'Bug seems to have taken care of that,' Diana answered.

She had to cut Penny off before she saw what was happening. Before she saw Sanjit.

Diana picked up a vase from a side table. Very pretty crystal. Heavy.

'This is nice,' Diana said to Penny.

Penny looked at her like she was crazy. Then Penny's eyes focused beyond Diana. Out of the window.

'Hey!' Penny said. 'They're trying –'

Diana swung the vase and caught Penny on the side of the

head. She didn't wait to see the effect but staggered, vase still in hand, to the kitchen.

Caine was still asleep. But he wouldn't be for long, maybe, not long enough. Penny's power of hallucination could wake the dead. She would send terrors into Caine's dreams and wake him as she had Bug.

Diana raised the vase over her head. It occurred to her in a moment of wry clarity that while Sanjit might not be the kind of person who would brain someone in their sleep, she apparently was.

But before she could smash the vase down on her true love's head, Diana's flesh erupted. Gaping red mouths appeared on her arms, gnashing with serrated shark's teeth. The mouths were eating her alive.

Diana screamed.

In some corner of her mind she knew it was Penny. She knew it wasn't real, because she saw the mouths but did not feel them, not really, but she screamed and screamed and her fingers let go of the vase. From far off came the sound of shattered crystal.

The red mouths were crawling up her arms, eating her skin, baring muscle and sinew, eating their way to her shoulders.

And then they stopped.

Penny stood there, snarling. Blood streamed from the side of her head. 'Don't mess with me, Diana,' Penny said.

'I could send you screaming off that cliff yourself.'

'Let them go,' Diana whispered. 'They're just nice kids. They're just nice kids.'

'Not like us, you mean,' Penny said. 'You're a stupid idiot, Diana.'

'Let them go. Don't wake Caine up. You know what he'll do.'

Penny shook her head, disbelieving. 'I can't believe he likes you, not me. You're not even pretty. Not any more.'

Diana laughed. 'That's what you want? Him?'

Penny's eyes gave it all away. She looked longingly, lovingly at Caine, still passed out. 'He's all there is,' she said.

Penny reached with a trembling hand and gently stroked Caine's hair. 'Sorry to have to do this, sweetheart,' Penny said.

Caine woke shouting.

THIRTY NINE

29 MINUTES

ASTRID FELL AND fell knowing it wasn't real, knowing it was all an illusion of some kind. But it was very hard to believe that when her clothing rippled and her hair flew straight up and her arms were reaching for the walls of a tunnel that couldn't possibly be real but seemed like it was.

But after a while falling began to feel like floating. She was suspended in the air and things no longer streamed past; they floated around.

Symbols, Astrid thought.

She was relieved to see that her brain still worked. Whatever was happening, whatever power was giving her this intense waking dream, it wasn't frying her brain. Reason intact. Words right there where she had left them.

Symbols. Neon symbols arrayed across a dark landscape.

Not even symbols, she realised: avatars.

There was a monstrous face framed with long dark hair that formed snakes. Dark eyes and a mouth that dribbled fire.

There was a female being with orange rays, like sunset beams spraying out of her head.

A male with a hand held up and a green light formed in a ball. This avatar was far away, at the edge of the dark playing field.

One avatar was neither male nor female but half of each sex. Metal teeth and a whip.

Nerezza. Orsay. Sam. But what was the fourth avatar?

It was this fourth avatar that seemed to be in contention between two manipulators, two players. One player was represented by a box. The box was closed but for one edge that shone so bright it was hard to look at. Like a toy box containing a sun.

Petey, Astrid whispered.

The other player she felt rather than saw. She tried to turn her eyes towards it, to see it, but it was always just out of range. And she realised that the light box was restraining her, not allowing her to see the opponent.

For her own good. Protecting her.

Petey would not let her look at the gaiaphage.

Astrid's mind flooded with images of other shadow avatars. Dark avatars. Dead. Victims in the game.

All of these were in neat little rows, like pawns lined up before the soul-killing emptiness that was the gaiaphage.

'Astrid!'

Someone was yelling her name.

'Astrid! Snap out of it!'

The game field disappeared.

Astrid's eyes saw the plaza, her brother just getting to his feet, and Brianna shaking her roughly.

'Hey, what's the matter with you?' Brianna demanded, more angry than concerned.

Astrid ignored Brianna and searched for Nerezza. She was nowhere to be seen.

'The girl, there was a girl here,' Astrid said.

'What's going on, Astrid? I just –' She stopped talking long enough to cough ten, twelve times in startlingly rapid succession. 'I just stopped Lance from beating some kid half to death. People all running around like nuts down on the beach. I mean, jeez, I take a day off to get over this stupid flu and suddenly it's craziness everywhere!'

Astrid blinked, looked around, tried to make sense of way too much information. 'It's the game,' she said. 'It's the gaiaphage. It reached Petey through his game.'

'Say what?'

Astrid knew she'd said too much. Brianna was not the person to trust with the truth about Little Pete. 'Did you see Nerezza?'

'What? The girl who hangs out with Orsay?'

'She's not a girl,' Astrid said. 'Not really.' She grabbed Brianna's arm. 'Find Sam. We need him. Find him!'

'OK. Where?'

'I don't know,' Astrid cried. She bit her lip. 'Look everywhere!'

'Hey,' Brianna said, and then interrupted herself to cough until she was red in the face. She cursed, coughed some more, and finally said, 'Hey, I'm fast. But even I can't look everywhere.'

'Let me think for a minute,' Astrid said. She squeezed her eyes shut. Where? Where would Sam have gone? He was hurt, angry, feeling useless.

No, that wasn't quite right.

'Oh, God, where?' Astrid wondered.

She hadn't seen him since he had gone off to deal with Zil and the fire. What had happened to make him run away? Had he done something he was ashamed of?

No, that wasn't it, either. He had seen the whipped boy.

'The power plant,' Astrid said.

'Why would he be there?' Brianna frowned.

'Because it's the place that scares him most,' Astrid said.

Brianna looked doubtful. But then her frown lines relaxed. 'Yeah,' she said. 'That would be Sam.'

'You have to get him, Brianna. He's Petey's best piece.'

'Ummmm . . . what?'

'Never mind,' Astrid snapped. 'Get Sam here. Now!'

'How?'

'Hey, you're the Breeze, right? Just do it!'

Brianna considered that for a moment. 'Yeah, OK. I'm outta –'

The 'here' was lost in the wind.

Astrid handed the game player to her brother. He looked down at the ground, oblivious. He felt the game player for a moment, then dropped it.

'You have to keep playing, Petey.'

Her brother shook his head. 'I lost.'

'Petey, listen to me.' Astrid knelt before him, held him, then thought better of it and let him go. 'I saw the game. You showed me the game. I was inside it. But it's real, Petey. It's real.'

Little Pete stared past her. Not interested. Not even seeing her, maybe, let alone hearing her.

'Petey. He's trying to destroy us. You have to play.'

She shoved the game at him. 'Nerezza is the gaiaphage's avatar. You made her real. You gave her a body. Only you have that kind of power. It's using you, Petey, it's using you to kill.'

But if Little Pete cared, or even understood, he showed no sign of it.

It was a panic run. Most of the population of Perdido Beach, all running and no one knowing quite why. Or maybe they all knew why but each had his own reason.

Zil loved it. Here at last was the total blind panic he'd hoped would result from the fires. Here was all order breaking down completely.

Kids on the beach stumbled in the sand. Some ran screaming into the water.

Drake, alive. Drake with his whip hand lashing at them, like he was driving cattle into the sea.

More kids sticking to the road, running parallel to the beach. Zil was with them, running with Turk beside him, looking for the freaks, seeing a kid whose only mutant power was the ability to glow brightly, harmless, but a freak and like all freaks he had to be dealt with.

Turk pulled up, raised his shotgun, aimed and fired. He missed, but the kid panicked and smashed face down against the kerb. Zil kicked him and kept running. He shouted in wild glee as he ran.

'Run, freaks! Run!'

But there were very few freaks in the mass of kids on the road. Too few real targets. But that was OK because the point right now was fear, fear and chaos.

Nerezza had told him it was coming. A freak herself? Zil wondered. He would hate to have to kill her, she was hot and mysterious and so much better than boring, pasty Lisa.

He spotted Lance ahead. Good old Lance, but he had lost his gun and his bat.

'I need a weapon!' Lance cried. 'Give me something!'

Turk had a nail-studded stick. He tossed it to Lance. They took off again, a pack of wolves chasing down a terrified herd of cattle.

The older kids were pulling away. But the fat ones, the young ones, they were falling behind, worn out or simply unable to keep up on shorter legs.

They were all crammed on to the curved road that led to Clifftop.

Zil pointed. 'That kid there. There! He's a freak lover!'

Lance got there first and swung the nailed stick. The kid evaded it and hared off the road, tumbling down the slope into bushes and coming to rest against a cactus.

Zil laughed and pointed. 'He's yours, Turk!'

And Zil was off again, with Lance at his side, Lance like a blond warrior god, like Thor, slashing away at everyone now, no longer differentiating between freak or non-freak, they could all die, all of them who had refused to join Zil. 'Run!' Zil screamed. 'Run, you cowards! Join me, or run for your lives!'

He paused for a minute, winded from running uphill. Lance stopped beside him. Others, half a dozen of them, the Human Crew faithful, each of them a human hero, Zil thought fiercely.

Then Lance's grin fell. He pointed. Back down the road they had just climbed.

Dekka, walking, but fast just the same.

Relentless.

Someone was beside Zil. He could sense her. Nerezza. He looked at her. Her throat was red, like the first stage of serious bruising. There was a cut on her forehead. Her eyes were bloodshot and her hair was all astray.

'Who did that to you?' Zil demanded, outraged.

Nerezza ignored him. 'She has to be stopped.'

'Who?' Zil jerked his chin towards Dekka. 'Her? How am I supposed to stop *her*?'

'Her powers don't reach as far as your gun, Zil,' Nerezza said.

Zil frowned. 'Are you sure?'

'I am.'

'How do you know? Are you a freak?'

Nerezza laughed. 'What am I? What are you, Zil? Are you the Leader? Or are you a coward who hides from some fat, black lesbian freak? Because right now you choose which to be.'

Lance glanced nervously at Zil. Turk started to say something but couldn't seem to find the right words.

'She has to be stopped,' Nerezza said.

'Why?' Zil asked.

'Because we're going to need gravity, *Leader*.'

Mary reached the top of the road, up to Clifftop. A series of smaller pathways led down to the cliff itself.

She looked back to check on her charges and saw the whole population of Perdido Beach seemingly following her.

Kids were spread all down the road, some running, some wheezing and gasping for breath. At the back of the crowd Zil and a handful of gun-toting thugs.

Farther off, kids who had fled to the beach were being herded back on to the road.

This second group fled from a different terror. From where she stood Mary could too clearly see Drake, driving terrified kids before him. Some were in the water. Others tried to climb over the breakwater and the rocks that separated Perdido's main beach from the smaller beach beneath Clifftop.

As the Prophetess had said. The tribulation of fire. The demon. And the red sunset in which Mary would lay down her burden.

Mary cried, 'Come with me, children, stay with me!'

And they did.

They followed her across the overgrown, formerly manicured grounds of Clifftop. To the cliff. To the very edge of the cliff, with the blank, inscrutable FAYZ wall just to their left, the end of their particular world.

Down below on the beach, Orsay sat cross-legged on the rock that had become her pulpit. Some kids had already reached her and gathered, terrified, around her. Others were scrambling down the cliff to her.

The sun set in a blaze of red.

Orsay sat very still on her rock. She seemed not to be moving a muscle. Her eyes were closed.

Below her stood Jill, the Siren, seeming lost, scared, a wobbly silhouette against the light show in the west.

'Are we going down to the beach, Mother Mary?' a little girl asked.

'I didn't bring my baving suit,' another said.

It was just minutes away now, Mary knew. Her fifteenth birthday. Her Mother's Day birthday.

She glanced at her watch.

She should be troubled, she knew, afraid. But for the first time in so very, very long Mary was at peace. The children's questions didn't reach her. The concerned, anxious, upturned faces were far away. Everything was finally going to be OK.

The Prophetess did not stir. She sat so calmly, unmoved by the madness around her, indifferent to cries and pleas and demands.

The Prophetess has seen that we will all suffer a time of terrible tribulation. This will come very soon. And then, Mary, then will come the demon and the angel. And in a red sunset we will be delivered.

Orsay's prophecy, as told to Mary by Nerezza.

Yes, Mary thought. *She truly is the Prophetess.*

'I can climb down to the beach,' Justin said bravely. 'I'm not scared.'

'No need,' Mary said. She ruffled his head affectionately. 'We'll fly down.'

FORTY

16 MINUTES

THE CLIMB DOWN to the yacht, the *Fly Boy Too*, had been enough to take a year off Sanjit's life. Twice he'd almost dropped Bowie. Pixie had banged her head and started crying. And Pixie could do some serious howling.

Peace had been peaceful, but fretful. Which was normal enough under the circumstances.

And then had come the part about getting them up on to the yacht. Easier than getting down the cliff, but still not a day at the beach.

Man, wouldn't a day at the beach be great? Sanjit wondered as he and Virtue shepherded the kids aft towards the helicopter.

A day at the beach. That would be so much better than glancing up at that looming cliff and knowing he was getting ready to fly them all straight into it. Assuming he even got the helicopter up off the helipad.

Most likely he wouldn't make it far enough to worry about

killing everyone on the cliff. More likely he'd get just enough altitude to plunge into the sea.

No point thinking about it. There was no staying here now. Not even if he set aside his worries about Bowie. He'd seen what Caine could do.

He had to get the kids off the island. Away from Caine. Virtue said there was something deep-down evil about Caine. Sanjit had seen Caine's eyes when he had talked back to him.

Sanjit wondered if Diana was right, that Virtue had some kind of mutant power to judge people. More likely he was just judgmental.

But Virtue had been right talking about evil coming. Caine had been within a heartbeat of smashing Sanjit against a wall. No way a creature like Caine was going to tolerate Pixie and Bowie and Peace, let alone Choo. He wasn't going to share a dwindling food supply with them.

'Like things will be any better on the mainland,' Sanjit muttered.

'What?' Virtue asked him distractedly. He was busy trying to strap Bowie into the back seat of the helicopter. There were only four seats altogether, the pilot and three passengers. But they were adult-size seats so the two in the back would be room enough for the three youngsters.

Sanjit climbed into the pilot's seat. The leather was creased and well-worn. In the movie the seat had been fabric.

Sanjit remembered that very clearly. It was about all he remembered.

He licked his lips, no longer able to put off the rickety fear that he was about to get them all killed.

'You know how to do this?' Virtue asked him.

'No! No, of course I don't!' Sanjit yelled. Then, for the benefit of the youngsters he twisted half way around and said, 'Totally. Of course I know how to fly a helicopter. Duh!'

Virtue was praying. Eyes closed, head bowed, praying.

'Yeah, that'll help,' Sanjit said.

Virtue opened one eye and said, 'I'm doing what I can.'

'Brother, I wasn't being a smart ass,' Sanjit said. 'I mean I am hoping to God or gods or saints or anything else you got.'

Virtue closed his eyes.

'Should we pray?' Peace asked.

'Yeah. Pray. Everyone pray!' Sanjit yelled.

He pushed the ignition.

He didn't know a particular god he should pray to, he was Hindu but only by birth, he hadn't exactly read the holy books or whatever. But Sanjit whispered, 'Whoever You are, if You're listening, now would be a good time to help us out.'

The engine roared to life.

'Wow!' Sanjit cried, surprised. He'd half expected, half hoped the engine wouldn't even start.

It was shockingly loud. It shook the helicopter amazingly.

'Um . . . I think I pull this,' Sanjit yelled.

'You *think*?' Virtue mouthed, the sound of his voice swallowed by the engine noise.

Sanjit reached over and put his hand on Virtue's shoulder. 'I love you, man.'

Virtue put a hand over his own heart and nodded.

'Great,' Sanjit said aloud though only he could hear his own voice. 'And now that we've had that touching scene, it's time for our heroes to go out in a flaming ball of glory.'

Virtue frowned, trying to hear.

'I said,' Sanjit shouted at the top of his lungs, 'I'm invincible! Now let's fly!'

Dekka saw Zil's crew split into two groups, to left and right of the road. An ambush.

She hesitated. It would be good right about now to be Brianna. Breeze wasn't bulletproof, but she was awfully hard to hit when she was going three hundred miles an hour.

If she kept going, they would shoot her down.

Where was Brianna? Still too sick to move, no doubt, otherwise she'd be in the middle of it. Brianna was not one to miss a fight. Dekka simultaneously missed her and hoped she stayed safely at home. If anything ever happened to Brianna, Dekka didn't know how she would go on living.

But where was Sam, that was the big question? Why was it

Dekka's job to walk this road? She didn't even know that she had to. Maybe nothing would happen. Maybe Drake, rampaging up from the beach, would take on Zil and the two of them would finish each other off.

Dekka would like to see that. Right about now. Right now before she had to keep walking up the road to Clifftop.

'Yeah, that would be great,' Dekka said.

Zil's punks were losing patience. They weren't waiting. They were working their way towards her on both sides of the road. Clubs. Bats. Crowbars.

Shotguns.

She could run. Live. Get away. Find Brianna and say, 'Breeze, I know you probably aren't going to feel the same way, and maybe this will just gross you out and you'll hate me for saying it, but I love you.'

Her body tingled with fear. She closed her eyes for a second and felt in that temporary darkness what it would feel like, death. Except that you couldn't really feel death, could you?

She could run away. Be with Brianna.

Except no, that wasn't ever going to happen. She was going to live out her days loving Brianna from a distance. Probably never even tell her how she really felt.

Out of the corner of her eye Dekka saw Edilio running straight at Drake from behind. He was alone, the crazy boy, going after Drake. Farther away, moving much too slowly, Orc.

Edilio could have decided to hang back, wait for Orc. Maybe wait too long as Drake laid into terrified children. But Edilio had not made that decision.

He wasn't waiting for Orc.

'And I'm not waiting for Sam,' Dekka decided.

She started walking.

The first gun fired. That creep Turk. It was as loud as the end of the world. Dekka saw the fire spray from the muzzle. Hot lead pellets hit the concrete before her. Some bounced up and embedded themselves in her legs.

Hurt. Hurt more later.

Dekka couldn't reach Turk or Lance or Zil with her powers. Not from this distance.

But she could make it really hard for them to aim.

Dekka raised her hands high. Gravity failed.

Dekka walked forwards behind a wall of dirt and dust and swirling cacti.

Sam was just at the twisted metal gate of the nuclear plant when he heard a rush of air and saw a blur.

The blur stopped vibrating and became Brianna.

She was holding something. Two somethings.

Sam stared at the objects in her hands. Then he stared at her. Then back at the objects in her hands.

He waited until she was done coughing, bent over.

'No,' he said.

'Sam, they need you. And they can't wait for you to snail walk all the way back.'

'Who needs me?' Sam asked sceptically.

'Astrid told me to get you. No matter what it took.'

Sam could not help but be pleased. 'So. Astrid needs me.'

Brianna rolled her eyes. 'Yeah, Sam, you're still necessary. You're like a god to us mere mortals. We can't live without you. Later we're going to build you a temple. Satisfied?'

Sam nodded, not meaning to agree, just meaning that he understood. 'Is it Drake?'

'I think Drake is just part of it,' Brianna said. 'Astrid was scared. In fact, I think your girlfriend may have had a really bad day.'

Brianna dropped the skateboard in front of Sam. 'Don't worry: I won't let you fall off.'

'Yeah? Then why did you bring the helmet?'

Brianna tossed it to him. 'In case you fall off.'

Edilio had trouble running in the sand. But maybe that wasn't why he couldn't seem to catch up with Drake.

Maybe he didn't want to catch up with Drake. Maybe he was scared to death of Drake. Orc had fought Drake to a draw once. Sam had fought him and come out on the losing end.

Caine had killed him.

And yet, there was Drake. Alive. As Sam had known he was. As Sam had feared. The psychopath lived.

Edilio stumbled and tripped in the sand. His automatic rifle hit muzzle first and fired, BAM BAM BAM into the sand as Edilio accidentally squeezed the trigger.

Edilio stayed on his knees. Get up, he told himself. Get up, this is what you do. Get up.

He got up. He started running again. Heart pounding like it would tear itself loose.

Drake wasn't far away now, just a hundred feet, maybe, not far. Whipping some poor kid who'd run too slowly.

Edilio had seen the results of that terrible whip. It had broken something in Sam, the pain of that whip.

But Edilio moved closer. The trick would be to get close enough . . . not too close.

Drake still had not seen him. Edilio raised the rifle into firing position. Fifty feet. He could hit Drake from here, but there were a dozen other kids in range just beyond him. Bullets didn't always go exactly where you aimed them. He could kill Drake. He might also kill the fleeing children.

He had to stall until the kids got out of range.

He lined Drake up in the sights. Aiming was hard with the weapon on automatic. The kick would be ferocious. You could aim the first shot, but after that it would be like spraying a fire hose.

Had to get Drake to stop. Had to let the kids get away.

'Drake,' Edilio said. But his mouth was as dry as the sand. What came out was a barely audible rasp.

'Drake!' Edilio yelled. 'Drake!'

Drake froze. He turned, not in a hurry, slow. Languid.

Drake smiled his feral smile. His eyes were blue and empty of anything but amusement. His dark hair was matted and filthy. His skin seemed to be smeared with mud. There was dirt in his teeth.

'Why, Edilio,' Drake said. 'Long time, wetback.'

'Drake,' Edilio said, his voice failing him again.

'Yes, Edilio?' Drake said with exaggerated politeness. 'Something you wanted to say?'

Edilio's stomach heaved. Drake was dead. Dead.

'You . . . you're under arrest.'

Drake barked a surprised laugh. 'Under arrest?'

'That's right,' Edilio said.

Drake took a step towards him.

'Stop. Stop right there!' Edilio warned.

Drake kept moving. 'But I'm coming to surrender, Edilio. Slap the cuffs on me, officer.'

'Stop! Stop or I'll shoot!'

Kids beyond Drake were still running. Far enough? Edilio had to give them all the time he could.

Drake nodded, understanding. 'I see. You're such a good

boy, Edilio. Making sure the kiddies get out of the way before you gun me down.'

Edilio guessed that Drake's whip would reach ten, maybe twelve feet. He was no more than twice that distance now. Edilio aimed for the centre of Drake's body, the largest target, that's what he'd read you were supposed to do.

Another step. Another. Drake advanced.

Edilio stepped backwards. Again.

'Oh, no fair,' Drake mocked. 'Keeping me out of range like that.'

Drake moved suddenly, with shocking speed.

BAM!

Click!

The first round hit Drake in his chest. But no other bullets flew.

Jammed! The gun was jammed. The sand was in the firing mechanism. Edilio yanked the bolt back, trying to –

Too late.

Drake lashed him, curled his whip around Edilio's legs and suddenly Edilio was on his back, gasping for breath and Drake was standing over him.

The serpentine hand wound its way around Edilio's throat. Edilio thrashed. He tried to swing the gun like a club, but Drake blocked it easily with his free hand.

'I'd whip you, Edilio, but I don't really have time for fun,'

Drake said.

Edilio's brain swirled, crazy, fading. Through blood-reddened eyes he saw Drake's smile inches from his face, savouring the close-up joy of watching Edilio die.

Drake grinned. And then, as Edilio lost consciousness, as he fell into a pit of blackness, he saw metal wires growing across Drake's mud-flecked teeth.

FORTY ONE

12 MINUTES

SANJIT HAD FORGOTTEN every single thing he thought he had learned about flying a helicopter.

Something about a lever that changed the pitch of the rotor blades.

Something about angle of attack.

A cyclic. Pedals. A collective. Which was which?

He tried the pedals. The tail of the helicopter swung violently to the left. He took his feet off the pedals. The helicopter had almost spun off the deck.

'Well, that works OK!' Sanjit shouted, desperately hoping to reassure the others.

'You should probably go up first, before you try turning!' Virtue yelled.

'You think?'

Now he remembered something. You twisted something to make the rotors give you lift. What was there he could twist?

Left hand. The collective. Or was it the cyclic? Who cared, it was the only thing that twisted.

He twisted it. Gently. Sure enough, the engine noise increased and changed in pitch. And the helicopter lifted off.

Then it began to spin. The helicopter drifted towards the bow, towards the superstructure while the tail spun the helicopter like a top, clockwise.

Like a Tilt-A-Whirl.

Pedals. Had to use them to . . .

The helicopter stopped spinning clockwise. It hesitated. Then it began to spin counterclockwise.

Sanjit was distantly aware that several voices were screaming. Five kids in the chopper. Five screams. Including his own.

Pedals again. And the helicopter stopped spinning. It was still drifting towards the yacht's superstructure, but now it was doing so backwards.

He twisted the collective all the way and the helicopter shot upwards. Like a ride Sanjit had been on in Las Vegas once. Like the helicopter was on a string and someone was yanking it towards the clouds.

Up and over the superstructure. Sanjit saw it pass beneath his feet.

WHACK! WHACK! WHACK!

The rotors had hit something. Bits of wire and metal poles flew away. The yacht's radio antenna.

The helicopter was still rising and still drifting backwards towards the cliff.

The other thing. The watchamacallit the cyclic the stick the thing near his right hand grab it grab it do something something something push it forwards forwards forwards. Spinning again! He'd forgotten the pedals the stupid pedals and his feet couldn't find them now and the helicopter had spun 180 degrees and with the cyclic tilted forwards was now zooming straight for the cliff wall.

It was maybe a hundred feet away.

Fifty feet.

In a split second they would be dead. And there was nothing he could do to stop it happening.

Diana ran across the overgrown lawn. Caine was ahead of her, faster, she had to catch him.

The sound of the helicopter engine was growing louder, closer.

Caine stopped at the edge of the cliff. Diana reached it, panting, a dozen feet away from Caine.

In a flash Diana understood what Sanjit had been hiding. Far below a white yacht lay crumpled against the rocks. A helicopter struggled aloft, spinning crazily this way and then that.

Caine's face formed a wicked smile.

Penny was just labouring up behind. Bug, well, he might be there, too. No way to know.

Diana rushed to Caine. 'Don't do it!' she cried.

He turned a furious face to her. 'Shut up, Diana.'

As they watched, the helicopter spun again and surged towards the cliff.

Caine raised his hands and the helicopter stopped moving forwards. It was so close that the rotor hacked apart a bush that clung to the cliff face.

'Caine, don't do this,' Diana pleaded.

'What do you care?' Caine asked, genuinely puzzled.

'Look! Look at them. They have little kids in there. Little children.'

The bubble canopy of the helicopter was no more than a rock throw away. Sanjit struggled with the controls. Virtue beside him, gripped his seat cushion. Three smaller kids were huddled in the back seat, screaming, covering their eyes, not so young they didn't know they were a split second from death.

'I guess Sanjit should have thought about that before he lied to me,' Caine said.

Diana grabbed his arm, thought better of it, and reached for his face. She pressed one hand against his cheek. 'Don't do it, Caine. I'm begging you.'

'I'll do it,' Penny said, appearing on Caine's other side.

'Let's see him fly when the cockpit is full of scorpions!'

The wrong thing to say, Diana knew.

Caine snarled, 'You'll do nothing, Penny. I make the decisions here.'

'No, you do what she tells you to do,' Penny said. She practically spit the words at Diana. 'This witch! Pretty girl, here.'

'Back off, Penny!' Caine warned.

'I'm not scared of you, Caine,' Penny shouted. 'She tried to kill you while you were unconscious. She –'

Before she could finish the accusation Penny flew through the air. She floated, screaming, in mid-air, above the thrashing rotor blades.

'Go ahead, Penny!' Caine bellowed. 'Threaten me with your powers! Make me lose focus!'

Penny screamed, hysterical, flailing wildly, staring down in terror at the flashing blades below her.

'Let them go, Caine,' Diana pleaded.

'Why, Diana? Why do you betray me?'

'Betray you?' Diana laughed. 'Betray you? I've been with you every day, every hour, from the start of this nightmare!'

Caine looked at her. 'But you hate me, anyway.'

'No, you sick, stupid creep, I love you. I shouldn't. I shouldn't. You're sick inside, Caine, sick! But I love you.'

Caine cocked an eyebrow. 'Then you must love what I do. Who I am.'

He smiled and Diana knew she had lost the argument. She could see it in his eyes.

She stepped away from him. She backed towards the cliff. Felt with her feet for the edge as she held his gaze.

'I've helped you when I could, Caine. I've done all of it. I kept you alive and changed your filthy crap-stained sheets when the Darkness held you. I betrayed Jack for you. I've betrayed everyone for you. I ate . . . God forgive me, I ate human flesh to stay with you, Caine!'

Something flickered in Caine's cold gaze.

'I won't stay with you for this,' Diana said.

She took another step back. It was meant as a threat, not meant to be final.

But it was one step too many.

Diana felt the sudden horror, knowing she was going to fall. Her arms windmilled. But she could feel that she was too far, too far.

And in the end, Diana thought, wouldn't it be better?

Wouldn't it be a relief?

She stopped fighting and toppled backwards off the cliff.

Astrid ran, pulling Little Pete behind her.

No way she could have known, she told herself as she panted and yanked and her heart pounded from the fear of what she would see when she reached Clifftop.

No way she could have known that the game was real. That it had become real when the last battery died. And that Little Pete's opponent in the game was no program on a microchip, but the gaiaphage.

It had reached Little Pete. It wasn't the first time. Somehow, in some way she might never be able to grasp, the two greatest powers of the FAYZ were linked.

The gaiaphage had tricked Little Pete. It had used Little Pete's own vast power to give life to its avatar, Nerezza.

Orsay, too, had once touched the mind of the gaiaphage. It was like an infection – once you had touched that restless evil mind, it had some kind of hold over you. A hook buried in your mind.

Sam had said Lana could still feel the gaiaphage inside her. She still wasn't free of it. But Lana had known it, been aware of it. Maybe that had given her a defence. Or maybe the gaiaphage simply didn't need her any more.

They reached the road to Clifftop.

But the way forwards was blocked by what looked like a tornado. A tornado named Dekka.

Dekka raised the whirlwind before her and walked steadily.

BLAM!

A stab of fire barely visible through the flying, swirling debris.

'Get her! Get the freak!' Zil bellowed.

Dekka kept moving, ignoring the pain in her legs, ignoring the slosh of blood filling her shoes.

Someone was running up behind her. She yelled back over her shoulder without looking, 'Stay back, you idiot!'

'Dekka!' Astrid's voice.

She came at a run, yanking her weird little brother along behind her.

'Not a good time for you to yell at me, Astrid!' Dekka yelled.

'Dekka. We have to get to the cliff.'

'I'm going wherever Zil is,' Dekka said. 'I have a right to defend myself. He started this fight.'

'Listen to me,' Astrid said urgently. 'I'm not trying to stop you. I'm telling you to hurry. We have to get through. Now!'

'What? What's happening?'

'Murder,' Astrid said. 'We have to get through. You have to get through!'

Someone came running at them from the side. He stepped too close to the weightless zone and went flying up, head over heels, spinning slowly.

He fired as he rose. Gun banging in random directions.

But now they were circling around behind her. They moved cautiously, far outside her field. She could see them scurrying from bush to hillock to cactus.

A bullet whizzed so close by her ear she thought it might have hit her.

'Get back, Astrid!' Dekka said. 'I'm doing all I can.'

'Do whatever it takes,' Astrid said.

'If I take Zil out the rest will run.'

'Then take him out,' Astrid said.

'Yes, ma'am,' Dekka said. 'Now get out of here!'

Dekka had last seen Zil off the road to her right, ahead, just out of range.

Dekka dropped her hands.

Thousands of pounds of dirt and debris that had headed skyward fell. Dekka ran straight into the storm, eyes closed, hand over her mouth.

She almost barrelled into Zil. She had emerged from the pillar of falling dirt and practically ran him down.

Zil, startled, swung a shotgun barrel towards her, but she was already too close. The barrel hit her like a club, smashing against the side of her head but not hard enough to stun.

Zil tried to back off, the better to take a shot, but Dekka's hand shot out, grabbed his ear, and yanked him towards her.

Now he managed to jam the barrel up under her chin, hard enough to snap her teeth together. She jerked back and he pulled the trigger. The blast was like a bomb going off in her face.

But she did not lose her grip on him. She yanked him closer still as he whinnied in pain and terror.

Dekka aimed her free hand down at the ground. Gravity simply disappeared.

Locked together now in a frantic, wrestling embrace, Dekka and Zil both floated upwards. The dirt and debris came with them. They were the struggling centre of a tornado. Zil yanked free at the cost of a ripped, bloody ear.

Dekka punched him. Her knuckles hit him squarely on the nose. She punched again and missed. The first punch had spun her away from Zil. Zil was trying to bring the gun around, but he was having the same problem she was with moving and fighting in zero gravity.

Dekka's eyes were closing, clotted with flying sand. She couldn't see for sure how high they had risen. Couldn't know for sure that it was enough.

Zil twisted and shouted in triumph. The shotgun barrel was inches from her.

Dekka kicked wildly. Her boot connected with Zil's thigh. The two of them flew apart from the impact, floating now ten feet apart. But still Zil kept the shotgun aimed at her. And the distance wasn't enough for Dekka to be able to drop him without dropping herself as well. Not yet.

'Look down, genius,' Dekka snarled.

Zil, his own eyes squinting, glanced down.

'Shoot me and you fall,' Dekka yelled.

'Filthy freak!' Zil shouted.

He pulled the trigger. The blast was deafening. Dekka felt the wind of buckshot flying past her neck. Something hit her, like a punch.

The recoil of the shotgun blew Zil back five feet through the air.

'Yeah. Far enough,' Dekka said.

Zil cried out in terror. A single vowel that went on for the ten seconds it took Zil to fall and smash into the dirt.

Dekka wiped dirt from one eye and squinted down.

'Higher than I thought,' she said.

FORTY TWO

6 MINUTES

MARY TERRAFINO CHECKED her watch. Minutes.

It was coming. Coming so soon.

'I just want you kids to know that I love you,' Mary said. 'Alice, back from the cliff. It's not time yet. We have to wait so that you can go with me.'

'Where are we going?' Justin asked.

'Home,' Mary said. 'To our real homes. To our moms and dads.'

'How can we do that?' Justin asked.

'They're waiting.' Mary pointed. 'Just outside the wall. The Prophetess has shown us the way.'

'My mommy?' Alice asked.

'Yes, Alice,' Mary said. 'Everybody's mommy.'

'Can Roger come, too?' Justin asked.

'If he hurries,' Mary said.

'But he's sick. His lungs are hurt.'

'Then he'll come another time,' Mary said. Her patience was

fraying. How much longer would she have to be this person? How much longer would she have to be Mother Mary?

Other kids were pressing closer now. They'd been driven up the hill, right up against the FAYZ wall by battles going on below. Drake. Zil. Evil people, awful people, ready to hurt and kill. Ready to hurt or kill these very kids unless Mary saved them.

'Soon,' Mary crooned.

'I don't want to go without Roger,' Justin said.

'You have no choice,' Mary said.

Justin shook his head firmly. 'I'm going to get him.'

'No,' Mary said.

'Yes. I am,' Justin said stubbornly.

'Shut up! I said NO!' Mary screamed. She grabbed Justin and yanked him hard by the arm. His eyes filled with tears. She shook him hard and kept screaming, 'NO, NO! You'll do as I say!'

She let him go and he fell to the ground.

Mary drew herself back, stared down in horror. What had she just done?

What had she done?

It would be OK, all of it OK, once the time came. She would be gone from this place. Gone and gone and gone, and all the children would come with her, they always did, and then they would be free.

It was for their own good.

'Mary!' It was John. How he'd made it past the fights

down the road and reached her she could not imagine. Yet, here he was.

'Children,' John said. 'Come with me.'

'No one is leaving,' Mary said.

'Mary . . .' John's voice broke. 'Mary . . .'

Sanjit was torn between staring in blank horror at the cliff wall just inches away from the tip of the whirling rotors, and the awful sight of a girl, the one named Penny, hanging in mid-air above those same rotors.

Caine stood at the top of the cliff, unafraid of falling. He wasn't a guy who *could* fall, Sanjit realised. Caine could step off the edge and like the Road Runner simply hang in mid-air, beep beep, and zip back to solid ground.

Not so the girl named Penny.

The other one, Diana, was pleading with him. What was she saying? Drop the girl? Crash the helicopter?

Sanjit didn't think so. He'd seen something very wrong in Diana's dark eyes, but not murder.

Murder lived in Caine's eyes.

Sanjit had the cyclic pulled all the way back. The rotors wanted to pull back from the cliff, but Caine would not let it go.

Diana stepped backwards. Walked with halting steps to the cliff edge.

'No!' Sanjit cried, but she was falling, falling.

It all happened in a heartbeat. Diana stopped in mid-air.

The helicopter was released from Caine's grip. It jerked suddenly backwards.

Penny fell. The rotor blades retreated.

She fell past the rotors safely and the helicopter roared backwards like it had been on the end of a stretched bungee cord.

Diana was thrown more than lifted back on to the grass. She rolled and sprawled and looked up just in time for Sanjit to meet her eyes for a split second before he had his hands full.

The helicopter was moving backwards but falling, like it intended to ram its tail rotor straight into the deck of the yacht below.

The other thing, the other thing, lift it lift it twist it twist it and up the helicopter went. It spun wildly around as Sanjit once more forgot the pedal but it was rising. Spinning and rising and spinning faster and faster and now Sanjit was jerked wildly as he fought to find the pedals.

Clockwise, slower, slower, pause, counterclockwise faster, faster, slower, pause.

The helicopter hovered. But far from the cliff now. Out over the sea. And twice the height of the cliff.

Sanjit was rattling with nerves, teeth chattering. Virtue was still praying, gibberish mostly, and not English gibberish.

The kids were in the back screaming.

But for a few heartbeats at least, the helicopter was not falling and not spinning. It was rising.

'One thing at a time,' Sanjit told himself. 'Stop going up.' He loosened his death grip, and the twist grip went back towards neutral. He kept the pedals right where they were. He did not move the cyclic.

The helicopter was pointing towards the mainland. Not towards Perdido Beach, exactly, but towards the mainland.

Virtue stopped praying. He looked at Sanjit with huge eyes. 'I think I pooped a little.'

'Just a little?' Sanjit said. 'Then you've got nerves of steel, Choo.'

He aimed and pushed the cyclic forwards.

The helicopter roared towards the mainland.

Brittney stared down at Edilio. He was face down in the sand.

He bore the mark of a whip. His neck was raw and bloody, as though he had been lynched.

Tanner was there, too, looking down at him.

'Is he dead?' Brittney asked fearfully.

Tanner did not answer. Brittney knelt beside Edilio. She could see grains of sand move as he exhaled.

Alive. Barely. By the grace of God.

Brittney touched his face. Her fingers left a trace of mud behind.

She stood up.

'The demon,' Brittney said. 'The evil one.'

'Yes,' Tanner said.

'What should I do?' Brittney asked.

'Good,' Tanner said. 'You must serve God and resist evil.'

She looked at him, eyes blurring with tears. 'I don't know how.'

Tanner looked past her, raising glowing eyes to the hill that rose behind Brittney.

She turned away from Edilio. She saw Zil fall to earth. Saw Dekka sinking slowly in a pillar of dust. Saw Astrid with her little brother. Saw children running up the hill, still panicked.

'Calvary,' Tanner said. 'Golgotha.'

'No,' Brittney said.

'You must do as God wills,' Tanner said.

Brittney stood still. Her feet did not feel the warmth of the sand beneath them. Her skin did not feel the slight breeze from the ocean. She did not smell the salt spray.

'Climb the hill, Brittney. Climb to the place of death.'

'I will,' Brittney said.

She began to walk. She was alone, everyone else ahead, she the last to climb the hill.

Dekka was just coming down to earth. Astrid was racing ahead, pulling Nemesis with her.

How did she know to call him that? She had known Little

Pete before, back in the old days. She knew his name. But in her mind the name Nemesis had formed when she saw him. And a surge of pure rage.

Is *he* the evil one, Lord? She stopped, momentarily confused as Astrid and Little Pete ran ahead.

Her arm twitched. Stretched. So very strange.

And her braces were turning liquid, leaving only a metallic slick on sharp teeth.

Zil lay groaning, his legs twisted at impossible angles.

Brittney passed him by.

She would meet the evil one when she reached the top. And then would come the battle.

'Everyone hold hands,' Mary said.

The children were slow to react. But then, one by one, their little faces turned to the sunset, they reached out for each other.

Mary's helpers, carrying the babies, stood in the line with all the others.

'It's coming, children,' Mary said.

'Hold tight to each other . . .

'Be ready, children. Be ready to jump. You have to jump so high to go to your mommy's arms . . .'

Mary felt it beginning, just as she had known it would. The time had come.

Fifteen years before, at this very hour, at this very minute, Mary Terrafino was born . . .

Sam could hear nothing but a hurricane wind in his ears. He could feel nothing but the manic gyration of the skateboard under his feet, rattling up through every bone in his body. That and Brianna's hands on his back, pushing him, and again and again grabbing him, righting him, guiding him on a ride that made the craziest roller coaster Sam had ever experienced look like a quiet stroll.

Up the road from the power plant.

Down the highway, slaloming through abandoned or crashed cars.

Then a blistering few seconds of tearing through town.

A turn so sharp he was airborne and completely off the board, flying through the air.

Brianna raced out in front of him, grabbed his two kicking feet and guided them back on to the board. Like a sack of cement. Sam couldn't believe he hadn't broken both legs, he hit so hard. But Brianna's hands held him steady, pushing and guiding him.

Then a blur and a sudden, shocking, gut-wrenching stop.

He was pretty sure he'd been screaming the whole time.

'We're there,' Brianna said.

Time stopped for Mary. People froze. The very molecules of air seemed to stop vibrating.

Yes, just as others had described it. The poof. The big one-five.

And there, oh God, her mother.

The mother of Mother Mary, Mary thought. Not beautiful, maybe, not so very beautiful in reality as she had become in memory. But so warm and so inviting.

'Come on, honey,' her mother said. 'It's time to lay down the burden.'

'Mom . . . I've missed you so much.'

Her mother held her hands out, a waiting hug. Waiting. Arms open. Face smiling through tears.

'Mom . . . I'm scared . . .' Mary said.

'Come to me, baby girl. Hold tight to their hands and come to me.'

'The littles . . . my kids . . .'

'All their mommies are with me. Bring them out of that awful place, Mary. Set them free.'

Mary stepped forwards.

FORTY THREE

0 MINUTES

ASTRID SCREAMED, 'GRAB the children! Grab the children!'

She leaped to get a grip on the child nearest to her. Others just stared. Kids gaped, stunned, as Mary stepped, as if in a dream, off the cliff.

Mary dropped from sight. She was still trying to take steps as she fell.

Her grip was tight. Kids fell with her. A chain reaction. One pulling the next, pulling the next.

Dominoes off the cliff.

Justin tried to pull back when Mary pulled him over the edge of the cliff. But he wasn't strong enough to loosen her iron grip.

He fell.

And the little girl who held his other hand fell after him.

Justin didn't cry out. There was no time.

Rocks rushed up at him. Fast as a time when he'd been hit in the face by a dodgeball. But he knew the rocks wouldn't sting and bounce away.

A rock monster opened jaws to receive him. Jagged stone teeth were going to chew him up.

Astrid's grip was too weak.

The child she'd grabbed was torn from her grip.

Disappeared over the side.

She turned away, eyes wide with horror.

Brittney was there, right there, staring at her. But her face was changing, twisting, a horrible mask of melting flesh.

And Sam!

Sam, staring.

Brianna, a sudden blur as she leaped off the cliff.

Mary felt her grip on the children loosen. They weren't falling, they were flying. Flying free.

Her mother held out her arms and Mary, free at last, flew to her.

Justin felt Mother Mary's hand simply disappear. There, firmly gripping his one moment.

Then gone.

Justin fell.

But behind him something fell faster, a wind, a rush,

a rocket. He was halfway to the rocks when the something fast hit him and knocked the air out of him.

He flew sideways. Like a baseball that had just been hit for a home run. He was rolling across the sand of the beach now, rolling like he'd probably never stop.

He hit the sand ahead of the others who, without Brianna's speed, simply fell towards the rocks.

'Well, if it isn't Astrid,' Brittney said with Drake's voice. 'And you brought the Petard with you.'

Brittney, whose arm was now as long as a python, whose braces had been replaced by a shark smile, laughed.

'Surprise!' The thing that was not Brittney said.

'Drake.' Astrid gasped.

'You're next, pretty girl. You and your idiot brother. Over the side. Jump!'

Drake lashed at her with his whip hand.

Astrid staggered back.

She reached for Little Pete. She grabbed his hand. But it slipped from her grip. Instead, she held the game player. She stared at it, uncomprehending.

Astrid took a step back in mid-air, tried to recover, windmilled her arms crazily, trying to maintain her balance. But she could feel the truth: she was too far.

And then, as she gave up, as she accepted the fact of death

and called on God to save her brother, something hit her hard in the back.

She jerked forwards. Both feet on solid ground.

'You're welcome,' Brianna said.

The impact had thrown the game player from her hand. It spun through the air and hit a rock. Smashed.

Drake drew back his whip arm.

'Oh, I've been waiting for this,' Brianna said.

'No, Breeze,' Sam said. 'This is my job.'

Drake whirled, seeing Sam for the first time. Drake's mud-stained grin disappeared.

'Sam!' he said. 'You really ready for another round?'

His whip snapped.

Sam raised his hand, palm out. Brilliant green light blazed. But the whip had upset Sam's aim. Instead of burning a hole through Drake's middle, he hit Drake's foot.

Drake bellowed in rage. He tried to take a step forwards, but his foot wasn't just burned – it was gone. He rested his weight on a charred stump.

Sam aimed and fired and Drake fell on to his back. Both his feet were gone now.

But even as Sam watched, the legs were regenerating. Growing.

'See?' Drake said through teeth gritted more in fury and triumph than in pain. 'I can't be killed, Sam. I'll be with you forever.'

Sam raised both hands.

Beams of green light burned away the new growth. Sam played the light slowly up Drake's legs. Calves. Knees. The whip hand thrashed and slashed, but Sam was out of range.

Drake screamed.

Thighs burned. Hips. But still Drake lived and screamed and laughed. 'You can't kill me!'

'Yeah, well, let's just see if that's true,' Sam said.

But then, a voice cried out. 'Sing, Jill! Sing!'

Nerezza, her face no longer covered with flesh but with what seemed to be billions of crawling cells that glowed a green not much different from Sam's own killing light.

'SIIIING, Siren!' Nerezza cried. 'SIIIING!'

Jill knew the song she was supposed to sing. The song John had taught her.

She had come to fear Nerezza. She'd feared her almost from the first. But then had come the moment when Orsay told Nerezza to go away.

The last words Orsay had spoken. 'I can't go on this way,' Orsay had said.

'What do you mean?' Nerezza had asked.

'You . . . you have to go away, Nerezza. I can't go on this way.'

That's when Nerezza had done the horrible thing to Orsay. With her hands around Orsay's throat. Squeezing. Orsay had barely seemed to fight back, as though she accepted it.

Nerezza had carried her to the rock and dragged her to the top.

'She'll be fine,' Nerezza had lied to Jill. 'And if you do exactly what I say, you'll be fine, too.'

Now Orsay stared through blank, empty eyes. She hadn't seen Mary lead the children to the cliff.

She hadn't seen Mary pull the children off the edge.

Hadn't seen them fall.

But Jill had.

Jill sang.

Tho' like the wanderer,
The sun goes down,
Darkness be over me.
My rest a stone;
Yet in my dreams I'd be
Nearer, my God, to thee,
Nearer, my God, to thee,
Nearer to thee!

Sam's killing light died.

Brianna stood still completely still.

Astrid froze in mid-cry.

The kids of Perdido Beach, all within sound of the Siren's voice, stopped, and turned towards the little girl.

All but three.

Little Pete stumbled towards his game player.

Nerezza laughed and reached down to give a hand to Drake, who was swiftly regrowing what he had lost.

'Sing on, Siren!' Nerezza cried, giddy, triumphant.

Sam knew in a distant, far-off way what was happening. His mind still worked, though at a tenth of its normal speed, gears turning like a windmill in the faintest breeze.

Drake could almost stand. In a moment he would come for Sam. He would finish what he had started.

The memory of pain bubbled slowly up within Sam. But he lacked the power to move, to act, to do. He could only watch helplessly. Just like before. Helpless.

But then, out of a corner of his eye, Sam saw something very strange. Something was flying very fast over the ocean.

He heard a distant thwap thwap thwap.

The sound grew louder, as the helicopter roared across the ocean.

Loud.

Louder.

Loud enough.

Sam tried to move and found that he could.

'No!' Nerezza cried.

Sam fired once. The beams hit Nerezza in the chest. It was enough to kill anyone. To burn a hole through any living thing.

But Nerezza did not burn. She simply looked at Sam with a look of cold hatred. Her eyes glowed green, a light so bright it almost rivalled Sam's fire for brightness. And then, she was gone.

Drake watched as his feet grew back. But not quickly enough.

'Now, Drake,' Sam said. 'Where were we?'

He felt Astrid at his side. 'Do it,' she said grimly.

'Yes, ma'am,' Sam said.

Sanjit had mastered the art of flying straight ahead.

He had almost mastered the art of aiming in one particular direction. You could do it with the pedals. So long as you were very, very gentle and very, very careful.

But he wasn't exactly sure he knew how to stop.

Now he was rushing towards land at amazing speed. And he supposed he might as well keep going a while longer. Especially since he didn't quite know how to stop. Exactly.

But then Virtue yelled, 'Stop!'

'What?'

Virtue reached over, grabbed the cyclic, and pushed it hard to the left.

The helicopter banked suddenly, wildly, just as Sanjit noticed the fact that the sky directly ahead of them wasn't exactly sky.

In fact, when you looked at it from the right angle it looked an awful lot like a wall.

The helicopter screamed over the heads of a bunch of kids who looked like they were watching the sunset from the cliff.

The helicopter went fully sideways and the skids screeched along something that was very definitely not sky.

Then it was free again but still sideways and sinking fast towards the ground. An empty pool, tennis courts, rooftops flashed by in a split second.

Sanjit eased the cyclic back to the right but completely forgot about the pedals. The helicopter spun a 360 in the air, slowed, fought its way up, and then hovered in mid-air.

'I think I'm going to land,' Sanjit said.

The helicopter came down with a crash. The plastic of the canopy cracked and starred. Sanjit felt as if his spine had been jackhammered.

He switched off the engine.

Virtue was staring and shaking and maybe mumbling something.

Sanjit twisted in his seat.

'You guys OK? Bowie? Pixie? Peace?'

He got three shaky nods in response.

Sanjit laughed and tried to high-five Virtue but their hands missed. Sanjit laughed again.

'So,' Sanjit said. 'You guys want to go up again?'

*

Drake bellowed in fear and pain as the green light ate its way relentlessly up his body.

Drake was smoke from the waist down when from his mouth came Brittney's voice.

Drake's teeth flashed metal.

The lean, cruel face of the psychopath melted from its own internal fire. Brittney's full, pimpled face emerged.

'Don't stop, Sam!' Brittney cried. 'You have to destroy all of it, every bit.'

'I can't,' Sam said.

'You must!' Brittney said through her screams. 'Kill it! Kill the evil one!'

'Brittney . . .' Sam said, helpless.

'Kill it! Kill it!' Brittney cried.

Sam shook his head. He looked at Astrid. Her face was a mirror of his own.

'Breeze,' Sam said. 'Rope. Chains. A lot of it. Whatever you can find. Now!'

Astrid spotted Little Pete. He was safe. Looking for his game. Searching, but not near the edge of the cliff, thankfully.

She forced herself to go to the cliff. She had to see.

She leaned out over the side.

Dekka lay on her back in a mud of bloody sand. Her

arms were both outstretched towards the cliff.

The little boy named Justin was limping up out of the surf, holding his stomach. Brianna had saved him. Dekka had saved the rest.

And where Astrid had expected to see small, crumpled bodies, children huddled together on the rocks.

Astrid, tears in her eyes, gave Dekka a small wave.

Dekka did not notice her and did not wave back. She slowly lowered her arms and lay there, a picture of exhaustion.

Mary was nowhere to be seen. Her fifteenth birthday had come, and she had gone. Astrid made the sign of the cross and prayed wordlessly that somehow Mary was right and that she was in her mother's arms.

'Petey?' she called.

'He's over there,' someone answered.

Little Pete had come to a stop near the FAYZ wall. He was just bending down.

'Petey,' Astrid called.

Little Pete stood up with his game player, shattered screen dribbling fragments of glass from his hand.

His eyes found Astrid.

Little Pete howled like an animal. Howled like a mad thing, howled in a voice impossibly large.

'Ahhhhhhhh!' A cry of loss, a mad tragic cry.

He bent into a backwards 'C' and howled like an animal.

Suddenly, the FAYZ wall was gone.

Astrid gaped in amazement at a landscape of satellite trucks and cars, a motel, a crowd of people, regular people, adults, behind a security rope, staring.

Little Pete fell on his back.

And in a flash it was all gone.

The wall was back.

And Little Pete was silent.

FORTY FOUR

THREE DAYS LATER

'HOW IS IT going?' Sam asked Howard.

Howard looked at Orc to answer.

Orc shrugged. 'Good. I guess.'

Howard and Orc had been relocated, given a new home. It was one of the few houses in Perdido Beach that had a basement. There were no windows in the basement. No electricity of course, so Sam had left a small light of his own burning there.

The only way in or out of the basement was down a flight of steps from the kitchen. There, at the bottom of the steps, they had nailed two-by-fours across and up and down, forming a thick grid work. The spaces between the two-by-fours was just three inches.

At the top of the stairs the door had been strengthened by having Orc shove a massive armoire against it.

Twice a day Orc would shove the armoire aside. Then he would stump down the stairs and peek inside. Then he would come back up and replace the barricade.

'Was it Brittney or Drake when you went down last?' Sam asked.

'The girl,' Orc said.

'Did she say anything?'

Orc shrugged. 'Same thing she always says. Kill it. Kill me.'

'Yeah,' Sam said.

'How long you think we can keep this up?' Howard asked Sam.

It was not a great solution, keeping the undead thing locked in this basement to be guarded by Orc. But the alternative was destroying it. Him. Her. And that felt a little too much like murder for Sam.

Astrid and Edilio had worked for a couple of long days to try and make sense of the disaster that had come to the FAYZ. All the individuals who'd had direct contact with the Darkness, had touched the mind of the gaiaphage, had been used like pawns in a chess match.

Orsay's power had been subverted. Her empathy and kindness had been turned against her as the gaiaphage filled her dreams with images drawn from her own imagination. She had shown kids a path that seemed to lead to freedom but led instead to death.

Little Pete had been tricked into believing he was playing a game. And it was his own powers that had been used to create Nerezza, the gaiaphage's main player.

Nerezza had guided Orsay and, when the opportunity arose on that last terrible evening, pushed Zil to attack.

Lana still refused to admit that the gaiaphage had been able to tap her own healing powers to bring Brittney and Drake back to life.

Drake, the Whip Hand, was in a sense, Lana's creation. The Darkness had used her to give Drake his whip. And he had used her to give Drake a second life. It was no wonder, Sam thought, that Lana refused to acknowledge that.

Lana had spent days healing the wounded. And then she and Patrick had walked out of town. No one had seen her since.

Sam and Astrid had talked honestly about their mistakes. Astrid berated herself for being arrogant and dishonest, and too slow to understand what was happening.

Sam knew all too well how he had failed. He had been terrified by his own weakness and had reacted by mistrusting his friends. He had become paranoid and finally, indulging in self-pity, had run away. Abandoned his post.

But the gaiaphage had underestimated Brittney. It had needed her power, her immortality as well as Lana's healing power, to bring Drake back from the grave.

Brittney had fought him every step of the way. Not knowing what she was fighting she had nevertheless resisted Drake's takeover of the body they shared. Even when the gaiaphage had filled her shattered mind with visions of her dead brother,

Brittney's faith and willpower had kept the demon she sensed inside her from escaping completely.

The gaipahage had wanted to break the will of the kids of Perdido Beach. It had wanted them to give up, to abandon hope. Only then would the kids of the FAYZ become its slaves.

It had failed in the end. But it had been a matter of milliseconds. Had Zil managed to delay Dekka just a little longer, or had Drake not been slowed by Edilio's heroism, the children who jumped with Mary would have died.

That would have been the fatal blow for the struggling little society of Perdido Beach.

They had survived, but barely.

And maybe they had done better than just survive: Astrid's laws were in effect. They'd been voted in by all the kids assembled the day after Mary's Big Jump, as Howard had dubbed it.

It was a bitter thing, to Sam, to think that after all she had done, Mother Mary was to be known for her final madness. Sam hoped she really was alive, somehow, on the outside.

There would be no grave in the plaza for Mary. There was one now for Orsay.

They might never know whether that brief glimpse of a world just outside the FAYZ wall was real or just a last trick of the Darkness. The one person who might know was talking even less than usual: Little Pete had fallen into something almost like a coma since he'd held his shattered game player.

He would eat. But that was all he would do.

If Little Pete died, God only knew what would happen to this universe that he had created. And if kids ever really guessed how powerful Little Pete was, and yet how vulnerable, how long would he be left to live?

'I asked how long you think we can keep this up?' Howard repeated.

'I don't know, man,' Sam said. 'I guess we take it day by day.'

'Like everything,' Howard agreed.

There came the faint sound of Drake's voice. A muffled howl of fury.

'He does that when he gets control,' Howard said. 'That and a lot of threatening. Mostly, "I'll kill you all!" That kind of thing. I'm kind of getting used to it.'

'It wants us to be afraid. It wants us to give up,' Sam said.

Howard formed his sly grin. 'Yeah, well, we don't want to do that, do we?'

'No. No, we don't.'

But that mad, screaming voice, even muffled as it was, still sent a chill up Sam's spine.

'You guys need anything?' Sam asked.

Howard answered. 'You mean, aside from a hamburger, a peach pie, a bucket of ice cream, a DVD, a TV, a phone, a computer, and a one-way ride out of crazy-town?'

Sam almost smiled. 'Yeah. Aside from that.'

He went back outside. The street was empty. The unreal sun shone high overhead. He doubled over and coughed. The flu that was still going around had finally caught up with him.

But he was alive. And that was all you could ever ask from the FAYZ.

READ A NAIL-BITING EXTRACT...

PETE

HE STOOD POISED on the edge of a sheet of glass. Barefoot. Perfectly balanced. One foot in front of the other. Arms at his side. That was the game now.

The sheet of glass went down and down and down forever. Like a shimmering, translucent curtain.

The top edge of the glass was thin, so thin it might cut him if he slipped or fell or took a too-hasty step. That top edge was a thin ribbon of rainbow reflecting bright reds and greens and yellows.

On one side of the glass, darkness. On the other, jarring, disturbing colours.

He could see things down there on the right side, down below his right hand, beyond the reach of his fingers. Down there were his mom and his dad and his sister. Down there were jagged edges and harsh noises that made him want to clap his hands over his ears. When he looked at those things, those people, the wobbly, insubstantial houses, the sharp-edged furniture, the claw hands and hooked noses and staring, staring, staring eyes and yelling mouths, he wanted to close his eyes.

But it didn't work. Even through his closed eyes he saw them. And he heard them. But he did not understand their wild, pulsating colours. Sometimes their words weren't words at all but brilliant parrot-coloured spears shooting from their mouths.

Mother father sister teacher other. Lately only sister and others. Saying things. Some words he got. Pete. Petey. Little Pete. He knew those words. And sometimes there were soft words, soft like kittens or pillows and they would float from his sister and he would feel peace for a while until the next jangling, shrieking noise, the next assault of stabbing color.

On his left, down, down below the endless sheet of glass, a very different world. Quiet, ghostly things drifted silently, shades of grey. No hard edges, no loud sounds. No horrible colours to make him start screaming. It was dark and so very, very quiet.

Down there was a softly glowing orb, like a faint green sun. It would reach out to him sometimes. A tendril. A mist. It would touch him as he stood balanced, one foot in front of the other, hands at his side.

Peace. Quiet. Nothingness. It would whisper these thoughts to him.

Sometimes it would play. A game.

Pete liked games. Only the left side would play his games his way; games had to be his way, the same way, always and unchanging. But the last game Pete had played with the Darkness had turned harsh and overbright. It had suddenly stabbed Pete with arrows in his brain. It had broken the game.

The sheet of glass had shattered. But now it was whole again, and he balanced on top and as if it was sorry the soft green sun said, *Come down here and play,* in its whispery voice.

On the other side – the agitated, jangly, hard side – his sister, her face a stretched mask beneath yellow hair, a mouth of pink and glittery white, loud, was pushing at him with hands like hammers.

'Roll over. I have to get this sheet out from under you. It's soaked.'

Pete understood some of the words. He felt the hardness of them.

But Pete felt something else even more. A strangeness. An alienness. Something wrong, a deep, throbbing musical note, a bow drawn over strings, that pulled his focus away from the left and the right, away even from the sheet of glass on which he balanced.

It came from the place he never looked: inside him.

Now Pete looked down at himself, like he was floating outside himself. He looked down at his body, puzzled by it. Yes: that was the new voice, the insistent note, the demanding voice more compelling even than the soft murmur of the Darkness or the jangly words of his sister. His body was demanding his attention, distracting him from his game of balancing on the sheet of glass.

'You're sweating,' his sister said. 'You're burning up. I'm going to take your temperature.'

ONE

72 HOURS 7 MINUTES

SAM TEMPLE WAS drunk.

It was a new experience for him. He was fifteen and had once or twice snuck a sip of his mother's wine. He'd drunk half a beer when he was thirteen. Just to see. He hadn't liked it much, it was bitter.

He'd taken a single hit off a joint back before the FAYZ. He'd practically hacked up a lung and then spent an hour feeling bleary and strange and finally sleepy.

It had never been his thing. He'd never been part of the partying crowd.

But this night he'd gone to check on the caged monster that was both Brittney and Drake and had heard Drake's vile, obscene threats and howling, murderous rage. And then, far worse, he'd heard Brittney's pleas for death.

'Sam, I know you're listening,' she'd said through the barricaded door. 'I know you're out there, I heard your voice. I can't take it, Sam. Sam, end it. Please, I'm begging you, let me go, let me go to Heaven.'

Sam had been to see Astrid earlier in the evening. That hadn't gone too well. Astrid had tried, and he had tried, but there was too much wrong between them. Too much history now.

He had kissed her. For a while she had kissed him back. And then he'd pushed it. His hands went where he wanted them to go. And she'd shoved him away.

'You know I'm going to say no, Sam,' she said.

'Yeah, I've kind of gotten that message,' he said, angry and frustrated but trying to maintain some semblance of cool.

'If we start, how long do you think it will take before everyone knows?'

'That's not why you won't sleep with me,' Sam said. 'You won't do it because you think it would mean giving up control. And you are all about control, Astrid.'

It was the truth. Sam believed it, anyway.

But if he were being honest instead of just angry, he'd have admitted that Astrid had her own problems. That she was filled with guilt and didn't need one more thing to feel guilty about.

Little Pete was in a coma. Astrid blamed herself, although it was stupid to do so and she was the furthest thing from stupid.

But Little Pete was her brother. Her responsibility.

Her burden.

After that rebuff Sam had stood awkwardly while Astrid

spooned artichoke and fish soup into Little Pete's nerveless lips. Little Pete could swallow. He could walk if she guided him. He could use the slit trench in the backyard but Astrid had to wipe him.

That was Astrid's life now. She was a nurse to an autistic boy with all the power in their world locked inside him. Beyond autistic now: Little Pete was gone. No way to know where he was in his strange, strange mind.

Astrid hadn't hugged Sam when he said he was leaving. Hadn't touched him.

So that had been Sam's evening. Astrid and Little Pete. And the twinned undead creature Orc and Howard kept watch over.

If Drake somehow escaped, there were probably only two people who could take him on: Sam himself, and Orc. Sam needed Orc to act as Drake's jailer. So he had ignored the bottles beside Orc's couch and 'confiscated' only the six-pack in plain view on a kitchen counter.

'I'll dump this,' Sam had told Howard. 'You know it's illegal.'

Howard shrugged and smirked a little. Like he'd known. Like he'd seen some gleam of greed and need in Sam's eye. But Sam himself hadn't known. He had intended to dump the cans out on the street.

Instead he had carried them with him. Through the dark streets. Past burned-out houses and their ghosts.

Past the graveyard.

Down to the beach. He'd cracked the seal, ready to pour one out on the sand. Instead he'd taken a sip.

It burned like fire.

He took another sip. It burned less this time.

He headed up the beach. He knew in his heart where he was going now. He knew his feet were taking him to the cliff.

Now, many sips later, he stood swaying at the top of the cliff. The effect of the booze was undeniable. He knew he was drunk.

He looked down at the small arc of beach at the base of the cliff. The slight surge painted luminescent curves on the dark sand.

Right here, right where he was standing, Mary had led the preschoolers in a suicide leap. All that kept those kids alive was Dekka's heroic effort.

Now Mary was gone.

'Here's to you, Mary,' Sam said. He upended the bottle and drank deep.

He had failed Mary. From the start she'd taken charge of the littles and run the day care. She'd carried that load almost alone.

Sam had seen the effects of her anorexia and bulimia. But he hadn't realised what was happening to her, or hadn't wanted to.

He'd heard nervous gossip that Mary was grabbing whatever meds she could find, anything she thought would ease her depression.

He hadn't wanted to know about that, either.

Most of all he should have seen what Nerezza was up to, should have questioned, should have pushed.

Should have.

Should have.

Should have . . .

Another deep swallow of liquid fire. The burning made him laugh. He laughed down at the beach where Orsay, the false prophet, had died.

'Goodbye, Mary,' he slurred, raising his bottle in a mock toast. 'Least you got outta here.'

For a split second on the day that Mary poofed, the barrier had been clear. They had seen the world outside: the observation platform, the TV satellite truck, the construction underway on fast food places and cheap hotels.

It had seemed very, very real.

But had it been? Astrid said no: just another illusion. But Astrid was not exactly addicted to the truth.

Sam swayed at the edge of the cliff. He ached for Astrid, the booze had not dulled that. He ached for the sound of her voice, the warmth of her breath on his neck, her lips. She was all that had kept him from going crazy. But now she was the source of the crazy because his body was demanding what she wouldn't give. Now being with her was just pain and hollowness and need.

The barrier was there, just a few feet away. Impenetrable.

Opaque. Painful to touch. The faintly shimmering grey dome that enclosed twenty miles of Southern California coastline in a giant terrarium. Or zoo. Or universe.

Or prison.

Sam tried to focus on it, but his eyes weren't working very well.

With the exaggerated care of a drunk he set his bottle down.

He straightened up. He looked at the palms of his hands. Then he stretched out his arms, palms facing the barrier.

'I really hate you,' he said to the barrier.

Twin beams of searing green light shot from his palms. A torrent of focused light.

'Aaaaahhhh!' Sam shouted as he aimed and fired.

The light hit the barrier and did nothing. Nothing burned. Nothing smoked or charred.

'Burn!' Sam howled. 'Burn!'

He played the beams upward, tracing the curve of the barrier. He raged and howled and blazed.

To no effect.

Sam sat down suddenly. The bright fire went out. He fumbled clumsily for the bottle.

'I have it,' a voice said.

Sam twisted sideways, looking for the source. He couldn't find her. It was a her, he was pretty sure of that, a female voice.

She stepped around to where he could see her. Taylor.

Taylor was a pretty Asian girl who had never made a secret of her attraction to Sam. She was also a freak, a three bar with the power of teleportation. She could instantly go any place she'd ever seen or been before. She called it 'bouncing'.

She wore a T-shirt and shorts. Sneakers. Unlaced, no socks. No one dressed well, not any more. People wore whatever was halfway clean.

And no one travelled unarmed. Taylor had a large knife in a nice leather sheath.

She was not beautiful like Astrid. But not cold and remote and looking at him with defensive, accusing eyes, either. Looking at Taylor did not fill his brain to overflowing with memories of love and rage.

She was not the girl who had been the centre of his life for all these months. Not the girl who had left him frustrated, humiliated, feeling like a fool. Feeling more alone than ever.

'Hey, Taylor. Bouncy bouncy Taylor. T'sup?'

'I saw the light,' Taylor said.

'Yeah. I am all about light,' Sam slurred.

She held out the bottle tentatively, not sure what she should do with it.

'Nah.' He waved it off. 'I think I've had quite enough. Don't you?' He spoke with extreme care, trying not to slur. Failing.

'Come sit with me, Taylor, Taylor, bouncy Taylor.'

She hesitated.

'Come on. I won't bite. Good to talk with someone . . . normal.'

Taylor rewarded him with a brief smile. 'I don't know how normal I am.'

'More normal than some. I was just checking on Brittney,' Sam said. 'You have a monster inside of you, Taylor? Do you have to be locked in a basement because inside you is some psycho with a whip arm? No? See? You are so normal, Taylor.'

He glared at the barrier, the untouched, unfazed barrier. 'Do you ever beg to be burned into ashes so you can be free to go to Jesus, Taylor? Nah. See, that's what Brittney does. No, you're pretty normal, bouncy Taylor.'

Taylor sat beside him. Not too close. Friend close, conversation close.

Sam said nothing. Two different urges were battling in his head.

His body was saying go for it. And his mind. . . well, it was confused and not exactly in control.

He reached over and took Taylor's hand. She did not pull her hand away.

He moved his hand up her arm. She stiffened a little and glanced around, making sure they weren't seen. Or, maybe, hoping they were.

His hand reached her neck. He leaned toward her and pulled her to him.

He kissed her.

She kissed him back.

He kissed her harder. And she slid her hand under his shirt, fingers stroking his bare flesh.

Then he pulled away, fast.

'Sorry, I . . .' He hesitated, his wallowing brain arguing against a body that was suddenly aflame.

Sam stood up very suddenly and walked away.

Taylor laughed gaily at his back. 'Come see me when you get tired of mooning over the ice princess, Sam.'

He walked into a sudden, stiff breeze. And any other time, in any other condition, he might have noticed that the wind never blew in the FAYZ.

HE IS THE MESSENGER
HE OFFERS YOU A GAME

WILL YOU PLAY . . .
OR PAY?

Think you know the
meaning of suspense?
Think again.

Read an extract from Michael Grant's chilling new series

THE MESSENGER OF FEAR

"We have to help her."

"She is past help," the boy in black said.

"She's standing, she's . . . Can you hear me?" I addressed this to Samantha, knowing how foolish it was, knowing that my words would fall into the inconceivably vast chasm that separates the living and the dead.

No flicker of recognition in those brown eyes, no sudden cock of the head. I was inaudible and invisible to her.

Then she began to move, to walk. But backward. Away from us, but backward, not awkward but with normal grace. As though she had always walked backward. Backward across what was now a suburban street. A car came around the corner, not fast, the driver seeming to check for addresses as he drove. If he saw Samantha he gave no sign of it. I was sure, too, that he did not see me or the boy in black.

The car moved forward normally. Across the street a dog raced along its enclosure, moving forward as well, seeing the car but not us. Only Samantha was in rewind, only she moved backward to the sidewalk, to the flagstone-paved path, to a front door which opened for her. Now it was opened by her but all in reverse. It was a disturbing effect, part of what I was now sure had to be a strangely elaborate dream. Dreams could play with cause and effect. Dreams could show you bullet wounds and staring girls and people walking backward. Dreams could move you from black-hearted un-church to sunlit suburbia without effort.

"A dream," I whispered. I looked again at the boy. He had heard me, I was sure of that, but his expression was grim, focused on Samantha.

The door of the house closed and should have blocked her from our view but we were now inside that house, though we had passed through no door. We were in a hallway at the foot of steps leading upward.

There were framed photos on the wall beside the steps, a family, parents, a little boy and Samantha. And other pictures that must have been grandparents and aunts and cousins. I saw them all as, without thinking about it, I began to ascend those steps. Even as Samantha walked backward up them.

She disappeared around the corner at the top but the boy in black and I arrived at her room before she did. By what means we came there I could not say, except that that's how dreams are.

I felt sick in my stomach, the nausea of dread, because now

I was sure that I knew what terrible event I would soon witness.

And oh, God in heaven, if there is one, oh God, it was happening, happening before my eyes. Samantha sat on the edge of her bed. The gun was in her lap. Tears flowed, sobs wracked her, her shoulders heaved as if something inside her was trying to escape, as if life itself wanted to force her to her feet, force her to leave this place, this room, that gun.

"No," I said.

She was no longer moving backward.

"No," I said again.

She raised the gun to her mouth. Put the barrel in her mouth. Grimaced at the taste of steel and oil. But she couldn't turn her wrist far enough to reach the trigger and yet keep the barrel resolutely pointed toward the roof of her mouth.

She pulled it out.

She sobbed again and spoke a small whimper, a sound so terrible, so hopeless, and then, she placed the barrel against the side of her head which now no longer showed the wound, the wound which was coming if she didn't–

BANG!

The noise was so much louder than in movies. I felt as if I'd been struck physically. I felt that sound in my bones and my teeth, in my heart.

Samantha's head jerked.

Her hand fell away, limp and blood-spattered.

Blood sprayed from the hole for a moment, then slowed to an insidious, vile pulsation.

She remained seated for a terribly long time as the gun fell and the blood poured and then, at last, she fell onto her side, smeared red over the pastel floral print of her comforter, and rolled to the floor, a heap on the carpet.

The gunshot rang in my ears. On and on.

"I don't like this dream," I said, gritting my teeth, shaking my head, fighting the panic that rose in me.

The boy in black said nothing. He just looked and when I turned to him for explanation I saw a grim mien, anger, disgust. Simmering rage. His pale lips trembled. A muscle in his jaw twitched.

He crossed abruptly, his first sudden movement, to the desk in the corner of the room. There was a laptop computer open to Facebook. There were school books, a notebook, a Disney World cup holding pencils, a dozen colorful erasers in various shapes, a tube of acne medicine, a Valentine's card curled with age, a photograph of Samantha and two other girls at a beach, laughing.

There was a piece of paper, held down at the four corners by tiny glass figures of fancifully-colored ponies. The paper had been torn from the notebook.

The boy in black looked down at the paper and said nothing. He looked at it for far longer than it could have taken to read the few words written there in blue ink. I knew, for I, too, read the words.

I love you all. I am so sorry. But I can't anymore.

- Sam

I found that I could not look up from the words. I felt that if I looked away I must look at the dead girl, and I didn't want to see her. She had still lived when she wrote these words.

Then I realized that he was looking at me.

"Why is this happening?" I asked him.

He touched the note reverently with one finger.

"Why am I here?" I asked with sudden vehemence.

"The same reason we are all here," the boy said. "To learn."

But I had lost patience with cryptic answers. "Hey. Enough. If this is a dream then I don't have to put up with you!"

"Mara," he said, though I had never told him my name. "This is not a dream."

"Then what is it, huh?" My voice was ragged. I was sick through and through, sick with what I had just witnessed, sick with what I feared about myself. "What is it and what are you?"

"I am . . ." he began, then hesitated, considered, and again showed that slight lessening in the grim lines of his face. "I am the messenger."

"Messenger? What's your message, showing me this poor dead girl? I never wanted to see that. I don't want it in my head. Is that your message? Showing me this?"

"My message?" He seemed almost surprised by the question. "My message? My message is that a price must be paid. A price paid with terror."

I reached to grab him angrily, but he moved easily out of range. I wanted to grab him by the throat though I had instead reached for his arm. It was not that I blamed him for what I was now enduring, it was rather that I simply needed to hurt someone, something, because of what I had seen, and what I had felt since waking to find myself in the mist. It was like an acid inside of me, churning and burning me from the inside.

I wanted to kick something, to shout, to throw things, to scream and then to cry.

To save that poor girl.

To wipe the memory from my mind.

"You're the messenger?" I asked in a shrill, nasty, mocking voice. "And your message is *be afraid?*"

He was unmoved by my emotion . . . No, that's not quite right. It was more accurate to say that he was not taken aback. He was not unmoved, he was . . . pleased. Reassured?

"Yes, Mara," he said with a sense of finality, as though now we could begin to understand each other though I yet understood nothing. "I am the messenger. The Messenger of Fear."

It would be a long time before I came to know him by any other name.

Calmer now, having released some of my boiling anger and worry, I turned my unwilling eyes back to Samantha Early. Her life's blood was running out, soaking into the carpet.

"Why did she do it?" I asked.

"We will see," Messenger said.

Michael Grant has always been fast paced. He's lived in almost 50 different homes in 14 US states, and moved in with his wife, Katherine Applegate, after knowing her for less than 24 hours. His long list of previous occupations includes cartoonist, waiter, law librarian, bowling alley mechanic, restaurant reviewer, documentary film producer and political media consultant.

Michael and Katherine have co-authored more than 150 books, including the massive hit series Animorphs, which has sold more than 35 million copies. Working solo, Michael is the author of the internationally bestselling GONE series, the groundbreaking transmedia trilogy BZRK and the MESSENGER OF FEAR series.

Michael, Katherine and their two children live in the San Francisco Bay Area, not far from Silicon Valley. Michael can be contacted on Twitter (@michaelgrantbks), Facebook (authormichaelgrant), and via good, old-fashioned email (Michael@themichaelgrant.com).

Praise for the GONE series

'Exciting, high-tension story told in a driving, torrential narrative that never lets up. This is great fiction. I love these books.' *Stephen King*

'I would sell my soul for the next instalment.' *Sunday Telegraph*

'Gripping from start to finish.' *Independent on Sunday*

'Absolutely addictive.' *The Bookseller*

'Levels of nastiness almost worthy of Dante.' *Guardian*

'Nail-biting.' *The Bookseller*

'A chilling portrayal of a world without rules.' *Reading Zone*

'A white-knuckle ride in a tense thriller.' *Big Issue Scotland*

'These apocalyptic but coherent resolvable narratives are handbooks for mental survival.' *Guardian*

'An exceptional page-turner. Escapism just doesn't get better than this . . . a series that will in time become a classic.' *Lovereadingforkids*